Yesterday Will Make You Cry

OLD SCHOOL BOOKS

edited by Marc Gerald and Samuel Blumenfeld

CHESTER HIMES

Yesterday Will Make You Cry

Old School Books

W · W · Norton & Company
New York · London

Editors' Note copyright © 1998 by Marc Gerald and Samuel Blumenfeld
Introduction copyright © 1998 by Melvin Van Peebles

YESTERDAY WILL MAKE YOU CRY copyright © 1998 by Lesley Himes
A different version entitled CAST THE FIRST STONE was published in 1953.
Copyright renewed 1980 by Chester Himes.

The publishers wish to acknowledge the generous help of the staff of Yale University's
Beinecke Library in providing the text of *Yesterday Will Make You Cry.*

The text of this book is composed in Sabon
with the display set in Stacatto 555 and Futura.
Composition by Crane Typesetting Service, Inc.
Manufacturing by Courier Companies, Inc.
Book design by Jack Meserole.

Library of Congress Cataloging-in-Publication Data
Himes, Chester B., 1909–
    Yesterday will make you cry / Chester Himes ; with an introduction
by Melvin Van Peebles.
      p.   cm. — (Old school books)
    Complete and unexpurgated text of Himes' first autobiographical
novel which was originally published in a different form in 1953 as
Cast the first stone.
    ISBN 0-393-04577-3
    1. Afro-Americans—Fiction. I. Himes, Chester B., 1909– Cast
the first stone. II. Title. III. Series.
PS3515.I713Y471998
813'.54—DC21   97-40364
                                                                            CIP

W. W. Norton & Company, Inc., 500 Fifth Avenue, New York, N.Y. 10110
http://www.wwnorton.com

W. W. Norton & Company Ltd., 10 Coptic Street, London WC1A 1PU

1 2 3 4 5 6 7 8 9 0

CONTENTS

EDITORS' NOTE

The publication of *Yesterday Will Make You Cry* not only makes up for an injustice but also may give Chester Himes the stature that has always been denied to him in his own country. Originally published under the title *Cast the First Stone*, this totally neglected novel has been largely out of print in the United States since its first release in 1953. What should be regarded as a disgrace may also in fact be a happy circumstance—for stored away on libraries shelves was the best thing that could happen to *Cast the First Stone*.

Although it hasn't lost any of its impact—it remains one of the most telling indictments ever of the prison system, offered what is more by an author who himself served seven years behind bars—*Cast the First Stone* was itself a castaway novel. The new edition we are presenting, under Himes's original title *Yesterday Will Make You Cry*, is not simply an editorial facelift with an occasional sentence restored here and there. It is a totally different book, much of which had simply been thrown away by Himes's editors at Coward McCann. They upset the whole structure of the book and reordered the chapters, even rewriting certain passages. In a letter addressed to John A. Williams dated November 6, 1962, the writer Carl Van Vechten, a very close friend of Himes, said, "People say bad things about him because he doesn't like most people and shows it. I admire his books: *Yesterday Will Make You Cry* is probably his best but it was so cut for publication that in that form it is worthless."

In order to fully understand the demolition work methodically carried out by Himes's editors, it is necessary to go back to the original project which the author had planned. *Yesterday* was no doubt the book which was dearest to his heart, where he would at last be able to express himself at the height of his creative skills,

7

where he would disclose his innermost self. The book, which cost Himes six years of hard work, appeared doomed from the start, a project the scope of which no one seemed to comprehend. Despite Himes's endeavors to produce several versions—each bearing a different title—the response was always negative. In 1950, Himes mailed his rewritten prison manuscript to Blanche Knopf. She had read at least one of his earlier versions and disliked it. She didn't like this one any better and returned it the following month. The novel then passed from publisher to publisher, and it seemed for a time that Holt might take it. A few months later, Himes learned that Holt had turned down *Black Sheep* (another of his tentative titles). In 1951, Himes got a new agent, Margot Johnson. She tried unsuccessfully to sell his prison book, now called *Yesterday Will Make You Cry*. On April 14, 1952, Margot Johnson finally sold the novel to Coward McCann; by this time its title had been changed to *Debt of Time*. In early May it was being called *Solitary*, and it finally became *Cast the First Stone*. Understandably, Himes had disputes with his editors at Coward McCann, and perhaps because of their differences, the novel, originally slated for publication in October, was put off until January 1953.

Himes's project was both crazy and daring. Himes had decided to tell the story of his life using the voice of a white man, Jimmy Monroe, which enabled him to draw a few red herrings across the trail and resolve what appeared at the time as an irrevocable contradiction: being a black man *and* a writer and demonstrating that it is possible for an African American to go beyond ghetto experience. In a remarkable biography entitled *The Several Lives of Chester Himes*, Michel Fabré and Edward Margolies have drawn an extensive list of all the autobiographical passages that appeared in *Yesterday Will Make You Cry*, but which had been carefully edited out in *Cast the First Stone*. For instance, the protagonist evokes his childhood in terms strongly reminiscent of Himes's own, but there is nothing of that in the earlier version.

The editors deliberately and relentlessly erased the tenderer and more artistic aspects to turn Himes's manuscript into a hard-boiled prison novel. For many publishers in those days, the only place where the black man was not an invisible man was in a prison cell. They wanted *Yesterday* to be a book for the masses, which reduced black existence to a caricature. Of course, that book was never to reach its audience. Himes had meant to write a personal novel, where he could simply tell the truth of who he was. This is the book we have rescued from oblivion.

Marc Gerald and Samuel Blumenfeld,
Editors, Old School Books

... HIS WONDERS TO PERFORM

Melvin Van Peebles

*L*OOKING BACKWARDS OVER HIS SHOULDER, CHESTER Himes begins his autobiography, *The Quality of Hurt*, thusly— "America hurt me terribly, whether rightly or wrongly is not the point. When I fought back through writing it decided to kill me. . . . When America kills a nigger it expects him to remain dead. . . . The desperate struggle for life informed me that the only place where I was safe was in my skin." Another time, in a foreword he wrote for a collection of his short stories and essays, he describes himself as a sensualist whose two main obsessions are Black Protest and Black Heterosexuality. He goes on to say, ". . . I am extremely sensitive to all the humiliations and preconceptions Black Americans are heir to . . ."

Sounds pretty grim, doesn't it? Fortunately, that was only half of the story, half of the Chester I got to know. (Nothing happens outside of a historical context, now does it? Back then, to a white American, even more so than today, a smiling black meant a buffoon.)

Chester's dour assessment of himself was a classic downtrodden intellectual's gambit of self-preservation. Actually Chester was resilient to the point of ebullience, a trait he tried hard to conceal. The simple truth is, for the survival of their sanity and their self-esteem,

African Americans often find it expedient to officially appear grim. Black Americans who wished to be taken seriously learned to suppress any hint of joviality, lest they be taken for minstrels.

I'm not exactly sure of the date, but it was almost the middle of the decade, 1963 or '64, somewhere in there, before I ever heard of, or laid eyes on, Chester. It had been a slow week in the mayhem department, which was my specialty, and my boss brought him up. To earn my keep, my boss, the editor of the feature section of the Paris-based weekly *France Observatur*, had the bright idea of assigning me to interview this guy who had just won some big French crime-writing prize.

So there I was wandering down this street on the Left Bank trying to match the numbers on my notepad with the right home. Finally I spotted my destination . . . strange the things that stick in your memory. . . . I remember it was on the ground floor and it was on the west side of a street that ran north and south.

As I started across the road, a little yellow roadster with a rumble seat parked out in front of the address caught my eye. It was beat-up but sturdy, old but still jaunty—old as in mileage, not as in antique. I thought I knew cars, but I had never seen anything like it.

Knock knock. No answer. I knocked again. The door was opened by a not quite medium built man with European features and caramel-colored skin, a dashing figure, in a matinee-idol sort of way, his rakish features made even more handsome by several wicked scars lining his face.

"Pardon me, monsieur, I'm looking for Chester Himes," I said in my best French. The man looked at me as if he didn't understand. "Chester Himes," I repeated this item, leaving out the rest of the sentence, figuring maybe my French accent was throwing him off.

"I'm Chester Himes," the man smiled and held out his hand. (Turns out it wasn't my accent, Chester didn't speak French.)

Chester led me inside. Keen reporter that I was, I hurriedly made mental notes as I followed him: probably in his fifties, gait stiffer than his years . . .

Chester worked in the front room of his apartment. A table, or maybe it was a desk, was placed up against the wall. It had a typewriter on it and a neat pile of paper on either side.

He offered me a chair and, simultaneously shaking his head, scowling and chuckling, he took one himself. I studied Chester as I sat down. I couldn't get a handle on him, he was a mind-boggling mixture of frail and ferocious, the likes of which I had never seen.

"Sorry about the door," he apologized. "I wasn't expecting you."

"The paper said they were going to call and that you would be expecting me," I apologized.

"Oh, they did . . . but shit, I wasn't expecting *you*." He grinned. "Hell, brother, I didn't know you were black."

"Well, hell back, brother, I didn't know you were black either."

He grinned at me and I grinned at him, and that moment was, like they say at the end of *Casablanca*, "the beginning of a beautiful friendship." Chester was twenty-five years my senior, but notwithstanding that or the fact that I kept putting my foot in my mouth that first meeting, we remained buddies for the rest of his life, until he passed away somewhere in Spain, in the mid-eighties, twenty years later.

Suddenly the ludicrousness of the situation overcame us. We both burst out laughing, and not polite white simpers either, but head-back, teeth-flashing, basic colored barbership peals of joy.

"Are you all right, Chester?" an English accent called from another room.

"Yeah, yeah, I'm okay," Chester choked.

Chester's ladyfriend-cum-watchdog, Lesley—later to become the last Mrs. Himes—a sharp-faced, pretty woman, stuck a startled head in the room just to be sure. Later I learned why Lesley was so surprised.

Turns out Chester was considered cantankerous and was not known for taking to strangers. The truth of the matter is he was a bottom-line, no-bullshit brother and suffered fools badly. He was often impatient with the patronizing literati milling around the hem of his garment anxious to ingratiate themselves. Chester loved to let his hair down, but he was also a very cautious man and rarely

13

got the chance. I had the privilege, along with Herb Gentry, a black expatriate painter, of passing hilarious hours in Chester's company.

After Lesley's head retreated back into the other room, Chester and I got down to the nuts and bolts of the interview. He pointed to the two neat piles on either side of the typewriter and explained that before he started on one of his "detective stories," or "action novels" as he insisted on calling them, he would count out 220 pieces of carbon paper and 440 pieces of typing paper. He would then place a sheet of carbon paper between every two sheets of typing paper so that way he would have an original and a copy of each page that he completed. He would then put the untouched pile on the right hand side of his typewriter and begin to bang away. After he finished typing a page he would put it face down on the pile at his left.

"What's the significance of 220 pages?" I asked, fascinated. "Are you into numerology or something?"

"Numerology my ass," Chester laughed. He explained that his contract with the publisher required that he deliver a manuscript of at least 220 pages. "When the pile on the right hand side begins to get low I know it's time to start winding the story up."

Like I said, Chester was a bottom-line kinda guy.

I pointed to a saucer with a woebegone sliver of toast. "Breakfast?" I queried. He nodded.

Figuring I'd add a human-interest touch, I started asking him what he put on his toast: "Jam? Marmalade? Maple . . ."

". . . Caviar," Chester cut in. "I like caviar. Shit, it's pretty cheap if you know where to shop for it."

"Well . . . uh." I staggered back to the main topic of the interview. "What got you into writing mystery novels anyway?"

"Money. Marcel Duhamel . . . he had read my three novels and translated my first novel, *If He Hollers Let Him Go*, into French. I ran into him one day after he had been made the publisher of La Serie Noire, that's the detective series I write for. He was the one who thought my style would be great for detective stories. I didn't see it, but he talked me into it."

"Talked you into it? How did he do that?"

"Like I just said, money. He gave me an advance."

Like I said, Chester was no-bullshit to the bone.

I asked him how it was that he became a writer in the first place.

"I had a lot of free time."

"Free time?"

"Seven and a half years of it in the Ohio State Penitentiary for robbery."

I sat there with my jaw flapping in the breeze, staring at the delicate featured, elegantly dressed man sitting across from me.

When I finally regained my composure, I started bitching about another innocent black man being railroaded.

"Innocent my ass, " Chester interrupted. "I was guilty as sin! They caught me red-handed. I still had the jewels on me. Originally the judge sentenced me to twenty to twenty-five years."

I started commiserating again. "That's where the scars are from, I suppose."

Chester fingered a gash above his eye. "Maybe some," he nodded. "But before I went to jail I was working as a porter in a hotel and I fell 30, maybe 40 feet down the elevator shaft."

"Jesus Christ!"

"Yeah," he chuckled. "Another white guy." Chester squinted over at me and observed the obvious: "You don't seem to have a lot of information about me, young man."

I just told him the truth. "No, sir," I nodded. "I don't know shit about you."

Chester wasn't offended; he understood, like I mentioned before, nothing happens outside of a historical context.

My lack of knowledge was more than some funny story, it was a significant, insidious fact, striking to the core of the African American artist's dilemma. Despite the fact that Chester, this literary giant, had been publishing essays, short stories, and novels for over a quarter of a century, I, a black American, had grown up, gone to college, and never once heard his name mentioned in the myriad literature courses I had taken. This spoke volumes about the walls of prejudice and the barriers of racism. Chester was your basic "invisible man." In the States (outside of music) we were only allowed one brilliant Negro per profession and Richard Wright, soon to be dethroned by Jimmy Baldwin, had beaten Chester to the wire in the protest novel department.

Never mind what history did, or didn't, allow—there we sat, grinning at each other like a couple of Cheshire cats, the bloody features of racism's canary dribbling from our respective chops. Me, a French journalist, and him an award-winning French writer.

"Where were you born?"

"1909, in Jefferson City, Missouri. The youngest of three boys. My mother was a tall regal woman, almost white, and my dad was a teacher, a short bow-legged black man."

We chatted away the rest of the afternoon. On the one hand he didn't take his "action novels" too seriously, but on the other hand he was proud of breaking the "detective writer" color barrier. Chester loved theories, he was full of them, the more outlandish the better. All of which were delivered in a disarming straight-faced manner. One of his favorites was that French were really light-skinned colored folks in disguise. "Don't they like pigs' feet just like we do? And what the hell do you think tripe is? Just chitterlings by another name! . . ."

I finally had to go home. When he opened the door to show me out the jaunty old convertible was still parked in the road out front.

"Boy, that car is some piece of work. I never saw anything like it."

"She's mine," Chester said.

(Frankly, I wasn't surprised.)

I managed to get my hands on English copies of Chester's first three novels. I sat down and read them in the order that they had been published: *If He Hollers Let Him Go* (1942), *Lonely Crusade* (1947), and *Cast the First Stone* (1952). The books were analyses-cum-accusations, racial and otherwise, of American society. All three were searing litanies of injustices, and as brilliantly written as any protest novels I had ever read.

In the first two books, Chester's style had been a judicious balancing act: half literary, half hard-boiled, judgmental yet dispassionate, incisively detailed but fast-paced. In his third novel, *Cast the First Stone*, Chester abruptly checked his tendency towards literary grace and veered towards pure pulp.

Upon reflection, looking backwards from the detective stories to the earlier protest novels, I realized that the pulp path Chester had taken in *Cast the First Stone* was the natural and direct precursor to the joyous, "vulgar," uninhibited, pure pulp fiction of his "detective stories." In fact, it seemed to me that Marcel Duhamel, the French editor who convinced Chester to begin writing his series of "detective novels," was only nudging Chester along the road he had already chosen for himself.

Chester called it like he saw it, and he had seen everything. Chester's writing was for real and it was no third-hand bullshit gleaned from some secondary source. Not only could Chester "talk that talk," but he had "walked that walk." Every sentence of every page was alive with authenticity. But simply chalking up his grip on the reader to street-smarts demeans Chester's writing genius. He was not only streetwise, he was a brilliant writer, period.

To people raised in cushier circumstances Chester probably seemed cynical and bitter. But Chester wasn't bitter, he was *angry*. Angry because of and about the racism he had suffered. Bitterness has a more diffuse quality; one would have to believe in justice, or Jesus, for that. Of course, Chester longed for justice and was incensed by its absence, but he was too pragmatic to spend his time waiting for the justice-Santa to come down the chimney with a stocking full of equality.

Chester's experiences and keen memory, coupled with his irreverent imagination, enabled him to recount the foibles and follies of the folks up and down 125th Street. Chester reinvented Harlem as metaphor for the plight of dark-skinned folks in America.

Chester was like that Dutch painter of the Renaissance, Brueghel the Elder. Brueghel called it like he saw it too, so unflinchingly in fact that doctors today, 400 years later, have been able to identify various maladies from studying the characters that he painted, diseases of which people weren't even aware. Chester saw America unflinchingly too as hilarious, violent, absurd, and unequal—especially unequal. All of the so-called "new" racial antagonism bursting to the surface in the streets of these United States (diseases people claim weren't even there) lay festering just below the pavement of Harlem in Chester's work years ago.

On one hand, Chester got a big kick out of what he called his "action stories." He would sit around with me chuckling over the hilarious adventures he'd put Coffin Ed and Grave Digger, his two cop heroes, through. On the other hand, I had the impression that there was something Chester deeply resented about his detective stories. Puzzled, I attempted to solve the mystery, but whenever I tried to broach the subject, Chester's face would cloud up. Then, always gracious with me, he'd say something funny to cover himself and change the subject.

Finally, I stopped asking. That's all I knew, that's where things stood with me on the subject of Chester's grudge for the next thirty years or so.

Anyway, the series was hugely successful; it not only resuscitated his career, it took it to new heights. Of course Chester's mere survival was an affront to the literary establishment back home, but he did better than merely survive. In France his detective novels were such a hit he became a celebrity. Eventually the news of Chester's stardom ricocheted back to the States. Chester's "detective novels" having already been anointed a winner overseas (and everybody loves a winner), they became a big success in America too, so big they even started making movies from them. Then, partly on the coattails of his "detective novels," Chester's serious writings were rediscovered and finally began to receive the attention they merited.

OK. A couple of months ago, I was contacted by an editor who asked me if I would like to write the foreword for a new edition of one of Chester's earlier novels. (I didn't realize a thirty-year puzzle was about to fall into place.)

"Sure," I said. "Which one?"

"*Yesterday Will Make You Cry.*"

"Never heard of it," I told him. "I thought I knew all of Chester's work."

"*Cast the First Stone* is the title of the expurgated version of *Yesterday Will Make You Cry*," he explained.

"Expurgated version?" I came back. "You mean the normal editorial correction, don't you?"

"A little more than that . . . you'll see," the editor said. "We're publishing the original version of Chester's manuscript exactly the way he wrote it. That's why we're using his original title too, not the one he had to live with."

Expurgated version!? . . . What the hell was going on?

Well, the manuscript arrived and I sat down and started to read.

BLAM! By the second page, I realized what a chump I had been! I had accepted without question the swinging of the pendulum towards pulp in *Cast the First Stone* as Chester's unmitigated intention.

On the contrary, *Yesterday Will Make You Cry* is Himes at the top of his game, literary as well as pulp sensibilities all rolled into one unique style.

What a fool I had been! Chester hadn't veered off toward the pulp genre, for which he later became famous, at least not of his own volition.

Turns out *Yesterday Will Make You Cry* had made the rounds of the publishing houses with successive waves of editors and agents imposing "improvements" on the manuscript, forcing him to delete his more literary touches. They jammed Chester's head in their toilet of racist preconceptions and pulled the chain and kept pulling the chain, flushing away what they felt were his uppity literary pretensions, forcing him to dumb-down his masterpiece before agreeing to publish it.

You think perhaps that saying Chester had his head shoved into the toilet of racism might be, uh . . . too strong a metaphor. Think again. What would you call making Chester reduce the literary device of flashbacks, including the back story of Jimmy, the central character's life? What would you call forcing Chester to change the original manuscript from the reflective third person to the more "natural" (i.e., primitive) first person?

Perhaps *Yesterday Will Make You Cry* might have been accepted for the literary jewel it was and published in its original form 45 years ago if Chester had been an unknown, or more specifically if his race had been unknown. Not that the national obsession about race has changed that much down through the years. The blurb copy, twenty years later, for the Signet 1972 reprint of *Cast the First Stone* begins with the patronizing . . .

"James Monroe was a cool cat . . ."

and ends with . . .

". . . a ruthlessly honest novel of a young black's agonizing discovery of his own emotions, his own identity . . ."

What damn "young black's agonizing discovery"? Jimmy Monroe, Chester's central character, was white! The writer of the blurb (twenty years later) still couldn't leap over the ingrained racial assumptions that all a black writer could write about was another black.

No wonder Chester had a grudge against his "detective stories." How painful it must have been to endure. What a bitter pill. What stomach-turning irony, forced to mutilate your work and then, adding insult to injury, having that mutilation become the map to greater fame and fortune.

Well, finally, here at last is the novel as Chester conceived it, the passionate story told for the first time as intended, and what an amazing book it is. Long denied his rightful place at the literary table, Chester is finally getting his due. *Yesterday Will Make You Cry* adds to the towering force of the man.

Chester loved having the last laugh, so I know somewhere out there he's a happy camper.

My momma used to always talk about "God and the mysterious ways of his wonders to perform." Now I know what she meant, this is a case in point if there ever was one.

. . . When I got back to the *France Observateur*, after that first meeting with Chester, and turned the story in, my boss asked me if I had a title for my article.

"Yeah," I said. "I'm calling it *The Unconquered*!!"

"Strange title, isn't it?" he asked.

"No," I grinned. "Not if you know Chester." And from that day to this I have never seen a description of Chester that I thought was a better fit.

Melvin Van Peebles
July 14, 1997

Book 1

Gray Clothes and Gray Lines

1

IT WAS THE FIRST NIGHT Jimmy Monroe, convict no. 57232, had been in the dormitory. It was all strange; everything was strange. After having been choked up for the past ten days, so scared and lost and alone, he could not realize that he was actually watching convicts play poker and laugh. He had thought he would never hear laughter again.

During the period of examinations and interviews by the doctor and deputy and chaplain, and God knows who else, of being measured and finger-printed by the convicts in the Bertillon office, all vague, confused, disconnected, meaningless movements, he had celled with the other newcomers up on 5th-K, the top range of the I&K cell block, a very old block with small, grimy, and very cold cells. He had been scared and choked up and had kept thinking of his sentence and of the outside world and of at last being in prison until he was solid sent with hard, dry tears.

Twelve of them had been transferred down into the coal company that morning. He was glad to get out of that dark, cold cell. But he could not acquaint his mind with the fact of convicts actually playing poker, and for money, too. It floated on the outside and would not go in.

Blankets were spread over the table. Old cards stamped with initials and cut into various designs served as chips. One of the game-keepers sold the chips of penny, nickel, and dime denomination, while the other dealt.

Jimmy couldn't get used to any of it, any of the entire dormitory scene. It wasn't real—convicts walking about and mingling with each other. The real prison was the one which kept coming back—

a prison of dark, dank dungeons with moldy bones in rusted chains, the prison that held the Count of Monte Cristo, Jean Valjean, Saint Paul—the real prison was the prison in his mind.

He was still scared but it had thinned out so that it did not jerk him around woodenly, stiff-jointedly; and he didn't feel it all the time. Only he knew it was still there, underneath the convicts gambling and walking around and talking.

"You, fish?"

He jerked around. A little red-headed convict wearing tight-fitting silk underwear and low-slouched trousers grinned at him.

"You talking to me, stud?" Jimmy asked.

"Come on, let's walk," the convict said, thumbing.

Jimmy turned back and stared at the game without replying. He felt peculiar, as if he was some one else standing there in a prison dormitory, not Jimmy Monroe. It wasn't real; nothing was real. Everything was a tableau; every time he blinked his eyes it was another tableau. His mind had stopped working four days ago when prison had first become real, and then suddenly, in the momentary flash of reality, it had again become unreal. Everything came through his senses and then stopped as though it had come into a mirror and there was nothing but the reflection caught in the mirror with no meaning. It was funny being there and not feeling it.

After a moment he turned back and saw the red-headed convict still standing there, looking at him queerly, and he nodded and swung in beside him. There were a number of other convicts walking in two's and three's in the aisle around the tables, and they joined the procession.

"What you in for?" the convict asked.

"Robbery," Jimmy told him.

"Ten to twenty-five?"

"Uh-uh, twenty. Twenty to twenty-five."

"That's what I'm doing, too," the convict boasted. "I stuck up a jewelry store. Who'd you stick up?"

"Oh, just some people."

They turned at the front by the doors of corrugated steel and came down the other side of the tables. Jimmy felt conspicuous; he had been feeling conspicuous all day, every time he moved. Looking at the red-headed convict, he noticed how smooth-skinned and round-muscled were his bare arms and body beneath the tight-fitting silk undershirt. Then he noticed that every one was watching them. It added up to something vaguely offensive; but he didn't get it. Just a faint hint of something that his mind wouldn't register.

"Ain't your name Jake?" the convict asked.

"Uh-uh, my name's Jim—Jim Monroe."

"My name's Henry Hill, but they call me Red," the convict said, grinning. He had a nice grin and freckles, Jimmy noticed, guessing his age to be about twenty-five. "Say, were you ever in Cincinnati, Jimmy?"

"Jim, stud—*Jim!*"

It was coming a little clearer now. There was something wrong about this red-headed convict, that was it.

"Oh, you don't like the *Jimmy*, eh? How old are you, Jim?"

"Twenty-two," Jimmy lied.

"Say, were you ever in Cincinnati? Seems as if I've seen you some place."

"Uh-uh, I'm out of Cleveland. Ever been to Cleveland?"

"Naw, but it sure seems as if I've seen you some place before."

It was just a feeling about this red-headed convict. Nothing Jimmy could be sure of.

"Man, you musta been to Cincinnati; I couldn't be mistaken."

Jimmy didn't reply, for abruptly his thoughts had gone away from Red, back to the dormitory. He began seeing things which he had been looking at unseeingly all day. Seeing them for the first time in a hard, cutting clarity . . . Dirty duffel bags chunked into fat unshapeliness with convict junk, hanging to bunk-frames . . . Pictures and photographs of convicts' relatives and sweethearts— sad-faced mothers, undernourished kids, family groups, simple-looking, over-dressed, whore types, shabby, mattress-shaped, hunky types, a girl in a bathing suit. Most of them were framed . . . Seeing the other convicts for the first time, also. Sitting on their bunks, reading, talking, some walking around, others playing musical instruments, making rings and cigaret holders and inlaid jewel boxes, coming in and out from between the bunks with the sliding, sidewise motion of crabs . . . And then he began to hear the noises peculiar to convicts—clumping of hard heels on concrete, yells, curses, off-key ballads, arguing, eternal arguing—all blended into a convict medley.

It came close and enveloped him—the noises and the sights and the smells of unwashed bodies—penetrating the blankness of his thoughts. And in the closeness he could neither see nor smell nor hear them anymore—only feel them. And feeling them there, in prison beside him, he became scared again.

"Want a cigaret?" Red asked.

He jumped. "Huh?"

"Want a cigaret?" Red repeated. "You smoke, don't you?"

"Sure, thanks. I had a carton but the suckers chiseled 'em."

Red had pulled out a bag of Bull Durham, but suddenly pocketed it again. "Come on down to my bunk and I'll get you a ready-made."

"Okay."

In passing the crowd about the poker game, Red squeezed against him. It gave him a funny feeling. "How do you keep warm?" he asked foolishly, drawing back from something slightly repulsive that the touch of Red's bare arm had brought up in him.

But Red put his arm about Jimmy's waist and hugged him. "I got my love to keep me warm."

Jimmy pulled away. "Yeh?" He didn't know what to say.

Red's bunk was in the far corner. It was shadowy down there, secretive. Red's bunk, like most of the others, was curtained, screening it from the aisle. Red sat down and pulled the curtain closed. "Sit down, Jim," he invited, patting a place beside him.

"Uh-uh, I'm going back out and watch the poker game," Jimmy declined, feeling ill at ease.

Red pulled a wooden box from underneath the bunk and unlocked it. He took a package of cigarets from the tray and handed them to Jimmy. "Keep 'em," he offered.

Jimmy took one and handed back the pack. "Uh-uh, this will do me."

"Aw, go ahead. Take two or three for tonight, anyway."

Jimmy took two more. "These will do me." He didn't want to feel obligated.

Red struck a match, holding the light. Jimmy leaned over and lit his cigaret and the red-head made a kissing sound. Jimmy jumped back, bumping his head against the bunk-frame. "Goddammit!" he cried.

"Oh, I didn't mean to make you hurt yourself," Red said, concernedly, jumping to his feet. "Here, let me see."

"Naw, it's all right," Jimmy said, drawing away.

"I was just kidding," Red said, seating himself again and taking Jimmy's hand. "Come on and sit down," he insisted. "You haven't got anywhere to go. Where you got to go? Got to catch a train or something? Sit down and let's talk."

Jimmy pulled away his hand. "Uh-uh," he declined. "I got to get a drink of water." He wanted to tell Red to go to hell, but he wasn't sure of himself. "Thanks for the smokes," he said, turning away.

Some one picked a clear melody on a mandolin, stopping him. A voice crooned a tentative note . . . "*Me and my shadow, walking down the avenue . . .*"

"Like that one?" the voice asked, breaking off. "*Me And My Shadow.*"

"Yeh, sure," Jimmy replied, feeling a strange embarrassment.

As he moved off, he heard Red say, "Come on, come on, cut it, Mike. I knew him in Cincinnati. We went to school together."

What the hell? he asked himself. Then he got it clear. What the hell! A sissy!

Coming out into the aisle, he heard some one snarl, "What was that punk trying to do?"

At first he thought the convict was talking to some one else and kept going. Then suddenly he stopped, turned. "Huh? You talking to me?"

"What was he trying to do? Was he trying to start any funny stuff?"

Jimmy started to ask the convict what the hell business it was of his, then thought better of it. The convict looked angry. He remembered that he was in prison and began getting scared again. He wasn't scared of the trouble; to hell with the trouble! What scared him was not knowing what the trouble might be. "Why, what's the matter?" he asked.

"I just thought he tried some funny stuff," the convict said. "These damn bastards are after every new kid that comes in here. I just thought I ought to tell you before they get you in trouble."

Jimmy blushed; then tried to look angry. "Yeah? You gonna tell me about the trouble? What kind of trouble? Tell me about it."

"You don't know him, do you?" the convict asked.

"I don't know you, either."

The convict brushed it off. "You don't like him, do you?"

"What's this?" Jimmy asked hotly. "What the hell you care? Who're you? You the law?" Cooling, he added half-conciliatory, "I ain't got nothing against him. I don't know him. He's all right as far as I know. What's the matter with him?"

"He's a rat," the convict stated positively. "He was the one who ratted on those ten fellows who were digging out the woolen mill."

Jimmy didn't know about the ten convicts who were digging out the woolen mill, but he was impressed. "Yeah?" A rat! It shook him.

"He's a damned degenerate, too. Half of these guys in here are sissies. Filthy sons of bitches. I don't like that stuff and I don't care who knows it."

Jimmy lost the effect then and was just sickened. "I don't either," he replied, through with it.

But the convict was not through with it. "I knew you wouldn't go for that stuff, Jim," he continued. "I read about you in the papers. You've been to college. I knew you wouldn't go for that stuff. I don't like that stuff, myself. I don't see how a man can love another man, do you?"

Jimmy's gaze jerked into the convict, seeing him. He was a tall, clean-looking man of about twenty-seven, neatly dressed, with brown, parted hair and regular features. His pants were pressed and his shirt starched.

"What's your angle, stud?" Jimmy asked insultingly. "What you tryna sell?"

"You look like too nice a kid to get in a jam," the convict said, talking fast as if he had been expecting Jimmy's reaction. "Me, I'm just a guy trying to be a pal and steer you right."

"Don't worry about me, stud," Jimmy told him. "When I get down I get down right. I been around, stud."

Without noticing they had drifted down the aisle. At the door they turned and came down the other side by the wash trough and the guard-stand.

"You're getting me wrong," the convict said, spreading his hands. "You could tell me a lot of things; there's too much that I don't know. I'm not jap-wise. But I've been in here long enough to know this joint. And I can tell you this, any one as good-looking as you is headed for a lot of things you wouldn't know about. And there's one thing you can't do; you can't fight everybody."

Jimmy drew his shoulders up and tried to look tough. Here it was again, the need of proving something. Always—*always!* Well, goddammit, hadn't he robbed a man and his wife in their house and been given twenty years for it? Well, what did he have to do now, kill some one? He tried to draw on being bad and showing off and never caring about a goddamn thing.

But ten days in prison had crushed it out of him. He was all confused and wounded and deep inside felt mangled. He was scared, and trying to keep from showing it, feeling that if he ever showed it, if people ever found it out, he was lost. But every now and then it broke through, stifling him, making him wooden-fleshed, torturing his mind into a lacerated frenzy. When it got too great it choked and thought stopped and he could escape into present tense. That was best—when thought stopped. He would go automatic. If he just didn't have to think about it, about anything. He had done it, and they had gotten him and given him twenty years and now goddammit let him do those twenty years without thinking about them, because everything was so hopeless.

They passed the bunks down at the lower end where two convicts lay belly down on a bunk with their arms about each other, reading

3 1

a movie magazine, while on the bunk next to them two old men mixed tobacco.

"What's your name?" Jimmy asked the convict.

"Walter—Walter Richards."

"What you in for?" He had to talk to keep from thinking.

"First degree."

"Who'd you kill, your wife?"

"No, a state trooper from Pennsylvania," Walter said. "There were two of them came across the line to arrest me. I was in Youngstown; I had just got in from Pittsburgh. I had brought in a load of green weed and was in the kitchen eating. They broke down the door and broke in—"

"And you let 'em have it."

"I killed one but the other guy lived."

"It's a wonder they didn't give you the chair," Jimmy remarked.

"They did," Walter said. "I was in death row eighteen months, three days, and two hours."

"Huh?" Jimmy was shocked. "In death row?" He looked at Walter with incredulity. A man who had lived with death for almost two years. But there wasn't anything about him to show it. "How'd you get out?" he finally asked.

Before Walter could reply, Red Hill came out from between two bunks and addressed Jimmy, "Want another smoke, Jim?"

"Huh?" Jimmy turned, and then felt himself beginning to blush again. Couldn't he get away from the guy? "Uh-uh, I got some left. I still got those two. Thanks anyway." He couldn't deliberately hurt the guy's feelings.

Looking at Walter, Red spoke to Jimmy, "Come on down to my bunk, Jim, I got something to show you. You know that fellow who was playing on the mandolin when you were down there before. He's going to play and I'm going to sing. We're practicing for Sunday service week after next. You know how to sing, don't you?"

Jimmy opened his mouth to refuse, but Walter didn't give him a chance. "He don't want to sing with you even if he does," he said to Red.

"I wasn't talking to you," Red snapped.

"I was talking to you," Walter challenged.

"Come on, Jim," Red pleaded, taking Jimmy's arm.

"He's coming with me," Walter stated and took his other arm.

"Goddammit, turn loose of me!" Jimmy snarled, jerking away from both and turning crimson. "What the hell is this?"

Walter made a threatening move toward Red. "Go on, go on, beat it, slut!" he grated. "Scram! Jim and I were talking."

"You ain't nothing but a whore yourself," Red accused. "You're one of those swap-up bitches. You go out in the coal shed so can't nobody see you."

Walter made as if to hit Red, but Red ran his hand into his pocket, stopping him.

Jimmy walked away from them both. Walter turned quickly and caught up with him. "I ought to go back and hit that slut in the mouth," he said, getting very fierce.

"You ought to have hit him when you had him, stud," Jimmy said, having lost his awe of Walter by the little argument. He was getting fed up with the whole thing. It had taken him down another peg; it kept him from thinking but it didn't give him anything.

"You don't believe that stuff Hill said about me?" Walter asked.

"Why should I?" Jimmy countered. "Is it true?"

"You know it's not true," Walter denied. "I just hate that stuff so much I don't even want anybody to hear my name mentioned in such respect."

They had just passed the latrine again when an elderly, serious-looking convict stepped from between two bunks and called, "Walter! Oh, Walter! Step here a minute."

"I'll be back in a minute," Walter said, turning away. "You wait here, Jim, I'll see what this fellow wants."

Jimmy went over to the poker game again, wishing he had some money. It was late, close to bed time, and the betting had slowed to a dribble. The winners were already cashing in their chips; only the losers were left trying to ring in the dealer. Jimmy was amused, watching them; it reminded him of Sugar Patton's joint. If he just had some dough.

While he stood there the lights flashed; the guard rapped his stick on the table top. All over the prison, the rapping of sticks could be heard. Bed time!

And suddenly, it was back on top of him—prison and his twenty years. He turned slowly and went over to his bunk, feeling numbed.

His was a top bunk next to the outer wall, directly beneath one of the high, barred windows. Hanging at the head was the wooden label with his name and number, while at the foot hung his aluminum coffee pail, which served in the place of a cup. He had stuffed his soap, tin comb, and face towel down into the pail, and had stuck his Sunday shirt of blue denim, and his white string tie underneath the mattress.

Many of the other convicts owned wooden boxes, some of which were made like trunks with wooden trays and fancy locks. They kept these underneath the bunks at night, and on top of them during the day when the floors were swept and mopped. In these they kept their personal belongings, things which they were allowed to buy with their own funds—tobacco, soap, combs and brushes, extra shoes, underwear, sox, and such. But all Jimmy had was what the state had given him: the suit which he wore and the extra shirt.

He took off his outer garments, keeping on his long cotton underwear with his prison number stenciled in the neckband. Since there was no place else to put them, he laid them on the foot of his bunk. Then he slid underneath the covers on his stomach and looked about.

Most of the convicts, like himself, slept in their underwear which they changed once a week at bath, wearing them continually one hundred and sixty-eight hours. However, a few owned pyjamas, and others, like Red Hill, wore shirts and shorts and slept in them.

As he watched, the guard took count, starting at one corner and going up and down the aisles between the bunks. The guard was old, slump-shouldered, pot-bellied, but now he walked rapidly and the convicts who weren't already in their bunks or standing nearby came running. The guard counted the empties, not the men. When finished, he went out to the center table and rapped his stick to signify the count was right. The convicts began moving around again; some went to the latrine, others went from bunk to bunk, borrowing magazines, tobacco, and such.

After a few minutes the outer lights went off; but every third light down the center aisle remained on all night. The convicts who bunked near the lights could read as long as they wished. Several convicts sat on their bunks, taking a last puff from cigarets. Smoking in bed was prohibited.

For a time the guard walked up and down the center aisle, but when the convicts were settled, he returned to his padded chair on the stand and opened a detective story magazine.

Jimmy turned over and looked at the ceiling. He couldn't get over the feeling that he was some one else. He couldn't be Jimmy Monroe, lying there on an upper bunk in a prison dormitory, looking at the low, flat ceiling. It just wasn't real.

"Jim."

He spun over.

It was Walter. "I brought you some matches," he said.

Jimmy took them. "Thanks."

"I couldn't get back. That guy got to singing the blues and I couldn't get away."

"Oh, that's all right."

"Good night."

"Good night."

After Walter had gone back to his bunk, Jimmy heard a high falsetto voice mimic, "Good night." And another reply, "Good night." Some snickering followed. He tried to ignore it.

Some time later he climbed down from his bunk and went to the latrine. The convicts on upper bunks had wooden stools to step on. Jimmy felt very conspicuous going across the floor under the center aisle lights. To make it worse, a number of convicts began hissing at him. He gritted his teeth and tried to look tough, but he didn't quite make it with his face so fiery red and his body dwarfed in the huge, flopping underwear.

As he stood at the latrine, Red Hill came out and joined him. "What'd that guy say about me?" he asked.

"He didn't say no more about you than you said about him," Jimmy grunted.

"What you want to do is wait and find out for yourself," Red told him. He was wearing rayon shorts which showed his round, hairless legs. In that prison of the eternal floppy, long-legged, cotton drawers, bare legs looked odd and slightly obscene.

Jimmy felt embarrassed, standing so close to him. "That's what I'm going to do, wait and find out," he said to Red.

Then he went back and climbed into his bunk and tried to go to sleep. But he couldn't go to sleep. All that stuff in Chicago kept coming back. He could see himself asking that pawn broker for five hundred dollars on the ring, and then standing there while the pawn broker called the police—for to have run would have made him cowardly.

He could feel the cops hitting him in the mouth, hanging him by his handcuffed feet upside down over a door, beating his ribs with gun butts until, with the live red pain eating out his guts and blood running down his unbearably hurting legs, he confessed. Confessed to highway robbery of the first degree.

But it was too new to stand much thinking about. He didn't want to think about it. He hated thinking about it. He felt like vomiting when he thought about it; he felt all ruptured down in his groins.

He thought a little of his mother and father and of Damon, but he had almost got past thinking about them. And a little of Joan, and of Benny, and of Sugar, and the boys out to the club; but he had got past most of them, too.

It was thinking of Chicago that hurt the most, but he couldn't keep from thinking of Chicago. He couldn't get past thinking of that. It came and went, and when it went he tried to get some sleep. But he hadn't got to the place where he could sleep much.

When he turned his head and looked out the window, he saw the moon and the sky and a guard turret with spot lights down the walls. He saw the guard silhouetted against the lighter sky, rifle cradled in his arm, the intermittent glow of the cigaret in his mouth. He saw the long, gray sweep of the walls against the deep blue distance. Just fifty feet away was freedom, he thought. And it would take him twenty years to make it.

WHEN THE LIGHTS CAME ON next morning, Jimmy put on his shoes and sox sitting cross-legged in bed, then lay on his back with his feet in the air and pulled on his trousers. He then sat at the foot with his feet dangling and put on his hickory striped shirt, vest, coat, and cap, jumped down on his stool, got his towel and soap out of his coffee bucket, and went over to wash.

It was always cold in the morning; the air was cold, the bunks were cold, the floor was cold, everything you touched was cold, and the water was icy. No one thought of washing underneath their arms in the morning. Jimmy tried the soap, but it wouldn't lather, so he knocked back his cap with his forearm, dabbed a little water on his face and smeared it around with the towel, then said to hell with it, it was his dirt, anyway.

When the breakfast bell rang, the guard knocked his stick and the men lined up down the wide center aisle in two lines, two by two in each line, the tall men at front, graduating down to the short men at the rear, and marched lockstepping with the snow in their faces and on their hands out across the road which led in from the West stockade, down the alley beside the three-storied red brick tin shop and storehouse building, and turned into the dining room through the side entrance.

It was a flat, one-storied building divided into two wings with the kitchen in the middle. Jimmy's company was the first to enter. They marched down the wide center aisle and filed in between the narrow, slate-topped tables, ten men to a table, twenty tables deep, and sat on their wooden stools with their arms folded until the guard knocked his stick. Then they took off their caps, put them underneath their stools, and looked at their breakfast.

Aluminum bowls were half-filled with soupy oatmeal over which had been poured a solution called "milk", but which, by the time the convicts arrived, had returned to its original form, the chalk settling in a white scum over the oatmeal with clear water on top. To the side were aluminum plates each containing one link of fried sausage which had cold-welded by congealed grease. Empty cups were lined against the front ledges of the tables. The utensils were made of some sort of lead-black alloy.

For a moment there was the usual dead silence of slow minds trying to decide whether to rebel or continue, broken only by the sound of other companies coming in and the scraping of stools and banging of stick. Then they began to eat.

A voice said dully, "Slop."

Another, addressed to the waiter who stood by the service table along the wall, said, "Get me some bread down here, boy."

The waiter brought a pan of whole-wheat bread, and the convict shouted, "I don't want no goddamn black bread, neither," taking out his spleen. "I want some white bread." Turning to the guard, he called, "Hey, cap, what about some white bread? Goddammit, I'm a working man, I want some white bread. It's bad enough to eat the rest of this goddamned shit."

The guard turned to the waiter, "Give 'em some white bread, boy."

"Attaboy, cap!"

"Tell 'im 'bout it, cap!"

"I'm gonna look out for my boys," the guard said.

After a moment the waiter returned with the mess sergeant.

"Who sent this boy after white bread?" the mess sergeant wanted to know.

"I did," the guard said. "These are working boys, they need white bread."

The mess sergeant gave him a long cold look. "You run your

goddamn coal company and let me run this goddamned dining room," he said.

That was that.

"Who wants to swap some meat for some oatmeal?" some one asked at large.

No one paid him any attention. Finally a convict replied, "I got some meat for you; and it ain't no cold meat with hard grease all over it."

"Give it to your mother," the first convict suggested.

Slowly, stolidly, without thought, Jimmy ate everything. Everyone else ate rapidly, and he was the last finished. Soon after the mess sergeant rang the bell. Everyone stopped, those who had come in last and those who had come in first. The guard knocked his stick and they got up and marched out. No more talking.

Most of the convicts in the company turned over toward the railroad spur which came in from the Northeast stockade, and went to work. Some rolled wheelbarrows without legs in an endless circle about the two coal piles flanking the track, up the incline to the crusher where lump was converted into slack, dumped, went around again. Others shoveled, putting a shovel full on each barrow that passed. Beyond the crusher others rolled the slack into the shed back of the power house.

Jimmy had not been assigned to a job as yet, so he, along with the other nine newcomers, followed the porters back into the dormitory, and were interviewed by the senior guard, captain Donald, who sat in the office at one corner, his feet propped up on the rough table, and bellowed at every one within earshot. He was a stoop-shouldered old man of about sixty-five with dirty-gray hair and a flabby, weather-red face. Washed out, blue eyes behind old-fashioned, gold-rimmed spectacles held a contemptuous expression as if he thought convicts were the lowest form of animal life. His mouth, filled with chewing tobacco and draining spittle, was the sloppy, uncontrolled mouth of a man beginning to dodder.

After telling each of the newcomers how hard the work was out on the coal pile, how cold it was, how tough his assistant, captain Wire, was on the convicts, how some of the convicts sweated and got chilled and caught pneumonia and died, after gloating over each of them in turn, he assigned each of them to outside work with the parting remark, "Ha-ha, I bet you won't do it no more."

Jimmy, however, was the exception. Captain Donald's daughter, Ellen, had been in a class with Jimmy at the university, and had asked him to sort of look out for Jimmy if he should happen to get in his company. So he held Jimmy for the last.

Right off Jimmy told him about his injury, and the fact he was still under doctor's care and drawing compensation. However, captain Donald was not impressed.

"You were strong enough to rob those people," he said.

But because of his daughter's request, he grudgingly assigned Jimmy to a job as porter inside the dormitory, which was supposed to be an easy job. It didn't make Jimmy any friends, he soon discovered, for almost all the convicts in the company had in applications for porters jobs. But it didn't matter. Jimmy felt he could do without the friends.

When mail was called after supper, Jimmy received a letter from his mother and a note from his father with a thirty-dollar money order enclosed, which he endorsed and had put to his credit in the cashier's office. Suddenly, every one wanted to walk with him, to give him something, or sell him something, or tell him what he could buy in the weekly commissary order which was to be turned in the following day.

Red Hill wanted him to come down and sing, and Mike, the little kid with the mandolin and the bedroom eyes, wanted to play for him. Every one called him Jim after that and knew all about him, about his sentence and his going to the state university and graduating and practicing medicine and law and one of them had it out that he had an interest in a gambling club in Cleveland.

The only thing Jimmy wanted to do was gamble, and he could have gotten credit in any of the games, only he didn't know it. So when Walter came out and asked him over to his bunk, he went because he didn't have anything else to do. He noticed for the first time that Walter was slightly taller than he, perhaps five feet ten, and that his hips were as wide as his shoulders. Evidently Walter had washed and cleaned up right after finishing work, for he was very neat in shined shoes, pressed trousers and an ironed shirt. He was also very pleasant and smiled a great deal, and the slight hardness which his face had in repose was dispelled, leaving a certain boyishness in his appearance.

Jimmy liked Walter's bunk. There was an openness about it which was lacking in the curtained gloom and secretiveness and suggestiveness of the bunks down in the corner by Red Hill's and Mike's. He lay across the foot while Walter sat at the head facing him.

"We look enough alike to be twins, only you have dimples and your hair is lighter than mine and your skin is smoother," Walter said, smiling at him with half-closed eyes. "Jesus, you've got pretty skin."

"Hell," Jimmy mumbled, blushing.

"Mine was smooth, too, but this water and soap in here roughens it." After a moment he added, "You better get a cap like mine. The dye comes out of those like yours and makes your hair come out."

"Yeah?"

He took off his cap and showed it to Jimmy. It had a long bill and was lined with black coat lining material. "See, it's got horsehair inside of the lining."

"Where do you get 'em?" Jimmy wanted to know.

"The fellows make them up in the tailor shop. I'll get you one."

"I'll pay you. How much do they cost?"

"Oh, that's all right. It won't cost me anything. They charge the other fellows fifty cents."

A little later the runner came around with newspapers and Jimmy subscribed to a morning and evening daily.

"Want me to get the same for you?" he asked Walter.

"Oh no, not for me. I want to read yours."

"Okay then."

Several other convicts sauntered up and joined in the conversation. They talked about the warden and the incoming governor and the outgoing governor and the parole board. Every one of them was some kind of a son of a bitch. The warden was a pig sonafabitch;

the parole board members were bastard sonafabitches; the governors were all crooked sonafabitches; everybody who had ever been a governor anywhere was a crooked sonafabitch, ". . . they always got their goddamn hands stuck out—"

They said he was lucky to get a porter's job and asked him if it was true about his being a college graduate. He said, sure, he'd gone to college since he was nine years old; and they said that was pretty young to start, wasn't it? They asked him how much he got in the stickup and he said five thousand in cash and eighteen thousand in jewelry, but no one believed him. They wanted to know how he got caught after getting clear to Chicago and he said the cops picked him up from his description on the circulars which the Cleveland police had sent out, and they said, disbelievingly, that's tough, and he echoed them.

When the runner came around with the magazines, he bought a *Black Mask* and a *Cosmopolitan* for himself and a *True Story* for Walter.

"Every time I see you write your number it shocks me," Walter said, watching him sign the order blank.

"Why?"

"So many men have come in since I have. Let's see, nine thousand and three hundred men have come in between you and me. That's a whole city of men. That's as many men as there are in a whole lot of little towns."

"How long have you been in?"

"A little over five years."

"You're an oldtimer," Jimmy joked.

"No, not yet," Walter replied seriously, continuing, "You know, sometimes I get to wondering how many of those nine thousand went out."

Later on he said, as if he had been thinking about it all along, "Jimmy, you certainly are good looking."

"Yeh?" Jimmy felt a blush coming up.

"Let's make like we're cousins," Walter suggested.

"I don't care; but every one will know we're not."

"No they won't. They haven't got any way of telling. Let's tell them we're cousins on our mothers' sides. Our mothers were sisters, let's tell 'em."

"It's okay with me."

"Cousin Jim. How does that sound?"

"Cousin Walter," he grinned.

Walter was delighted. "We're cousins. I wish you were my cousin for real. I feel like I'm your cousin for real."

"Aw, hell."

"Everybody has seen us together ever since you came into the company yesterday. They'll think I knew you before. I told a couple guys you were my cousin, anyway."

"We're just a couple of old cousins in the bighouse," Jimmy grinned.

But Walter was all excited. It was in his face and eyes. His eyes were bright blue and now they were brilliant with excitement. "We ought to cut our arms and mix our blood and then we would be real blood cousins."

"Hell, we don't have to do that."

"We ought to do something."

"No, let's just say it and let it go at that."

"Oh, all right. But really, Jimmy, we ought to do something to seal it."

"We could cut the warden's throat," Jimmy joked.

But Walter was serious. "Oh, all right. But really we should."

In the rigid severity of the days that followed, and in the nights, especially in the nights when the girls he once had known came back to lie with him, brushing their fleshless lips across his passionate mouth and caressing his tingling body with the dead, formless fingers of memory, he had plenty cause to remember those words of Walter's—"But really we should"—and wonder.

3

*T*HERE ARE MANY HAZARDS IN PRISON, but none greater than the hazard on friendship. Jimmy learned that the day Walter was transferred to the 5-E dormitory. For weeks he and Walter had been nurturing a growing affection for each other. And then, just before dinner that day, the deputy's runner came with a transfer slip for Walter. Hacked off. No way to prepare for it, no way to brace himself against it. Just like walking down the street with a twin, and he steps off the curb and gets run over. Just like the time he and Damon were playing in the basement with explosives—that sudden bright flash and Damon was gone forever.

It was in the evenings when they had talked, their eyes warm and their voices slightly blurred from a feeling of intimacy, that Jimmy missed him most.

Chicago came back first. That one night in Chicago and those two whores who he had had, showing them the diamond rings so huge they laughed and kidded, "What Woolworth store you been raiding, Dimples?" That next day riding down to the State Street Station. Goddamn, what had he been thinking about. Had he been paralyzed? Would Chicago always be coming back like that, a memory to haunt him forever? Would he never get past it. Wasn't it bad enough to get the goddamned twenty years without having to keep remembering what a fool he had been in Chicago?

Red Hill tried to be his friend. Red said he had been in twenty months and had never had a friend, not a real pal, anyway. But Jimmy had gone sour on Red. "Tell it to the wind, stud," he said.

Big Ole, one of the gamekeepers, gave him some credit in his poker game and he won a couple of dollars, but kept playing until he had lost it back again.

And then he got fired from his easy porter's job. Since the night before it had been snowing continuously, so captain Wire kept the company indoors that day. Captain Donald had stayed at home. When the porters had finished sweeping and mopping, the head porter, who had disliked Jimmy from the first, ordered him to go over to the planing mill and get some shavings for the floor. Jimmy got his coat and cap and then saw that two of the three barrels were filled and the other two-thirds full, so he said to the head porter, "To hell with you, you baby raper. Even if we needed shavings I wouldn't go out in this snow."

The head porter was an old, gray-haired, nasty-looking convict with a cast in his left eye, called C&O after the railroad over which he had hoboed so long. On top of being evil, waking up each morning with a grouch that kept him cursing and muttering to himself all day, he was a rat of the first order. He told the guard on Jimmy.

Captain Wire called Jimmy down to the office and asked him what was the matter he couldn't get the shavings.

"We don't need any; that's simple enough, isn't it?" Jimmy said.

"C&O supposed to be the judge of that," captain Wire replied.

"It don't need no goddamn judging," Jimmy muttered.

"You can either go get shavings today or go outside with the wheelbarrow gang tomorrow," captain Wire told him.

Jimmy said, "Yeh," and let it go at that.

Captain Donald returned the next day and decided that it was clear enough for the convicts to go back to work, especially since he didn't have to go out with them. When Jimmy started inside with the other porters, captain Wire yelled to him, "Come on out and grab a wheelbarrow, Monroe. You've lost your happy home."

Jimmy got all tight inside. "Hell with you, stud," he muttered.

Several convicts warned him that he would get into trouble, but he told them, "If twenty years ain't trouble it'll have to do."

Captain Donald let Jimmy come inside, but C&O wouldn't let him work. So that morning and thereafter Jimmy climbed up in the night guard's stand and sat with his feet on the railing while the other porters swept and mopped, then he got down and joined in their card games.

After ten days of this, captain Donald locked him outside one morning. Jimmy hadn't expected it. Dressed in light-weight oxfords, and without gloves, he couldn't have worked outside if he had wanted to.

"Hey, cap, let me in," Jimmy called. "You locked me out."

Captain Donald unlocked again and stuck his head out the door. "Get a wheelbarrow and commence pushing, Monroe," he ordered. "I've had enough out of you."

"But I'm not able to," Jimmy argued. "You know I've got an injured back. I'm drawing compensation for total disability and you expect me to push a wheelbarrow."

"Well, stand out there and watch the others," captain Donald snapped, and locked the door again.

"That's what I'll do," Jimmy snarled.

At first it was just on the outside, on his bare hands and face and ears; and then it was in his skin and slowly underneath his skin, down in his chest and around his bones—the cold. Then it was in his bones, in the marrow, creeping up his spinal column to his brain, filling his brain and leaking out his eyes and down his nostrils in an endless glacier; it came out the roots of his hair in long needles of obscene, goddamned, unearthly cold. And then it was in his soul, in his spirit, and he couldn't stand it anymore and went over and hammered on the steel door and called in a voice as cold as his mind, "Open this door and let me inside, I'm freezing."

Captain Donald cracked the door and looked at him. "What's the matter, what's the matter? Tired of standing?"

"I'm cold."

"I thought you liked to stand."

Jimmy didn't reply.

"Are you ready to roll?"

"I ain't ready to do nothing," Jimmy snarled. "I'm freezing, I tell you."

Captain Donald snickered, then closed the door and locked it. Jimmy wanted to fight somebody, anybody. Pulling his cap down over his eyes, he set out for the deputy's office. Captain Wire called to him, but he didn't look back. The deputy was out, so he went next door and sat down in the vestibule of the court room to wait for him. Kish, the big Greek runner for the hole, came up and tried to start a conversation, but Jimmy didn't feel like talking.

Several guards came in, looked at him, and went away. The dinner bell rang and the companies marched past, then marched back. Jimmy still sat there. Just before supper captain Donald peeped in.

"You're going to the hole," he said.

"That's fine," Jimmy granted.

After supper the deputy warden came in. He was a tall, straight man with a shock of gray hair, sharp aquiline features and a thin beaked nose which along with his bright gray eyes, sharply sardonic behind rimless spectacles, gave him the appearance of a gray eagle. He walked rapidly, his head bobbing up and down and his body shaking with a nerve affliction which had caused the convicts to name him "Shaky Jack."

A sergeant of the guards followed with two other convicts accused of refusing to work, and the deputy sentenced the three of them to the hole without trial. They changed into overalls in the room beyond the courtroom where Kish bunked, then the sergeant opened the heavy steel doors of the "Correction Cells", and ushered them into separate cells.

When he closed the outer doors and turned off the lights, it was pitch black in the hole and absolutely silent. For a moment Jimmy stood stock still, listening, but he could not hear a sound, although he knew the other two fellows were in there somewhere, and perhaps others. He stuck out his hand and felt around; but with the loss of vision in the solid darkness, his mental perspective lost focus, and he had a sudden, swift sensation of floating. He groped quickly for the walls, bumped his shin against the steel slab projecting from the back wall, and cursed.

Somebody laughed, then a voice called tentatively, "Jimmy!"

"Yeah?" He wondered if it was the fat convict who had looked vaguely familiar.

"This is Julius . . . Julius Moore. Remember me? I was in the county jail with you in Columbus."

Sure, old Julius Moore; he had celled with him. "Yeah, sure, stud, I remember you. What say, fellow."

"What'd you do, break your parole?" Moore asked.

Jimmy frowned. "What parole?"

"Didn't you get a five-year bench parole for forgery?"

"Oh yeah, sure, that's right." He had forgotten about it, as he had forgotten about everything but Chicago, it seemed. "But I got a different rap this time," he said. "I'm doing twenty years for robbery."

He could hear Moore's breath suck in. "Twenty years! Jesus Christ! You musta stuck up a bank."

"No, just some people."

"Hell with what you in the stir for!" a voice said. "What you punks in the hole for?" It sounded as if it came from a deep hollow down in the earth somewhere.

At first no one replied, then some one giggled. Jimmy thought it must have been the third convict who had been put in with them who giggled; he had seemed a little simple minded.

Finally Moore challenged, "Who's a punk?"

"Aw, I didn't mean no harm, buddy," the voice replied. It was laconic, indifferent. "I know you ain't no punk. Got a cigaret?"

After a time Moore said, "No."

"Got a cigaret paper?"

"No."

"Got a match?"

"No. We ain't got no makings at all, buddy."

"You ain't? Well, don't call me no buddy, you goddamned punk. You bastard. You fat gunsel."

"Aw, shut up, you screwball," Moore said. "You're stir simple."

"Your mother's a screwball," the voice replied. "Your sister's stir simple. Your grandma's a whore." He said it with such flat indifference that Jimmy had to laugh. Moore didn't reply.

After a moment the voice asked, "Ain't you even got a butt?"

"Kiss something, rat!" Moore yelled.

"Aw, shut up, you fat louse, I wasn't talking to you," the voice said. "I'll catch you out there when I empty my pot in the morning and knock you on your fat can."

"I'll meet you!" Moore shouted in an agitated voice. "I'll fight you. I'm not scared of you."

The laugh kept coming up in Jimmy until he felt queer; it couldn't have been that funny, but in the darkness with so much locked up ferocity floating all around him, he felt like lying on the floor and laughing until he cried. "Hit him in the mouth," he called in a laughter-filled voice.

After that no one said anything. Jimmy sat on his bunk. The darkness closed in and the silence became tangible. His shoulders drooped forward, his head bowed as if from the weight of the silence. His mind would not penetrate the darkness and his thoughts turned into themselves. He wished some one would start talking again because all he could hear was his own heart beating like a trip-hammer, and his thoughts became broken and scattered. He tried to say something himself, but when he opened his mouth to speak his voice would not come out.

Suddenly, a high-pitched, insane shriek knifed into the silence, "*Get out of here! Get out of here, I say, Go!*"

Jimmy jumped to his feet, kicked into something, making a startling clatter, and in dodging, slammed into the wall with a crash. "Goddamn! Goddamn!" he sobbed, cold sweat coming out on him like showers of rain.

"That you, Jimmy? What the hell's the matter?" Moore asked with quick concern.

"I don't know," Jimmy confessed in a shaky voice. "I heard somebody scream and I jumped up and knocked into something."

"Aw, that punk's just blowing his top," the voice said.

"Then it wasn't you that screamed?" Moore said.

"Naw, that's what made me jump. Do you know what I bumped into?"

Moore laughed. "That's your bucket."

"Bucket? Water bucket?"

Some one giggled.

"Not hardly," Moore said.

Jimmy began to smell it then. He had knocked off the lid. "Jesus Christ, is this what we use? Don't they ever wash it out?"

"Sure, you'll have to wash it out in the morning."

"Me? Hell, I won't use it." Feeling in the darkness, he located the lid and put it back into place, then he said, "I wonder who that was screamed."

"Aw, just some sonafabitch blowing his top," Moore said callously.

"It was his baby sister," the voice said.

"Aw, go to hell, you stir simple bastard," Moore told him.

In the backwash of his sudden emotion, the cold sweat chilled Jimmy to the bone. And again that laugh began growing until he could visualize it crawling about inside of him.

"Ha-ha-ha," he laughed. "Ha-ha-ha, I'm cold as hell."

"There's some blankets over there somewhere," Moore called. "Take it easy, kid."

"Ha-ha-ha, hope I don't find that ghost looking for blankets, ha-ha-ha." The thing was getting the best of him. "Ha-ha-ha." Goddammit, he wasn't tickled . . . "Ha-ha-ha."

A Negro's voice came from the lower end, "This guy's in the cell ri' next to me—crazy sonamabitch." His voice was ragged. It was the first time he had spoken and Jimmy was almost as startled by his voice as he had been by the scream. "Dare wuz 'nuddah guy in dat cell though ev'body wuz tryna poison him. He saw ghostes, too. Saw him uh-settin' dare uh-talkin' 'bout, 'Ah sees yuh. Go 'way, Ah sees yuh.' Wonder wassamatter in dat cell."

"Ha-ha-ha," Jimmy laughed. "Goddamn, it's cold."

"Dass what dey says w'en dares a ghost around," the Negro said.

"Aw, shut up, you black sonafabitch," Moore called.

"Get out, now! Get out now!" the maniac whimpered.

"Ha-ha-ha, has he got on yellow gloves?" Jimmy called, wondering where he had heard that before. "Has he got on yellow gloves?" The thing was getting cross-wise his nerves, but he couldn't for the life of him keep down that laugh . . . "Ha-ha-ha."

Suddenly, he heard an abrupt scuffle coming from the maniac's cell.

"He done grabbed him!" the Negro yelled in a panic stricken voice.

"Ride him, cowboy," the indifferent voice encouraged.

"There he goes! *Out that window there!*" the maniac shrieked.

Jimmy slammed against the bars and strained his eyes in the darkness. He heard the Negro come to his feet, heard his startled exclamation, "W'ut goddamn window!" He could almost see the whites of his eyes gleaming in the darkness.

He felt his brain begin to crack, his skin begin to burst, his bones begin to snap. He felt himself flying into pieces of laughter. He tried to hold himself together, but he could feel himself breaking all apart . . . "Ha-ha-ha . . ." Because there wasn't any window. There never had been a window in the hole. Nothing but a wall of solid stone, keeping out the light, keeping out the world, keeping out sanity.

And then he was laughing, terribly, horribly, hysterically. Moore was shouting, "Butt your head against the wall! Butt your head against the wall! Come out of it, Jimmy!"

"Aw shut up you fat slob and butt your own goddamn head against the wall," the indifferent voice called, bringing Jimmy back to normalcy. "I bet you got a fat mama, you fat stinker. I bet your mama's got some good stuff. I'd like to have your mama in here with me."

"Dirty screwball!" Moore screamed, his voice getting out of control. "Dirty, stir-simple bastard!"

Some one giggled.

"Fat gump," the voice heckled. "I wish I had you over here with me, you fat, funky punk. I bet you're a whallapaloosa, you fat, funky gunsel."

Engaging in a duel of very low obscenities, they finally became very friendly with each other, and in a spirit of good fellowship, Moore asked the convict his name.

"I'll tell you if you give me some of that fat stuff," the convict said, and Moore became angry again and said he would meet him out at the drain the next morning when they emptied their buckets and knock out his teeth.

After that the silence came again. Jimmy took a deep breath and lay down on the cold slab of steel. In the excitement he had forgotten about the blankets; now he began to explore about the cell floor with his fingers. He found them stuck in the corner underneath the slab—three small, torn pieces of dusty blanketing.

"I found my blankets," he called to Moore. "At least I found something that feels like blankets."

"You're lucky," Moore called back. "A lotta cells in here ain't got no blankets."

And then he heard the distant scream of a locomotive whistle. Suddenly, he could see that long line of coaches gliding through the night with their chain of yellow-lighted windows, filled with people going somewhere, going anywhere . . .

"Am I?" he asked.

Finally, he lay down again. Maybe he could go to sleep, he thought. He lay in one position for what seemed like ages. At first he felt the cold. He tried to arrange the blankets so as to give him the most warmth. He said to himself, "I'm tired, I'll go to sleep." A bedbug bit him, then another. His throat and neck began to itch intolerably. And then a trickle of pain leaked into his body. It began at the hip bones, at the base of his spine where the pelvis bone hinges, flowed slowly down his legs, up his spine. Mind over matter, he said to himself. I won't think about it. I'll be asleep in a minute.

And then it came in a rush, a throbbing part of him from the top of his matted head to the bottom of his feet, alive and crawling like the cockroaches on the floor, like the maggots in his mind. He jumped to his feet and involuntarily yanked at the door. It made a squeaking sound and he let it go as if it was hot. Suddenly, he could see his mind standing just beyond his reach, like a white, weightless skeleton. He had the oddest desire to push it and watch it float away.

"Jesus Christ, I'd do another life for a smoke," the voice said, its indifference gone now. "I'd cut a bastard's throat from ear to ear for half a cigaret. I'd shoot a sonafabitch in the eye for two puffs off a good old *Camel*."

Tears of sheer gratitude came up in Jimmy's eyes to hear a human voice.

"Goddammit, I want a fire!" the voice shouted. It was getting him now. "I want something to eat! I want a sirloin steak with some hot brown gravy and some porterhouse rolls and a dish of fried onions. I want the pig's wife! I want the governor's daughter! What the hell you doing, you fat, funky, ugly, rotten, sneaking, dirty, low, degenerate, sonafabitching bastard! You can't go to sleep! What the hell you tryna go to sleep for? Let's sit up and talk about your good old mother, God bless her good old soul."

In the silence of that night, there were seventy-two thousand, six hundred and forty-nine hours—Jimmy counted them. But when the convicts talked, the time went faster.

In the morning the deputy asked Jimmy if he was ready to go back to work, and Jimmy said, "Yes sir." He was sent back to the coal company. Captain Donald gave him a job sweeping off the wheelbarrow path. It was an easy job, the other convicts said.

However, the next day he was transferred into the school company.

*T*HE 5-F DORMITORY TO WHICH THEY transferred Jimmy was the coal company dormitory over again, only it was long and narrow and also housed Negro convicts down in the lower end next to the latrine. It was the north half of a long, weather-stained, flat-topped, wooden building which lay in the areaway back of the hospital and the hole and the combined Catholic chapel and school building like a huge frozen lizard. The east wall extended along the other side, less than fifty feet away; and at the southeast corner, so close that voices could be heard on execution nights, stood the squat, brick death house. The 5-E dormitory where Walter bunked comprised the south half of the building.

Jimmy was assigned to a lower bunk on the center aisle next to the guard stand—"Right under the gun," Walter said when he told him about it—where upon awakening each morning he had his choice of looking at the convicts don their grayed and sweat-stained underwear and sweat-stiffened socks which they wore from week to week, and their bagged stinking trousers which they wore from year to year, and their gaunt patched coats which they seemed to wear forever; or he could raise his eyes and look beneath the sagging upper mattresses out of the west window at the back of the hospital, so early in the morning still asleep, housing tuberculosis and syphilis and cuts and lacerations and contusions and infections and operations and skulls cracked by guards' sticks and fakery and death, with the mattresses thrown out beside the front entrance every morning to be taken away and burned, grim reminders to the long lines of convicts who marched by to breakfast that the convicts who had last lain on them would not need them anymore, or anything else anymore, except a six-foot plot in Potter's Field and some words by the prison Chaplain.

Displeased with that, he could turn around and look across the aisle, overtop the unmade bunks, out of the east window, at the stretch of dark gray wall against the reddening sky, cutting out the rising sun, the smell of burnt gasoline, and the unforgettable perfume of a woman's hair.

Or he could lie in bed and pretend that he wasn't going, and watch the others spread their sheets and make their bunks and form a ragged soap-and-towel procession down to the lower end where the wash troughs were located by the latrine, and where the Negro convicts would have a skin game roaring as if it had been going since the night before.

In the evening after supper he could sit and watch the evening promenade, up the aisle on one side, down on the other, up and down, mile after rectangular mile, which straightened out and put together would have extended a good way out into freedom, but which ended up each night at the bunks from which it had started. Or he could watch the amateur prize fighters who worked out in the area in front of the guard stand; and he could smell them, too.

At night he could roll over on his stomach and watch the nightly latrine brigade with their open drawers and felt house shoes stolen from the hospital. Or he could read by the eternal drop light overhead; or listen to the steady, planted stride of the night guard making his rounds; or watch the furtive slitherings of those bent on degeneracy and maiming, and bent sometimes on murder as was the case of the Negro convict called Sonny who slipped up on another Negro convict called Badeye while he was asleep and cut his throat from ear to ear. It was a sort of gurgle that Jimmy heard, for it was late and quiet. When he got down there, peering over the shoulders of the convicts in front of him, he saw Badeye lying there with blood bubbling out of his mouth in large and small and very fine slavering bubbles, like the mouth of a dog gone mad, only the bubbles in Badeye's mouth were bloody and not quite so frothy, and the blood was running out of his nostrils and down his black greasy skin on the dirty gray sheet. He saw where the blood had spurted out of his throat over the dusty blanket and on his dirty cotton underwear and on the bottom of the mattress on the bunk above. Badeye's arms were half drawn up, and he was flopping very slightly, but after a while, as Jimmy stood there, even the flopping stopped and Badeye was lying there in such a pool of blood he could hardly be seen.

Or he could talk to the night guard whom everyone called captain Charlie, who had taken a liking to him. They talked in whispers, of crime and punishment, virtues and vices, religion and atheism, and in the end captain Charlie would always remark of the pity that a boy his age should have to come to prison.

Or he could roll over on his back and close his eyes and say that he was back in Cleveland in the Far East Restaurant listening to Guy Lombardo's Royal Canadians; or he could say he was on the road at night doing a cool seventy with the sound of the cutout behind him, catching up with him only when he passed through some small town with the heavy-leafed tree limbs hanging low over the road and the white, vine-clustered houses reflecting the sound. He could say he was in Ashtabula the night he drove Johnny down to catch the boat; or back at State again standing on the library steps flirting with a girl. He could say he was in Chicago, too, and had sold that ring and was on the way to Tijuana for the December races with eight hundred bucks in his pockets. But he couldn't make himself believe that, no matter how hard he tried, or how tightly he closed his eyes, or how much he might curse fate or luck or destiny or whatever people called it. Sooner or later, anyway, all of his thoughts would come back there from wherever they had gone, no matter how far, how many miles or how many years, and he'd feel again that sickening, unbearable chagrin as acutely as when the judge had sentenced him. And he would wish to God that he had gone to sleep when he had had the chance.

Just by trying hard enough he could keep from thinking of his mother and father and brother. Or of any of the other things that hurt in memory. But if he thought at all, his thoughts would always come back to Chicago, and thinking of Chicago made him want to vomit. It was not what had happened to him in Chicago. It was the way that it had happened. He never wanted anyone to know how he stood in that pawn shop, defiantly waiting for the police to come and get him and send him back to twenty years, simply because to have run would have made him cowardly.

There were many things about that dormitory, things that happened there and things that happened elsewhere while he was bunking there, which afterwards he could remember without at all remembering the dormitory—not the mechanical aspect of breadth and length and height and bunks and tables and such; that was like the color *red* that one never forgets; but the living, pulsing, vulgar, vicious, treacherous, humorous, piteous, taudry heart of it, the living convicts, the living actions, the living speech, the constant sense of power just above, the ever-present hint of sudden death that kept those two hundred and fifty-three convicts with their aggregate sentences totaling more years than the history of Christianity with the confines of that eggshell structure, to live on, day after day, under the prescribed routine and harsh discipline and grinding monotony which came to all after a time.

And there were convicts, too, whom he could remember without remembering the dormitory as a whole, as if by telescoping back into retrospect he could pick them out, where they stood, what they said, and how they looked, without seeing beyond the radius of the vision of the telescope, like sighting a deer at three hundred yards.

There was Walter at the hole in the partition, asking every passing convict who came near enough to hear to tell his cousin, Jimmy Monroe, that he wanted to speak with him until he found one willing to go the twenty or thirty steps out of his direction that delivering the message would entail.

"Hello, cousin," Jimmy would say, bent over to the hole. "All I can see is your eye. It looks funny," he would laugh.

"I can see all of you," Walter would say.

"Can you? Do you still love me?" Jimmy would tease; he had reached the stage where he could tease again.

"I love you like I see you," Walter would say. "All of you."

"I saw an ad in the paper," Jimmy would say. "*Lazarus* has on a shoe sale. *Florsheims* for eight, seventy-five. Two pairs for sixteen dollars. Do you want a pair?"

"You're not kidding, Jimmy?"

"Naw, I'm going to get a pair for myself."

"I need a pair, but I don't know. You won't be straining yourself?"

"Eight dollars! What the hell! I'll get you a pair, I don't care what you say. You're my kid, I've got to keep you looking pretty."

"Don't say that, Jimmy."

"Well, hell, you don't have to be so serious. I was only joking."

"I'll make it up to you," Walter would promise.

And Jimmy would say, "Aw, hell!" and laughing, add, "What difference does it make if you still love me?"

And Walter would reply, "Always," with so much feeling that Jimmy would blush.

By that time they'd have to get away and let some other "cousins" talk.

And there was Lippy Mike, the head porter, a big, wide-shouldered, athletic-looking, black-haired Irishman, who held his shoulders high and square and walked with a swagger. The other convicts seemed afraid of him because he had a reputation with a knife, and a scar over his deep-set, insane-looking eyes as mute evidence of its authenticity; and for all those who still disbelieved, he carried a knife with a blade six inches long. He was the most overbearing, arrogant person Jimmy had ever known; and he assumed more authority than the guards, themselves.

"After this when you're transferred, Monroe, bring your sheet and pillow case," he had said to Jimmy on his arrival, assigning him to a bunk. "Thursday's laundry day. Be sure to have your sheet and pillow case on top of your bunk. And take everything off the floor in the morning."

"Anything else, captain?" Jimmy had asked.

Mike had pinned those fanatical blue eyes on him, his shoulders high and square and the butt of the knife sticking out of his left breast pocket, and had said in a tin-hard voice, "I'm not your Goddamned captain, punk. I'm Mike!" And then after a full moment during which he just stared at Jimmy, he had lifted his voice and had called, "Papa Henry, give this boy a sheet and pillow case." And with that he had walked down the aisle, high-shouldered and swaggering.

When Jimmy had said, "Go to hell!" Mike had been too far away to hear.

There were the guards; one of whom was captain Bear, big and beer-bloated and slovenly, with tobacco ashes down his vest, and a stubble of gray beard, and the heart disease which finally killed him; and the other, captain Chester, who had a narrow, nasty, greasy face and a sloppy mouth, and narrow shoulders, and a pot belly, and skinny legs, looking young in the face and old in the body, with premature gray in his hair, and who convicts swore they had caught masturbating more than once.

And there was Haines who had been in the county jail with him the time he had been arrested for forgery. He and another convict called Booker were running a poker game. Jimmy began taking a spell on the deal and selling chips for them. It gave him something to do besides lie on his bunk and think. And he could talk to Haines, too, because Haines always treated him like a big shot; whereas he couldn't talk to most convicts, because to most convicts he was just another punk.

Haines was a school porter when Jimmy was first transferred into the company, but the guard caught him washing shirts one day and had him transferred into the coal company. After that Jimmy took over Haines's part of the game to run for him.

There was the school, too. Situated on the first floor of the weather-darkened, gray stone building which also housed the Catholic chapel, it consisted of eight rooms, four on each side, and six grades, since two rooms each were required to hold the students in the first and second grades.

The desks were regular classroom desks which had been donated to the prison, along with the castoff books, by the school boards of various cities. Blackboards extended full-length across the front of each room, while the windows which more often claimed the students' attention were at the back.

And there were the latrines, one on each side, sort of added features after the school had appeared, with their eternal gurgle of water and everlasting stink and red and blue tags which the students were required to carry when leaving a room and hang on nails outside the latrine to announce not only their destination but their purpose.

And there was the time when McGee, a Negro porter, got into an argument with Panic Slim, another Negro. Panic Slim threatened to cut McGee's throat when he went to sleep that night. So when the lights had been turned out, McGee prepared for him by stringing wires completely about his bunk and stacking coffee pails behind them so that if he dozed off during the all-night vigil he intended keeping, Panic Slim would stumble over the hidden wires and fall into the pails and sound the alarm. But as it happened, McGee fell asleep as he had feared, and forgot all about Panic Slim's threat.

Awakening in the middle of the night, he got up and started to the latrine, stepped into the pails with a startling clatter, broke to run and tripped over the wire, and fell headlong into the aisle. Judging from the ensuing commotion, as he threshed about in the wires and buckets and bunks, yelling at the top of his voice, "Oh, he's got me, cap'n, he's got me!" awakening the entire dormitory and frightening Jimmy numb, he must have thought Panic Slim was really killing him.

It was happenings such as these that Jimmy remembered separately, with no connection one to the other, and with no continuity; and without the feel and sight and smell of the dormitory.

And on the other hand there were two things about the dormitory which brought back the whole living, pulsing, stinking scene so vividly that he could see it and live all through it again, and feel that hurt that he had then felt, being away from all those things that he had then liked, as he had then been young and hot-blooded and passionate and had liked the living, tangible things—women and going to bed with them, drinking whiskey and getting drunk, gambling and winning, sports to watch and to play, a car to own and to drive, the moving picture shows, and nights in a park, sunsets on Lake Erie seen alone, clouds after a rain, and springtime which had always been as tangible to him as a woman's kiss; and being always conscious of those endless years that he could not afford to think of then, that he had tried so hard not to think of that pretty soon he had lost all thought of anything that went beneath the senses of sight and hearing and smell and feelings. But still he had thought of them, those endless years away from things; he had thought of them with his eyes and ears and nose and skin; he had thought of them with the coldness of being out in the weather and with not enough clothes to protect him, and with the sight of guards clubbing convicts over the head with loaded sticks, and with the smell of unwashed bodies and dirty latrines, and with the sounds of sticks banging for bedtime.

The first of those two things was Guiseppe playing *I Can't Give You Anything But Love, Baby* on his mandolin every morning just before breakfast, the loud bell-clear notes carrying all over the dormitory.

He could never understand why that should have affected him so that hearing it years afterwards, when prison had become natural and the dormitories commonplace, he could see the dormitory again as he had seen it then, those gray convicts who in after years become just other fellows, and those gray winter mornings with the fog and the walls and the deserted morning look of the prison yard, and feel again that utter sense of being lost in a gray eternity.

The second was Chump Charlie's radio which Dean, one of the deputy's runners had bought for him. Sometimes at night, after the lights had been put out, captain Charlie had let him play it if the other convicts did not object; and the program which invariably he had tuned in had been the senseless prattle of some old man called Anderson, who had come on and had never gone off, it seemed, with the words, "Hello, li'l old world, doggone you!"

It was always an utter mystery to Jimmy why all those convicts had liked that phrase so well.

Years later when he had learned more about such things, he could remember old man Anderson, and Chump Charlie, and the radio, and see again Chump lying there so proud, his Indian blood darkening his skin, and remember the important way he acted about owning a radio, as if the seed of Dean, whom they said was his old man, had spawned the radio within him and he had birthed it.

THE GUARD WHO WAS ON DUTY at the visiting hall looked at the pass and gave it back to Jimmy. "Return this to your mother," he directed. "She needs it to get out again."

Then, ushering Jimmy into the hall at the end of the A&B cell block, the guard searched him, directed him to leave his cap and gloves on the table there. Jimmy was afraid the guard might take his cap as it was tailored against regulations, so he turned it down atop his yellow pigskin gloves to hide the lining. When the guard ushered him around the corner of the C&D cell block into the long, gloomy visiting hall, with the sheer tiers of cells rearing overhead like the caves of cliff-dwellers, he was still thinking about his cap.

Tables had been placed end to end down the concrete range of 1-C, the same kind that were used in the dormitories, only these had been scrubbed. The same backless benches paralleled them. The visitors sat on the inside, next to the cells, and the convicts sat across from them. Several visitors, all women, had already arrived. They had spread lunches on the tables. The convicts ate and did most of the talking, while the women just sat and listened.

Jimmy walked down behind the benches. When he saw his mother, he stopped and stood there for a moment, very still, looking at her and seeing her look at him, and seeing her love for him in her eyes even at that distance. Right then he loved her more than he ever had, or had ever loved himself, or anyone in all his life. His love for her overwhelmed him.

She stood up and held out her arms and he hurried forward into them. They leaned across the table and kissed each other. He lost sight of her, but he could feel her hands holding very tightly to his arms, and after she had released him and he had sat down, he could still feel them. Neither of them had spoken.

"I brought you something to eat, James," she said finally, moving her hands around in the basket. "I brought you some scalloped oysters. You always liked scalloped oysters." Her voice sounded very thin and hollow, as if it came out of the front part of her mouth instead of her throat. It reminded him of how he had tried to say, "That's all right, that's all right," when the judge had sentenced him, only to find that his tongue had stuck to the roof of his mouth and his throat had become solid and inflexible. He had only been able to move his lips in all of his face and mouth and throat and chest, and he had not been able to make any sound with them at all.

"Did you, mother? Let me help you, mother," he said, but he did not look at her.

She had been looking at him; now she looked at the basket in which all the while her hands had been moving without accomplishing anything.

"Here is the table cloth . . . and here are the napkins . . . and here are the plates," she recited, taking them out of the basket.

They spread the table cloth very carefully, taking a long time as if when they were finished they would find themselves facing each other without anything at all to do or say. She smoothed out the wrinkles, and then began to take out the silver, piece by piece; and then the food. But it did not seem real to either of them— neither their funny, ridiculous actions, nor their being there, in that grimy, gloomy prison, sitting across from each other.

There was a dish of scallopped oysters and some potato salad and some bread and butter and a jar of jelly and some cakes.

"I didn't bring you anything to drink," she said in that light, weightless voice. "I couldn't find anything to put any liquid in."

Since he had first looked at her, he had not looked at her again. He had been staring at the table cloth and at the food; and now, when she spoke, he raised his eyes and glanced beyond her, through the open bars into a cell where the two bunks had been chained up for the day, at the basin in the cell, and at the shelf which held two pictures of two young women and a large white jar and three bottles and two combs and one brush and a whiskbroom, and at a wine-colored lounging robe hanging on a line strung obliquely across the cell, deep-colored against the yellow calcomined walls. But he did not look at her.

"That's all right, mother, I don't want anything to drink." His voice sounded muffled and he cursed under his breath. "We get plenty to drink, all we want to drink," he added, trying to sound more cheerful.

"You look well, James."

His fork touched an oyster and moved it on the plate. "I feel fine, too, mother."

She was wearing a brown, woolen dress and the light brown imitation caracul coat which she had worn, he recalled, for the past five winters. "Do they feed you well enough, James?"

"Oh yes, they feed us pretty good," he replied, attempting to smile, but succeeding only in spreading his lips into something of a grimace. It made him feel sick all up in his face, under and around his eyes. The muscles and the skin of his face felt sick, and his eyes felt sick such as his stomach sometimes felt. He knew that she wanted him to look at her; but his eyes were too raw and open, showing too much that would intensify her suffering. He sat there with his lips spread, toying with the oyster. He would have traded every hope of freedom for the power to smile. It struck him odd; he had never never never felt that way before.

"Do-do they hurt you any, James?" she asked.

If something hurt you, you didn't think about it . . . "No, mother. It's not all that bad." Then he told her about the routine and discipline . . . "I was a porter in the coal company at first but now I'm in school."

"I should think that would be nice," she remarked.

"It's all right; it's fine."

"You're not eating anything, James," she observed.

He stole a glance at her and quickly looked away. "I'm not hungry, mother. We just finished dinner."

But he noticed in that brief glance how red her eyes were from crying, and how swollen her eyelids and the flesh all around them were. Her face seemed loose; the skin was slack and fell in folds beside her jaws. It was as if some inner support which had held it in shape for all those years had broken apart. Her hair, showing beneath the brim of the made-over felt hat, was grayer.

And suddenly he knew that it was not only because he did not want her to see the sickness and guilt and remorse in his own eyes that he did not look at her; but also because he, himself, did not want to see the grief and sudden age showing in her face, as if not seeing it would keep it from being there. But he knew that it was there. He had known all along, even before he had allowed himself to think of it, that it would be there.

"I-I thought you liked oysters cooked that way, James. That's why I fixed them," she said, and he could hear a tear on each word, so high and light and damp and filling up. She was trying so desperately not to cry.

"I do like them, mother." He moved an oyster, lifted it to his mouth, lowered it. "How's Damon, mother?" If he had put it in his mouth he would have vomited. "Did he graduate, mother? Did-did you go to his graduation, mother?" Funny, he could not remember ever having called her *mother* before—it was always *mama*.

"Yes, his father bought him a blue suit. He graduated this past Friday. I didn't write because I planned on coming to see you. He received a medal for scholastic honors."

"He did?"

"Yes, they would have given him the valedictorianship if he had attended for the full four years."

"That's fine," he said. "That's great."

"But you're my baby, Jimmy," she said. "You're my baby." And suddenly she was crying. "Oh, my baby! My little baby!"

Oh, my God, and *this*, he thought . . . saying, "Don't cry, mama, please don't cry." Touching her hand. "I'm all right, mama! I'm all right!"

"Oh, my poor little baby! Why did you do it? Why did you do it?"

On top of all the goddamned rest, he thought . . . pleading, "Don't cry, mama." Holding helplessly to her hand. "Please don't cry." Thinking, all those tears and all that love, that pure and holy love, that mother's love, now, when it can not help and does not matter . . .

After a moment she regained her control and dabbed at her eyes. When she took her hands down and held them in clasped restraint on the table—her red, work-coarsened hands with cracked nails and hardened arteries—he could not look at them without crying, too, so he kept looking away.

"Every one was so nice," she said in a choked voice. "They thought it so remarkable for him to do so well."

"That's swell," he said.

"They are going to give him a scholarship."

"They are? That's swell. Where's he going to college?"

"He's going to Athens, I think. He hasn't decided yet."

"That's a good school."

They were silent for a time. It was difficult to talk of anything but Damon; they were apart; they had always been apart, in separate worlds.

"Do you still say your prayers, James?" she asked.

Hesitating, he lied, "Yes, mother."

"Things are not so hopeless as they seem, James," she said. "The warden says that if you behave yourself and stay out of trouble you will receive time off."

"Did you see the warden?"

"Yes, I was here before the visiting hour started and he came out of his office and talked to me. He said that you appeared to be a nice boy."

"He did?"

"He said they all liked you very much."

"He did? I haven't talked to him yet."

"He said that in twelve or thirteen years you will receive a hearing by the parole board and that if you behave yourself in the meantime you will be paroled."

Twelve or thirteen years . . . "He said that, too?"

"Do try to be a good boy, James," she said. "You are young yet; you still have time to change."

"I will, mother; I'll be a model con—" he broke off. "I mean a good boy. I'll be a good boy."

She took a Bible from the bottom of the basket and gave it to him. "I want you to have this, James."

At sight of the book he gave a start, then caught himself and said, "Thanks, mother." He took the book and thumbed through the pages, forcing himself to say again, "Thanks, mother, this is very nice."

It was a very old book with a worn, soft-grained leather binding. The words, *The Holy Bible,* were printed in gilt on the front, and written in ink on the fly-leaf was his mother's maiden name and the date, "June 13, 1895."

"I had that before I was married," she said.

The leaves were very fine and slightly yellowed from age.

"The time is up, madam," the guard announced from behind her. They had not seen his approach.

Her fingers, folded on the table top and held so carefully, went rigid. Her whole body went rigid. Down the table the other visitors stood, kissed, and prepared to leave.

He stood, also, and she clambered slowly to her feet. They kissed again. Her lips were trembling and breaking up beneath his, and he prayed, "God, please don't let her cry anymore."

As before, he could feel her hands holding very tightly to his arms, and when she let go of him, he could still feel them on his arms.

"Tell Damon I said hello, mother," he said, looking at the food and at her nervous hands tearing her handkerchief to shreds; and at the funny-shaped box on the floor of cell No. 8.

"Goodbye, James. I'll try to get down next month. Be a good boy and read your Bible."

"Yes, mother, I will, mother. Goodbye, mother."

In all that time he had not looked at her again, and now he turned away, still not looking at her, because he knew if he looked at her again he would think of all those things which she had done which might, or might not, have been responsible for his being there. So he held the Bible tightly in his hand, but it was just so much dead weight, and went down the range, not looking at her. When he came to the table where he had left his tailored cap and pigskin gloves, he passed blindly by, having forgotten them.

But just before he stepped through the doorway into the prison yard, something inside of him made him turn and look back. Down at the other end of the long, dim-lit range, flanked on one side by the C cells rising in a sheer steel cliff to the concrete ceiling sixty feet overhead, and on the other by the grim cell house wall with its barred dingy windows keeping out the sunlight, he saw her standing there after all the others had gone, very small in the middle of all that immense masonry erected to confine convicts such as he, picking up the food which he had not eaten after she had prepared it and brought it down to him, and putting it back into the basket to take home for a warmed-over meal, so slow and so old, her suffering discernible even from where he stood; and against his will he thought of all the times that she had said to him, "James, do try to be a good boy, the things you do hurt mother so." Remorse came up in him in overwhelming waves.

MANY THINGS HAPPENED to Jimmy the months following his mother's visit; but thought was not one of them. They happened in sight and in feeling and in smelling and in hearing. But nothing lingered, neither the shocks nor the scares nor the laughs nor the hurts. Nothing had a past or a future; and when the feeling or action happened, stirring up its sensation, that was all. He could not bring it back to conjure up that laugh again, nor could it come back of its own account to bring those tears.

He could not think; he could not remember. Slowly, without his realization, his mental process underwent a change. Where, before, there had been girls outside the walls; now there were only walls. Where there had been hurts; now there were only shocks. Before, each moment had been all past, hurting with a deep ache of remorse; or all future, hideous with the thought of twenty years. Each happening had brought back its picture, the slow, virginal birth of a smile on the girl's lips he had just kissed; the tight, mounting suspense of watching lazily pirouetting dice. Had stirred up an old poignancy. Or had filled him with a lingering dread, connecting the inside with the outside, and the time with eternity.

But that night following his mother's visit, he lost it. Between the hours of nine and five, he burnt it all up. What was left was a nineteen year old man lacking the qualities that would have made it human. Now to this man, named Jimmy, each moment was absolute, like a still life photograph. Each happening lived and died, unrelated to the ones that came before or those that came afterwards. A day was no longer the seventh part of a week, but in itself infinity. Everything was an odor, a sound, a picture, hot or cold, blunt or sharp, aching or irritating. The tone of voice was the thing that offended in being called a son of a bitch.

In this absoluteness there was no past. No outside world. No thought. No memory. He lived inside a pattern, an old and musty pattern that some convict had used before he got there, and which some convict would use after he was gone; he lived by seeing, smelling, feeling. If he had never lived before, it wouldn't have made any difference as it was all in the pattern.

It was simply that his mother's visit tipped him into that stunned stage of senselessness which permitted him to do time. In that way it helped, for any old-timer could have told him, you do time on top of each moment, no more, no less, for the past will drive you crazy and the future kill you dead. Things happen, and that's all. *How?* you do not think of. And *why?* you do not care.

He wrote a note:

"Dear Haines—I haven't got a cent, pal. I let that hunky, Big John, have a nickel's worth of chips for a monkey he had carved from a peach seed, and he took it and made a monkey out of me. He broke the game. When time came to pay off, Booker claimed broke—you know, I think that guy's a little ratty. Anyway, I had to pay him off myself; and then I had to owe him 95¢. As soon as I get hold of something I'll send you a ball or two—Jimmy."

He flipped the note towards Haines when they passed the coal company on the way to dinner. The note hit a convict by the name of Hawkins in the face. Hawkins grabbed for it, missed it. Captain Donald noticed the motion, then saw the note when it fell to the ground. Five minutes later he came over where Jimmy's company was seated and ordered Jimmy, Booker, and Big John to get up and march ahead of him to the hole.

Booker hesitated. "What have I done?" he wanted to know.

"Come on, come on, no back talk," captain Donald rasped.

But when they had gone as far as the hospital, Booker balked. "I ain't going to the hole unless I know what I'm going for. I ain't done nothing."

"Gambling, that's what," captain Donald accused as if he relished the fact. "You and your henchmen have been running a big poker game every night."

"What the hell you got to do with that?" Booker muttered. "You ain't my guard."

Captain Donald raised his stick and swung, catching Booker, who had been walking ahead of him, squarely across the back of the head. Falling forward in a sudden arc, Booker caught himself halfway to the ground, turned slightly and staggered off balance. The blow had knocked his hat askew and when he kept turning out of his stagger, it fell to the ground, and his hair flagged thinly across his forehead. Jimmy spun about, facing captain Donald, and backed from the sidewalk.

Seeing captain Donald draw back again, he switched his gaze to Booker's face, saw his loose mouth and wide eyes as he came in; and then he saw the stick lay across Booker's forehead just above the eye and underneath the flagging hair, heard the meaty sound. He saw the dead white slit come into the skin as if it had been slashed with a knife; saw the red blood gush; saw the light of consciousness leave Booker's eyes as still in a crouch, he fell into captain Donald's legs. It was a series of dull paintings, gruesome in subject and overly realistic in treatment. Only when captain Donald drew back and hit the unconscious figure draped against his legs did it come to life.

Blinking out the nausea, Jimmy cried, "Goddammit, don't hit him again! Don't hit him again! Can't you see he's down?"

Captain Donald had his stick raised. Turning slightly, he struck at Jimmy. Jimmy caught the blow on his arm and backed away, through the ankle deep slush. Captain Donald came forward and Jimmy turned away from him, walking rapidly toward the hole, a stubborn pride holding him to a walk, and fear urging him to run, until his nerves were like a million tiny hands, twisting his flesh into quivering disconnected charqui. With every step he braced himself for the blow across the head, his ears straining for the sound of footsteps behind him because his pride would not let him turn his head; telling himself that if captain Donald hit him and did not knock him out, he would kill him; all the while trying to decide whether the indignity which he had already suffered was worth dying for. He went as far as the court-room vestibule without looking back, feeling as if he would fly into a million pieces at the slightest touch.

"They're taking Booker to the hospital," Big John said, catching up with him.

Looking in that direction, Jimmy saw two nurses lifting Booker into stretchers. "They're right at the hospital," he said foolishly. "What do they need the stretchers for?"

And then he was sweating, all up in his hair and underneath his eyes and back of his neck and in the palms of his hand. He could feel it on his legs, turning icy cold as it came through the skin.

In a few minutes captain Donald, followed by the Deputy, and Mr. Blue, the Personnel Officer, came into the vestibule. Mr. Blue was a short, pot-bellied man, with a wrinkled, toothless, owlish face, who, despite the fact that he was pigeon-toed almost to a deformity, still managed to swagger. Sometimes during court sessions he was allowed to act as prosecutor—the chaplain, to make the farce complete, being defense attorney—and had over the years built up a reputation as the dirtiest, meanest, lowest, rottenest officer in prison. Jimmy had heard that once Mr. Blue had been a famous attorney, but seeing him now for the first time, found it difficult to believe.

"I'll put this punk in the soup company," Mr. Blue said, giving Jimmy a look and rearing back with his hands on his hips, his bloated, frog-like body pulling his uniform into a surrealistic caricature. "And this one in 1-K," acknowledging Big John with a glance.

"Give them a week in the hole first." Then turning to captain Donald, he asked, "What in the hell have they been doing anyway, goddamn 'em!"

"Wait a minute—" Jimmy began. "I haven't even had a trial."

Ignoring them all, the deputy pushed Jimmy and Big John into the court room, pulled captain Donald in after them, and closed the door in Mr. Blue's face.

Captain Donald exhibited the note and a stale, dry piece of bread which he claimed he had found underneath Big John's mattress. The Deputy put Big John in the hole, ordered Jimmy to be transferred back to the coal company; then stood up and went out, passed Mr. Blue without a glance, looking more sardonic than ever, his head bobbing up and down and his eyes aloof and indifferent.

Captain Donald assigned Jimmy to rolling coal as soon as he was transferred. Then he came outside to ride him.

"Look at him, fellows, here he is," he said. "Thought he was too good to be in the coal company and got transferred into school so he could loaf. Over there running a gambling syndicate. Look at him! A big shot! Got one fellow's head cracked and another put in the hole. Look at him, right back here in the coal company."

But Jimmy beat the rap. Just before supper he went to the hospital on sick call, complained of an aching back, and got hospitalized. Captain Donald fumed, but he couldn't do a thing.

Housed in an old, two-storied, weather-stained, wooden building with a gabled roof and cupola, shaped like a cross, the hospital was a congested madhouse, staffed by convict nurses and headed by a civilian, doctor Drew, a sloppy, fleshy incompetent who had failed in private practice, and after accumulating more than twenty-five thousand dollars in debts, had finally found his place in prison. Jimmy had heard that doctor Drew, upon losing his third patient on the operating table in a single afternoon, performing hemorrhoid operations, which was the extent of his surgery, had cried in an angry voice, "What the goddamn hell they keep dying for? They'll make me lose my job!"

Jimmy was assigned to C-ward. Situated on the ground floor in the south wing with a sun porch to the east and cots with top and bottom sheets, it was the most pleasant place he had been since entering prison. Three nurses were on duty at the time, all clad in white shirts and tight-fitting white trousers, and smelling of perfume and pomade. One, smaller and nicer looking than the others, came into the bathroom while Jimmy was bathing and offered to wash his back. So Jimmy let him, enjoying the smooth touch of his hands.

For supper he had steak and fried potatoes, bread and butter, his choice of milk or coffee, and a slice of apple pie. Lying there after he had finished, with his stomach full and two white sheets caressing him, and no one to swing their stinking feet down in his face, he felt magnificent. Grinning, he said to the cute little nurse, who's name he had discovered was Harry, "I could lie right here and do my twenty years, so help me."

Winking, Harry replied, "And I could lie there and help you do it, dimples."

For a moment Jimmy did not know whether to blush or expand. Finally, he sputtered, "What *is* this?"

The nurses kept him there by showing a temperature on his chart until they all had had a try at making him. Then they put his temperature back to normal and the doctor discharged him.

That happened in five days from the time he flipped the note until the time he left the hospital. Separate days, unrelated to those before or after. He never knew how long Big John stayed in the hole; how long Booker stayed in the hospital. He never saw either of them again. He did not think to ask about them. He did not think about them at all. It happened, and that was that.

He was transferred to the soup company. Ostensibly created for convicts who had stomach trouble and couldn't eat the main line food, its diet of oatmeal and chalk-water for breakfast; soup, bread and coffee for dinner; the same soup thinned out and warmed over for supper, made it a perfect punishment company for those who had incurred Mr. Blue's disfavor and whom he could punish in no other way. As a consequence it was filled with white and colored agitators, degenerates, and stirbugs, who greeted Jimmy on his arrival with that decayed enthusiasm of men who have lost their pride. Throughout the prison it was known as the "Three-C Company"—cranks, cripples, and cocksuckers.

It was celled on the 2-1 range of the I&K cell block, the last of the old, crumbling, dark, damp, dim cell blocks of a past era. According to rumor Civil War prisoners had been held there; it was Jimmy's conviction there had been no change, not even in the moldy, stagnant atmosphere. There was no sanitation. Tin buckets were used and placed on the range each morning to be collected and cleaned by the bucket company. There was always an argument, and generally a fight, when one of the inmates had to take a purgative without being joined by the other.

In the crevices of the rotten wooden bunkframes, and underneath the mattresses, bed bugs perpetuated by the thousands, literally by the millions, and grew obese on convicts' blood, little difference it making to them whether the blood was four-plus or negative. Neither fire nor water nor fumigation could exterminate them.

In a sort of fatalistic effort to keep them out on the rotting wooden range, once the cell had been deloused, convicts encircled the fronts of their cells, the legs of their bunks, and the chains hanging from the walls with axel grease. But nothing kept them out of the beds at night, nor actually killed them. During fumigation they went into some sort of coma, to come alive, vicious and ravenous within a week.

Jimmy learned the trick of trapping them with a shiny tin lid placed on the floor, and on quiet nights when he could not sleep, would lie and listen to them drip from the ceiling like a slow leaking faucet onto the shiny surface until it was black with them. Burning those, he would catch another tin, perhaps. And by that time he could sleep.

It did not do to try to burn them out, for then they would only come out the crevices and hide in the bed coverings, after which he would have to sit up all night.

But Jimmy lived. He didn't die. In that dark and gloomy cavern where it seemed only fungi could possibly exist, subsisting on a diet which would conceivably starve an infant, he gained ten pounds. He talked a great deal to his cell mate, joked and kidded with the others when they went to the idle house each day, and laughed like hell the time the guard, Calahan, told a group of visiting women that the refuse buckets stacked up outside the block to air were ice cream containers for the quart of ice cream each convict was given every Sunday.

The soup company happened.

His compensation was cut off. He had been receiving seventy-five dollars monthly. He had two hundred dollars to his credit in the cashier's office. So it did not matter.

On the first day of March—a cold and dreary day, with a sagging second story sky dripping pure forlornness and the bleakness that comes alone to prison; gray top, gray bottom, gray men, gray walls, dull-toned and unrelieved—Jimmy was taken along with other new convicts to the chapel to hear the warden.

When they had all been seated, the warden appeared on the stage. It was the first time Jimmy had seen him. He was the remnant of a big man gone to seed, dressed in an expensive suit made for the man which he had been before, and much too large in the shoulders for the remnant of the man which he had become, and much too small in the waistline for where he had all gone to. His head was practically bald, and his face, seamed and sagging, looked as if it had melted through the years and had run down into his jowls which in turn had dripped like flaccid tallow down onto his belly. His shoulders had sagged down onto his belly, too, so that his whole skinny frame seemed built only to keep his belly off the ground. His hands were sick and white, laced with frayed blue veins, and on the third finger of his right hand he wore a diamond the size of a robin's egg.

He held out his sickly, white, vein-laced hands, and spoke one sentence, "In these hands, I hold your destinies." Then he turned and walked away. The convicts were returned to their companies.

That happened.

Several nights afterwards, Stepp, a Negro convict on 1-I, was yelling to some convict on 3-I, and the guard, walking down the second range, stopped in front of Jimmy's cell, took the cigar out of his mouth, spat over the railing, and barked, "Pipe down! Pipe down! What the hell you think this is, a levee camp?"

"Come down and make me," Stepp called back.

The guard reddened. He was a young, medium built, dark-haired man with a bluish growth of whiskers and a Clark Gable mustache. He wore his pin-striped, double-breasted blue suit unbuttoned so the convicts could see the .38 special hanging in its shoulder sling; and after seeing the gun, the convicts would smell narcissus perfume, whiskey, and cheap cigars. It always made Jimmy frown a little.

"I'll come down and break your skull, you black nigger bastard!" the guard snarled.

"Come on," Stepp said.

Some one laughed. The guard rushed down the range, tugging at his gun.

"Will he shoot him?" Jimmy asked his cell mate, a little fat, thin-haired convict by the name of Lardy Stark.

"Naw!" Stark said. "He ain't even going down there. Stepp's one bad nigger. Got some old white canvas gloves he puts on and battles those roaches as fast as they can gang up. Man, he can knock you down without even drawing back. I've seen him fighting so many roaches they'd hit each other's sticks hitting at him, and every time he'd stick out his fist he'd knock one down."

"Yeah?" Jimmy didn't believe it; Stepp was not his hero. "Why don't they shoot him?" It was just a question.

"Aw, Shaky Jack thinks he's crazy. He won't let them shoot him."

After a moment Jimmy heard the guard's voice below. "What's the matter with you, Stepp?"

Then Stepp's reply, "Aw, take it easy, punk. Gimme one of those good-smellin' seegars you're smoking."

"You know it's against regulations to talk out of your cell—"

"Aw, forget it, punk. Gimme a seegar and tell me 'bout your women."

After the guard had gone, Jimmy could see the bluish smoke coming up over the edge of the range from Stepp's cell. He had to laugh.

But the next night, with two other Negro convicts as stooges, the guard played a different role. But the night before was gone; the incident with Stepp forgotten. Jimmy took his ringside seat at the bars as if it was a new show entirely, and not just another scene.

After lights-out, the two convicts in the cell next to Stepp's got into a fight, and the guard went down to quiet them.

"Oh! Oh! Please don't hit me no mo', cap'n. Please don't hit me no mo'. Ah wasn' doin' nuttin. It's him. He walks all night an' keeps me 'wake." Jimmy heard.

"Hot Britches got him a man," Stark observed.

"What the hell's the matter with you black bastards?" Jimmy heard the guard snarl. "Every goddamn night you get into an argument."

"It's him," the same voice accused. "He walks and talks to hisself."

"What's the matter with you, nigger?" the guard asked.

There was no reply.

"Smart nigger, eh? Come on out of there!" Jimmy heard the click of the lock, the creak of the door as it was opened. Then the guard's voice again, "Come out or I'll blow you out!"

"Aw, let that poor bastard alone, he's crazy," a voice called from Jimmy's range.

"Come out, goddammit!" the guard shouted.

Jimmy stood up and pressed his face close against the bars so he could see onto the outer edge of the bottom range. When the convict came out of the cell, coat half on, cap on backwards, he got a look at him. The convict was coal black and pure African-looking.

Stark stood on the stool to get a better view. "That's Perry," he whispered. "He's nuts."

Jimmy saw the guard kick Perry. Perry started to run, then suddenly stopped, looking back over his shoulder at the leveled gun, and grinned, his eyes white slits in his wet black face. "Ah ain' gonna run," he said, grinning. "Ah ain' gonna run. Ain' no need uv shootin' me 'cause Ah ain' gonna run."

"You better not, you black bastard," the guard grated, pushing the other convict before him, taking them both down the aisle bound for the hole.

After the sound of the outside door opening and closing, Jimmy went back to bed.

"Tickle Britches is trying to be like Two-gun Tracy," Stark said. "We had a punk roach in here named Tracy. Man, he was a sport. Talking about dressing—"

But Jimmy wasn't listening. About five minutes later, just as he was about to doze off, he heard distant gun shots—one, then two more, then one, then a fusillade. Then abrupt silence.

"That was inside!" Stark exclaimed, jumping to the bars again.

"Say, you hear that shooting?" a voice asked from above.

"Yeah, sounded like it was inside," came the reply.

"Wonder who it could be?"

"Damned if I know. Did they take that nig—that colored fellow out?"

"I don't know."

"Hey, down there! Hey, down there on 1-I! Did they take that fellow out?"

No reply. The colored convicts weren't talking.

"Hey, they just killed Perry," a convict called from one of the first cells on either the first or second range, Jimmy couldn't tell.

"How the hell you know?" some one asked.

"Cap'n Baker just came in . . ."

"Where?" . . . "Where what?" . . . "Who killed him?" . . . "Was he the colored fellow?"

"The dirty sons of bitches! Who did it?"

"Short Britches shot him first—"

"He says Short Britches shot him—"

"Shut up, goddammit, I can hear him!"

"Kish and Short Britches—"

"That rotten stool pigeon mother—"

". . . and the night captain were beating him with a pipe out in front of the hole and he broke and ran."

"They wanted him to run."

"Short Britches shot at him first, then the night captain. Neither of them sonafabitches can't shoot. He ran around behind the hospital down by the coal company. The wall guard cut loose at him with his Tommy gun—"

"Them goddamn dirty . . ." All the convicts joined in cursing all the guards. It was fine fun.

But it didn't bring Perry back to life. Well? That happened.

One day Brownie and Russell got into a fight up in the idle house, and the big, good-natured guard, called Big Irish, went down to part them. It was during the dull hours of the afternoon, and Big Irish, desiring to finish his afternoon siesta, did not take them to the hole.

However, Elkhart, another guard, gray-haired and squat, with a blunt, mean face, wasn't satisfied. He rushed in between the benches and jerked Brownie out. Squeezing past Russell, Brownie drew back and hit him on the nose without warning. Blood spurted from Russell's nose as he struggled to his feet. Brownie hit him again. Then Elkhart drew back and hit Brownie across the back of the head with his stick. Brownie went down without a grunt.

Four convicts jumped up and ganged Elkhart. He tried to protect himself, but they were on him like white on rice. One jerked his stick and slugged him across the head until blood matted in his hair. He slumped down between the benches and the convict bent over and kept slugging him on the head.

Before the head guard, fat and lazy, sitting on the stand by the door, could get to his feet, a convict threw a tin cuspidor of sawdust and tobacco spittle in his face. Then a mob of other convicts grabbed him by the legs and yanked him out of the stand, down on the floor, and began kicking him. Blood flecked from his mouth.

Three other guards were on duty in the idle house. About five hundred convicts were assembled there. Big Irish tried to plead with them. A convict snatched the chair from behind him and hit him across the head. The two remaining guards ran for it. The last Jimmy saw of them, they were smothered by convicts.

Cuspidors were thrown. Windows were smashed. The noise which had begun as a confused babble of excited voices rose to a shrill, loud, continuous wail, ear-splitting and nerve-shattering.

Benches were splintered. It seemed as if Elkhart and the head guard were being killed.

Jimmy jumped to his feet and started for the doorway, but Chump Charlie clutched him by the arm. "Keep your seat," Chump warned. "That's the only way to keep out of it."

Jimmy sat down again, but the excitement ate into him. Then he heard a voice yell, "Let's make a break!"

"Goddammit, let's go!" another voice took it up.

"Let's crush through the front gates!"

"Let's go get the warden!"

"Kill the goddamned pig!"

A concerted movement surged toward the doorway. Five hundred wild-eyed, disheveled, howling convicts.

"Let's break down the stockade gates!"

"Down with the stockade gates!"

"Kill the bastard!"

"Bastard son of a bitch!"

"Shoot the son of a bitch in the guts!"

It was then that Jimmy saw the guns. Two convicts at the front of the mob were waving them about. They must have taken them from some of the guards, he thought. Suddenly, he could see them shooting their way to freedom. The thought bit into him, gutted him, jerked him to his feet again. Goddamned if he was going to be left behind! Goddamned if he wasn't going with them! His body tautened. He took a step. His legs trembled.

At the door the mob abruptly stopped, as if they had run into an invisible wall. Backed up step by step. Suddenly all except the two convicts with guns broke for their seats. Those two stood as if paralyzed, turning dead white in the drain of blood from their faces. Their hands shook as if the strength had gone out of them.

What Jimmy saw come through the doorway shocked him deeply, violently, as he had never been shocked before. If you had not seen those freedom-crazed, wild-eyed, loose-haired, raving convicts surging in a solid, seemingly invincible mass toward the doorway, screaming of freedom; if you had not felt the tight cold scare, the compelling excitement, the taut pull of impulse, turning you rigid, freezing your scalp into one great sheet of ice, setting fire to the breath in your lungs, stretching your eyes until they ached, as Jimmy had, then you wouldn't understand.

One man came through that doorway. Just one man. Sergeant Coty.

He wore a dark blue cadet cap low over his eyes and a black slicker buttoned around his throat and wet with rain. He came steadily through the doorway, his bare hands at his sides, his lips tight and bloodless, his face a burnt red, raw-edged and hard as baked clay, his eyes a half-hid tricky gleam beneath the low-pulled visor of his cap. He came across the floor, neither hurrying nor hesitating; came up to the two convicts holding the guns, drew back in the same hard, unhurried motion, and slapped one of them his length on the floor. The other broke to run, but Coty caught him by the collar, and holding him at arm's distance, slapped him until his face was raw and swelling, red and turning blue.

Then he said, "Stand over by the door." His thin, bloodless lips did not seem to move, but his voice came out loud, harsh, uncompromising.

The convict hastened to obey. But the other convict climbed to his knees and lunged for one of the guns which they had dropped. Jimmy did not see the motion of Coty's hand. The first he saw of the gun it was already in Coty's hand. He heard the five spaced shots, the sound of each falling separately and distinctly and then ceasing, and then another, separately and distinctly and ceasing; and when the last had sounded, he knew the convict was dead. He had seen a man shot to death.

In the utter silence following the last spaced shot, Jimmy heard first the stifled breathing of the five hundred convicts; the hard, fast thumping of his own heart. Then from outside on the yard, a guard's stentorian bellow, "*Companeee! . . . March! . . .*" And through his head, from ear to ear, their shod feet scuffing his bare brain, convicts began marching in the rain.

Below, the looms of the woolen mill beat their slow and melancholy music, deliberately, indifferently, mockingly, eternally. He

81

heard the melody very distinctly. He kept on hearing it . . . That happened . . .

Then near the end of April, Spring happened, and made him want to cry. Grass came out in bright green spots here and there on the barren yard, tufts about the hospital steps, on the sunny side of a stack of lumber. Birds sat on the electric wires and cheeped.

"Say, did you see the buds on that tree, Jim?" A whispered voice in line as they marched by to dinner.

"Buds? Tree? What damn tree?"

"The cherry tree in front of the hospital."

"Saw, I didn't even know there was a tree—"

"There's trees all over. Last summer I was picking some cherries and Mr. Blue came out his office and says to me, 'What you doing picking cherries off this tree?' and I says just like you, 'What tree, Mister Blue—'"

"*Cut out that talking!*"

Jimmy had not seen the trees. He had not seen the statue of *Omphale* out in front of the deputy's office until they cleaned it; nor any of the flower plots on each side of the dining room doorways and in the sunken garden west of the dining room around which they marched twice each day, and in the corners where the main walks crossed, until the flowers bloomed.

But he had known it was Spring just the same because his blood came alive.

"If I had a woman I could make it-," he said one night.

"Why don't you stop by Chump's, he's been trying to get you to give him a play," Stark said.

"And have him birth another radio?"

Stark didn't get it.

One day the sun dipped down and summer happened. It was heat and that live wire edge.

7

I<small>N</small> S<small>EPTEMBER THE COMPANIES</small> in the I&K cell block were broken up and scattered about the institution. Some went to the new G&H block, some to the E&F dormitories, some to White City, some to the A&B block. The block was being torn down; a new one, similar to the G&H block, was to be constructed. Jimmy was transferred back to 5-F.

It was just before dinner and the company had come in from school to wash up. After he'd made his bunk, he sat at the table, smoking. Several convicts came up and spoke to him.

"I see you got back, Jimmy."

"Yeah."

"Know you're glad to beat that 6-H rap."

"You said it."

Most of them he did not recall; but the little hump-backed, sharp-faced convict who sat down beside him seemed familiar.

"Hello, kid, did you make that nine?"

Then he remembered him—George Blocker. He had been up in the idle house for a time.

"What say, Blocker, how you doing?" Jimmy felt glad to see him.

"Slow," Blocker grinned, his long yellow fangs giving him a wolfish look. "The chumps in here won't gamble."

In appearance Blocker resembled the third paragraph of a weird story. Beneath a flag of light-colored, unkempt hair, almost colorless eyes looked out in a dead, fixed stare; but his fingers, slender and unnaturally long, were quick and alive, and his fingernails were the longest and cleanest Jimmy had ever seen on a convict.

Jimmy said, "No wonder, your fingernails scare them."

Lippy Mike swaggered up, pushing over the other convicts,

reached down and took the cigaret from Jimmy's lips. "Hi, kid," he greeted.

Jimmy burnt up. "What the hell's the matter with you, fellow?" he snarled.

Then Mike burnt up. "I was just playing with you, little punk," he grated. "Here, take the damned butt back."

Jimmy brushed it away. "Keep it, goddammit. Just don't play with me like that."

Mike threw the cigaret on the floor and stepped on it. "Hey, pappy!" he called.

"Coming, Mike."

"Bring this punk a bag of tobacco." Then turning to Jimmy, he said, "I'm going to give you a bag of tobacco, punk, and don't you ever speak to me again."

"To hell with you!" Jimmy spat.

"What?"

Jimmy jumped to his feet. "You heard me."

Mike had his knife half out when he saw Blocker crouched to one side with a long shiny dirk in his hand. He tucked his knife out of sight, looked at Jimmy and said, "You take it easy, little punk."

"You take it easy, your goddamn self," Jimmy snarled.

Mike wheeled and walked away. It was not until Blocker said, "If that chump had started anything, I was going to gut him," that Jimmy saw the knife and realized it was Blocker who had really stopped Mike.

"That sonafabitch," he muttered, his face still stinging.

"Take it easy, kid, you're on fire," Blocker grinned. "There's only one thing to remember; you can't fight a chiv with your dukes."

They became inseparable and a short time later began running a poker game. From the start they got a heavy play; Jimmy did most of the dealing and the players thought him easy. Blocker seemed content to stand around and watch, taking over occasionally when the going got tough. All he ever said to Jimmy was, "There's only one thing to remember, kid; never give a sucker a break. That's the one rigid rule. Never let the 'gator get to the pond; he'll give you more trouble than the days are long," grinning that wolfish grin.

The poker game happened. One night Jimmy won a hundred and twelve dollars on a pair of deuces; another night he lost seventy-six dollars on three aces, letting a player fill to a straight. A guy swung a chiv at Blocker one night, missed him, and cut the lip off the player sitting next to him. Another night Lippy Mike called a convict a name and told him if he didn't like it to pat his foot; the convict got a scantling stick and split Mike's forehead from hairline to nose; and Mike got up, blind from the blood in his eyes, and had a knife fit, stabbing everybody in reach.

The poker game happened every night. The days turned around it. But other things happened which claimed Jimmy's momentary attention.

Deacon Gardner, a Negro convict doing life for wife-killing, held a prayer meeting in the dormitory. Beau Diddly, a Negro convict doing life for rape, got so happy he leaped aloft and dived head-first into a commode and seven stitches had to be put into his head where the spirit split it.

The ugliest, roughest, toughest convict in the dormitory turned out to be a girl-boy, and broke down and announced that he had always been that way.

Every night right after supper the convicts gathered for mail. Those who hoped to receive letters and those who didn't and those who knew there was no one in all the world to write to them, ganging about the guard as he read the names and numbers. Sometimes it was trouble; sometimes it was death. Nothing a convict could do about it whatever it was.

Within the hours there were laughs, scares, shocks, happening and were gone. And now and then the unusual, cutting obliquely across the pattern like a diagonal furrow across a plowed field, bringing its peculiar sensation as if the scalp had been suddenly torn from reason; leaving its backwash of distaste to fill out its moment before forgetfulness, such as the happening of Neal.

Jimmy became aware of Neal following him about and staring at him shortly after he had returned to the dormitory, but had thought nothing of it at the time. Then it began to get annoying. Ofttimes while dealing, he would feel Neal's gaze on him and glance quickly up to catch him staring. And nights, if he happened to the latrine, he could feel Neal watching him all the way down and back. It gave him the creeps, for Neal never smiled at him, never spoke. When Jimmy caught him staring, he'd just look away.

He was a small built, fat-jawed young man with rotting, tobacco-stained teeth, and very carefully parted hair, pomaded to his skull. His shoulders were slightly stooped and his stomach bulged like that of a pregnant woman's. He did not look to be more than twenty-five, but his actions were those of a man past fifty.

In two months time he did not approach Jimmy, nor say one word to him—just stared. Then one night Jimmy straightened up from the fountain with a mouth full of water to find Neal standing over him. He jumped back, blowing water and strangling.

"What the hell you keep watching me for, fellow?" he choked angrily, squeezing the water from his nostrils.

"I-I want to talk to you," Neal faltered.

"And I want to talk to you, too," Jimmy challenged, following Neal to his bunk.

"Sit down, please," Neal begged. "I want to tell you something."

After Jimmy had sat gingerly on the edge of the bunk, Neal began, "Jimmy, I know this is going to sound queer, but I can't help it because it's true."

"Go ahead," Jimmy told him. It sounded like the beginning of a beg.

"A long time ago," Neal said, "I was standing on a platform of a depot in a little town in Mississippi named Port Gibson. I was just a little boy and my mother was with me and we had come to town on Saturday. I'd said I wanted to see the train come in and she had taken me down to the depot and we were standing on the platform. When the train came in, I saw you. You were looking out a window. I fell suddenly in love with you, and when the train pulled out I began crying. When my mother asked me what I was crying about, all I could say was, 'He's on that train.' She asked me who and I told her the little boy I dreamed about all the time.

I cried for a week, and I never did forget it. When I grew older I used to think of you more and more and I knew that some day I would meet you. I knew it just as I knew I was living. And all that time I've loved you; I've never loved anyone else." He sat there, talking in a solemn, serious voice, his brown eyes filled with a soft humid expression.

"Er, look," Jimmy stammered. "You sure you haven't got me mixed up with some one else." To know that he had been loved so many years by this infirm-appearing convict with his rotted-out mouth and filthily bloated stomach was a shocking realization.

But Neal was positive. "No, I know it's you. I'd know you in a million years, among a million people."

"Well, I don't know just what to say," Jimmy floundered embarrassedly. "I'm glad you found me, I guess. I mean—yes, of course. I mean—if you want anything just let me know—you know, some smoking or toothpaste or—"

"I don't want anything," Neal said.

"Say, I got to go now," Jimmy said, getting up. "I got to spell Blocker on the deal. Take it easy now." And he was gone.

Back at the game he asked Blocker, "Say, do you know a fellow named Neal? Bunks down in the corner."

Blocker looked at him curiously. "Quiet sort of fellow?"

"I know him," one of the players said. "He's a good kid."

"What's the matter with him?" Jimmy asked. "Is he crazy?"

"Not as I know of," Blocker said. "No more than half these guys in here. I think he'll go, but that ain't no crime. They say one time don't make you a girl-boy anyway. Why?"

"Oh, nothing in particular. He called me over to his bunk and told me a funny sort of story."

"Come on, come on, let's gamble," another player grumbled. Then turning to Jimmy, added, "Don't you know when a fellow's trying to get you to put him on?"

But Jimmy knew that this was different. Although he avoided Neal as if he was the plague, he'd still catch Neal watching him. Then one night Neal sent for him. At the time Jimmy was lying on his bunk, reading a magazine, and didn't want to be bothered. So he sent word he'd be down after awhile.

About an hour later a convict named Cook stopped at his bunk and asked him what he had been doing to his old lady.

"What old lady?" Jimmy challenged.

"Neal. Ain't he your old lady?"

"Hell, I hardly know the fellow."

"Well, he's down there crying because you won't come and see him."

"Jesus Christ," Jimmy groaned.

He got up and went down. "What do you want, boy?" he asked gruffly.

"I just want you to sit and talk to me," Neal sobbed. "You don't have to do anything but just talk to me. That won't hurt you."

Jimmy sat way down at the end of the bunk so he wouldn't touch Neal. He listened for a time, but he couldn't stand much of it. Finally he jumped up and said, "Look, goddammit, I got enough of this. Go find somebody else to love. I ain't the fellow."

The guard caught Neal smoking in bed that night and sent him to the hole. They found Neal hanging the next morning.

That happened . . . A prison break happened.

Blocker told Jimmy about it first thing in the morning. "Didja hear, kid, all of 1-C broke out last night." He had gotten it from the convict who bunked next to him who was said to be a rat. The convict had gotten it from the night guard who was said to be a liar.

But Jimmy was excited, nevertheless. "Yeah? 1-C!" He whistled. The red-shirt desperadoes of 1-K had been transferred to 1-C when the old I&K block had been wrecked. "Last night? Whataya know! Here we were sleeping away."

Another convict, looking more excited than either of them, stopped long enough to volunteer, "Wasn't all of 'em. Just twelve. The rest wouldn't go. What you know 'bout that?"

"Wonder how they made it?" a fourth convict said.

"Must have tunneled," a fifth ventured.

"Tommy Garet tunneled out there two years ago and was almost ready to lam when some one squealed on him," a sixth supplied.

"Wasn't there; was in 1-K he tunneled out," a seventh corrected.

There was a crowd. All over the dormitory they were grouped in tight knots, discussing it. They were as happy as if it had been a holiday.

"Was Tommy in this bunch?" Jimmy asked at large.

"Must have been," a convict reasoned.

"I bet he was the leader," another said.

"I bet Jiggs was in it, too. And Bobby Burns—"

"And Johnny Grogan—"

"And Red Hart . . ."

They called the roll.

"When they miss 'em?" somebody wanted to know.

"I don't know; when the night guard counted out, I guess."

"Hell, they count them guys every hour."

"Well, the last hour they counted 'em there was twelve short," a convict cracked, enjoying his own humor.

"Hey!" a voice called. "They got it on the radios."

The groups dissolved in a rush for radios. By the time Jimmy got near a radio, so many other convicts were ahead of him he had to climb on top of a bunk in order to see it; not realizing in his excitement that he could hear it without seeing it.

". . . Patrick Michael McDermot," the loud, metallic voice of the radio intoned. "Patrick Michael McDermot . . . Answers to the name of Pat McDermot . . . Five feet, five and one half inches . . . Five feet, five and one half inches . . . Weight: one hundred and thirty-two pounds . . . Weight: one hundred and thirty-two pounds . . . Blue eyes . . . Blue eyes . . . Brown hair . . . Brown hair . . . Probably dressed in gray prison uniform . . . Probably dressed in gray prison uniform . . . Serving a life sentence for first degree murder . . . Serving a life sentence for first degree murder . . . Very dangerous if armed . . . Very dangerous if armed . . . Very dangerous if armed . . . *Caution;* do not attempt to capture this man as he is very dangerous . . . If seen, notify police . . . If seen, notify police . . . *Caution;* do not attempt to capture this man as he is very dangerous . . . If seen, notify police . . . Henry Raymond Busch . . . Answers to the name of Ray—"

"Pat wasn't in 1-C; he was in the heart trouble company," some one interrupted.

"Weren't none of 'em in 1-C."

"Shut up and let us hear!"

"Fuck you, son of a bitch!"

They hung about the radios until the breakfast bell rang, then there was a mad scramble to get dressed. There was no semblance of order in any of the lines en route to breakfast that morning. The dining room buzzed with talk.

"If that Pat McDermot's got a gun it'll be just too bad."

"You sure ain't told no lie. That Busch is a desperate sonafabitch, too."

"Yeah, but not like Pat. They'll never get Pat without some one getting killed."

"Man, that's one gun battle I'd sure like to see."

But when the convicts left the dining room, they braced themselves against the sight which greeted them, straightened up in line, put their caps on right, buttoned up their lips, and stepped smartly. For while they had been eating, twelve machine guns had been mounted on tripods over the yard, and three more atop the front cell house overlooking the prison.

Jimmy read in the newspapers that evening that only five men had escaped. They had crawled up the ventilator shaft in the C&D block and had lowered themselves by a rope of sheets from the roof to the front yard. The night guard had missed them shortly after twelve.

Pat McDermot was captured the following day. A housewife on the outskirts of town saw him slinking through her backyard and called the sheriff's office. A feeble old gray-haired deputy sheriff, named Williams, whom Jimmy remembered from his time in that jail, went out and found Pat hulking in the back shed, too cold to fire the pistol which he held in his hand.

A week later Busch was shot and killed in a public park in Philadelphia. A third of the five was arrested and returned from

Kansas City, Kansas. Three weeks later one of the remaining two walked back into the prison and surrendered, explaining that it made him nervous to be hunted by the law. By then Jimmy had forgotten about it . . . Happened and was gone . . .

Christmas happened. On Christmas Eve way up until morning, as they had the night before, the boxes came; some getting two, some three, some even four. Jimmy received one from his mother and another from his father. In his father's box was a twelve-pound bag of flour which must have been mistaken for sugar which the convicts were allowed to have. Jimmy took a long hard breath, touched by the picture of the old man, confused and alone, trying to get a box together; then he threw it in the waste can and went to dealing stud . . . Gone . . .

An execution happened . . . They were in school that afternoon, baiting their teacher as was their custom, when some one exclaimed, "Here comes the professor!" They jumped up and rushed to the windows in a sudden disruption of routine.

A tallish, bald-headed man with a seamed, ravished face, accompanied by a stoutish woman in a fur-collared coat with a dark felt hat pulled low over her face, holding a handkerchief to her eyes as if crying, came down the walk. The man was bareheaded and dressed in a prison-made blue suit with a white shirt and dark tie. He smoked a cigar. The woman walked close to him, on the far side, holding to his arm. They walked slowly, talking earnestly. Behind them, about twenty feet, followed the deputy warden and a guard, also talking earnestly. It was as if they were on a tour of inspection.

"That him?" some one asked.

"Sure."

"I don't believe it," Jimmy said.

"That's him all right, kid," Blocker verified.

Candy yelled out the window, "Take the cigar out your mouth, you rape-fiend murdering bastard!" Other convicts yelled obscenities.

The deputy turned and motioned them away from the windows. But as soon as he had turned his head again, they rushed back and remained there until the professor and his wife, he smoking his cigar and she crying into her handkerchief, had rounded the corner and passed from sight.

"That's the way you go to the chair if you're a big shot," Blocker observed.

As soon as they had returned to the dormitory from supper, they sought points of vantage at the windows. The time of execution, they had learned, was 5:45.

"There she is, kid," Blocker said. "The cooker."

From where they stood, Jimmy saw the death house, etched in the twilight glow. It sat a square, squat building of dull red brick, about the size of a two-car garage, in the southeast corner of the prison, an angular blot superimposed upon the gray stone of the south wall. Its black slanting roof stood out very distinctly above the dull-red brick, and the areaway stretching out in front of it, down between the dormitory and the wall, was a window of failing light. The guard turret to the left, atop the corner of the wall, was outlined against the darkening sky. Muted bubbling of convicts' conversation drifted out of the windows to lose itself in the twilight haze.

There was the brick walk, leading from the prison yard, chopped abruptly off by a waist-high iron railing. To the right was the green door. Jimmy wondered fleetingly how the professor had felt after having come his bitter half mile from death row to be stopped at the dull green door. He wondered if he had thought of the young girl whom he had murdered.

In the slow waning of light, the glare of the prison lights became more obvious. A group of noisy, chattering, well-dressed men came down the walk and entered the death house.

"Who the hell are they?" Jimmy questioned.

"Reporters mostly," some one replied.

"The warden was with 'em. Didn't you see him?"

"So was the doctor."

"Yeah?"

"They're witnesses," Blocker explained.

"The warden officiates," another convict supplemented. "And

the doctor sticks a needle through the dead man's heart after they take him out the chair. That's to make sure he's dead."

"I don't believe it," Jimmy said.

Later, the purr of a motor sounded. Jimmy saw the black sheen of the hearse as it idled across the rough areaway outside. The chrome steel of its trimmings glistened against the dullness of the wall. It turned, backed up to the green door and came to a stop, waiting.

Some one began whistling *Ramona* tunelessly, monotonously. It got on Jimmy's nerves. "Goddammit, cut out that whistling!" he snarled.

"Take it easy, kid," Blocker said, grinning wolfishly.

The sky brightened in a last brief flicker and then, suddenly, it was dark. After a time a sullen whine, very faint, came from within the squat, dark building.

"'*Murder seems such a little thing when you are doing it,*'" a convict quoted. Jimmy spun about. It was Hall—Shakespeare, the convicts called him. From Hall's expression, Jimmy couldn't tell what he was thinking.

"An asinine remark," Jimmy challenged. Hall let it pass.

The door of the death house opened from within, and some one beckoned. Two men from the hearse took an open wicker basket inside, brought it back closed, shoved it carelessly into the hearse, climbed into the driver's seat and drove off. A woman screamed once. And then it was eerily quiet. Jimmy could hear the breath spurting from Blocker's nostrils. He could feel a vein throbbing quickly, steadily, in his own temple. He went back to the poker game and lost erratically . . .

But the days did not stop. Coming and going through the rooted prison; the everlasting pattern. If you could live out the days, you would make it, no matter what your sentence was. If you could live out the days, Johnny Time would spring you. And if you died, you went out, too. Everybody left sooner or later, the quick and the dead. An execution happened and the professor went back to town.

Then along about the end of April, Easter happened. If you did not get a card on Easter, you were pitiable, you were the saddest convict Jimmy ever saw.

And Hall standing there—Shakespeare—unsmiling, doing his second-degree life because he had killed the slut whom he had married, and by whom he had happened to have a child, not having received a card then or at any time during the five years he had been in prison, quoting doggedly, " *Then to the lip of this poor earthern Urn I leaned, the Secret of my Life to learn: And Lip to Lip it murmur'd—"While you live, Drink!—for, once dead, you never shall return.'* "

"Don't tell me—*Shakespeare!*" Jimmy said facetiously . . .

Just happenings . . . Like ripples in the alligator pond . . . While below, in the stagnant depths, slime collected . . .

FROM THE DORMITORY WINDOWS they saw the fire trucks come through the stockade gates. They heard the clang of bells, the motor roar. They saw convicts running across the yard; the sudden surge of Negro convicts from the wheel barrow company, carrying blankets in their arms; then the white convicts from the dining room company. Guards came running. Everyone was running.

Excitement ate into them, gnawed at their control. "That's bad!" some one exclaimed. "That's bad! That's goddamn bad! Too much smoke."

Another convict said, "Goddammit, I'm going out! My brother's on 5-H. I'm going out! Everybody else is out. Goddammit, I'm going out!" He broke from the jam and ran down the aisle toward the door.

"I'm going out, too!" Jimmy said, breaking after him.

The day guard was standing in front of the door, clutching his stick in one hand and his coat in the other. It was just before the change of shift at six, and he was hoping to get away before the trouble started.

"Get out of my way, I'm going out!" the convict said to him.

"Now, boys—" the guard began.

"I'm going out, too," Jimmy echoed.

The guard got tough. "Get back, get back, both of you, you can't go out here!" he said, raising his stick.

"The hell I can't!" the convict said, arching a long swing and hitting the guard just beneath the eye.

The guard brought the stick down in a vicious arc, but the convict caught it in mid-air. Jimmy hit the guard in the stomach with his left fist. The guard grunted and doubled over, dropping his coat. The convict brought an uppercut and caught him in the face. Jimmy pushed him to one side. Just as he fell, the door opened from the outside and a convict called Dean came in, bareheaded and panting.

"Get some blankets, boys," he gasped in a ravished voice. "Hurry and get some blankets; the boys are burning to death over there. Oh God, it's terrible; they're burning to death in their cells."

Jimmy snatched a blanket from a bunk and started running. He skirted the back of the hospital, turned at the northeast corner. The early night had settled over the prison and lights yellowed in the beginning darkness. A stiff wind blew from the north, with a coldness left over from winter. He was coatless and hatless; he could feel the chill of the breeze through his shirt, on his head. Turning at the northwest corner of the hospital, the whole face of the yard opened to his view. Sudden shock jolted him to a stop.

Smoke rolled up from the burning superstructure about the I&K block under construction in black, fire-tinged waves. The wind caught it and pushed it down over the prison yard like a thick, gray shroud, so low he felt that if he reached up he could touch it with his hand. Flames, shooting through the windows and roof of the cell house, seen through the smoke, were a page torn from Dante's *Inferno*. Buildings were shadows in the crazy pattern of light that streaked the black blanket of smoke. It was startling, like something suddenly discovered; like the night itself had been discovered and the fire in the night had been discovered.

Beside the I&K cell house, joining it, was the G&H cell house, housing the G&H block, crammed with living convicts; a huge red-brick monster with a thousand fiery eyes, sucking in the flame and the smoke upon the living, writhing convicts in its belly. Sight stopped there, and thought, and conjecture, and memory; even the night stopped there.

Jimmy never knew that it was only in his imagination he heard those convicts, a hundred yards away, crying, "Oh God! Save me! Save me!" over and over again. The words spun a sudden cold-tight fear through his mind.

He took a tentative step forward, another; he could feel himself trembling. In front of him, yellow light shining from the open door of the hospital cut a kaleidoscopic picture into the confusion of the yard, showed convicts coming, going, running. Thousands of convicts were aloose; they were all running, yelling, a sinister shad-owgraph against the backdrop of the burning cell house.

He took another shaky step, and abruptly the confusion swallowed him, made him a part of it, pushing out the memory of old Blocker, of the dormitory, of the prison, of life itself, leaving with him the compelling urge to run.

And he was running again, across the yard, with a high-stepping sense of being too tall to stay on the ground. He ran harder, lifted his feet higher, until he was churning with motion, going nowhere. He stepped into something and looked down at it and saw that he had stepped into a burnt-up convict's stomach and had pushed out huge globules of vomit through the tight-clenched teeth and over the black-burnt face. And then he saw them, prone gray figures on the bare ground, spotting the face of the yard, and still more were coming—figures of charred and smoke-blackened flesh wrapped snugly in new gray blankets for which all that winter they had cried and could not get, and now they had them, and he thought queerly, involuntarily: *They don't need the blankets now; they don't need*

*the blankets; goddammit, they don't need the blankets; can't you
see they don't need the goddamn blankets!*

Suddenly a variegated color pattern formed before his eyes—
black, smoke-mantled night, yellow light, red flames, dead convicts
in gray blankets, crisscrossing into maggotty confusion. And he was
running again, plowing through the sense of confusion, past the
front of the hospital, feeling that each step he took was on a different
color, smelling the odor of death clogging in his nostrils—life and
death and smoke and fire and the night.

To the left was the white glare of confusion in the hospital, gray
bodies on the linoleum floor and white-clad nurses bent over them;
to the right was the black confusion of the yard with bodies lying
in the semi-gloom amid the rushing, cursing convicts, being stepped
on and jostled and cursed for puking down some one's shirt. At
the fringe of the light where the shadow began, smoke was a thick,
gray wall. He ran forward into the wall of smoke. For an instant
he could not see. Some one bumped into him, knocked him to his
knees. His head struck the railing beside the sidewalk. Out of the
sudden hurt the sound of voices filled his ears, like a roar,

"Gangway! Live one! Live one!"

Four convicts swept by into the stream of light, up the hospital
steps. They carried a writhing body—a *live one!*

Getting up, he went down and stood on the sidewalk in front
of the deputy's office. His blanket was gone and his hands felt light
from missing it. He fanned himself for a cigaret, had none. A convict
rushed by with a butt dangling from his lips. "Gimme a draw,"
Jimmy said, and the convict tossed the butt without stopping. Jimmy
caught it and stuck it in his mouth, and after a puff suddenly realized
that this was the first time he had smoked after another person. He
started to throw the butt away, then saw the bodies on the yard,
and stuck the butt back in his mouth, thinking, "Why, goddamn,
who am I?"

Standing there, puffing on the butt, motion swirled about him
as if he was standing in the center of a spinning wheel. The deputy's
office was the hub of the confusion; everything spoked out from
there, or spun out across the yard like a ribbon of tissue tossed

97

from an upper window. Everything passed him; he saw everything; it was like watching a barrage of fireworks from the top of a jag. His mind could not acquaint itself to the swiftly passing sensations, the rapid change of vision, the utter finality of the spoken word, the absoluteness of the moment, the sheer obscenity of every curse; nor to the sudden, startling necessity of bridging the gap from life to death. Quickly, shockingly, the incidents came into his consciousness, and as quickly, as shockingly left; the live ones and the dead ones and the strings of greenish vomit down the yellow-lighted walks. He felt only an increasing nausea.

He saw the stream of people coming in from the outside, doctors and priests and reporters and policemen and one woman nurse, mingling shoulder to shoulder with the three thousand slavering, running, always running convicts. They pushed by him, over him.

And suddenly he was running again, high-stepping and churning. He ran over toward the burning cell block. The acrid fumes were thick over there. He began to cough. Running and coughing, and suddenly he stopped a short distance from the cell house door, having forgotten by then what he was running for.

The scaffolding about the half-constructed I&K block was burning furiously; the smoke and flames leapt across the well into the G&H cell block where the top ranges of convicts were locked in their cells. He could hear those strangled screams, those unended prayers, those curses and coughs and gasps and moans and wails of the locked-up convicts.

Outside, water covered the ground. Fire hoses writhed in the mud like huge, floundered snakes. Two fire trucks were backed to the cell house door; the others were down at the end of the cell house, beyond the Protestant chapel. Water bouncing from the hot stone sprinkled his face.

He started through the doorway into the burning cell house, slowly, cautiously. Then he heard a voice scream, "Oh, you bastards! Get me out of here, get me out of here! You lousy, goddamned sons of bitches! . . ." Choked off . . .

He backed out of the doorway, trembling violently. But those muffled screams followed him . . . "Oh, God! OhhhhHHHHHH,

God! OhhhhhHHHHHHH GodddDDDDDDD! Get me out of here! Get me out, I say! What the hell you tryna do, kill me? You tryna kill me? Oh, you dirty bastards, you tryna kill me?"

"Why doesn't some one do something?" Jimmy cried.

"Why the hell don't you?" a convict nearby said.

"There's some one up there somewhere unlocking the lower cells," another convict volunteered.

Jimmy bent over and peered up through the smoke, but all he could see was the bottom of the cell block, dripping water and slime and those horrible, choked half-prayers, half-curses.

A big Negro convict called Eastern Bill suddenly loomed in the doorway with a limp figure draped across his shoulder. The unconscious figure strangled and vomited. Jimmy looked at the slimy, clotted filth, felt his stomach turn over.

"Get a blanket and give a hand here," he heard a voice say.

All his life he had wanted to be a hero. Ever since he first read the *Iliad* and became a worshipper of Achilles. All of his life! And now was his chance. He felt his lips twitching as a wave of nausea swept over him.

"No can do," he said in a low, choked whisper, backed away. He just couldn't do it, that was all. Just couldn't do it.

A policeman pushed him aside to let four men pass with a body on a blanket. He stumbled over a fire hose, sat down in the slop. He jumped up, looked around. And then he was running again, through the confusion, high-stepping, churning. His mind was a gray daze. Blue-coated firemen passed his vision; their loud, mega-phoned voices reached his ears. In his eyes were the sight of police-men, of living convicts lugging the dead, of smoke and flame and water and prison guards. He could not help but think of these convicts who were working overtime at being heroes as men who had committed murder, rape, arson, men who had cut little living girls open with butcher knives to insert their oversized organs, who had mutilated women and carved their torsos into separate arms and legs and heads and packed them in trunks, who had stolen automobiles and forged checks and shot down policemen, working like hell, now, in the face of death to save the lives of other men

99

who had raped their baby sisters. It got sharp and hurting in his mind and he stopped and shook his head. He was on a tide and the tide was carrying him away from everything he had ever known or seen or heard or thought; he wanted something to grab to; and there was nothing.

And then he was running again, running and gasping and shoving and running and cursing and striking out with his fists and slipping and falling and getting up and running; and it seemed as if he was standing still while the chaos rushed past him, pulling him, clutching his garments, choking him; and then he was running and fighting and struggling. And then he was at the chapel, a hundred feet away.

He tried the chapel door, found it unlocked, and walked inside. In the vestibule, just inside the doorway, a convict stood crying, repeating over and over again with a slow, dull deliberateness, "Damn God! The bastard! The lousy bastard! Damn Him!"

Inside, several convicts were shooting dice on the floor of the aisle in front of the pulpit. He stopped, listened to the snapping of their fingers, the rattle of the dice. It was an odd sound.

One of them looked up and saw him. "What you shoot, Jimmy?"

Jimmy shook his head, feeling his face break crookedly. And then without warning, his mind snapped loose in grotesque fantasy . . . God and the devil gambling for the souls of the dying convicts . . . I bet this nigger murderer. He cut his wife into black, bloody hash . . . All right, I'll put up this hunky rape-friend. He ravished his five year old daughter . . . Omnipotence touched him and he saw the whole universe standing there before him in its bleached skeleton . . .

Then he heard a slow run on the bass keys of a piano, heard the crackle of flame from the fire outside, saw the red glare through the frosted panes.

He looked toward the rostrum. The cover had been rolled from the grand piano and a slim, curly-headed youth formed a question mark on the stool, playing Saul's *Death March* with a slow feeling. A pencil streak of firelight, coming through a broken pane high up behind the stage, cut a white stripe down his face. His cheeks were wet with tears.

Then the slow, steady beat of the bass notes hammered on Jimmy's mind like measured blows from a hard fist. "Don't you know people are dying outside, you goddamn fool?" he shouted.

The youth stopped and looked around. "I'm no fool," he said after a wire-tight moment. "I'm playing their parade march into some red hell."

Worms began crawling in Jimmy's stomach; little white maggots and long slimy worms, crawling in his stomach. He backed out of the chapel into the chaotic night, feeling those worms crawling in his stomach as if he, too, was dead and in the ground and already rotting.

Everything was gone, the touch of Omnipotence, the skeletoned universe, present tense. Everything was dead and stopped and gone and nothing mattered.

Outside the scene had changed as if another act had come upon a revolving stage. A snarling jam of convicts, who but short moments ago had been sweating heroes, were now jammed in a ragged, surging, snarling mass about a circle of policemen who stood about the cell house door with submachine guns held at ready.

He heard a voice say, "The walls are falling!"

He saw a policeman's legs begin to tremble as the convicts pushed closer. The moment hung on so thin a thread that he felt an almost uncontrollable urge to throw something at the line of policemen to set it off.

And then a crippled convict broke from the line of tight-jammed convicts and ran toward the policemen in a hobbling, one-sided gait. A young policeman raised his gun and aimed. The convicts tensed. And then the deputy rushed into the scene. "Men! *Men!*" he cried. "The walls are *not* falling." The tension eased.

Jimmy turned away, feeling a queer, perverted disappointment. And suddenly he was running again, arms churning, knees pumping. At the end of the walk he stopped, undecided.

Two convicts were talking. "There's Yorky!" one said. "He won a couple of Cs up in the idle house yesterday."

The other convict looked at him. "No need letting the worms get it."

Jimmy turned away, went over to the school. Walter was coming out of the lavatory. He hadn't seen Walter in months; hadn't even thought about him. But now he felt as if they were very intimate. He pushed Walter back, pulled the door shut behind them. "Where the hell have you been?" he asked.

"I was looking for you," Walter said. "Then the deputy sent me over to the A&B block to knock the locks off the doors. They lost the keys." He was smiling and his face looked very clean and his lips looked very red.

Fresh from that greasy, grimy chaos, that sweating, soot-blackened, vomit-spattered mass of humanity, Jimmy thought Walter was the prettiest person he'd ever seen. Putting his arms about Walter's waist, he backed him into the wall and kissed him, and when Walter tried to pull away, he said, "Don't, goddammit, let me kiss you."

Walter looked at him with a hesitant, peculiar expression, then returned the embrace, and for a moment they clung to each other, kissing each other. Jimmy could hear the water running in the commode; he could feel the pressure of Walter's body and his lips; but he didn't get anything of what he had hoped he might.

After a time Walter said, "I got to go."

Jimmy released him, feeling nothing. He didn't know what he had hoped for; but he didn't get a thing. No excitement, no passion, no change; just the lingering feeling of the pressure of his lips.

"I've got to go up in the tin shop," Walter said, still looking at him with that peculiar expression. "Cap Hardy wants me to go up there and keep a lookout on things for the rest of the night."

"Okay," Jimmy replied, without looking at him.

After Walter had gone, he went outside again and stood on the edge of the sidewalk, wondering what he had thought he might get from kissing him. And suddenly, without realizing it, he was running again. But before he had gone far, a convict at the corner of the deputy's office stopped him. "Send a telegram home," he said. "Tell the folks you're living."

"Gimme two," Jimmy said, taking two of the yellow Western Union blanks.

He returned to the school room and filled out one to his mother and the other to his father. "I'm living," he wrote, and then, looking at it, thought he should add something, and wrote, "Thank God," but after a moment he crossed out the "Thank God" and wrote instead, "Because I wasn't in the cell block where the other convicts died."

Then he couldn't recall his mother's address. When he returned the telegrams, he said, "I can't remember my mother's address."

"That's all right," the convict said. "Just put the city on it."

"Oh, now I remember," Jimmy said, and scrawled on the address.

Then he went over to the edge of the sidewalk and leaned against the low railing, looking out over the yard. The prone, gray bodies got into his eyes again—white men, black men, gentile, Jew—but in his eyes they were just gray humps on the bare ground, all alike.

Looking at them, he didn't feel a thing, neither pity nor sorrow nor awe nor fear—nothing. It was like looking at newly plowed earth; the earth was turned and there they were, rows of dirt. He saw Lardy Stark there with the stink gone out of him, with the voice gone out of him, lying very still and very dead, no longer swaggering and poking out his fat belly and imagining himself a prize fighter; he saw Mother Jones, long and black and dead; and Brownie, small and delicate and white and dead. He saw them all, hundreds of them lying on the ground, and they looked all alike to him, with their teeth bared and vomit in their lips and their bodies grotesquely twisted and their hands, with the flesh scorched and burned, gripping at something, and their eyes, wide open with sightlessness, staring at something; and from somewhere, with no connection whatsoever, the phrase came to him: "*While you live, Drink! For, once dead, you never shall return . . .*"

He picked his way through the bodies to see if he knew any of the others. Some one began crying at his side. Because it sounded phony, he turned around, saw a black boy with a hippo-spread of lips, called Broadway Rose, kneeling on the ground beside the body of a little brown-skinned convict who was burned around the mouth.

"Oh, lawdamercy, what will I do?" Broadway blubbered. "Mah man's dead!"

"You dirty black bastard, robbing a dead man," Jimmy said dispassionately.

"What the hell you got to do with it?" Broadway snarled.

Jimmy didn't feel a thing; he just drew back and swung at the shiny black face because he felt that it was something he should do. He missed, went sprawling over a corpse. The soft, mushy form gave beneath him; the sudden contact with the dead electrified him again.

He jumped to his feet, shook himself; but the worms began crawling about in his brain again. They were mashed in the middle and they crawled slowly just beneath his skull, dragging their mashed insides. He could feel their legs gooey with the slimy green stuff that had been strung out on the sidewalk.

And then he was running again, away from the slimy worms that were crawling in his brain. Running blindly over the corpses, stepping in their guts, stepping in their faces. He could feel the soft, squashy give, the roll of muscle over bone. He put his face down behind his left hand, lowered his head, plowed forward.

A moment later he found himself standing in front of the entrance to the Catholic chapel, feeling a queer, light-headed desire to laugh. He went up the stairs, inside the chapel, leaned against the door frame beside the basin of Holy Water, wondering how many basins of Holy Water it would take to put out the fire.

Candles burned on the white altar, yellow flames cascading upward to a polished crucifix. A well of peace amid chaos. He saw the curved backs of several convicts bent over the railing before the images of the saints, bringing back to mind the words: *I believe in God, The Father Almighty, Maker of Heaven and earth . . .*

He never knew whether he said them aloud or not. Then they were gone, and there was a sneer on top of his teeth, underneath his lips, in his eyes . . . *I believe in the power of the press, maker of laws, in the almighty dollar, political pull, a Colt's .45 . . .*

He turned and went downstairs, around beside the school, back toward the dormitory. Two convicts were standing in the shadows, talking.

"Tuck clipped the screw and took the keys away. That's how those chumps got out. He's the one unlocked 'em."

"Tuck, eh? That simple bastard?"

"Sure, him! That's how they got out. He just did make it. Brought the kid out with him. That's what I call love."

"You goddamn right, a sucker's gotta love his fellow man a hell of a lot to risk his life like that."

"Fellow man, hell!" the convict spat. "I wasn't talking about any damn fellow man; I was talking about the kid. You know, that yellow-haired punk called Lively that Tuck's blowing his top about. That's all he was after."

That was a hero, Jimmy thought. His thoughts got hurting. The sound of running feet came as a relief. Up the darkened areaway, between the hole and the dormitory, the deputy and a fireman came into view. And then, from within the dormitory, a voice yelled, "We're burning down the joint!"

A convict stepped into the doorway of the dormitory, holding an empty can in his hand. Jimmy caught the faint stench of gasoline. He saw the stab of light from the deputy's hand torch. He saw the convict in the dormitory, a suddenly embossed picture on the black night, tall and lanky and starkly outlined. He saw the abrupt stretch of the convict's eyes, saw the sag of his mouth, heard the ejaculation, "What the hell!"

He saw the fireman draw a pistol, jam it into the convict's guts; heard the convict's grunt; saw him back away from the pressure of the gun. He heard the clanking of the can on the wooden steps, heard the convict's loud laugh, saw him draw back his foot to kick the fireman in the face. The picture hung. Jimmy watched, feeling the moment like an electric shock. He saw the flash of the gun, heard its roar, heard the laugh choke off. He saw the convict double slowly forward, fall down the steps, land on his face.

The moment held him, continued shocking him. And abruptly the shock left, and he was free. And he was running again.

Out in front of the deputy's office a convict with a crocus sack of tobacco stopped him. "Here, take a bag, kid," he said, thrusting out a bag of Bull Durham. "Take two bags; take all you want. There's plenty more over to the commissary. We're looting the joint, taking everything."

Jimmy took the bag, tore it open with his teeth, rolled a cigaret. He didn't have a match, so he stuck it dead in his mouth. Some one ran by him and said, "Come on, kid, they're getting new clothes over to the commissary."

And he was running again, through the bodies, past the fire trucks bunched at the end of the chapel, through the mud, the spray of water coming from the hoses, underneath the ladder of the hook and ladder truck, up the commissary stairs. He changed trousers, snatched up a new coat, went downstairs again.

"They're firing the woolen mill!" some one yelled.

Several convicts broke in that direction. Jimmy broke after them. Inside the woolen mill, convicts were sprinkling gasoline, lighting it. Jimmy gave a look, heard the roar of the fire trucks behind him, and began running again.

He ran down across the ball diamond, looked up at the guard tower in the northeast corner of the wall, curved back toward the dining room, high-kneed and churning, his mind a blank. Inside the dining room, several convicts sat to the tables, eating steaks. One of them looked up and said, "Go on back to the kitchen and get something to eat, kid, they're giving it away."

"And wash your face," another said.

Jimmy started toward the kitchen, but halfway there he began running again, out of the dining room, down the areaway. At the stairs leading up to the tin shop, he halted. There was something he wanted; something he ought to do. Then he thought of Walter. He didn't know whether Walter was what he wanted or not. He hesitated a moment longer, then went up the steps.

Walter was sitting in the guard's office, reading a magazine.

"What you doing?" Jimmy asked.

Walter looked up; his eyes stretched. "Jesus Christ!" he exclaimed, "What's the matter with you?"

Weakness swept Jimmy in waves; he felt as if he would faint. Resting the palms of his hands on the desk top, he leaned his weight on his arms.

"Why don't you wash your face?" Walter asked. "Your face is black. What the hell's the matter with you, Jimmy, your eyes look crazy as hell."

"Listen—" Jimmy began. His tongue felt thick.

Walter came around the desk and put his arm about Jimmy's waist. "Come on and sit down," he said. "You're letting it get you, Jimmy. What the hell you been doing? You been bringing those stiffs out the block?"

"Listen—" Jimmy said thickly, pulling away from him. "I want you."

Walter froze. "I don't understand what you mean," he said.

"Listen, don't give me that stuff," Jimmy muttered. "You know what I mean."

"You don't know what you're saying, Jimmy," Walter said. "Come on and sit down." He put his arm about Jimmy again. "Come on and sit down and take it easy. You've got too excited."

"I know what I'm saying," Jimmy grated thickly. "I want you to-to—I want you for a w-woman. I don't want no more of this goddamn cousin stuff."

Walter took his arm away and asked, "You wouldn't want me to do that, would you, Jimmy?" There was no condemnation in his voice; it was a question, that was all.

Jimmy didn't know whether to say yes or no. For a moment he just stood there; then he rubbed his hand down his face as if to wipe away something, bowed his head, licked his lips.

"Damn you!" he said and turned away.

At the bottom of the stairs he hesitated again. Whatever it was he wanted, Walter didn't have it. He wandered around to the back of the hospital and ran into Blocker. A convict called Pete was sitting on the ground in front of Blocker with three blankets wrapped about him.

Pete looked up and said, "Old Blocker saved my life. If it hadn't been for old Blocker I'd be dead right now. Old Blocker saved my life. Yes sir, old Blocker—"

Blocker grinned, his teeth looking like yellow fangs in the dim light. "Damn, kid, looks like you been fighting smoke."

"I'm tired," Jimmy said.

"Sit down and take it easy, kid," Blocker told him. "Here, wait a minute." He dragged Pete back against the hospital wall and made a place beside him for Jimmy. "Here, sit down and take it easy."

Jimmy slumped down beside Pete. Blocker sat on the other side. They talked intermittently.

"Man, I thought I was a gonna," Pete said.

About three minutes later, Jimmy said, "Yeah?"

Later on, Blocker said, "I saw him laying there on the yard and straightened him out a little. I said to myself, this chump owes me four bucks and I'll never get it if he croaks."

Some time later, Pete said, "Old Blocker."

They felt very friendly, sitting there in the darkness back of the hospital. The fire and the confusion and the lurid chaos seemed a long way off.

"I wish I could go to sleep," Jimmy said.

Blocker rolled and lit a cigaret. "Why don't you?" he asked.

Jimmy leaned his head back against the building. Above, the sky was cloudless; stars were scintillating jewels in the black onyx of night. There was a pale, wan moon, remote and merciless. Beyond, the everlasting walls connected the earth with the sky, closing in a world.

"I can't," Jimmy said.

Some one came around the corner of the building from the yard.

"How's the fire going?" Pete asked.

"It's about all over now," came the reply.

All over. That was a funny thing to say, Jimmy thought. *All over now.* What was all over now?"

Book II

A Flood of Tears

1

BEFORE THE FIRE, despite the fact of its submergence beneath the level, endless, monotonous, unvarying, unmoving, eternal stretch of prison days, there had been a humanism in Jimmy Monroe, an un-dead spiritual affinity with the world beyond the walls— memories and feelings and dreams and desires. Heartaches and loneliness and yearnings and nostalgia, soft, impressionable, intangible emotions which all along had kept him afloat like the belly of a ship in the ocean of humanity.

The ineffably poignant stir of emotions caused by raindrops striking gently against a window pane, a curtain of shattered brilliance against the lights of the raining night, as soft and insistent as the filter of water through porous stone.

The unaccountable gladness in a perfect day. The rare, heart-choking beauty of tulips in the morning. The softness of breasts imagined in a pillow of tamped cotton as solid as rock in his arms in the night. The inexpressible gallantry of a smile. The charm of a gesture. The enthusiasm in eyes. And thoughts in the darkness, the gutting loneliness, powdery dry and agate hard, trampling down the lushness of his heart. But always stirring, touching, moving, fingering the softness in his soul.

Before the fire he had always felt that he was as good, if not better than anyone on earth, and that no matter what he had done or what had happened to him, he still belonged to the outside world. All these feelings deep inside of him, but still there, buoyant and lifting, like the love of God felt beneath a lighted altar, supporting all the dead weight of living out his youth in a prison.

And the knowledge that in the world there was right and there was wrong, guiding you even though it hurt you, restraining you even though you hated it. Even the bitter memories, the hurting memories, the memories which scalded but yet had had meaning, keeping you above the oblivion of the prison.

The memory of the days of his life which had protected him against the high stone walls and the tiny barred cells and the breathing, eating, stinking, crying, cursing, fighting convicts who were the backwash of humanity, lost to the world he had saved.

Even the memory of the judge's gaze leveled on him appraisingly from behind the high court desk, the weight of it on his face, on his lowered lids, the weight of it on his brain and down into his heart. The fear that had burnt a thin sickening fuse through his consciousness, diffusing his vision. But making him know from his reactions that he was still a human being, that he still belonged.

He had never forgotten his frightened prayer, "Oh, God, please don't let him hurt me," nor the pressure of the deputy sheriff's grip tightening on his arm. He had stood to a stiff attention before the judge's desk.

The people whom he had robbed stood at a distance to his right. The man and his wife. They were white-faced and ill at ease. He turned and looked at them and although they did not move they gave the impression of shrinking away from him. His fear suddenly left him and he felt superior toward them as if they, not he, were the ones accused.

He let his gaze linger on them for a moment in insolent condescension, then looked about the courtroom to see if there were other spectators. There were none. He felt an inexplicable humiliation, as if he had received a dreadful slight. There should have been spectators and one or two newspaper reporters, he thought. After all, he had been front page news. Perhaps they had lost interest because he had entered a plea—a plea of guilty to highway robbery in the first degree. The phrase sounded ponderous and vicious and heavy with a sinister weight.

He switched his thoughts quickly from it, to his mother and father and brothers. But he did not care that they were not present.

He did not want them to be. What was the use? They couldn't help him. They didn't know what it was all about.

His attention snapped back to the judge. It seemed as if he had called his name and was asking him something. He noticed how the judge's lips smacked together after each word. Then he listened to the last of the sentence: ". . . to say before I pass sentence?"

A dozen things leaped into his mind that he could say, like: "Shoot the works," or "Take it easy on this curve, your honor." Something smart and snappy that would get in the headlines . . . But he couldn't say them. If somebody had been there to see and hear him. Somebody who counted, like Sugar Patton from the Green House gambling club. Or newspaper reporters. Or even Benny. Maybe he could have said it then. But those people there did not count.

He slowly shook his head and looked out the window, down at the dirty snow on the Public Square. Then he recalled that his attorney had assured him that he would only be given a short term in the reformatory. He said to himself, "I'm only nineteen years old. I'm not going to get more than a few months in the reformatory at the most. I'm a college boy." He felt like whistling . . .

The judge's voice floated into his consciousness again: ". . . You have taken ten years from the life of each of these persons by your vicious crime . . ." His lips curled. Then the voice was gone and he thought fleetingly of his two victims standing there, but he did not feel any emotion toward them at all.

On the slush-covered street below a fat man was trying to maneuver a rusty sedan into a parking space. He ought to cut it short now, he was thinking. His hand moved in exasperation when the fat man failed to cut short. There're so many people who don't know how to park a car, he thought. He'll never make it now. He shook his head. *Never make it!* Queer how the words repeated themselves in his mind . . .

The judge's voice penetrated his consciousness again in a quick, stinging stab, and he jerked his gaze to the judge's eyes: " . . . *to be taken to the state penitentiary where you shall remain incarcerated at hard labor for a period of twenty years.*"

His gaze came sluggishly back to the courtroom, crawled up the black severity of the judge's gown. The wide focus of his interest narrowed to needle-point fineness as realization slowly dawned on him, and in all the world there was only the judge's veined face, sitting there at the tiny end of the funnel of his vision, mouth closed in utter finality. " . . . *for a period of twenty years* . . ." His eyes widened until they seemed to spread all over his face. Then abruptly he turned blind.

Time passed, he did not know how much, in which the world stood still, then the deputy took him by the arm and guided him back to the county jail where he was placed back in solitary confinement where he had been since getting smart with the head jailor a week before.

He was stunned. He had been so assured, riding down a steep hill toward a blind end, enjoying the speed and the wind in his face and the pavement rising up over the hood, leaning back in complacent ecstasy—to find quite suddenly, when the end was immediately ahead, that there were no brakes.

His glazed vision moved over objects unseeingly, as if he was sleep-walking. When they brought him his supper he stared at it uncomprehendingly for long seconds before saying, "Oh, oh yes, supper, yes, sure. Sure, I want it."

His window gave a dust-dimmed picture of the corrugated infirmary roof, a window-spotted square of red-brick wall. Sunlight briefly touched the wall in passing, and then the deepening darkness closed in about him, tightly smothering, and he thought about twenty years away from things.

For a deep, wild instant sudden fear engulfed him. He was at last afraid. Afraid of the darkness about him, of the darkness stretching out before him. Afraid of what might happen to him.

He felt that all the world was against him. That people wanted to hurt him. He had never felt like that before. He hadn't believed that people would actually hurt him. Of course, his mother and father had whipped him. And several employers had fired him. And school officials had censored him. But this was different. This was final, irrevocable, more like being crushed to death in a hideous vise while being conscious of it but unable to stop it. Something that you couldn't forget and cease to think about because it was still happening to you, and would continue to happen for twenty years.

He couldn't understand why it should matter so much either to the judge or to the people whom he had robbed, that, out of all the dull, stolid people in the world, all the plodding, unimaginative people—out of all the people who lived their vague and humdrum lives hoping for nothing better—they would choose him to hurt like that. He actually couldn't. His hopes had been so high and his dreams so brightly burning. What he had done did not seem at all that consequential in the scheme of important things for them to want to hurt him for it. He hadn't hurt the people, not much, not like they had hurt him, anyway.

It did not occur to him that he had it coming, that he had been building up toward it for almost all of his life. That on the scales of compensation his life did not balance. It would not have occurred to him then anymore than it ever had, for not one thing which he had ever done in all his life had ever seemed important. The important things had never been the things he did but the things he had dreamed he did. That had been his life, all inside of him, not really happening in this world of mass and matter and living people.

He knew, of course, that he had done a whole lot of things during his life which his mother had called "ugly". *Ugly* had been her favorite word to describe most of the things he had done. But what she had never seemed to understand was that most of the things he had done, he had not wanted to do. There had been things inside of him that had needed proving. He never knew just what they were. Perhaps being so girlish looking as a little boy had had something to do with it. Or perhaps it was being away from other little boys during the first years of his life. He never knew. But the things he had done had somehow seemed to prove them.

That had been at first, when the necessity of adapting himself to this living world had first entered into his awareness. Afterwards he did them because he did not care one way or the other.

115

*T*HOSE FIRST YEARS of existence left queer memories in his mind, diffused and sketchy, with no continuity or chronological order; here and there an incident sharply recalled like a thin red gash across his brain.

There was the big rambling house which needed painting, with its nine draughty rooms and banging doors and splintery, wooden floors covered in spots with threadbare carpet, situated in the heart of the Mississippi delta seven miles from the nearest railroad station, in which he was born on the 14th of August, 1909, the last of three male children, and christened James Buchanon Monroe.

And there was the twelve-acre garden in which they all worked on summer days; and the soybean field over toward the Norwood's side; and the pecan tree in the corner of the back fence; the fig tree with its split purple fruit growing up over the eaves of the front porch; and the dusty loft where Damon and he played on rainy days and listened to the drumming of the rain on the shingled roof. Damon was little more than a year older than Jimmy, and they had been inseparable in those days, like fingers on the same hand.

And the open space beneath the house with the tall brick pillars in the front and the short ones behind where the land slanted upward. Once his father killed a full-grown rattle snake trying to crawl up into the house. And the church over to the right with its wedge-shaped roof and peeling paint and weedy graveyard and scrubby, scarred trees in front where the horses were tied on Sundays. And there was Cindy, the black mammy and grinning cook and wash-woman and maid and nurse all rolled into one.

He could remember faintly the dogwood trees in bloom, and gathering greasy pecans in the fall, and his father's mouse-gray buggy horse named Maud, and the cow named Ruth, and the chickens and guineas and turkeys, and the dog they had to kill because he sucked eggs, and how old "Billy Goat" with his tobacco-stained whiskers split his leg with his knife blade and sucked the poison out the time he was snakebit. And the time when he was nine and Damon ten his father took them to the station. How Damon broke and ran when the train came snorting in. But he, Jimmy, did not run. He did not run because he did not believe that it would hurt him. And the time his mother whipped him for slipping off with his father's shotgun and going hunting. She whipped Damon, too, but she always seemed to whip Jimmy the worse.

He remembered his mother best as a strange, harsh, violent woman, given to uncontrollable outbursts of temper; and for the accusations and vilifications she heaped upon his father. It was not until years afterwards that he discovered her attitude stemmed from delusions of grandeur, and that in marrying his father she felt that she had taken a step down in life and was bitterly regretful forever afterwards.

And there were the study hours and recitation periods and recesses in the large, book-lined library where his mother taught him and Damon the fundamentals of academic knowledge. She swore that no child which she brought into the world would ever attend a "backwood's school in the company of poor white trash," as she referred to the school where his father taught. His oldest brother, Harry, seven years his senior, was away to boarding school most of those years they lived in Mississippi.

But out of all those hazy memories, the times which stood out clearest were the times he slipped away with some book or other, usually some ancient Greek or Roman legend, and read and dreamed. Their mother had forbidden them to play with the neighboring children—"vulgar maniacs" she called them—and after a time they didn't want to; they discovered they could entertain themselves.

The *Iliad* made a lasting impression on him, and for many years afterwards, even after he was almost grown, the sullen, invincible character of Achilles was his hero. Having confused the characters of Hector and Paris in his mind, he always thought of Paris as the one whom Achilles chased around the walls of Troy. After that there were only two kinds of people in the world—those who ran and those who chased them.

Little by little, the incidents and situations of books, the language and atmosphere therein, the virtues and vices, wove themselves into a pattern of reality in his mind, submerging the realistic and material happenings of this blooded, living world into a vague unreality. He came to feel that the things he did and the things which happened to him, such as eating and studying and sleeping, each absolute within itself, were things which did not count, and were only to be forgotten and passed on to an oblivious past; the real things were the things he read and the things he dreamed and the castles he built and the armies of mail-clad soldiers he led through the forests and along the sunken Mississippi roads. An abyss grew up between him and this peopled world which nothing ever bridged until he went to prison.

The war came and passed, remembered only as big black letters across the face of newspapers and the elders shaking their heads and muttering something about the "bloody Huns" and Eastern and Western "fronts", and funeral services for empty caskets . . .

3

IN NINETEEN-HUNDRED and twenty-one he was twelve years old. He would rather have been Achilles than any living human. Had he been asked to name the one woman through all history who represented the highest in womanhood he would have named Penelope.

It was then his father moved to Pine Bluff, Arkansas, and began preaching in a small wooden church. Damon and he entered high school in the ninth grade, which was the first school either of them had ever attended. He still believed in Santa Claus.

The students called him "Galahad", quoting in asides: "His strength is as the strength of ten because his heart is pure." He was rather proud of it until he discovered that it was something queer and funny to be called; then he fought them. He didn't want to fight. No one ever really knew how much he hated fighting, and how sickeningly afraid he was to fight. But when some one hurt you, you fought them. That was what all the heroes and knights did. And if you won they stopped.

If you could not fight them, then you did not think about the hurt and it could not hurt. He learned that all by himself. No matter how hurt you are, if you do not think about it, it can not hurt. He became capable of doing most things he wanted to do, no matter how frightened he was, for being frightened was something you couldn't help; but if you didn't think about it, it could not hurt. That was how he overcame, somewhat, the fear of people which he had when first thrown into contact with them.

But God was different from People. He was afraid of God in a different way for He could hurt you and there wasn't anything you could do about it. Like the time He made Damon blind. They were experimenting with chemical explosives in the basement.

Jimmy knew that God had caused it to happen because just a few minutes before his mother had told him that God was going to punish him for being so ugly that day; and he was on the lookout for something. God was a huge unseen Being just above who swooped down and punished you when you needed punishing. But his mother had meant that God would punish him, Jimmy. And God had swooped down and put out Damon's eyes. God didn't have any right to do that, Jimmy thought. He, Jimmy, had eyes; God could have put out his eyes.

He never forgot Damon's tiny stricken cry; he could hear it just as plainly and piteously and heartrendingly years afterward in the solitude of a prison cell, looking at a bar-blocked square of sky, remembering things. And the way Damon cupped his black-burnt face in both of his hands and ran blindly into the wall. Jimmy never

119

forgave God for that. His mother took Damon to St. Louis to the Barnes Hospital; but God, Who had taken his sight, never gave it back.

The loss of Damon's companionship left a lonely hole in Jimmy's heart which nothing ever filled except Joan for one short moment when he held her in his arms, and that had been like a sun-cloud drifting by—white and soft and *gone*. His mother didn't count; she had never counted. All she ever did for him, it seemed, was whip him; and in between the whippings she forever nagged as if something gnawed within her, clamoring to be released. She never understood him; at first because she did not try, and later because he would not let her.

He turned to other kids in school, but that only made it worse. They did not like to talk to him or play his games. It wasn't that they disliked him; they thought he was all right in his way, reading books all the time and doing the strangest things ever. And when he laughed it always seemed to startle them.

He began to wonder why he was so strange and different from other boys. It wasn't just being girlish-looking with silly yellow hair and big blue eyes with long gold lashes; it wasn't having dimples either, although that was something that gave him plenty fights. It was something else and he didn't know what it was. But whatever it was, it worried him a lot because he didn't want to be different. So he watched the other boys to learn the things that impressed them, and then he went to extremes doing those things. Whatever some other boy said he had done, Jimmy actually went and did it. And when he could not do it better than all the others, then there was nothing in it for him.

It was then that he came to believe that he had to prove something. At first he did not care much for doing it. It was like fighting—something that you had to do to prove you weren't scared.

He learned to smoke and curse and play hookey from school because that seemed to make him like other boys. They lived on West Second Street and the freights came down West Third. He learned to ride them clear out past the crossing where they turned, and over to Sixth Street where they began to pick up speed. Once he climbed into an iron Mountain boxcar and rode it all the way to Little Rock; but that turned out to be disastrous when his father found out.

He started off by treating little girls with story-book chivalry. He kept it up until they laughed at him. Then he wanted to fight them, too. He wanted to beat the little girl next door in the face with his fists for telling him that there was no Santa Claus. He wanted to hurt her as badly as she hurt him. But he didn't. There was something inside of him that kept him from; something that told him little girls were like damsels in distress whom the knights had always rescued. And of course you didn't fight damsels in distress, you rescued them—everyone knew that.

It was something of the same feeling which kept him from wanting Katie—that and the fact that he had not reached the age of puberty. He was on his way to the shooting range by the lake in Battleville to watch the marksmen shoot clay pigeons, and he saw her lying naked on the grass in a little dell. She started to run when she saw him. He didn't know what made him run after her. But after he had caught her and thrown her, she had quit struggling, and there was nothing else for him to do. He felt that any other boy would have done the same; at least any boy like Luke Hardy or Jake or the tall hatchet-faced Clem who chewed tobacco and spit in the inkwell. So he did. It wasn't much different from going to the bathroom, but the idea of it was something else.

Afterwards he was terrified. He ran all the way across Battleville and down the hill and across Pullen Street and down the railroad tracks to West Second and home. But he didn't know what to do about it, so he kept mum and quit thinking about it, and after a time, to his great surprise, he didn't even care.

It was that way with everything. Being bad and showing off and trying to prove something when in his mind things were so utterly different that he couldn't really see why he should.

It was much the same with school athletics. He liked football and baseball and tennis after he had learned to play them. He liked to come in fast from short to meet a high bounder and whip an underhanded throw to first to nail the runner stepping on the bag.

It was great fun to trick an opponent up to the net and smash hard drives at his face, or run skyey punts back through a broken field. It was something of Achilles chasing Paris around the walls of Troy. Only he never told anyone he thought it was like that.

But in school the games were different. There were the hours of practice which weren't play at all, but more like hard and tedious work to learn to play. He thought it so reversed and nonsensical that he never would have gone out for any of the teams if he had not found out shortly before that all the girls called him sissified because of his looks. That was something else again which called for proving. He made three letters in his tenth year of high school, which was his second year in any school.

Next was the long train ride to St. Louis; crying all the way, crying down in his heart and trying to keep a straight face so his father wouldn't notice. He was saying goodbye to first love. It was as if he knew that he was saying goodbye to something he would never feel again.

He didn't know why he should have loved her in the first place. He hardly knew her. He had only met her on the tennis courts the day before, and that night he had taken her out on Cherry Street to a carnival.

That was one of those memories—not the girl, but the feeling . . . Walking along in a wash of silver moonlight, holding hands, not ever wanting to part. Discovering each other, telling each other a little of the things they dreamed, and listening raptly while the other told. Finding out how much they loved each other from the moment they first met. And then saying goodbye for keeps; but making believe it was not so. Saying goodbye late that night and crying and not ashamed.

At first he remembered her with an etched clarity which he thought he would never lose. He remembered her face and her features and her body and the way she walked and laughed and smiled and the color of her eyes and the different tints of her dark brown hair and the crinkles in the corner of her very red mouth.

And then he could not remember how she looked at all. She

was gone and that was that. Afterwards he remembered her as a feeling because she was the first girl whom he had ever loved.

HE DID NOT LIKE ST. LOUIS. He started off not liking it and never changed. He went to school and played spectacular football and baseball and made the track team and the students applauded him. And he did not care. He was very popular. He asked the girls right off for what he wanted and did not play around. And afterwards he hated them for giving in, and forgot that they had. He smoked in the school basement and slipped out for lunch against regulations; and learned his lessons miraculously well. And in the end he was expelled.

His father had made a payment on a home in St. Louis, and being unable to get a job teaching, or a church, was forced to resort to other work, carpentry and selling insurance and taking small building jobs on contract. Damon was attending the blind school out on Grand Avenue, learning Braille and how to play the saxophone among other things. Harry was going to college out to Washington University and doing some kind of work about the campus. His mother seemed more contented there than ever before. And he smashed that serenity like a broadaxe through a skull by getting expelled from the public school system. It was a wonder he escaped the reformatory—but that was saving up for him.

At that time he was fifteen. What he did not understand was why they made all the stink about it. After all, it was not his idea. The boys around about had said that she was hard to make, and so he made her. Others had taken girls down into the basement. The *modus operandi* was not original. Of course they had run when

Mr. Sawyer, the manual training instructor, returned from lunch. And Jimmy had not. He never knew just why he hadn't. He could have gotten away if he had and there wouldn't have been anything said about it at all.

That was a trait that remained with him. Many times he could have run, and escaped. But when you ran, that made you Paris and the one who chased you Achilles; and that was all wrong, for you were not Paris—*never!* You were never scared of consequences like Paris had been, for you never admitted to yourself that there were consequences.

He took all the blame that they would let him take, but the girl was sent to a "home" in spite of it. He was sorry for her, truly, when he discovered that she was an orphan. But what could he do?

There was a session in the parlor. His father and mother talked to him. But what was talk? Be good, they said. But what was that? Something that when you were, people thought you queer. And when you weren't, they merely thought you bad. And if you had a choice to make, you'd always rather be bad.

It was near the summer vacation so he got a job delivering for a drugstore out on Delmar Boulevard past Union Avenue, and forgot about it. He worked from ten in the morning until two in the afternoon, then went back at six and worked to closing time which usually was some time after midnight. He was paid five dollars a week.

He liked the job. He liked it out at night. People seemed different at night. He was able to say things to them that he was afraid to say during the day.

He was given a bike and he learned to ride it bare-handed. The soda clerk gave him all the ice cream and sundaes he could eat, and the boss gave him plenty of candy. He stole his cigarets, but didn't really care for smoking. It made people stare at him—and so he smoked.

There was a red-headed girl named Sarah who ushered in the theater across the street. She wore tight fitting dresses and rolled her hips when she walked along the street. He stopped her once and tried to make a date. He sounded scared even to himself. But she surprised him. She said, "Sure, catch me when I get off some night—and bring three dollars."

He gave his mother what he earned each week and had never had three dollars at one time. So he began to look around for some way in which to get it. He had never intended giving it to Sarah. But she had given him the idea. Three dollars was something good to have; it offered possibilities.

There was a refund on soda water bottles delivered in the neighborhood. He had been bringing them back to the drugstore and returning the refund to the customers. But after he got the idea of having three dollars all his own he began to slip the bottles from the storeroom and hide them in the foyer of the apartment house next door. When he returned from a delivery he'd pick up one or two and keep the refund for himself. He made several extra dollars that way before he found the storeroom locked one day. The boss grew cold and stopped giving him candy, and for a time he watched his step.

And then he said to hell with it. Five dollars a week was no great fortune for a person his age. He would quit the job and look around for something better. So the morning of his next pay day he stole two eighteen dollar Kodaks and an Ingersoll watch and a quart of maple nut ice cream and several packages of chewing gum and a package of Chesterfield cigarets and a knife. He hid them in an empty Coca Cola barrel in the basement.

He never did discover just how the boss found out about it. But that day at noon his boss took him down into the basement and confronted him with the swag and accused him of stealing it. The ice cream had melted and leaked all over everything.

No one will ever know how frightened he was, nor how badly he wanted to confess and get it over with. But when something was happening to you, something that could hurt you, you pretended that it wasn't, and if you pretended hard enough to the bitter, final end, then it wasn't. That kept him from confessing. All his boss could do was fire him; although he knew Jimmy had stolen the stuff, he couldn't prove it.

At first Jimmy had been afraid to go home. He dreaded it; he hung around on the street hoping to make a date with Sarah. Hoping for anything to happen that would keep him from going home and telling his parents that he had been fired for stealing.

And then suddenly it occurred to him that he didn't have to tell them at all. He could tell them that he had quit because he figured he could get a job that paid more money.

That's what he did. They said all right. It was as easy as that.

Thinking about it afterwards he called himself a fool for being scared of anything at all. How could they have possibly known what he had done without his telling them. For that matter, he reasoned, how could his boss have proved that he had stolen those things unless he had confessed. So he concluded that it was best never to admit doing anything of which he was accused of doing— there was nothing at all to gain by it and everything to lose.

He got another job as busboy downtown in a saloon. Of course, in 1924 they called it a "soda fountain". The pay was fourteen dollars a week, and he made tips besides. He told his father that he had another drugstore job, a better one. Now he was an assistant soda jerker and made eight dollars a week. His mother said he could keep a dollar for pocket change, but he insisted that she take all eight. She thought he was getting better. He kept the other six and the tips he made and was doing fine. It was just as easy as that.

It was a place where prostitutes hung out. Their "cokes" were loaded from a bottle underneath the counter; or else they went back in Dinty's "office" and got things called "bangs". But Jimmy liked to talk to them; he never knew why. And strangely, they liked to listen to him—especially if he gave them a dollar, which he usually did. In the corner of the dim and dingy taproom on Washington Avenue in St. Louis that winter in the early twenties he slipped silver dollars across grimy tables and talked to drunken whores of shining paradises and enchanted dreams and hopes that grew up to the stars—and that winter in St. Louis they listened for a dollar.

Why he ever did it, he never knew. Not to prove anything that he knew of. Not because he was sorry for them. Just because he wanted to.

At first he could talk to Damon. And after Damon hungry whores in St. Louis. And after them no one. He smoked cigarets and talked his dollars away and earned the name of the "One Dollar Kid" all up and down the avenue. He drank a little whiskey, too, but not too much for fear his mother might smell it on his breath.

That fall when school opened his mother wanted to send him away to a military academy. He didn't want to go. He begged and pleaded with them to let him stay. He'd never make it in an academy, he knew. He said that his pay had been raised to twelve dollars a week and that if they would let him stay and work another year he'd save every cent he made and pay his own way.

Finally his father said, "He's young, one year away from school won't hurt him."

He had his way again. He would have had it, anyway. He would have run away.

And then one night he was talking to a dark-eyed woman who had once been very pretty; but by then she looked a little tired about the edges of the mouth, a little weary in the lids of her eyes; and in the dim light her face showed slightly slanting lines. She had come in and ordered a "coke" and he'd said, "Look, want a dollar?"

He never forgot the startled look that came into her eyes. "I'm the one who should be paying you," she said. "But there isn't that much money in all the world to pay for what you have, kid."

And then a fellow named Joe who hung around the place came in and snatched her pocketbook. He stuck his hand down in it and when he didn't find any money he brought it out and hit her in the face.

Jimmy thought to himself, I've always been a fool. *Always!* So he jumped right straight over the counter and hit Joe in the stomach. He didn't want to fight him. But the woman made him think of damsels in distress. So he went to her rescue . . . *Always!*

He poured hard fast blows in Joe's midriff until he'd knocked him down. And then he stood chivalrously over him and waited for him to get up.

Joe came up with a blackjack in his hand and beat Jimmy across the face and head until he'd backed across the cafe out into the street. A grinding bitter tartness went all through him before he felt the pain. Finally Pebo, the bouncer, came out and stopped Joe from beating him to death. Pebo pushed Joe away and turned to Jimmy and said, "You're too fresh, kid. Go in to Dinty and get your money and beat it. You're fired."

When the tight bitter tartness gave way a sudden flopping hurt filled his head and blood trickled from his nose. But when his head had cleared enough for him to think, he wasn't angry, nor even scared. He was humiliated. That kind of beating was something that one man did not take from another, he told himself.

Perhaps he wouldn't have done more than think about it for a time and then have forgotten it, if he hadn't seen the gun. But when he went into Dinty's office to get his pay, he saw the big blue revolver gleaming dully from an open bureau drawer. There was no one about to stop him so he picked it up and put it in his pocket and slipped back into the street.

He could feel the slow trickles of blood from his nose and in the roots of his hair, and his head throbbed like a hot day on the delta. He went down the street looking for Joe. He didn't want to beat him; he didn't even want to get even with him. He wanted to kill him. He wanted to see him dead.

Reason had deserted him; and his destination was not the place but the act. Street lights were beacons lighting his purpose, not his footsteps; and the world was the place whereon he walked. He was Achilles and Joe was Paris and time had dropped back to the walls of Troy.

If you thought about it being 1924, then you would think about jails and prisons and scaffolds for murderers and the inexorability of the law, and you would get confused and not do what you intended to do after all. So he would not think about the time.

It was lucky for him that Dinty and Pebo caught up with him before he caught up with Joe. They had him arrested, and the police took him down to the central jail and locked him in a cell. There were a couple of drunks in the cell occupying the slab of steel placed there for a seat. And there were bars across the front, and tobacco spittle down the dirty concrete walls.

He became frightened. He fought against it. But it grew in his brain and burst through his skull and ran down into the cell and filled the cell with something white and frozen which blinded him; it grew so large that it encompassed prisons and chain gangs and convict camps like he had seen from the train in Mississippi with prison guards on horses with long rifles and imagined days of unending, heartbreaking labor cleaning swamps and digging ditches and breaking rock. It overwhelmed him, numbing his senses and clamping him in a frozen embrace like a body in a glacier.

And then the jailor came and let him out. His father was there to take him home. He did not ask him how he had found out that he was there. He felt such a deep warm gratitude toward him then that he was not able to think of anything else.

There was another session in the parlor. For once his mother did not scold him. She seemed so shocked, so stunned, as if she had just discovered that the world was coming to an end. He felt a queer desire to laugh at her. It was nothing, anyway, looking back at it from the brightness of the day. He had made a big enough fool of himself for them to let it go at that, he thought.

Finally his father talked to him of right and wrong, and of the things that people did who wanted salvation. But he did not care so much about salvation, nor did he think his father could tell him much about the things he cared about—the things before salvation. He had seen those prostitutes down there wearing furs and diamonds and living in houses bigger and finer than any in which he had ever lived—some of them.

But he sighed and acted as if he was impressed by what his father had said. That made it easier. Soon it was over. He went outside and down the street. He saw a blind beggar on the corner and gave him his last dollar bill. Now that was doing good, he told himself, and felt squared all around.

When Christmas came they moved again; this time to Cleveland, Ohio, where his father bought another home.

So his boyhood passed.

IN SOLITARY CONFINEMENT in the county jail for getting smart with the head jailor. Alone with twenty years. Alone in the darkness of the night. Thinking of girls and boys and incidents and places; thinking of those unimportant things that had gone to make up his existence. Wondering how it all tied up with the life he had lived in his imagination during all those years; the life of red adventure and noble deeds and rescuing beautiful damsels in distress; the life of a millionaire playboy and a great statesman and a famous general; the thousand and one lives during those listless years of existence . . . Thinking of his senior year in East High School and how he had disliked it, and wondering if that dislike had anything to do with his being in a cell. Or if he had liked any of the things that he had disliked, would it have made any difference . . .

HE GOT OFF TO A WRONG START in East High School in Cleveland. The principal had him on the carpet the very first thing and laid down the law. He said, "Okay," and let it go at that.

That was the way it was during that year. Everything was dull and uninteresting, and he went along, doing as little as he could to make it any better and telling himself that he did not care. That was after the beginning. In the beginning he did try.

The students there did not make friends with him, in fact they

130

did not seem aware of his existence. It was that as much as anything else which made him dislike it so. He started out looking for ways in which to make them notice him. He knew well enough that he could not afford to get into trouble, so he tried for the basketball team; but he played too rough and soon they did not care to play with him at all.

Next he turned to study. For a time he poured into his studies with a diligence new to him. But there were many students who studied diligently at all times and who were just as smart, if not smarter, than he. So he quit. He couldn't be the best, so there was nothing in it for him.

When Spring came he went out for football practice. But it was mostly routine with no chance for individual performance. So he quit that, too.

Finally he said to hell with everything and went back into his shell and dreamed that he was great and famous with a yacht and a fleet of limousines and several mansions and a thousand suits of clothes and just too many girls and East High school could go to hell.

That summer when school let out he got a job washing dishes in a restaurant on 105th Street. He made the mashed potatoes and swept the floors and washed the dishes and was paid twelve dollars a week.

After he had been there for a month the second cook took sick and he persuaded the boss to let him take the job. His pay was raised to sixteen-fifty, which was six-fifty less than the job paid, but he didn't mind. He could fry fairly well so the boss kept him on and fired the second cook when he came back to work. A gnarled and knotty bum had taken his dishwashing job.

There were three waitresses, one of whom was a big blond Scandinavian with a broad face and blue eyes and a strong round body. She wore tight uniforms which made her hips stick out; and her skirts were split down the side showing her thigh when she took long strides. Every time he saw her walk, his stomach drew up and he went weak. But he couldn't get anywhere with her. There was a big truck driver from the warehouse next door who had the inner track.

One day he went down to the men's dressing room to take a smoke and caught the dishwasher peeping through a hole in the partition which separated the men's and women's dressing rooms.

"Why, you dirty peeper!" he accused, pushing him away.

Then he had bent down to the hole, himself, intending to tell the girls to cover it. He could have covered it, himself, but he thought it was the big blonde at whom the dishwasher had been peeping and that by warning her he could get himself in solid. But it was the skinny lean-eyed brunette and when he spoke to her she screamed. The boss rushed down and the dishwasher accused him of peeping.

So he lost another job. It had been a good job and he hated losing it. He got another one, however, driving a delivery truck, but soon school opened and he gave it up.

He had saved almost a hundred dollars, all of which he spent on clothes before his mother had a chance to stop him. That fall in school he was the sport. He had all the girls he wanted. But he did not keep any of them for long. He just liked to win them.

That January he graduated. But even that was by a fluke. The 5 in the 50 which his Latin teacher had given him had so resembled an 8 that his grade had been recorded as 80 instead of the 50 which it actually was. The mistake was not noticed until after he had received his diploma, and when the principal requested that he return the next semester and review the course, he told him: "Not me, I didn't like it the first time." Perhaps they were a little tired of him by then for they did not bother.

Before he had a chance to feel what being finished with high school was really like, his eldest brother, Harry, was killed in an automobile accident in Santa Barbara, California, and his parents decided right off to send him to college. He was all they had left now, with Damon blind, they pointed out. It was up to him to make good for the family. If he failed now, they all failed, and everything they had struggled for would be in vain.

He caught the spirit of it, and for once was not afraid of trying, even if he couldn't be the best. This one time he was going to play it out to the very, very end. He owed his parents that much.

He got a job with a painting contractor in the middle of February. It paid twenty-five dollars a week. He'd save his money, he resolved, and help pay his way through college. It was working with an aim. It gave him a new feeling of self-reliance, a certain buoyancy, like treading water gives.

The tenth day he went to work, he fell to the sidewalk from a thirty foot scaffold. He just made a step and it was thirty feet. He watched the sidewalk come up and hit him and he didn't feel it. Just a heavy hard push all over and through him and a new leaking, misplaced, slightly smothering sensation inside. It wasn't until he tried to push himself up with his left hand that the pain shot through his brain in a white sheet of flame. He looked down at his arm and saw his hand flopping to one side on a piece of rubbery, bloody flesh. The bone had punctured the flesh of his arm and stuck out at a crazy angle, white and jagged at the end where it had snapped completely off just above the wrist. Blood had run down on the sidewalk and on his shirt and pants and a few tiny drops of it had collected in the white jagged end of the broken bone like red ink shaken on a clean white blotter.

He looked away from it and cried, "Help! Help! Help!" in a scared, monotonous voice. Then the world went away and came back and went away in waves; there was the damp sidewalk slanting up toward the blue sky and then bug-eyed faces drifting by; and then the ambulance came and took him to the hospital.

That made it a perfect score. Harry dead, Damon blind, and now Jimmy in the hospital.

The doctors soon discovered that two of his vertebrae were fractured and that he was injured internally. His arm was put into splints and he was placed on his back and given shots of morphine and the next morning early the doctors performed an operation.

At first he did not think about it. The morphine helped; the countless, endless shots of morphine. All day long he grinned with dimples in his cheeks. He is so brave, they said—the stern-faced supervisors and the blank-faced doctors and the pretty nurses. He is so cheerful.

All day long.

It was in the darkness of the night that he cried. In the darkness of the night when there was no one about to see him. It was something that you did not let people see you do. It was for babies and women; and if you could not help it, you did it in the dark and did not let on.

Later they put him in a ward. He saw several men die while he was there. One night he saw an intern go haywire and curse a dying patient into eternity. And another night he heard a man with an arm horribly bloated from blood poisoning pray himself somewhere.

The man ran a hemorrhage; his arm started bleeding shortly before eight o'clock when it was being soaked. And all that night it bled, slowly, continuously, while he recited the Lord's Prayer over and over and over: "*Our Father Who Art in Heaven* . . . Lord have mercy on my soul . . . *Hallowed Be Thy Name* . . . Have mercy, Jesus . . ." Growing weaker and weaker and weaker.

Jimmy lay there in the darkness and listened to that unended prayer and his mind spurted and flared and blew off horrible pictures of death and bright red hells and lost souls dropping one by one into the fiery pits until his very brain felt lacerated. When the voice choked to a gurgling end and came no more, Jimmy heaved a sigh of relief.

If you lived it all today then you wouldn't have to worry about tomorrow. That was the best way, he told himself. But it didn't help.

His father and mother visited him each day. His mother cried and his father looked sad. Damon was the cheerful one. Damon said it wasn't so bad that it couldn't have been worse. He knew.

An agent from the State Industrial Commission came and signed him up for compensation. He was granted eighteen dollars and seventy-five cents weekly. When he began to mend, a driving irritation came which made him exceedingly nervous. Cigarets seemed to help. He smoked them in chains. It was then that he formed his real and lasting smoking habit.

His arm looked queer and bloated when the splints were taken off and he had little faith that he would ever use it again. His fingers were dried and brown; he thought of beggars he had seen with dwarfed and dangling arms. It put a nauseating fear down in his heart.

No matter how hurt you are, if you do not think about it, it can not hurt, he told himself again. But looking at that brown dried hand, it did not work. He could not keep from thinking about it. He thought about it until he bruised his mind.

He worked his fingers by the hours and massaged his arm with cocoa butter in a frantic sort of rush, thinking about it. He wanted results that he could see right off. After a time when he could actually see the results, he cried like a baby; he cried during the middle of the day when every one could see him. He did not care. He was that happy. Finally he was able to close his hand. That was the most ecstatic moment of all his life.

And then one morning at the end of three months he surprised every one by walking down the ward holding to the cots for support. In two more weeks he was given a back brace and discharged.

He took long walks through the parks and wore his brace religiously, and after a time he began to pick up weight and regain his strength. He went to picture shows and out to Euclid Beach and rode the buses around about. It wasn't so bad. He took Damon around with him at times and they tried to talk to each other again; but they never quite made it. There were always those years between them when secret things had happened to both of them.

One day he discovered that he could play a little tennis. From that time on he knew that some day he was going to get completely well. There followed a period of experimentation with women which proved successful. No one knew how exultant he was.

HIS COMPENSATION ACCUMULATED and by September he had saved four hundred and fifty dollars. He bought three new suits and an overcoat and all the accessories and packed his trunk and went to college. He had decided to become a doctor.

Sixty dollars went for fees, and one hundred dollars for a second-handed roadster. He was exempted from gym and R.O.T.C. His college education began.

He found the girls easy to meet and willing to learn. He had a lot of fun. There was no one there to see that he studied, so he didn't. His room and board cost only ten dollars weekly. That left nine for spending money. The town was cheap. His car made speed. And so did he. The girls all seemed to like his speed. He quit wearing his back brace because it showed beneath his clothes and he didn't want any one to know that he was slightly crippled.

He was invited to many parties; and he went to many others without invitation. And then he began chiseling in on the upper-classmen's girls. Pretty soon they put thumbs down on him. They ostrasized the girls who allowed him to date them. The girls said he was too fickle to take the gamble. And so he became a pariah. In less than two months he couldn't get a girl. He said, oh well, I had them first, and let it go at that.

From that time on he came to know a lot of "joints". He met a lot of part-time prostitutes who seemed to go for him. Pretty soon the university was just a place where he went to spend unpleasant hours, it seemed.

His *German* professor soon discovered that he did not want to learn the *German* language and stopped trying to teach it to him. He had an argument with a chemistry instructor and quit lab. He never understood why they didn't kick him out right then and there. It would have saved a lot of trouble.

He went to all the football games and when Michigan played there that November he helped break down the stadium gates. Thanksgiving week found him in Chicago for the Army-Navy game. He bought a porcelain goat of many colors and rooted for the Army. When finally he returned he was forty dollars in debt. He never paid it. He would have. He intended to. But he never had that much to spare at one time after that.

His car went across a gambling table the second week in December. He got drunk to commemorate its passing and stayed drunk until the Christmas holidays. He thought that he was going to be dropped after that quarter, anyway, and did not care.

The quarterly finals caught him in a stupor. He turned in a blank paper to his *German* professor. It didn't seem that he did much better in anything else. But he passed in all four subjects, which meant that he had to come back after Christmas. He didn't know whether to be glad or not for that. He went home Christmas. His father and mother were proud of him. All they knew was that he had finished the quarter, so they had hope.

The second week in January he was expelled.

It all happened at a fraternity prom. He crashed the door with a notorious prostitute. He was drunk and quoting Omar: "*You know my friends, with what a brave Carouse I made a Second Marriage in my house: Divorced old barren Reason from My bed, and took the daughter of the vine to Spouse . . .*"

The dean sent for him the next day. "My son," he said, "it is with deep sorrow that I must do this. You are a brilliant youth; you have one of the highest I.Q.'s of any student to matriculate in this University . . ."

A film of tears came over Jimmy's eyes as he walked from the dean's office. He was saying goodbye to a period of life which on the whole had been rather pleasant. For a long and melancholy moment he stood on the steps of University Hall, watching the gray dusk settle slowly over the snow-covered campus. He knew as surely as he knew that he was standing there that he was never going to amount to a damn. It put a sadness in his heart. He brushed his hand hard down his face and descended the steps and went along the walk toward High Street.

He had been to college . . .

THE NEXT YEAR WAS KALEIDOSCOPIC. He found something terrifying in the dogged certainty that he was never going to amount to a damn.

He was eighteen and the problem of existence was presenting itself to him. He wanted all of his dreams to come true overnight. He did not want to wait for them; he could not bear the thought of long and tedius years of work throughout his life. It gave him a feeling of being trapped, as if eternity had left him stranded. He did not know which way to turn, and not knowing went haywire.

So if he could not have a fleet of Rolls Royces, he could have a second-handed touring car with an aeroplane cut-out. What difference did it make that he parked it on the next street and walked home so his parents wouldn't learn that he had bought it.

And if he could not charge forth on a white steed and rescue beautiful damsels in distress, he could come down the avenues at a roaring sixty in his second-handed car and pick up strays and strumpets whose only distress was boredom. And so he did.

There was a countless array of them, in cafes and cabarets, at Euclid Beach and Gordan Park and Crystal Springs and the Palais D'Or. There was Anne with her black bushy hair and sculptured body and sleazy mind who worked in a beauty parlor on 105th Street. And Jacky who lived down on Carnegie and had a husband who had been some sort of ham prize fighter. She wanted something else again from all the rest. Once he was overcome with such a loathing for her that he jumped up and screamed, "I hate your soul!" She prostrated herself before him and begged him to stay and he was so sickened he kicked her in the stomach and ran out of the house. And there was Cleo with her manifold operations and vulgar speech. She was amusing in her inimitable way. And there were others like the polish on his car who were lost in the dust. And there were those who demanded their price and cared no more than he.

He met them in dim-lit booze joints with the victrolas playing, and in prohibition night clubs, and took them for rides about town and got them drunk. He kept a bottle of bad gin or worse bootleg in the pocket of his car.

The best of the heap was Margaret Brown, a corn-silk blonde with violet eyes and a wide and luscious mouth. She acted something like he thought a virgin should and she swore he was the second man who had ever had her, and she was twenty-two. He drove her to nearby towns and out on lonely country roads. Anywhere with her was swell.

She gave him a deep and demonstrative love in her own soft way, and perhaps he would have gone for her if she had let it grow. But he got the idea she was rushing him, which she was because she had to. It came to a head when he was taking her home from a room one night. She turned to him and asked, "Do you really love me, Jimmy?" She was in dead earnest.

There were two fellows in the back seat and they stopped talking to hear his reply. So he said to her, partly for their benefit, "I never thought of you in just that way, baby."

The next morning she left town to have her baby somewhere else.

At first he missed her. But after a time he told himself that she was gone, so what. Next he turned to dice. A guy named Mitchell took him to a place called "Charlie's" where he could get his gamble, so Mitchell said. The third night they cleaned him. He always had a sneaking suspicion that Mitchell had in some way tricked him. So after that he cut out and went his way alone. Which after all was his best way, he told himself.

He put it down to learning and all would have been well if the monthly payment on his car had not come due. The finance corporation sent a collector to his house and his mother learned about the car.

That brought about another session in the parlor. He confessed everything, that he had bought the car and owed a payment and was broke. He said he had lost his money out of his pocket, but no one believed him. He certainly couldn't blame them much for that. His mother asked him where he kept the car and he told her. She told him to bring it home. He did.

The next day she had him arrested, charging him with taking her bank book and cashing a check for five dollars on her account. It shocked him at first that she would do a thing like that to him, but after the shock wore off he thought Damon might have done it, and since he didn't have a chance to ask him, he didn't deny it.

The police had him in the jail again. When they took him to the juvenile court that morning, his father came over and spoke to him, but his mother didn't even look his way.

When called upon to testify, his mother told the court that he had been drinking, smoking, gambling and running around with loose women, and that he had spent the money he was supposed to have been saving for college buying a car. All of which was true enough. Then she asked the court to give her the power of attorney to draw his compensation from the State Industrial Commission. She wanted to save it for him, she said.

It suddenly dawned on him that the whole thing was a frame-up manufactured so she could draw his compensation. He stared at her like some one he had never seen before. Not so much because she wanted to draw his compensation; he knew she would save it for him. But the way she had gone about it. You just didn't treat your own children in such a way, he reasoned.

He never told anyone how much she hurt him when. Nor did he ever feel the same toward her again. He told the court to hell with it, and turned and walked away. And no one tried to stop him. He would have died right then had a hand been raised in the least restraint.

His father saved him. "Don't bother him, please," he begged the court. "The boy's been hurt. Let him go. I'll post bail. And if you want him again I'll bring him in."

The judge motioned to the jailors to let him go. His father ran after him and said, "Come on home to dinner, son."

"All right, I will," he promised.

Outside he stopped on the sidewalk for a long and bitter moment, watching the cars go by. He wished his mother had not done that to him. A person had to believe in something, no matter how bad he was, he told himself. Then he took a deep breath and said aloud, "Hell!" and went over on Euclid to a matinee show.

The organ was playing, "*Among My Souvenirs.*" Words formed in the turmoil of his thoughts: *There's nothing left for me of things that used to be* . . . He got up and went out into the afternoon crowds. He would have hurt some one then just for nothing. He ate a hamburger sandwich and went home.

And then, two weeks later, one rainy summer day, as he was trying to beat a Cedar Street car up the hill by Ashland Road, he wrecked his car. He cut in front of the street car trying to keep from hitting another car coming fast out of Ashland Road and did not see the other street car coming from 55th until he smashed into it. He wasn't hurt. He was immune, he told himself, and laughed. But his car was a wreck.

At the garage he was told that it would cost one hundred and thirty-two dollars to put it into shape. He said, "If I had a hundred and thirty-two dollars I'd buy another car." The finance corporation tried to collect, but when they discovered that he was a minor they gave it up.

And so he became a pedestrian once more. His mother seemed quite pleased, but he hated it. It left him at loose ends again; left him walking in a driving world.

Then Indian Summer came on with its bruised, splashed sunsets and its wind-stirred pageant of color. In his unguarded moments he felt lonely enough to cry. Dreams no longer sufficed. Perhaps it was because school was opening and he wasn't going. It gave him a feeling of being left behind. Or perhaps he missed the companionship of students. He didn't know. But he knew that he had to do something or go somewhere or he would go crazy.

He began drinking and haunting cheap dice games. It was at one of these that he met Benny, a big, red-headed, loutish youth with gangster ambitions. Benny's idea of being a gangster was to swagger about with a pistol stuck in his belt and talk about bank jobs through the corner of his mouth. He had a pistol, too, a long-barreled, Spanish-type .38.

The second time Benny noticed Jimmy at the game, he approached him. "This is small time stuff," he grated through the corner of his mouth, waving at the dice game. "You got it in you, I can tell. You're a gangster like me. Come on, I'll show you where there's some real dough which can be clipped by two gangsters like us."

He took Jimmy across town and showed him a Cleveland Trust branch at the corner of 105th and St. Clair. "It's a cinch," he said through the corner of his mouth. "Now take on Saturday nights when they stay open late—"

"Why! Why! You brought me way out here to show me that!" Jimmy exploded. "You brought me past the First National and the Federal Reserve and the Guardian Trust—to show me that! What's the matter with the Federal Reserve? Why, I oughta—"

He left Benny standing there and went home. His mother was waiting up for him. She often waited up for him during that year. She came and stood in the doorway of his room. There was cold cream on her face and her hair was tied up for the night. Her voice flicked at him, "You just watch, you're going to end up in the penitentiary or on the gallows yet. Running around all hours of the night with I don't know what kind of people. Throwing away your chances to be somebody in life. You're going to regret every single bit of it. You just watch what I tell you."

Jimmy disliked her a little standing there. Otherwise she did not touch him. Perhaps if she had told him what could have been gained by being different, instead of what he would lose, he might have listened. But he did not care anything at all about what he might lose. He didn't think he had anything to lose, anyway. When she left he closed the door and put out the light and went to sleep and forgot it. It was always like that.

In some way Benny discovered his address and the following Sunday showed up at church time. "Jesus, this a swell pilch ya got here," he said to Jimmy, flicking ashes on the parlor rug and looking all about. It was a good thing Jimmy's mother was at church. He got Benny out of there before she returned, too.

But after that he and Benny went about a lot together. Benny always made it plain that he considered Jimmy the leader. He called Jimmy "Boss", and nominated himself his "bodyguard". It flattered Jimmy although even then he realized that it was rather funny. As a matter of fact he was developing into a common sneak thief.

It was strange, perhaps, but he could always see himself from other's perspectives. He knew all along that he was little better than youths like Benny, and getting worse all of the time. It hurt him, too, realizing it. But on the other hand it gave him an odd feeling of importance, of being a bigshot at least to the pool room crowd. There was no guarantee that he would ever have more than that no matter how he lived, he argued with himself.

Then again, it helped him pass the time. He and Benny discussed crooked cards and dice and planned on putting them down in different games; they "cased" bank and payroll "jobs" and timed spectacular robberies down to the last second. But in the end they merely went into some confectionery store or other and Benny swiped a pocket full of chewing gum or something while Jimmy bought a package of cigarets. That was the way it went. Jimmy didn't really want to commit a serious crime; he just wanted to feel that he would if he wanted to.

And then one night he came home to find his father and mother in the midst of a violent quarrel. He soon discovered that they were quarreling about him; his mother charged his father with being too lenient on him. And in return his father accused her of running Jimmy from the house by her constant nagging. She called him a vulgar name. There was the sound of breaking glass, a sudden scuffle, and his mother's choked scream. Jimmy felt a chill run down his spine. Rushing into the room, he found his father choking her.

Blood streamed from a gash on his father's forehead and a shattered mirror lay on the floor.

In that first full sight, they lost him. Before that, he had felt that he owed them something of respect, a semblance of honor, even if he had hardly ever agreed with them. But after that he didn't feel he owed them a single goddamned thing. They had turned into somebody else again.

He pulled his father away and stood there, feeling ill at ease and wishing they'd stop screaming at each other. He didn't know what else to do; he wanted to ask them to stop but he couldn't trust himself. Finally his father left the room, dressed and left the house. The week following his mother sued for divorce. They all moved out and put the house and furniture up for sale. Jimmy went to room with his father in a boarding house. Not because he wanted to especially, but he didn't know of any other place to go. Damon went to room in the home of a blind friend.

His father was working in a carriage company and was away all day. Jimmy was away all night. They seldom saw each other although they roomed together. Jimmy ate in restaurants and lived in dives.

He knew that he was to blame for that sudden disruption of their home. He didn't try to excuse or justify himself. He, Jimmy, was to blame. So what?

Damon went away to a special preparatory school that fall. Everything seemed so broken and gone. Once or twice each week, Jimmy visited his mother in her room on the West Side. But when she wasn't nagging at him she talked about his father with such a bitterness he hated coming to see her. One day he told her harshly, "I don't want to hear all that, mama."

They both went into a hurt, numbed silence. Jimmy wanted to say, "I love you, mama," because he pitied her so. But the words would not come out.

It was then he became assailed with the sense of drifting, like a bloated corpse through a still sea, going nowhere. One night having nothing else to do, he walked out to Lakeside Park and watched a full moon turn Lake Erie into crumpled tinfoil. The air was crisp with the first snap of winter. Close up the waves seemed as beckoning fingers, tugging at his heart. It was as if they whispered, "Come on to sleep, come on to cool, deep, caressing sleep. You'll never be tired anymore . . ." He was so tired. *So tired!*

He caught himself standing on the edge of the pier staring down at them with a queer intensity. He never knew what he might have done if two girls had not passed close by just then. He turned and stared at them. They were strolling along arm in arm, laughing. He pushed between them and said, "Kiss me, baby."

One of them gasped and broke away, but the other one turned toward him with wide, startled eyes. He clutched her in his arms and kissed her brutally, again and again. She did not struggle. After a moment he released her. "I'm sorry," he said in a low, thick voice, turning away. Her voice stopped him, "If it made you feel any better—" Then the other girl returned and she broke off.

He went home to think about what she might have meant by that, and found his father sleeping in the middle of the bed. He crawled in on the edge to keep from touching him, and lay there hating him all night long with a blue, double-edged hatred that spawned the thought of getting up and knocking out his goddamned brains. He was grateful for morning.

The following week he was subpoenaed to appear as a witness in his parents' divorce proceedings. He stole a car and drove down to Columbus. It was bad enough for them to get a divorce without his having to say anything about it one way or the other, he told himself.

It was the day before Thanksgiving. The day after Thanksgiving he was arrested for forgery. He had cashed eight checks in stores up and down High Street. Even then he could have squared it by returning the money and the things he had bought. He had always been a fool. *Always!* For to confess, he had reasoned, would have made him Paris.

The police lost patience and locked him up. When he was tried the following January, his lawyer entered a plea of guilty over his protests and the judge gave him a bench parole. The fact that he had been injured and had once attended the State University there kept him out of prison. His mother and father had been divorced by then. And all it had cost Jimmy not to have to testify was a couple of months in jail. It hadn't been bad. There'd been a colored guy called Booker who kept them entertained singing, "The sun's gonna shine in my back door some day," or "Three white horses running side by side, you stole my good gal, now just be satisfied . . ." His cell mate had been the Julius Moore who had been in the hole with him. Jimmy learned about crooked dice, short cons, how to pick pockets and play whores. It hadn't been bad.

His mother lectured to him when he returned to Cleveland. She was sitting in a chair at the foot of her bed and Jimmy was standing by the dresser. He noticed that her hair was rapidly graying and that there were deep lines about her eyes and mouth that had not been there before. He noticed, also, that her hands folded in her lap would not be still. And he knew that he was to blame. All right, he was sorry, he told himself. But what was being sorry? Had it ever straightened out the past? Had it ever made anything better than what it was. Not as he could see.

If he had a choice to make, he'd rather not be sorry. He'd rather not care. But being sorry was something that he owed to his mother or father or whoever wrote the rules. So he was sorry.

She said, "James, if you don't intend to go back to school why don't you try to get a job in an office where there is a chance for advancement?"

"That's just what I'm trying to do," he assured her. "I was talking to Attorney Bruce and he told me that there would be a clerk's job open soon down at the main office of the firm and that if I kept in touch with him he'd give me a chance at it. I'll be able to learn enough down there to pass the bar exams in five or six years . . ."

He felt a little guilty telling her that lie, but when he saw how much it cheered her, he felt justified. He really wanted her to be happy; it was such a rotten break for her to wind up in a two-bit rooming house. And if so small a thing as just one lie could cheer her, he'd tell a dozen, a thousand. He walked around to the foot of the bed and kissed her, then started away.

Her voice came after him, "James, why don't you try to be a good boy; the things you do hurt mother so."

It was just as if she had slapped him. But he wasn't angry. He just felt a dull, detached pity for her. Being good seemed such a futile aim. She and his father had been good, he supposed. And what had it got them? If they were examples of the benefits of being good, to hell with it, he told himself. But he only said, "I will, mama. I'm going down and get that job. Now don't you worry about me." He closed the door behind him.

The job he got was at the *The Green House,* Sugar Patton's gambling joint. He ran the errands and spelled the dealers and took turns in the cage where the horse race bets were booked. His salary was thirty dollars a week and his hours were from noon until the joint closed, which was when the last potential sucker left.

The people with whom he came into contact seemed to give him a certain homage and soon he came to feel that he was something of a big shot. All he needed was cash to go out for himself.

That gave him ideas. Even if he didn't go out for himself, cash was always something fine to have. So he gambled on the races trying to win a stake, and often ran his money into hundreds before he let some long shot chop him down. He played in the dice games, too. He was a reckless gambler, always, and nothing made him bet so much as for a crowd to gather around. But the stick-men carried him along with all the rest when they put the chilled dice in. Finally one of them told him that Sugar only let him play because he was a good "shill"—a come-on for the suckers. He quit the job.

It was the last of May. All in all it had been rather interesting, he thought afterwards. Riding around in big cars and dropping in on the various dice games about the town with fifty or sixty dollars to play big shot. Being treated as a big shot, too, by the hangers-on and riffraff. It had kept him from thinking about those certain things that he had been missing—such as his home and family and the feeling of going forward which school had given him no matter how he had taken it. He felt that he was being left behind. It filled his mind with a frantic sort of desperation.

The first of June came and went before it dawned on him that it was Spring. For three days he was crazily lonely. He only left his room to eat. He began to dream of girls then. Not about the kind he saw each day; about the kind that he had never seen. In the end they turned out to be Penelope knitting in her window, and all his boyhood came back and haunted him for days.

ON THE FOURTEENTH DAY of August that year he was nineteen years old. He was tired and lonely. He was perhaps the most tired and lonely nineteen year old boy in all the world. Fearing that his mother would visit him, he went downtown and rented a hotel room and stayed locked up all day. He did not want to see anyone. He pulled down the shades and lay there in the semi-darkness, thinking of being sorry, and of not being sorry; of caring and of not caring. Wondering what was the right thing and what was the wrong; and if the end would be just a hole in the ground and worms and the dark close embrace of earth. Without flowers; without tears. And if it was, so what? If nobody cared for him then to hell with everybody.

For the week following he was drunk. Doggedly, sickeningly drunk. Heat began growing in his mind in a thin, steady flame. At that time he was five feet, eight inches tall, and weighed one hundred and forty pounds. He had a typical schoolboy build, slightly athletic but not ruggedly so. He had clear-cut patrician features and wide blue eyes with lashes as long as any woman's. His hair was crinkly and golden, and his skin was clear white, the kind that bruises easily and blushes easily, too.

He had reached the stage where he was afraid to think of the next day coming up. It was then he met Joan. She was the second woman ever to touch him. Perhaps the only reason she touched him was that he was in the mood for it. He kissed her the very first moment he saw her. They were at a party. He saw her when he came in and took her in his arms and kissed her. It must have done something to her immortal soul for she grew to worship him.

She was a little solemn-faced girl with bangs and big brown eyes full of being frightened and a lower lip hanging down and just beginning to tremble. When they were together she was laughingly happy; but when it came time to part, she looked as if she wanted to cry. That was the story.

Perhaps she had a lot to cry about at that for he was not the easiest person in the world for a little girl to love. And she could not have been over seventeen.

He tried to appear a man of the world before her, but she did not seem very impressed by it although she did think that he was older than he was. Once she caught him staring at a sunset and told him that he was the prettiest person that she had ever seen. And he blushed. Another time she told him, "You're not so tough and casual, Jimmy. Not as much as you try to be. You're soft and sentimental inside as a girl in love. You have a great, grand mind full of beautiful dreams and ideals and—"

"Not always beautiful—" he cut in and then caught himself and changed the subject. That was the nearest he had come to confessing his dreams since that night long years before on Cherry Street.

He could never quite figure out what it was about him that incited her smiling desperate love. He knew he was good looking, but he knew, too, that it wasn't that. Maybe it was the boundless generosity of her soul, he finally reasoned. She gave him everything she had—her love, her time, her thoughts, her concern, her body and her soul. He knew that she loved him more than she loved her mother or father or sisters or brothers. And once with a queer divination he knew that there would never be another woman who would love him with the same boundless, unreasoning, unquestioning devotion; who'd be willing to go where he went, whenever he went, if it happened to be down into hell—just to be with him.

And he threw it away like a mother tossing a butt into the gutter.

It happened one night in front of a corner drugstore. She told him that she thought she was going to have a baby. He knew that she was living over all the moments that he had held her in his arms. He knew she was thinking of the life growing inside of her which she would bear for him. He knew how proud she must have felt, how glorious, exalted.

He waited patiently for her to have her moment. Then he said, "I know a swell guy in the pool room here who's just crazy about you, Joan. I'm going in and get him and send him out. Marry him, Joan. I'm sorry, but I can't."

He felt a surge of pity for her as he watched her turn sheet white and stiffen slightly as each of his words sunk into her consciousness. He thought, "You're too young to be sacrificed like this." Then he turned away from the stark, unrelieved hurt in her eyes and went into the pool room. But before he closed the door behind him he looked back at her, standing there in dumb, slavish obedience, and he almost went back and said to her, "Darling, I can't do this to you. I'll marry you, honestly I will."

But he couldn't. He just couldn't, that was all. He could not see her as what life held for him. She couldn't be the end of his long lonesome dreams, nor the pinnacle of his high hopes, he argued with himself. She was just another girl—and he was Jimmy. He could not marry her. He closed the door behind him and sent Eddie out to her. She married Eddie.

But afterwards, thinking about it, it hurt him more than anything that had ever happened to him. No one had made him do it. He did it. That was what hurt. It appalled him to know that he could do a thing like that. An overwhelming, stifling remorse filled him. It was as if he had passed up the opportunity to have made his one eternal bid for happiness; as if in the end, in the final analysis, he had failed himself. He couldn't understand what made him do it. He just couldn't understand.

He said to himself, trying to relieve the hurt, "She's gone—so what?" But it stayed on his mind. He tried not to think about it; but he could not keep from thinking about it.

150

He picked up two hoodlums in a pool room one night and robbed a national guard arsenal of fifty army automatics. There was a lot of agitation in the papers the day following. The chief of police ventured the opinion that a new racket was in the making and put on a hundred extra policemen.

The next night they kicked in a fur store window and stole a half dozen cheap fur coats. And the day after they were caught trying to sell the guns. They had him in jail again.

His confederates signed confessions after a session with several detectives in the "consultation rooms". Jimmy ducked the "consultation" because he was a patient of the Industrial Commission. So he didn't sign the confession. Later he got a chance to send a message to the other two. He promised to get them an attorney if they took the rap and let him go.

They did, so the federal prosecutor released him. The afternoon papers carried their pictures and Jimmy felt rather important since he had beaten the rap. But the next morning he was arrested for the larceny of the coats.

He was arraigned before a woman judge. He wore a white slipover sweater and knickers into the courtroom and did not look a day over seventeen. The judge looked at him and reprimanded the detectives for bringing him into municipal court. When they explained that he was nineteen and should know better, she fined him twenty-five dollars and costs and gave him a suspended sentence.

His father came down and paid the fine and he was free once more. But the last two times in jail had frightened him. Never again, he told himself. And he meant it.

When Damon left for school the following month, Jimmy took him to the station, and stood there for a long blind moment after the train had pulled out.

October was like kissing his last chance goodbye. He became moody and silent and stayed indoors. He tried to write stories for a time but could not keep his mind on it. He tried the picture shows. He took long walks. He went to gyms and worked himself into utter exhaustion. But in the end he came to feel like a powder keg on fire. It was as if he knew that he was going to do something crazily desperate and was trying to restrain himself.

He tried reading but that only spread his emotions to the surface so that everything touched him. He read of love and life and of people achieving things and finding happiness—and cried. He slipped off from his better intentions one night and gambled again. He won a hundred and sixty-four dollars and quit winner for once. On his way home he ran into Joan. She looked piqued and slightly faded and a little older than when he had seen her last. She told him that Eddie was at work and begged him to come home with her.

She was living in a three-room attic apartment. It was rather nicely furnished although the furnishings were cheap. Suddenly, looking at her odd-shaped body beneath loose hung clothes, he filled with a weighted, hammering remorse. He took the money he had won and shoved it into her hand and ran out of the house before she could stop him.

His compensation was temporarily stopped the week before Thanksgiving. The doctors promised to recommend him for renewal, but said it would be a month or two before his case was heard. Now with the rest, he was out of funds.

Never again, he had said. So he went out and robbed a man and his wife in their home in Cleveland Heights and caught a train for Chicago. He was arrested the day before Thanksgiving and brought back and given twenty years . . . *Twenty years . . .*

He clutched his tin drinking cup in both hands and raked it savagely across the vertical bars, making a loud, burring sound. And then he screamed, "ALL RIGHT, GODDAMMIT, YOU GAVE ME TWENTY YEARS! ALL RIGHT, GODDAMMIT! ALL RIGHT!"

And then he lay down on his bunk and cried.

But that night after the prison fire as he sat behind the hospital with Blocker and Pete, these memories died. Only the dead and dying convicts were left within his mind, and he could not bear them, could not hold them, could not think about them . . . Dear God, please make them go away, he prayed . . .

As he sat there trying to push them from his mind, trying to fight off nausea, to smother the flare and sputter and lurid burning that kept going on in his mind like a continuation of the fire itself, trying to unhook the whole damn thing, his mind with its thoughts and flares and sputters and smoke, trying to get it off, frantically, like the quick jerking disrobement of a blazing garment, in his too abrupt awareness of the reality of death, change came into him like a chemical reaction, so rapidly you could see it with the eye.

For he reached the conclusion that night that everything he had ever seen, or had ever done, or had ever dreamed of doing, would in the end betray him. That no matter what you had been, or ever hoped to be, a foot of greenish vomit hanging from your teeth would make you much the same as any other bastard.

Book III

Shall Become the Same at Last

1

IN THE EERIE QUIETNESS of sunrise the ghosts creeped back into their graves and the slow footsteps of time sounding faintly across the prison yard stirred them from their sleepless torpor.

"Let's look her over," Blocker said, stretching.

"Okay," Pete said, climbing shakily to his feet.

Jimmy followed, feeling dirty and disheveled, weary and stiff. His joints were a thousand years old and only emptiness was inside of his head, inane and queer, making him want to cackle like an idiot. But he knew if he laughed it would sound too weird.

Rounding the corner of the hospital they came into the line of police reserves extending from wall to wall, a barrier separating the cell houses from the industrial buildings, erect and silent and somber in the early sunrise.

"Jesus, all the police in the world," Pete observed.

Blocker gave his sly, chuckling laugh. "Better watch yourself, kid," he winked at Jimmy. "There's the law."

"I bet they'd cook and eat those dead convicts," Jimmy said.

Blocker jerked about and looked at him. "Take it easy, kid," he soothed, adding after a moment. "You need some sleep, your eyes have gone back into the middle of your head."

"Hey, where you boys going there?" one of the policemen questioned.

"None of your goddamned business," Pete replied, teetering on his unsteady legs.

The policeman reddened. They walked past, slowly, indifferently, secure in the knowledge that no cops would molest them that morning.

"You hear that rotten bastard?" Pete asked Blocker in a treble tone. "After I damn near burnt to death last night."

"I know you don't want that stuff."

"I ought to go back and hit him in the mouth."

"Why didn't you hit him when you were there?" Jimmy asked. They looked at him. "Take it easy, kid," Blocker repeated.

"Jesus Christ, your eyes are red," Pete noticed.

As they came into the yard they saw the stark photography of the sunlight on the dead. They looked very dead in the sunlight. Jimmy could feel how dead they were, looking at them lying there in the muddy prison yard. A truck was backed up to the middle walk and a dozen or more convicts brought the bodies over and stacked them inside of it like logs. The deputy stood to one side directing. "Hurry up, hurry up, get them away before they begin to spoil."

Continuing across the yard, they entered the G&H block and climbed to the top ranges. Across the well stood the charred skeleton of the wooden scaffolding of the partly-constructed I&K block, in which the fire had started. The wooden framework of the roof above them had been burnt and patches of the roof had fallen in, showing irregular patterns of sky. The cells, with their grimy, smoke-blackened walls, contained partly burnt mattresses, scorched clothing, the charred personal effects of the convicts; here was a Sunday shirt with a sleeve burnt off, a bathrobe burnt down the middle of the back, a pack of soggy cigarets, a twisted shoe. Everything was wet and water stood in shallow puddles down the ranges. Seeing a blanket-draped object hovering over a commode, Pete raised the blanket, and they saw the body of a convict bent over the commode, its head rammed down into the water.

"My God!" he exclaimed, backing away, and suddenly stopped and vomited on the floor.

Jimmy looked at the body dispassionately. Its hair was partly floating in the dirty water, and there were red welts about the back of the neck and behind the ears, and a big hole burned in the back of the shirt. Its hands, their skin drawn tight over white bones in a death grip, clutched the edges of the commode as if the convict had been trying to ram himself down the sewer when death came.

"Come on, kid, let's get out of here," Blocker said, taking Jimmy's arm.

Jimmy spat, turned and left. A Negro convict, called Shortdrawers, went into the cell and looked about. "You know him?" he asked, pointing at the body.

Jimmy, lingering by the door to watch with detached interest, shook his head.

Shortdrawers disconnected a half-burnt radio which lay at the head of a bunk. "He don't need this," he grinned. His teeth were decayed and tobacco-stained, and grinning he looked like a small, dirty animal.

"He don't need that," Jimmy agreed, turning down the range after Blocker and Pete.

The cells were squirming with them, like maggots in a piece of rotting meat. They took everything which was even remotely valuable, or had ever been of any value; they took things that would never be of any use to them, but which they had always wanted, and now had a chance to take from the soot-blackened, burnt-out cells.

"They won't find any money, I bet," Blocker commented. "Most of the guys who had any money, had it on them, and they've already been cleaned."

"I just hate to see it," Pete disapproved.

"We'll get our share of it just as soon as they start to gambling, won't we, kid," Blocker said to Jimmy.

"Let's eat," Jimmy said.

They were told at the dining room that breakfast would not be ready for an hour or more, so they walked slowly about the institution, through the cell blocks and dormitories, to kill time. Most of the convicts whom they saw were sleeping, sprawled across bunks in two's and three's, fully dressed, their clothes wrinkled and twisted about their bodies, their mouths open and snoring, some with saliva drooling from the corners. To Jimmy, they seemed no different from the dead. He stretched out on a bunk for a time while Pete and

Blocker played cards at the table. He was very sleepy, but he could not sleep.

Later, when the bell rang, they went to the dining room and had bacon and eggs. There were no lines, no companies. The convicts came over singly and in groups, filling the empty seats, while the policemen stood outside and watched. There was very little talk. They ate doggedly.

Coming from the dining room, they saw the last truck-load of bodies drive away. "Go wash up and get something to eat," the deputy directed the men who had just finished loading it.

"They got bacon and eggs for breakfast," some one volunteered.

"Hell, come on, we can wash up in the kitchen," one of them said. "I'm hungry."

Jimmy, Blocker, and Pete went over and sat on the front steps of the hospital, watching the growth of activity on the yard. Jimmy was so sleepy it filled his nostrils and his eyes and ears and head and trickled through his bones and burnt into his flesh like acid; he felt as if his nose was bleeding and his body was ruptured; he felt that he could sleep a thousand years, but when he closed his eyes the fire began to burn again, underneath the eyelids and in his eyes and in his brain, and he could not keep them closed.

The convicts milled exhaustedly about the yard, sat in doorways and on the railings and leaned against the buildings, talking listlessly about the fire, too stunned to be violent, too weary to be vicious, but determined, it seemed, to show with their last remaining ounce of energy that they were no longer to be governed.

They were very orderly that morning. Word had spread that two companies of soldiers were patrolling outside the walls. A semblance of martial law was declared, although at first no proclamation was issued, and the police were replaced by national guardsmen and little apple-cheeked sailor boys with their tight-fitting blue trousers. To Jimmy, sitting sleepily in the sun, it meant nothing. He noticed it, and that was all.

If he could only go to sleep . . .

Once they got up and went to the latrine. Returning, they found their seats taken by another group of convicts. They trudged across the yard and sat with a score or more of others on the stone steps of the Protestant chapel until the bell rang. Then they went to the dining room and ate. The food was like knots in Jimmy's stomach.

Two broadcasting chains had installed microphones near the front gates and announcers were interviewing various convicts concerning the fire. The three of them walked down that way and stood in the crowd. Most of the convicts who were interviewed recounted their deeds of heroism in loud, choppy voices as if they had to shout to make themselves heard outside. One, called Hard-walking Shorty, began by shouting, "I'm a man of a few words but lotsa action," and before he had finished, by actual count of the laughing, booing convicts assembled there, had saved four hundred and ninety-nine convicts' lives, and would have saved an even five hundred, Blocker joked about it afterwards, if the warden had not become tired of the drivel and had the lines cut about then.

But that afternoon the qualities of character which made these men criminals began to come alive. In the absence of discipline, these men ceased to be human; they reverted into slavering, lustful, wanton beasts. They did the things which they had always wanted to do; they gambled and argued and degenerated, they had that punk they'd always wanted to have. Beginning that night, and during the days following, they ran wild like packs of wolves, stole from each other and robbed each other with knives at throats in the darkness. They raped each other; they raped the pink-cheeked sailor boys whom they caught alone after dark; they raped the national guardsmen; they would have raped the guards, a thing some of them had wanted to do for a long time, had the guards been present. But most of the guards remained outside the walls during that period.

That night, sitting in a slow stud game in the dormitory, Jimmy and Blocker learned that a convict had changed in civilian clothes taken from the commissary, picked a pass from a reporter's hat, and walked through the front gates. He was the only one to make an escape during the confusion. None of the others, among whom were the condemned men, attempted an escape in the face of the soldiers surrounding the prison.

Only the dead tired and the dead themselves slept that first night following the fire. Jimmy was among the former, but he couldn't sleep. He was afraid to close his eyes. It was not mental; it was physical. He could actually see the fire, and feel the heat from it, underneath his eyelids and in his eyes and in his brain.

The following morning, a committee of twelve convicts was formed to direct a campaign of passive resistance against the warden, who, by now the convicts had learned, had stood outside the front gates with a shotgun in his hands all during the fire, prepared to shoot down any convict whom he saw trying to escape. Having always been a rat, he had now become the personification of all rathood. Nor was he just a rat only; his mother before him was a rat, and his daughters after him; and he was many other things, the vileness of which the convicts did not have the vocabulary to express.

Too weak to stand from lack of sleep, Jimmy sat on the ground and leaned against Blocker's legs to listen.

"Do you think we're going to let that son of a bitch govern us anymore?" asked Wolf, chairman of the committee, pointing a dramatic finger to the back window of the warden's residence which overlooked the yard, and in which the warden then sat watching him through a pair of binoculars. "Do you know what he said when the hall guard told him that the block was on fire? He said, 'A little smoke won't hurt them, it'll make them appreciate the fresh air more.' Do we let that pig-faced bastard get away with that?"

"No!" they shouted in unison.

"A thousand times no!" Jimmy echoed in a weak voice.

Several convicts turned to look at him. Blocker said, "Take it easy, kid."

"Old man Hall is another lousy son of a bitch we want to get. We don't want to kill him or anything like that. We just want to get him out of the prison . . ."

"I'd like to get him out here in the yard," a convict interrupted. "I wouldn't kill him either; but I'd make him call me daddy."

"We don't want none of that," Wolf roared. "But we want him out of here. We don't want to riot, boys. We don't want to destroy any property. We don't want to harm any of the guards or officials;

just ignore them if they say anything to you. But we ain't gonna take any more orders from a bunch of bastards that'll let our comrades burn to death in their cells like rats. No, by God, we won't!"

The convicts screamed and whistled.

"We don't do a lick of work until they give us a new warden, and a new deal. We want some consideration. We're human beings just like everybody else. The deputy's all right."

The convicts screamed and whistled. Sitting there, too weak to stand, afraid to sleep, Jimmy said, "And the convicts cheered."

"Come on, kid, I'm going to take you back to the dormitory and let you try it again," Blocker said, helping him to his feet. They had lost Pete sometime during the night. "You got to sleep sometime."

"Sure, I got to sleep, I'm a human being," Jimmy grinned.

All the remainder of the day, he lay on his bunk, pressing wet towels to his eyes to ease the burning. But the burning was there, whenever he closed them; and he could not keep them closed long. Open, they became raw and stinging and dry. Chump Charlie got a bottle of argyrol and bathed his eyes, and then they were huge, yellow-ringed, staring orbits, sunk deep into his head. Combined with his white, drawn face, and deep, black circles underneath the yellow rings, he looked like walking death.

But that night, he was up again, he and Blocker making the round of poker games. He saw it that night as he had not seen it before. Like carrion lying in the sun, it was, and the coming of the maggots to worm in squirming, sickening frenzy through the polution of rotten flesh, and then the stink, the awful stink, which lasted longer in the end than even the sight of the white, fattening maggots in the black, rotting flesh.

In the school, where bunks had replaced the desks for those who had celled in the burnt block, he saw that night an indescribably lewd act of degenerate sex staged by two naked, sex-mad, marijuana-jagged convicts. He went outside and stood sucking in the air, trying to get the dirt from his lungs; he wanted to bend over and eat the earth; he wanted to tear his regenerative organs from his body; his senses were outraged. But the next moment it was not there; it was gone, and he was only sleepy. God in Heaven, he was sleepy.

So he went over in the dormitory and sat and listened to one of the twelve radios owned by the Negro convict who before the fire had not owned one, and who sat there in the middle of them like a sheik in a harem.

The next night, up on 5-C, Jimmy saw the prostitution. Convicts clad in feminine undergarments, bright colored kimonos, silk stockings and such, brought into them by the vest edition soldiers, paraded up and down the range to be inspected by those who had won in the gambling games. Many of the cells were curtained across the front, and from within came the odor of perfume and sweat, and the sounds of rumbling.

That Sunday, which was the following day, Jimmy attended the exercises in the Protestant Chapel, which the Negro Deacon Gardner explained were being held in commemoration of "our dear dead comrades." A fat-faced fag sang *My Buddy Misses Me*, and crocodile tears poured down his cheeks like showers of rain.

But Jimmy thought nothing of it; he could not think of anything. His mind would not concentrate, and there were spots before his eyes. He was no longer sleepy, but utterly, terribly weary. He could not walk across the yard without sitting to rest.

The next day, one week following the fire, he was caught in what was afterwards termed a riot, and in his condition, the excitement was too much. Entering the C&D block from the yard with Blocker, he noticed several convicts arguing with two guards who stood behind the grilled gate in the guards-room, an anteroom between the first and second of the five main gates leading to the outside.

"To hell with you convict bastards!" one of the guards shouted in reply to some statement one of the convicts had made. "Eat what you can find. Eat each other. Dog eat dog—"

And before he could finish convicts began coming from the ranges in a tidal wave. Although protected by a concrete wall and the grilled steel gate, the guard became panicky and drew his gun, firing a shot before the other guard could stop him. From the direction of the second range a convict screamed, "He got me!" And the convicts surged into the gate, mashing the breath from those in front, and hurling imprecations at the guards which could be heard clear out on the street.

Suddenly, Jimmy was running again. His knees came up, came down, came up . . . The ranges and the bars and the angles and the men slanted precariously, first one way, then another, then they melted and ran together in a huge boiling mass as his eyes went out of focus, and then the blackness came . . .

They told him it was Wednesday evening. A fellow by the name of Blocker had left him a toothbrush and some tooth paste and several packages of cigarets. The bed rocked gently from side to side as the long white hospital ward rose and fell. Faces drifted by his vision in a slow adagio dance, and one of the nurses laughed and said, "The M's still got him." He closed his eyes again and saw endless green prairies and heard running water as if a swift-flowing stream passed through rapids.

When he awoke again it was Thursday noon. Now the ward surrounded him in sure-angled perspective, and his mind was alert. He felt strong and ravenous. The nurses told him that they had given him enough morphine to knock out a horse. "Well, I ain't a horse," he grinned. After dinner they released him.

At the steps he met Blocker coming to visit him again. "See you're back, kid," Blocker chuckled.

"You're still living, anyway," Jimmy observed. "Man, that sleep was beautiful."

"You look like a different person, kid," Blocker told him.

"Feel like one, too."

Blocker took him down to the ball diamond and showed him the wire-enclosed stockade with machine guns mounted at each corner and armed soldiers marching in pairs up and down each side. Inside, five hundred convicts milled about, sullen and silent.

"That's what we just missed, kid," Blocker informed him. "The soldiers grabbed every one in the C&D block. I got out by helping to carry you to the hospital."

"A riot, eh?"

"That's what the papers said."

"Well, I'm a cripple," Jimmy said.

"Me, too," Blocker echoed.

That night a nine o'clock curfew was established and notices were posted to the effect that convicts caught on the yard after nine o'clock would be shot on sight. Friday morning the convicts in the stockade burnt down their tents. The guard was doubled, but no new tents were issued.

At noon, several hundred convicts rounded out of school and the A&B block were lined up on the yard and identified. New wooden labels were issued to those who had destroyed theirs, and after being divided into companies of fifty-eight each, the convicts were locked in the cells of the A&B block. By then the cell locks which had been damaged the night of the fire had been repaired. As new companies were formed, the guards returned from the honor dormitory where they had been passing the days since the fire, to take charge of them.

One morning Jimmy and Blocker picked up their boxes and moved into the cripple company, which was then housed in the 1-E&F dormitory, on the ground floor of the E&F cell house. And they remained indoors. For outside, on the yard, machine guns had been mounted at the corners of a series of squares so as to cover every inch of the prison, and were manned night and day by gun crews. Pickets walked with rifles, stopping and searching every convict who dared to cross the yard. Going back and forth to the dining room under the dead eyes of those Browning machine guns was an ordeal in itself.

That second Sunday, Jimmy and Blocker were standing by the window which looked out into the street, marking some cards preparatory to putting down a poker game, when behind them a tall colored convict said, "I caught you!"

Jimmy jumped, and then laughed guiltily. "We'll make him the lookout," Blocker laughed.

While they were looking at him, the top of the convict's head flew up into the air. He had been making his bunk, and now, on the white sheet which his hands still held, a gooey mass of brains appeared. They were still looking at him, and his mouth was still grinning as it had been before he lost the top half of his head, but his eyes were gone and blood was coming out over the edges of his skull, running down in his ears and down his nostrils, and his hands, which had been spreading the sheet, gave it one terrible jerk, pulling the sheet down over him as he fell between the bunks.

Jerking his vision away from that sight, Jimmy bit off the screams with his teeth, his mouth going sharp and on edge and unbearably tart as if he had drunk a glass of lemon juice. He looked at the cards, his vision clinging to him as he tried to hold his mind with sheer force of will, and when he saw the clots of brains on them, the words came out of him in an inhuman scream, "Keep your goddamned brains off of my cards!" And then he was trembling from the after-shock, and Blocker was clipping him lightly on the chin, saying, "Take it easy, kid."

A white convict had also been decapitated, and his head left hanging from the iron girders where it dripped blood until two nurses came from the hospital and dislodged it with a stick. When they learned that these deaths were the result of an accidental burst of machine gun fire, coming from a machine gun stationed a hundred yards distant, many were actually afraid to venture as far as the dining room for their meals, and remained indoors, keeping below the level of the window casements, until hunger drove them out.

In the hard days that followed, the incident was forgotten and overwhelmed by memory of the other hundreds dead, but Jimmy's involuntary remark became a classic, and was oft quoted in poker games when some player took too long to study another's hand, "*Keep your goddamned brains off of my cards.*"

Monday following, the prison got tough. It did not get tough gradually, but all at once. That morning at nine o'clock two hundred and forty guards, dressed in new tan uniforms with shiny puttees and Sam Browne belts and smart military caps, marched into the institution and took over, although the soldiers remained to the end of the week to assist in reclassifying the convicts.

A completely reorganized guard personnel had been effected, and the force doubled. Young, athletic men, has-been prize fighters and second-rate wrestlers, neighborhood bullies and flop house bouncers, big, beefy ex-policemen who had been expelled from various police departments throughout the state, had been hired to replace the rheumatic old time guards. Twelve yard lieutenants, of whom Cody was the head, had been created in place of the old guard sergeants; and a bull-necked, ax-faced, self-deluded popinjay with a gas-tank belly and a mile of shoulders was named Inspector, and given the authority which the deputy warden, who had been the convict's hero, had held before the fire. He and Stout held court.

A riot squad was created. With headquarters in one of the rooms of the Protestant Chapel, they stood at the top of the wide chapel stairway when the lines marched across the yard. Dressed in neat tan uniforms with their shiny Sam Browne belts supporting side holsters in which they wore ring-handled forty-fives, the two at each end carried knapsacks of tear gas bombs, the two next to them submachine guns propped thigh-high, while the lieutenant in charge strutted proudly up and down before them, his restless eyes on the marching lines. It was power on parade, an ever-present reminder that the wages of rioting was death, rioting being a term which, at that time, covered a multitude of minor infractions, the wages of most of which were death, anyway. And God help the convict who got out of line.

They soon earned the name of "Head-hunters," breaking from their stiff, proud line of six abreast to bludgeon a convict's head into a bloody pulp at the least sign of commotion.

Radios were confiscated and stacked in the hole and left there to rot over the years; newspaper were banned. Writing privileges were revoked, and visiting prohibited. Nor was the mail that was received delivered. It was the warden's prison after that. "I hold the destiny of you four thousand convicts in the palm of my hand," he had said. And he did. It was rumored that he was afraid to come into the yard, until one day, as the lines were coming from dinner, he came into the yard with some visitors and stood on one side of the walk to let two thousand convicts march behind him on the other side, insolent in his contempt for them.

At the first signs, hundreds of convicts made for the protection of the cripple company. But there was only room for a few, and most were caught in the awful grind which came.

The convicts in the stockade were labeled agitators and returned to the C&D block where they were kept under machine gun surveillance and given two abbreviated meals a day. They were the "agitators"; they took the fall for everything that had happened or would happen. They took the fall for all of the humiliation which the warden had suffered from the roastings he received in the newspapers. They took the fall for the rout of discipline, for the starting of the fire, for the convicts' deaths who died in the fire.

The Committee of Twelve were rounded up and put in the hole, where they remained until their fingernails dropped off and their hair came out by the roots, until one hung himself, another went blind, and three contracted tuberculosis. The convicts who had cheered them on, now called them fools.

A convict on one of the top C ranges shouted at a guard on the first range, calling him a bastard. After failing to discover the identity of the convict, the guard lieutenants took the one hundred and fifty convicts on the three top ranges out of their cells, one at a time, and beat them into insensibility; then locked them back to live or die. Coming on at six that evening, the night guards discovered fourteen delirious, bloody-headed convicts, and thinking that they had been fighting among themselves, locked them in the hole, where two died and six went crazy before the Inspector let them out next morning.

Only the lieutenants and the head-hunters were permitted to wear pistols, which saved many a convict's life, for, given authority the first times in their lives, suddenly discovering that they held the power of life and death over numerous other humans, those new, big-bodied, little-brained guards became as brutal as people can become.

"Talking in line!" one would say, jerking the convict out.

"But, cap, listen—"

And before he could finish, his skull would be split and his body stretched its length on the ground. With orders to whip a convict's head as long as his head would last, they went entirely crazy.

The soldiers were withdrawn on Saturday. Sunday morning twenty-five hundred convicts were lined up on the yard, given wheelbarrows without legs, and set to rolling heavy loads of sand, gravel, and cement between a merciless gauntlet of guards, stationed on each side of the line, twenty feet apart. The old woolen mill was being wrecked and a new industrial building, in which the prison industries would be centralized, erected.

The washer, where the sand was washed and the gravel sifted, was placed in one corner of the prison, the cement mixer in the other, while the building under construction was across, forming the tip of an isosceles triangle, the borders of which the trudging feet of convicts trampled into the ground. They rolled all that Sunday until five-thirty, and all the following Monday, and the following Summer, and all day the Fourth of July. Old men and young men. Feeble and strong. All alike. In the blistering heat. Falling in dead faints over the legless wheelbarrows to be revived with a bucket of water to get up and roll some more. With bandaged heads festering under bloody bandages.

That prison was as tough as a prison can become.

But Jimmy and Blocker, having seen the handwriting on the wall, had beat that rap. They were crippled. And the crippled company was moved down into the brick building, where, what now seemed like a long time ago, in some former life, Jimmy had celled in the coal company dormitory when first coming to prison.

JIMMY HAD SEEN HIM several times during the two weeks immediately following the fire, in school and up in the Catholic chapel and around on the yard in different places, and always the heavy-set, cripple fellow had been with him. But it was not until they were transferred into the company about a week after it had been moved into the old coal company dormitory that Jimmy learned who he was.

"What say, Lively," he greeted, pushing him a card.

The other one sat across the bench from Lively and reached for the card coming his way.

"What you guys trying to do, Tuck, squeeze me?" Jimmy asked jokingly.

"Just going to try to keep you from squeezing us," Tucker replied good-naturedly. "We know you're slick."

"I'd like to squeeze you all riiiight," Lively said, looking sideways at Jimmy through the corners of his eyes. He had a high, beautiful voice like a choir-boy's, only it was slow and slurred and drawn out in a delightful drawl. Now it contained a saucy note as a girl's in witty repartee.

"I'd like to squeeze you all riiiight, too," Jimmy mimicked.

"You ain't mannnn enough," Lively blushed, throwing him a quick side glance, then looking down at his hand, then over at Tucker.

"Yes I am mannnn enough, too," Jimmy stated, feeling a laugh grow inside of him.

"Naw you're not, you ain't nothing but fish," he contradicted, blushing redder, his swift side glances giving him a sort of roguish bashfulness like a bride on her wedding night.

"What's fish?" Jimmy asked.

"You're fish," Lively slurred. "You're a minnow fish."

"Maybe he don't play that," Tucker pointed out, grinning.

"He doesn't have to play it, I'll play it for him," Lively said.

Looking at his long, wavy, pure golden curls and mischievous blue eyes that threw roguish side glances, Jimmy dealt off too many cards. "Look what you made me do," he said.

"I ain't surprised at nothing a minnow fish does," Lively teased.

Although his features were not regular, his nose hooking slightly to one side, and his mouth much too wide and marred by a small bluish mark at one corner which Jimmy thought to be a birthmark, there was a quality of laughter within him which caused him to appear extremely good looking. He did not look exactly girlish, but he left that impression by the feminine lilt in his voice. On the other hand, perhaps he thought him so pretty, Jimmy admitted to himself, because of all the other boy-girls in prison who, though they wanted to be thought of as pretty, were horrible. There was no particular reason for him putting Lively in that class, but at the first sight of him he had, and strangely, he had not felt at all repelled.

Tucker's voice, saying, "Maybe he can beat you playing it," brought him back, and he looked at Tucker, feeling pleasant all inside because he thought Lively pretty.

Heavy-voiced and good-natured, Tucker was just the opposite of Lively, dark and hairy-armed, wide-shouldered and athletic appearing for all of his slight limp. He carried himself in a careless, unruffled manner; and his round face and cropped hair gave him a sort of stolid look. However, the two of them appeared very close and understanding of each other's moods.

"Me," Jimmy said, flashing Lively a look, "I'm the best ever did it."

Lively gave a spontaneous burst of high, clear laughter, alive with contagion, and slurred in a laughter-streaked voice, "I'll bet you are."

And although Jimmy knew that Lively was laughing at him, he wanted to laugh also; it made him want to laugh, only it was so delightful listening to Lively laugh, he did not want to spoil it. He felt light and warm and full inside as if he had kissed a beautiful girl, cleanly and with pride.

Finally, he asked, "What are you laughing about, boy?"

"I'm not going to tell you, little minnow fish," Lively said and continued to laugh, his blue eyes turning to light gray and shining with mischievousness.

Jimmy was greatly attracted to him. A few hands later he broke Tucker, and could have broken Lively, but kept letting him win. When he had him beat, he'd shuffle in his hand and push him the pot; he wanted to hear him laugh again. But Lively divided his winnings with Tucker until Jimmy grew peeved and broke them both in a pot. From then on he felt an antagonism toward Tucker which troubled him because many times he would have liked not to feel it. When they left he quit and called Blocker to deal, but Tucker borrowed some merchandise and they returned, so he stood around to watch them play.

"Why don't you go away, fish," Lively said. "You're bad luck. I bet you're bad luck to yourself."

"He is, kid," Blocker said. "He's so bad luck they got him in here for something he didn't do."

"I bet them have at that," Lively agreed, giving Jimmy one of those quick side glances. "He don't look like he'd do nothing, anyway."

"He wouldn't do anything," Blocker assured. "He ain't got sense enough."

"I wouldn't do anything," Jimmy admitted. "You could sleep with me."

"I know I could," Lively stated. "I bet if I had some spurs I'd ride you."

Tucker was taking it in with a grin.

"Why don't you try him and see what he'd do," Blocker said to Lively, winking at Jimmy.

Looking at the large, spreading knuckles and long, ill-shaped fingers of Lively's hands, Jimmy recalled a phrase he had read somewhere: Plough shaft hands. "Where are you from, Minnesota?" he asked.

Blocker snorted. "With that Kentucky drawl."

Of course. But not to be outdone, Jimmy kidded, "Naw, he looks like he's out of West Virginia."

"I'll bet you he's from Kentucky," Blocker persisted.

"How do you know so much?" Lively asked.

"You can't fool me, boy," Blocker boasted. "All I need to do is hear a sucker talk and I can read his history."

"Well, you read mine backwards, 'cause I'm out of New York."

"You'd have to change your voice to make anyone believe that," Tucker said to Lively, laughing.

"Come to think of it, he does look like one of those Kentucky moonshiners," Jimmy observed. "Boy, I bet your grandpa made many a barrel of good old Kaintecky moonshine. Yes sar, it seems to me as if I seen you all 'round dar, comes tuh think about it, uhrunnin' 'round dar in yo' shirt tail."

"You-I bet if you-that's all right, I bet if you ever came down there and I saw you I'd shoot your shirt tail off," Lively stammered, trying to keep joking, but Jimmy could see that he was plenty burnt up.

That night, after they had gone to bed, Lively leaned over the edge of his bunk and said, "I started to hit you in the mouth, little old Jimmy Monroe." His voice was loud and drawling and full of mischief, attracting every one's attention.

"Why didn't you, Lovely?" Blocker chuckled.

"You know my name, you call me by my name," Lively snapped.

"I told you you were going to get it," some one cracked at Jimmy.

"Lovely don't bluff, neither," Blocker egged. "I betaman he'll hit you in the mouth."

"You watch out I don't hit you in the mouth," Lively said to him.

"Don't get yourself hot, Lovely," Jimmy called. "I'll have to come over there and cool you off."

Lively started laughing. "Come on and cool me off then, I'm hot."

"You didn't get mad when he called you Lovely," Blocker pointed out.

"I don't mind him callin' me anything," Lively slurred in his high, soft drawl, and hearing it, Jimmy could see his face, roguish and bashful and blushing. "All right, baby," he laughed.

"I don't mind you callin' me baby, either," Lively told him.

"Boy, you sound sweet enough to squeeze," Blocker said.

The night deputy came in and they had to stop, just as Lively was getting burnt up again.

"Why do you dish it out when you can't take it?" Jimmy asked him the next morning.

"I don't have to take it," he replied belligerently.

174

"Okay, Mr. Villa, you'll learn," Jimmy prophesied condescendingly. "After you've been around in this joint a little while, you'll sing a different song."

"Whataya mean, fish, I've been here seven years."

"Whatttt!" Jimmy exclaimed. "You don't look as if you're more than seven years old," and Lively started laughing. Jimmy enjoyed hearing him laugh with his blue eyes changing color and his hair falling down into his face more than anything he knew.

Although taller than Jimmy, with a big-boned framed, he weighed less, being thin for his height. When he mentioned it, Lively told him, "You ought to have seen me when I came in."

"How did you look?" Jimmy asked, trying to get the picture of him with those golden curls seven years younger.

"I was stouter, I hadn't lost a lot of weight like now; I'm about twenty pounds under weight now, but I weighed about one-fifty-five then."

"I'll bet you were a dream," Jimmy said.

"I was in good health, too."

"Were you in fire?" Jimmy asked suddenly.

He said, "Sure, I was on 2-H," and then it came to Jimmy where he had heard of him before—the two convicts talking back of the hole the night of the fire: *That's what I call love.*

"Oh, you're the kid who made a hero out of Tucker," Jimmy sneered, and Lively flared, "What do you mean by that?" And then Jimmy flared, "Just what I said. You get mad too goddamn quick, you can dish it out all right, all right, but you can't take it. Who the hell do you think you are?"

Lively burnt a solid red and stalked away, but after a moment he came back and said, "I'm his friend, that's why he did it. You don't know the meaning of friendship, do you?"

"Yes, you're his friend, but is he your friend?" Jimmy gibed. "Would you have gone down that range to get him?"

Lively's scorn was towering. "You're just like all the rest, you don't even know what friendship is."

"There's a whole lot of things I don't know what is," Jimmy cracked. "But those what concern you, baby, I intend to find out."

During the days that followed, he learned that Lively made friendship into something of a fetish which he worshipped and which ruled him. Before the fire he had been out to the Brick Plant; that was the reason Jimmy had not seen him. Endeavoring to impress Jimmy with the value he put on friendship, he told him of how he had jumped on the younger Blossom brother, taking up for a friend. By their reputation, the Blossom brothers were very tough hacks, the older of whom was the Brick Plant deputy, and the younger his assistant, and it was hard for Jimmy to believe him until he discovered that the story was well known. Lively had taken Blossom's gun away from him, and had knocked him down; and then had put up a good fight with the other guards before they knocked him unconscious and set him inside with a cracked skull. But Jimmy acted as if he didn't believe it just to get Lively's goat. "I bet you were swapping up with that boy; and anyway, he did most of the fighting, I hear."

After that they were always spatting. Unbearably piqued at Jimmy's half perverse, half amused refusal to admit that he, Lively, would have attempted to save Tucker's life the night of the fire had he celled in Tucker's place, in the first cell, and Tucker in his, in the last, Lively fumed about it in a frantic sort of way.

To make it worse, Jimmy took every opportunity to taunt him about it. "You're nothing but a punk sponging off of people and calling it friendship," he jeered. "You don't even own your life, even that belongs to Tucker."

Lively wanted so badly to fight him that it came all up in his eyes, but he was afraid of what the other convicts might think. Discovering this, Jimmy took advantage of it, having himself a fine time. One night, after waiting for the dormitory to become quiet, he leaned from his bunk and said, "Oh, Lovely, let me be your friend," and from that distance, he could feel the heat in Lively's face.

"You better lay off Lovely," Blocker chuckled. "He's a prize fighter. Look at what he did to Blossom."

"Oh, Blossom was his old man," Jimmy said in a low voice,

and Lively jumped down from his bunk and challenged him, "What did you say, rat?"

Spreading his hands, Jimmy replied, "Don't shoot, Mr. Villa. All I said was that Blossom was an old man and you don't get no credit for whipping him. You got to whip some young hack be—"

"Naw he didn't," one of the cripples cut in. "He said Blossom was your old man."

"You know I wouldn't say that about you, Lovely," Jimmy denied.

"You better not," he grated, stalking back to his bunk.

"It wouldn't be true," Jimmy persisted. "And I wouldn't say anything that wasn't true, Lovely."

"And don't call me Lovely anymore. My name's Lively. Clermont Lively."

"Because that would make you a bigamist," Jimmy went on. "And you're not a bigamist, are you, wifey dear?"

"You just wait, you just wait!" Lively stammered, tears of pure rage in his voice. "You just wait."

"I'll lighten up if you beg me," Jimmy offered.

"You go to hell, you goddamn dirty rat!" Lively shouted.

But after that Jimmy stopped teasing him, anyway, and even apologized for what he had said. And finally, when Lively remained unmoved, admitted, "I do believe you would have saved Tucker's life, sho nuff," adding, "Honestly I do," in a more serious tone, because he wanted Lively to laugh for him again. He had heard him laughing with Tucker and Jew Baby and Bob down in the corner, and it had been like a needle in his nerves.

The dormitory had become full of little cliques. Tucker and Lively and Jew Baby and Bob formed one, and there was another with Horn and Dawson and some other convicts, and a clique of degenerates, and a clique of one-legged men, and a clique of one-armed men. It was as if every one had established family life. The cripples, of whom there were only about one-third despite the fact that it was a cripple company, were naturally a clannish lot, but since most of them were broke, their cliques did not bother Jimmy. The others, however, annoyed him, for he and Blocker, remaining in the field and operating the only poker game to which all of the cliques had to come sooner or later, had to act as arbiters, settling arguments between the cliques as a whole or between various members of different cliques, usually because of something in the past, Joe Doe had put this punk down, and George Blow had picked him up, now Joe Doe had another sidekick, and none of them spoke to each other. It was worse than the Bronx.

Some time in June, after the prison had settled down to a routine following its reorganization seizure, convicted prisoners who had been refused admission since the night of the fire, were now accepted. Having accumulated in county jails throughout the state for the past two months, they were committed in droves.

Several were put into the cripple company, one of whom was a blab-mouthed, lisp-voiced, petty robber out of Toledo, the typical cartoon convict who talks through the corner of his mouth of jobs in the double G's and shoots off his jib about his million dollar moll and his crate—"Cost eight G's, Jack."—and how things were in Atlantic City last winter and the time he had the double G's on Twenty Grand, or maybe it was Clyde Van Deussen that year, and then, "Save me a drag, buddy."

At that time they were shaving the newcomers' heads, and this fellow's head contained the most amazing assortment of deep, fluted crevices ever seen this side of a corrugated roof. There were several deep wrinkles running lengthwise his head, which were cut off front and back by wrinkles running crosswise until the top of his shaved head resembled nothing so much as some new system of irrigation trenches. When he talked, his eyes blinked, and the irises and pupils rolled out of sight underneath his eyelids which quivered frantically over a line of clear white as if he was totally blind, and his eyebrows would rise, lifting his forehead, and all those rows of wrinkles would squeeze into a dense crop of knots.

Of medium height, heavy set, with a narrow face, bad teeth, a left arm half paralyzed from gun shot wounds, and split nail on his right thumb where it had been cut at one time and had grown out over the scar in a long, ugly claw, he called himself Claw Hammer, but the convicts dubbed him Wrinklehead, and Wrinklehead he remained.

The first night was Wrinklehead's night, if he never had another one. He sat on his bunk and talked all night, telling them of the outside, bringing them up-to-date on the wrinkles and rackets, of the prisoners who had been held in the county jails and the stories which they had heard over the grapevine, what the papers had said about the fire and the riot and the warden; and then he started on himself in tongue-tied dramatics, shooting policemen and whipping sheriffs and robbing banks and playing havoc in general with the good citizens of Toledo, until some one yelled, "Hey, bring a bucket to catch this blood," while all the time his forehead was corrugated and his pared head knotted and his eyelids fluttering like a humming bird's wings with the irises rolled up in his head, leaving him white-eyed and blind as a bat, and, as Stepp pointed out, "Doan looks to me like you could see enough to even protect yourself, fellah, much less do nobody else no harm."

They had transferred Stepp into the company a short time before, not having any place else to keep so crazy a convict, and at night he would stand between the bunks while a gallery hemmed him in, and do his exercises, which consisted of weaving in and out, below and over, the bunk frames with his feet planted, moving his body so quickly they could not follow the flow of motion, and never once touching the bunk frames, which was a miracle of motion for one whose shoulders were wide enough to brush the bunk frames standing still. Jimmy tried it and bumped his head against the frame the second time he tried to straighten up.

Since most of the convicts who could afford it had their hair cut in the dormitories, Stepp also cut hair. He had a pair of old shears and a comb, with which he cut hair better than the barbers with their clippers and accessories, which lacked a great deal of being a miracle, however. Jimmy bought a razor from one of the barbers for a buck fifty, being cheated, he knew, and let Stepp use it in the dormitory to perform his tonsorial services. After that Stepp did all of Jimmy's barbering free of charge.

Then Blocker told Jimmy of the fits which Stepp had, resulting from the numerous blows he had received on the head. Stepp said the world would spin and whirl and turn black.

"If he ever has one while shaving you, it'll be just too bad," Blocker warned.

After that Jimmy kept an eye on him, and if he didn't look right, he would make him stop, although that snarling-mouthed, evil-looking colored man never looked wholly right to Jimmy.

Little duck-shaped, jumpy, fast-talking Candy, who was later to become a good friend of his, and big Jew Cohen were also moved into the dormitory. First off, Cohen stopped in the poker game and offered to bet Jimmy a dollar that he could "tee-roll a coon can deck" by taking out nine cards, which was a Negro's trick. They broke up the poker game and devoted the remainder of the evening trying to see if they could do it, and when all of them decided that it could not be done, persuaded Roy Jones to bet Cohen the dollar. Cohen did it, of course, and picked up the dollar, and Blocker chuckled, "By God, it was worth it to see how it was done."

About that time they got old, stiff-necked, Arizona Horsecollar, who claimed he had got that way from being hung once, but others, who knew him, declared that it came from drinking canned heat; and a little one-eyed, bow-legged, bald-headed Negro convict called Pork Chops. Horsecollar had a high, shrill laugh, similar to a horse's neigh, and a hoarse, thick, vibrating voice no louder than a whisper, and sitting in a poker game, he would raise the pot five cents and look around, and whisper in that hoarse, vibrating, canned-heat voice, "I'll bet a bilikin 'til his teeth rot out," while Pork Chops annoyed every one intensely by playing on an instrument which he called a "Git-fiddle", a combination of a guitar and a violin, he said. It was played by picking and bowing at the same time, and looked to Jimmy like nothing so much as pure and unadulterated junk, and sounded like hell. To make it worse, he also sang.

But though it annoyed the others, it did not bother Jimmy. It was all very distant. Like the fire. The fire was very distant during that June; it might have happened in another world during a lost era; it might have been Rome burning while Nero played "*Nearer*

My God to Thee." It was gone, and at that time, it had not returned. Everything was very distant that June.

During the latter part of the month, when the mail was finally distributed, Jimmy received a huge stack of letters from his parents, the first of which were very frantic, becoming less frantic as the postmarks grew more recent, and then more anxious than frantic, and finally reassured which must have been when the papers got more news concerning the dead, but still very much concerned, wanting to know, of course, how he had fared during the awful, horrible catastrophe, and how he now was, and did he need anything or want them to do anything, and was he behaving himself and praying and being a good boy. He did not know until then how distant they were, also. It seemed as if it had been a long time ago, perhaps in the life before, when he had had parents and had loved them; it seemed, in fact, as if he was a leaf of a tree, from which, when he fell and became earth again, it would not matter because he had never felt anything for the tree in the first place. Thinking of them, of his mother and brother and father, brought no love, no concern or anxiety or pity or sympathy, just the provoking thought that he would have to write to them, and he did not know what to say.

When the letter heads were passed out the following Sunday, he wrote to his mother, telling her hello and to say hello to Damon and that he was fine and all was well, lovingly . . . The letter was collected with the others, impersonally, and put into envelopes, indifferently, and in due time she received it, and was comforted, he hoped.

During the days they lay on their bunks and talked, or played Whist or Hearts, and if they had to gamble, shot dice in the corners where they could not be seen by the kill-crazy hacks outside, with their blood-filled eyes, who seemed to hate their living guts because they did not have them out there in that never-stopping, endless, rolling line; in fact those guards seemed to grudge the cripples their very afflictions which kept them in the dormitory.

The line passed by their door, coming between the tin shop and storehouse building and the dining room, around from in back of the wooden dormitory. It was nothing to count two dozen blood-stained, white-gauze caps where the skulls beneath had been split with sticks and patched up and returned to the red hot July glare to fester and fever and run into delirium and insanity and death.

Sometimes they would stand behind the bench which had been put across their doorway and watch the passing line, speaking to acquaintances with the flicker of an eyelash, an imperceptible nod, but never with the uttered sound, unless, of course, they were Stepp, who was crazier than ever and talked to whom he pleased, as loud as he pleased, when he pleased, wearing his white canvas gloves. Once Jimmy saw Walter, but did not speak and did not feel a thing; and if Walter had ever been a pal of his, he could not recall the feeling, looking at him pass.

Their day guard was a huge-bellied, white-haired, white-mustached, round-faced old man called Old Man Thompson, left over from the old regime, who would grin in their faces and talk about the other guards as if they were dogs, and if they, the convicts, agreed with him, would slip over to the inspector, who was open to all dirt, and tell him so and so was an agitator and have him transferred out into the line, as he did Jew Baby's Bob, and then see him pass bowed down under a wheelbarrow of wet gravel and click his tongue, saying indignantly, "It's a damned shame, by God, that's what it is! A damned shame, coming right in here, by God, and taking that boy out there and making him do that work, by God!" looking about at the others to see if they were properly impressed. "Yes sir, a damned shame! That boy was cripple, too," shaking his head, and knowing full well that the boy in question was no boy at all but a big, grown man, strong as an ox, and had fully deserved to be transferred into the line if for no other reason than that he was a degenerate, only by another method than that to which he had resorted. "A good boy, too, by God," he would say, shaking his head and sounding so sincere that Jew Baby was taken in by it and tried to get him to go over to the inspector and put in a plea to get Bob back. In fact, they were all taken in by it. Old Man Thompson would do them a favor—"Boys, if I only could . . ." They could gamble all day for all he cared—"But the lieutenants . . ." They could cook mulligans on Sundays—"But not this Sunday, boys . . ."

They gambled at night, which was enough. Too much for Jimmy after Tucker discovered that he would lend him money because he wanted Lively in the game—or at least Jimmy always suspected Tucker of having such motive, perhaps because he felt guilty about letting him have the money for that reason.

With his twangy, tantalizing voice and coquettish manner and yellow hair, Lively had him going. He'd watch him brush his hair at night and try to imagine how he would have looked at seventeen had he had been a girl. He got a kick out of him saying, "You're fisssshhhh . . . He's fisssshhhh . . ." Everybody was fish to let him tell it.

"You're fish yourself," Jimmy would laugh.

"Your hand's fishy," he'd reply.

Jimmy would look down at his hand and Lively would break out laughing. Then Jimmy would catch it, and deny, "I don't do nothing like that. I dream of you."

"I chased a rooster once," Lively would say, blushing and looking as guilty as if he had been forced into confessing it, and Jimmy would ask, "How was it?" and he'd reply, "Good, you ought to try it," and start laughing. He was irrepressible.

Jimmy certainly liked that dormitory. Perhaps it was seeing the others in the line catching the hell he was missing that made him like it so. He found it interesting; something was always doing. Between Wrinklehead trying to put the bee on some one for a blip— "Man, let me drive a tack. Man, I can gamble, they call me 'Gambling Claw,' "—in his tongue-tied voice with his wrinkled head and blind white eyes, the lids fluttering so he couldn't see, much less gamble; and Horsecollar betting his chips like a man on a slide, wheezing in his hoarse stage whisper, "I'll bet a bilikin underneath the table. Gotdamn me, I hate a bilikin worse than God hates sin," and getting broke on the same hand, sitting there with his head to one side on his stiff neck and saying, "Who wants to stake a gambler. Man, give me something and let me break these bilikins." And Stepp cursing out the lieutenant called Razor Back for throwing his stick against the window, both of them breaking for the door to stand there and look at each other, one with a forty-five strapped to his waist, and the other with white canvas gloves, feeling as safe in them as if they were the river Styx and he was bathing in it.

"Boy, by God, don't you never give me no more of your sass!"

"Who the hell is you, punk?"

"By God you'll find out!"

"When?"

Just looking at each other.

And Candy losing seven dollars in the crap game, and the simple-minded Negro degenerate who was stuck on him, saying, "I'll get you something," and returning with a package wrapped carefully in newspaper and tied with a red string, which he gave to Candy, looking senile and proud with his gap-toothed mouth half open like an idiot; and Candy opening the package and taking out seven dirty plugs of chewing tobacco and two half used boxes of penny matches and everybody laughing at him, standing there with the plugs and matches, not knowing what to do or say.

And Lively laughing. He could laugh for Jimmy's money, anytime.

ON THE SUNDAY FOLLOWING JULY 4, 1930, the cripple company was moved back to the 1-E&F dormitories, the ground-floor dormitory of the E&F cell house which extended halfway across the front of the prison from the main entrance, above which was the warden's residence, to the southwest stockade, forming a right angle with the G&H cell house.

Since the confiscation and burning of their wooden boxes, the convicts had been given flour sacks to hold their personal belongings. By then Jimmy had accumulated such a quantity of things—blankets, a bathrobe, shoes, pyjamas, sox, extra trousers, and their cards, chips, and gambling devices—his sack would not hold it all, and he had to get Candy and Al and Red Ziehm to carry some of it in their bags.

Halfway across the yard, the inspector and a flock of guards descended on them for a shakedown. Jimmy lost his extra trousers. Several wooden boxes were found, and a varied assortment of the things which cripples collect, such as bones, peach seeds, pieces of various kinds of wood, string, rope, wire, tin, and pieces of stone used for sharpening knives, and all the handmade tools, such as knives, saws, files, etc., used in "mush-faking", which is the prison term for the manufacture of knickknacks, were all confiscated. The cripples put up a squawk until the inspector slapped one-legged Kerensky sprawling; thereafter they restrained themselves to sullen muttering.

Heavily barred windows were spaced evenly down each side of the dormitory, those on the inside opening to their view the whole of the prison yard. They could see the construction company rushing to completion the new I&K block, and the other intra-wall activity, the main line marching to meals, runners scurrying here and there with transfer slips, visiting passes, parole board passes, and the yellow passes which meant *going home,* the nurses walking after supper, visitors peering about, night guards patrolling the yard, and the condemned men going to the death house.

While on the other side, the windows opened onto the deep green, velvet spread of lawn, with its beautiful fountain and immaculate rock garden, where, on those hot summer days when the water was cut off for hours inside, the sprinklers cast their long, thin, iridescent streams of water in the sunshine. Beyond was the sidewalk, and the asphalt street.

Across the street was an ice cream plant where twenty-two women worked—the convicts had counted them—coming out at noon in their crisp, tan-and-white uniforms; and in two weeks time the men in the dormitory not only knew each of them by sight, having given each a name, when they came and left and their days off and who was late and who was sick and who had changed the style of her hair and who looked as if she had a hangover and who got too much of it the night before and who had the widest can and who the best shape and who the largest bubbies, but one fellow by the name of Manuel swore that he had had them all and was starting all over again with the little wasp-waisted blond.

Unlike the others, who came and went, Martin stood in those windows eternally. He fell from one hundred and eighty to one hundred and twelve pounds, went into tb, and died; and there was another who turned gray, looking out those windows; and a third who had to be taken to the state asylum for the criminally insane. Some learned, of course, that there was nothing in a drug store that would kill them quite as dead as standing inside of a prison, looking out; and of course, some didn't.

But the passing women's jiggling buttocks in bright print dresses, whatever reactions they inspired in other convicts, left Jimmy cold. When Candy or some one called, "Hey, Jim, come look at this baby," he went and looked, but he could not imagine himself getting any of it like they said they could.

The others could have the women in the street, he decided; he would take Lively. Eventually, he told him of his preference, and Lively declared that he had never done anything like that, and even if he had, he would not do it for Jimmy, as Jimmy was not worthy.

"What the hell you mean I'm not worthy," Jimmy sputtered.

"You don't put enough value on friendship."

"I suppose you're saving it all for Tucker. He's worthy, ain't he? He saved your life."

They were by themselves at the time and Lively did not get as angry as he would have had others been around.

"Sure, he's worthy. He's a real man. He's my friend."

"You're a goddamned friendship freak," Jimmy snarled. "To hell with the friendship angle; how much is it worth in dollars and cents."

"Even if I did something like that, I wouldn't do it for money,"

Lively informed him. "All the money in the world couldn't make me do it."

"Oh, a man's got to save your life."

"I ought to hit you," Lively grated. "You know damned well that Tucker never thought about anything like that. And if he ever asked me, I couldn't. I don't love him."

"Well, so here's where love enters," Jimmy sneered. "Say, listen, you wouldn't do it because I've been keeping you in smoking and soap and gambling funds these past two months, would you?"

"You haven't given me nothing!" Lively shouted.

"Where do you think Tucker got it from? Heaven?"

"I don't know. Tucker's business ain't my business—"

"Aw, you're a lie!" Jimmy growled. "You know damned well I let Tucker have all that junk—I don't know how much, twenty or thirty dollars worth, I haven't kept count—but you know damned well I let him have it on account of you. You're not so dumb or innocent. You've been had all right, all right."

"If I have, you'll never know it. And you'll—"

"And I don't care to know it, either. I'm talking for my own self. Here the last past month or so I've been giving my stuff to keep you up and here you are handing me a lot of cut-rate jive about you don't know what I've been doing. What the hell did you think I was doing, making a play for that hairy-bodied ape?"

"For two cents I'd knock you down and kick you," Lively gritted in a high, tight voice, his face blotching red.

"Okay," Jimmy said, turning away. "Just don't send Tucker over to me to borrow anything else."

Lively ran after him and spun him about and hit at him. Jimmy caught the blow and they clinched. Passing, Jew Baby and Columbus Johnson stopped, and Jew Baby jumped straight up into the air. "Say, what's this? Say, Johnson, what's this? Look at this, Johnson, look at this!" He was boy-girl crazy. "What's going on here?"

"Looks as if Jimmy's getting lucky," Johnson observed, his face widening in its slow grin. "Or maybe it's Lively getting lucky. Which is it?" he asked them.

In his abrupt cessation of anger, Lively wilted, looking red and guilty and flustered.

"Kiss me," Jimmy said, still holding him tightly.

"I'll kisssss you," Lively drawled roguishly, pushing him away.

"Go ahead and kiss him," Jew Baby egged, falling against Johnson.

"Hey, get the hell off of me," Johnson said, pushing him.

Lively looked furtively at Jimmy, then his gaze slid off, crawled along the floor. He patted Jimmy on the hips and said, "I'll kiss you, fissshhh."

"Sure, I'm fish," Jimmy said. "Kiss your little baby fish."

"I'll kisssss you," Lively repeated, and then leaned forward and kissed Jimmy quickly on the lips.

"Well sir!" Johnson exclaimed, looking at Lively with a new interest in his eyes.

Jew Baby jumped up and down, clapping his hands. "Old Monroe! Old lucky Monroe! Old lucky chump!"

"Not like that," Jimmy told Lively. "Come on, let's do it again."

But Lively pushed him away, looking guilty enough to hang. "You sure do make me mad sometimes," he declared, and they walked down the aisle. Jimmy put his arm about Lively's waist, and Lively did not move it.

"You're gonna make me hit you yet," he said.

"I know how you're going to hit me."

"I'm going to hit you with my fist." And then he started laughing. And as far as Jimmy was concerned, those distant women out there in the street went straight out of sight.

At first, Jimmy and Blocker brought gambling back to the prison in a big way. While Old Man Thompson sat in the cool up front and snoozed, they ran the largest game they ever had. Starting with poker, soon a mob of players slipped in from the yard to take a hand, runners from the deputy's office and Bertillon and transfer departments, construction company foremen, honor clerks from the front office, Matt Brock and Coky Joe, Polack Paul and Hunky Harris, Chin the Chink and Stack O' Dollars, Mike the Pipe and Hank the Crank, old man Dean and Death House Jeff, and two colored convicts called McGhee and Deep Morgan, who wanted to play Georgia Skin, so they turned it into a skin game with Blocker taking one side and McGhee or Coky Joe or some one else the other, while the remainder piked.

That was the fastest game Jimmy ever saw in prison. So many were piking, when one fell, he couldn't get a card until the next deal. Once Blocker charged four drawn cards twenty-five dollars each, turned himself a ten, and doubled off, and threw cards in a forty-foot radius.

Dean lost nine hundred and fifty-seven dollars in four days, and although, being a Spanish War veteran, he drew a pension of forty-two dollars monthly, he never did get over it. Death House Jeff and McGhee and Polack Paul won most of the money in the long run, although nub-fingered Lightning got into the game one morning with a blip, with one white nickel, helped the blind cards on the first two deals and ran it into four dollars, drew for the four dollars and raked in seventy-two when the deal was down, and played his next three cards through, and he couldn't stuff his greenbacks into a coffee bucket. He drove that blip to a solid grand, and then lost it that afternoon before supper, and sold his Sunday's pie for a bag of smoking.

Wrinklehead and Horsecollar and Jew Baby and Cohen and Roy Jones, all the nits and vocal gamblers, got tree-top tall swallowing bets. Jimmy swore that he heard Wrinklehead talking in his sleep one night, shouting in his tongue-tied voice, "Thow down! Thow down, chwump! Bet tha thome mo! Bet tha fo' double G's," and Horsecollar, seven bunks distant, and dead asleep, also, answering in his canned heat whisper, "Let your money beat your mouth down, bilikin. I'll bet a bilikin 'til he fall over dead! Throw down yourself, bilikin! Money on the wood makes betting good! Goddamn my soul, I hate a bilikin worse'n God hates sin."

Although Blocker was considered one of the best skin players in prison, he was in bad luck. Sometimes Jimmy spelled him in the side, but his luck was no better. They got them both in the end.

And the moment they were broke, as if he had timed it, the

inspector walked in and broke it up. He didn't put anyone in the hole, however, which was telling that most of them were his rats.

"He'd have broke it up long ago if we'd been winning, kid," Blocker said, standing bent over the table with his hunched shoulders drooping and his hair down in his face and sweating like rain.

"I believe that," Jimmy replied, sweating himself. His eyes felt hot and dirty-looking and his lips were flattened into a line. All inside of him was drawn tight, and he remained that way, his eyes and his lips and the drawing tightness, for he did not know how long, although it was a month or so later that Columbus Johnson's Belle said, "Jimmy! Don't keep your mouth so tight. Smile. I haven't seen you smile in ages."

"Well, they got us, kid," Blocker said, gathering up the blanket. The inspector had taken the cards and chips.

"They got us," Jimmy echoed.

Carefully folding the blanket, taking eons, they went over to their bunks.

"You got any left out front, kid?"

"I don't know, maybe a dollar or so." He felt hollow inside and as scared as he had ever been before. He had always been afraid of being broke in prison, so very much afraid—and now he was. But Blocker held him up, again, his colorless eyes predatory, and his grin wolfish. "All we need is a deck of cards, kid, and we'll find the chumps."

And then Jimmy had to curse out Wrinklehead. "You're too goddamned familiar all of a sudden, fellow," he snarled.

All the convicts whom before, had been flunkeying for them for a handout, now wanted to get chummy. Jimmy cursed out Tucker for his sanctimonious sympathy, and Belle for his friendliness. He wanted neither their familiarity nor their sympathy nor their friendliness; he wanted their money. He knew, however, that in their hearts they were all happy to see them fall, they had been so high and mighty.

And although every one knew that they were rocky, they never admitted it. Jimmy slipped his bathrobe over to the dining room dormitory and pawned it for three dollars, and they bought some cards and chips and tried to start their poker game again. But now the players made them show their bank, they had to put the cash on the table and declare themselves, and then only a few played. In the end they had to take turns with Tucker and Heads in order to get a play; they would run the game one day and Tucker and Heads the next, and even then there would just be the four of them playing, sitting there for hours on end, turning down hand after hand, waiting for a sucker.

However, Lively seemed to like Jimmy better; perhaps it was because Jimmy had more time to devote to him, and then again, perhaps he was also impressed by the leveling effect. In the evenings when Tucker had his game down, they would walk up and down the aisles together and talk about themselves. Those were the only times Jimmy felt relaxed; Lively's laughter was a tonic.

In a moment of confidence. Lively told him that he and his brother, Buck, had been jointly indicted for murder, but that he had taken the rap to free Buck, who had been in ill health at the time.

"Where is he now?" Jimmy asked.

"Oh, he's dead. He died the second year after I entered."

And Jimmy couldn't help but think what a waste it had been, his taking the rap, although Lively swore that he had done the actual shooting. However, he heard it differently a little later.

"Hell, that punk ain't killed nobody," his informant stated. "He was a damn fool to take the rap for Buck. Buck never was no good, the sneaking rat. He caught this fellow drunk outside a saloon and slipped up and shot him down in cold blood. They'd had an argument a short time before about a bet in a crap game. This punk in here wasn't even there when it happened; he came up later, after they'd taken the gun away from Buck. I don't know why he took the rap unless it was because they figured out he was just a kid and wouldn't get much time for it."

And after he had heard it, Jimmy became blindly angry with himself for listening, because he did not want to be touched by it, or by anything. He did not want to go through all that emotion of being sorry for some convict again. He was through with that, he told himself. He had enough troubles of his own.

Later, Lively told him that his people had spent a thousand, three hundred and fifty dollars for his defense, and that it had killed his father when he was sentenced to second degree life. His father had died the month he had entered. A sucker for every shyster lawyer who came along, his mother had broke herself trying to get him pardoned, and had been forced to return to a small farm in Kentucky. He had three sisters, two of whom were married and living in Akron and Youngstown, and the third, just a kid, who was going to high school in Louisville. He showed Jimmy their pictures once; all of them were rather pretty, but the youngest was a dream.

"I could go for her if I didn't want you so badly," Jimmy told him, and he quit speaking. It was nothing new, however. After a day or two he always made up.

One night Lively told Jimmy how every one had been after him when he had first entered, and how a convict tried to rape him once. "They got so bad the deputy let me choose my cell mates," he said.

"Every word you say convicts you more and more," Jimmy said. "If you haven't been had, nobody in this whole joint has."

"That ain't nothing," Lively drawled, looking at him through the corners of his eyes, and blushing. "One or two times won't make you a girl-boy."

Jimmy laughed. "Why don't you give me a break, then?"

"I might if you were worthy."

"Well, for chrissakes, tell me what I have to do to be worthy."

"It's not what you do, it's the way you feel."

"Well, how does a person have to feel? If I wanted you anymore than I do now, I'd explode and go right up in a puff of smoke or something."

"Naw you wouldn't," Lively teased, laughter slurring his voice, "You'd get yourself a jockey."

Jimmy had to laugh again.

192

After a moment Lively said, "If you were in love, you would know what I mean."

"I am in love," Jimmy argued. "I'm in love with you. I couldn't be anymore in love."

"Oh, no you're not," Lively contradicted. "If you were you wouldn't always be thinking about what you want, yourself."

"Don't you think I think about the things you want. I've been going nuts trying to figure how to get you some shoes."

"That's not what I want. That's not what I mean. I don't mean that at all."

"Well, that's what you need. And just what do you want, anyway?"

"You wouldn't understand if I told you."

"Maybe not, but listen, let me tell you one thing. You're going to find out in the long run that your best friends are the ones with the stuff on the line. You'll find out one of these days, and then you'll know that I'm the best friend you'll ever have."

Shortly after that he and Blocker beat Dean out of five dollars, and at Blocker's insistence, he spent it to buy a pair of black shoes from Chump Charlie. Lively quit speaking to him. Why, he did not know. Lively gave one look at the shoes and walked away from him. He tried to talk to him, but he would not reply; he wrote him a couple of notes, but he tore them up without reading them. He became very friendly with Tucker again, and finally, Jimmy said to hell with him, why worry about that gunsel, although he did not mean it.

Lying awake one night about a week later, he saw Tucker slip down to Lively's bunk and try to crawl in beside him. He awakened Blocker, although most of the others were awake, it having become their favorite pastime to lie awake at nights and watch each other so they'd have some one to call a boy-girl the next day.

Evidently Lively rebelled, for Tucker sat up on the side of the bunk, and for a long time they talked, gesticulating angrily every now and then.

The next morning every one was talking of how Tucker had propositioned Lively and had been turned down. They took Tucker's side, reasoning that since he had saved Lively's life, Lively owed him that much, as he was that way, anyway. Openly, Jimmy agreed. "Sure, he ought to have given old Tuck a break," he said. "Little selfish punk. All for himself. That's the way these kids are."

But secretly, he was elated. He would have had a fit if Lively had let him.

All that day and the following, Lively lay on his bunk and refused to speak to anyone. Passing once, Jimmy noticed that his eyes were red as if he had been crying. Coming back, he stopped and said, "What's the matter, keed?"

"Go to hell!" Lively cursed.

"Okay, sucker," Jimmy said.

That afternoon, in the poker game, they teased Tucker about it, and he replied, "I wouldn't care so much if that gunsel didn't owe me seventy-five sacks of weed."

"And his life on top of that," some one added.

"Aw, I don't count that, he would have done the same for me if he'd had a chance."

"Don't be so noble, sucker," Jimmy sneered.

At that time tobacco cost two for fifteen, ten cents straight; and seventy-five sacks amounted to five dollars and sixty-five cents. All that Jimmy had at the time was a dollar and a half, so he took his new shoes down to Chump Charlie to pawn, but Chump wouldn't let him have but three dollars. Blocker had some tan shoes, so he pawned them to old man Childs for thirty sacks of tobacco. Wrapping this together with an envelope containing three dollars and forty cents and a note, he called Wrinkledhead. "I want you to give this to Lively," he instructed, "But don't let anyone see you give it to him. Go up to the front of the dormitory and slip down behind the bunks and put it underneath the blanket on the bunk next to his. Then tell him where to look."

Then he went back to the game and became engrossed in peeping at his hole card. A few minutes later, his face scarlet and so furious he could not talk, Lively rushed over to the game and hurled the tobacco and the money and the note across the table at Jimmy. "You goddamn rat!" he shrilled.

Jimmy ducked, and the junk scattered all over the floor. His face went beet red. "I was just trying to help you, sucker," he snarled.

Lively jumped up on top of the table and kicked at him; and he grabbed Lively's foot and jerked it out from under him. Lively fell on his back across the table, and he leaned over and hit him in the side. Lively kicked him on the shoulder. And then the others parted them.

"I knew it; I just knew it," Johnson cracked.

"Take it easy, kid," Blocker said, holding Jimmy by the arm. "What the hell's it all about."

Jimmy did not reply. Tucker and the others finally got Lively back to his bunk, but he would not tell them what it was about, either.

After collecting the tobacco and all of the money except the forty cents in change, which some one had copped, Jimmy went to his bunk. But the note was missing. That night Horescollar turned up with it and tried to shake Jimmy down for two dollars.

"Wait, I'll get it for you," Jimmy promised, going down to Blocker's bunk.

He and Blocker returned with a knife apiece, and putting them on Horsecollar's throat, took the note. Jimmy's first impulse was to tear it up, then he handed it to Blocker. "I'm a chump, ain't I?"

Blocker read: "Dear Lively, you can take this and pay that sucker those 75 sacks he keeps cracking about you owe him. I don't want to see you owe anybody. Now won't this convince you that I'm thinking about you? Jimmy. P.S. And don't you think, just between you and me, that one good turn deserves another?" He grinned. "It's a good thing we got this or we might have had to fight Tucker and his whole gang."

But the next day Horsecollar told every one what was in the note, anyway, and they got down on Jimmy for trying to cut out Tucker. Tucker got heartless mad, but all he did was blow off, and he didn't do that when Jimmy was about. However, after that they were always cool to each other.

And then Jimmy's eyes got really bad. He could feel all the dirty heat boiling up in them, and all the rotten tightness growing in his head until it took an effort to keep from walking up to convicts and hitting them in the mouth. In the evenings, he walked the aisles alone; the poker game had become intolerable, and he did not want to talk to anyone, not even to Lively, he told himself. Lively began walking alone, also; and when they passed they did not speak.

And then one day Jimmy asked, "Well, are you over it?" and Lively smiled, and that was it. In the reaction, he completely lost his head. He put that golden-haired punk before every one, and wanting him was utterly degenerating in its savage intensity.

Lively needed shoes, Jimmy thought, as if he could not wear the prison brogues that two-thirds of all the convicts always wore; and he needed a tooth brush, and some pyjamas, and some other things; so he wrote to his mother, who had gone to St. Louis to work, and who was having it as tough as any decent, old woman can ever have it, being broke and alone and needing work in a strange city during the dark days of the depression after having lived twenty-seven years of married life with a husband who had supported her in a home of her own, for some money and some shoes for a convict in prison whom he wanted to make.

His mother sent him ten dollars and a pair of tan brogues at a sacrifice he'll never know, and which no one but a mother will ever make. And because the shoes were too small for Lively, his mother having bought them to fit him, he blew up and had a fit temper and hurled the shoes halfway down the aisle, talking of sending them back to her, and only being restrained from doing so by Blocker, who said, "Take it easy, kid. She got the shoes to fit you. What the hell else could you expect? How was she to know you were trying to keep up one if these gunsels?" And even then he did not feel ashamed. He spent all of the money buying Lively another pair of shoes and some other things, and when writing day came around, wrote his mother a most ungracious, thankless letter, complaining about the small amount of money she had sent, and about the shoes not being the right size; complaining about how tough he was having it with nobody ever thinking about him. The prison censor, who was warden's daughter at that time, tore up the letter and sent him the pieces with a warning that the next time he wrote to his mother in such a manner he would be put in the hole.

He did not care. It had him, making him as rotten and lousy as a man can become. And he did not care. He never knew why Blocker did not tell him to go to hell and cut out from him. Every day he took their joint funds and every cent which they could rake and scrape from the poker game and spent it on Lively, but never once did Blocker squawk, not even when he took the bank one day in the middle of a game and bought Lively two pairs of summer underwear, which he did not need as it was early October with wintr coming on fast. When time came for the winners to cash out, they did not have a thing to pay them. That killed the goose which laid the eggs. Afterwards they did not even have a game.

And what did he do it for? He didn't know. What does anyone do such things for? he asked himself. Because he wanted to, he guessed. Perhaps in the end, after all his high and mighty resolutions, he had become sorry for the son of a bitch. Or perhaps it was from wanting him so badly that he could not sleep at nights, so badly that his weight began falling as if he had contracted galloping consumption. Or maybe it was both, churned together into a squashy, messy, dirty mess in his mind, like the greenish, stinking scum on top of a stagnant pool.

And what did he get out of it? The chance to hear Lively laugh, to run his fingers through his hair, to have him do his hair in various ways for the pleasure of seeing it; the chance to kiss him once, lying fully dressed underneath a blanket one cold October afternoon with a group of convicts standing behind, hemming in the radiator, kidding them, and a couple of other times down in the latrine in the cold, both nervous for fear of some one seeing them, and getting nothing, absolutely nothing, out of it. Being jealous of him, too, was something he got plenty chances to do: The time Matt Brock took him over to the chapel to work, Matt being the kind of chiseler one could always bet on getting something big for the little favors he bestowed: And the time he was talking to him, sitting across the table from him, watching his eyes change from blue to smoky gray and back to powder blue and then deep green and then a lighter blue with a touch of violet, growing deep, then shallow, serious, then laughing, and listening to him laugh, and to his slurred, high, choir-boy voice, watching the roguishness in his face, playing furtively with his hair, getting charged with emotion, and then Kippy Mike stopping by the outside window and calling him, "Say, Lively, come here," in his arrogant, overbearing manner, and Lively getting up to see what he wanted, leaving Jimmy so jealous, that had he been a chameleon, he would have turned a vivid green. The chance to listen to him talk of how a person could love another, deeply, genuinely, desperately, and feel no urge of sex, like Damon and Pythius, only when it came to that, Jimmy exploded and said, "I'll bet the truth was never told." Mostly, he got the chance to hear, over and over again, how unworthy he was.

THERE WAS NO WARNING. They were given five minutes to pack. The cripples, with definite proof of their afflictions, like the stump of an arm, were put into 1-B. Part of the others were scattered throughout the cell blocks, part transferred to the second and third floor dormitories.

Jimmy and Blocker were put in 3-E&F; Lively in 2-E&F; all in the wheelbarrow gang. Separated from Lively, Jimmy went nuts. In the evenings, catching the guard at the front, he climbed over the wire enclosure and shinned down the corner joist to the dormitory below, where he snatched a few scared moments with him. The third time his guard caught him sneaking up the stairs, and had not the second-floor guard, who was the same captain Charlie who had been his night guard a long time before in 5-F, lied for him, he would have been transferred into the G&H block, which the convicts called Siberia.

After a week, Jimmy said, "Hell, I'm not going anymore, I'm cripple, I can't do that work. I'm going over to the deputy's office and sit there until they transfer me."

"I'm with you, kid," Blocker stated.

When the line broke up after breakfast, they slipped back to the court-room vestibule, and there they sat. Later in the morning, when the word got out, they were joined by Wrinklehead, Horsecollar, Columbus Johnson, Babe, Candy, Jew Baby, and a number of others. Just before dinner, the inspector came in and gave orders that they were not to be fed. When supper was over, they were allowed to return to their dormitories. But the next morning after breakfast they were transferred into the four-man cells of 2-B, where Blocker was put in #5 and Jimmy in #12 with a consumptive-looking convict named Boyer who had just been returned from the insane asylum to which he had been sent from prison six years before for cutting the throat of another convict while he had been shaving him in the barber shop, and a one-armed, short, heavy-set, slow-talking, former West Virginia coal miner full of coal, God, and the Bible.

He sent word back by the runner for Lively to try to get transferred into the remaining bunk. Lively was transferred the following morning, but the convict who had been transferred with him, greasy, oily, ignorant Cook, was put into Jimmy's cell, and Lively into the next cell down. An egg would have cooked on Jimmy's head.

Every one knew how he regarded Lively, and it seemed to him as they all hushed to listen when he began to talk, so instead he wrote, "Dear Lively, I'll have some money pretty soon and I'll see if I can't get you transferred over here with me. I'll get the clerk to change you and Cook. That'll make it better, don't you think. I'll have some money soon."

"Don't think of money all the time, Jimmy," Lively answered. "Is everything worth so much in dollars and cents to you? Do you think I came over here because I figured you were going to get some money? If I had been looking for a friend who could give me something, I could have gone over to 5-E with Matt or to 5-F with Kippy."

That irritated him. He did not want to be considered any less able to support a kid than Matt or Kippy or anyone else. So he wrote, "If you've got to keep bringing them up all the time, you can go to hell on over there where they are." But he did not send it; he tore it up. And then, glancing around, he caught Cook's sly, oily gaze on him, a sort of leering expression which seemed to say, "I know what it's all about, but I wont tell," which infuriated him, although he could not keep from blushing. He felt suddenly young and inexperienced and utterly incapable of handling the situation.

After a time he wrote a reply to Lively, "Dear Lively, you know it isn't the money that counts. I only love you so much and want to do so much for you that it makes me feel terrible not to have any money and not to be able to even get you in here with me when it would only cost two dollars."

"I'd like to be in there with you, too, Jimmy," Lively wrote in reply, "but we can't now and we'll have to make the best of it as it is."

That set him up until the next morning when Tucker, who had been transferred into 1-B with the cripples, called up from below to kid Lively; then he turned green again. Two days later, Stout formed a company of prison degenerates, and Columbus Johnson's Belle and Boyer, who was in the cell with him, along with several others, were transferred there.

"I'm going to try to get you in here with me in Boyer's bunk," Jimmy wrote to Lively. "I think I can borrow two bucks."

"Don't try it now," Lively replied. "Old Stout might find out about it and transfer us both away to different cell blocks and I don't want to be away from you."

"I won't if you'll give me a break," Jimmy wrote. "I'm going nuts over here with you so close and still so far away. I can't sleep anymore thinking about you."

"I've never told you this before, but I'd do it for you, Jimmy, if we had a chance," Lively wrote. "I would have a long time ago but it was so open in the dormitory and I didn't want anyone to

200

know it. You have to be so careful in this place; you can't afford to let anyone know your business. No one in here can ever say I've done anything like that because if I have, I've never let anyone see me."

Jimmy's elation was so transparent that Cook observed, "Got it all straightened out now, eh, kid?" Fishing his razor from its hiding place, Jimmy would have cut him, he was so infuriated, had not Gay grabbed him.

"You don't want to do anything like that," Gay said, then turning to Cook, "Why don't you let this boy alone, he ain't bothering you."

Pocketing the razor, Jimmy sat down and wrote Lively a reply, "When we go out to march tomorrow morning, you fall out when you pass the deputy's office as if you are going in to see the deputy and then cut around behind the school building and on the next round I'll fall out and meet you back there and we can go in the back room of school. Don't anyone ever go in there anymore. And old Button doesn't pay any attention to us."

Twice a day, their guard, a tall, leaning-forward, rail-thin, Ant-eater-looking, modern edition of Ichabod Crane, whom they called Button, marched them around the yard a couple of times for exercise, and Jimmy hoped they would not be missed if they slipped from line. He was desperate.

"I will, Jimmy," Lively wrote, "but you'll have to give me a break, too. I want you to give me a break, too. All along I've wanted you as much as you have wanted me."

Reading that, the blood rushed to Jimmy's face and stung him blind. Tearing the note into shreds and hurling them into the commode, he shouted, "So that's the way it is? So that's the way it's always been?"

He heard Tucker's laugh from below. "Take it easy, kid," Blocker called from his cell. A snicker ran through the block, and some one said, "What's the matter with those two whores up there; they mad 'cause they can't get together."

Enraged, Jimmy yelled, "Go to hell, all you rat sons of bitches!"

The night guard, whom they called Pipe, came by and said, "Aw, pipe down up there."

"Here, take this," Lively said in a tense, tight whisper, sticking a note through the bars. Taking it, Jimmy read, "Keep your damn mouth shut and your business to yourself or I'll come out there in the morning and knock out your teeth. That's the reason I haven't ever before now, I figured you couldn't keep it to yourself. Your mouth's too big. That's the trouble with you."

Cooling, after a time Jimmy wrote a reply, "I would, but you know how those things are in here. Every one would be taking advantage of both of us. We'd have to be fighting all the time. You know, there's an old saying that there must be at least one man in every well-regulated family."

Almost immediately he received an answer, "I didn't mean any of it, Jimmy. I was just testing you to see if you were worthy. I know you don't do anything like that. I'm going to bed now, I'll talk to you tomorrow and let you know my answer."

But the next day Lively was transferred into 5-D, the company of degenerates. And that almost killed both of them. If ever a convict looked sick, he was Lively when he marched to dinner that day, with all the convicts in all the other companies craning their necks to see what new "whore" had been caught. As long as he was in the company with other convicts, he could have denied it; but once in 5-D it was like a label on a can. He was a "whore"; and that was that.

The only reason they could see for the transfer was that Matt Brock, who was the inspector's rat, had managed it through spite because he could not get Lively into the 5-E dormitory with him.

Seeing Lively there, and knowing how he felt, Jimmy was sick, too. He wrote, promising to do everything in his power to get him out of there, but without money, there was not a thing that he could do. He felt helpless and hurt and frustrated.

In order to see Lively at mass on Sundays, he put in a request to join the Catholic church. And though he was ordered to attend catechism classes for a period of six months, and be confirmed before attending masses, he attended the following Sunday and every Sunday thereafter. They could only put him in the hole, and that was nothing.

Winter came on, with its stark, stripped, gray days, small of stature and hard of heart, frostbitten and sharp-visaged, bitter and sardonic, barren and bleak, with their sagging ceilings and mono-toned patterns, through which the convicts marched in long gray lines of lock-stepping legs, with pulled down visors and bare hands, with weather-reddened faces and slightly stooping shoulders, across a blackened stretch of prison yard, to a vague and distant freedom, to the end of a natural life, to a grave in Potter's Field and worms and a dubious eternity, to dreams in the offing and a woman's white smile, to a fortune in gold and disillusionment, underneath the precariously hanging sky, before the weighted glare of the headhunt-ers, while a prison band played *Sousa's March* in the driving sleet.

As those winter days wore on, they wore Jimmy to the nub, to the white, meatless bone. Each day, during the few minutes between the time the cells were unlocked and they were marched to dinner, he and Blocker ran a furtive, hurried crap game in the end cell, which they fattened with every nickel they could scrape. All of the money which his mother sent to him, all he could get by selling his shoes and gloves and finally his sox and underwear and all the other things which he had accumulated, went into those games. He did not remember them once winning. After spending a week to carve some six-ace flats, a shooter picked them up and made seven straight eights. The ace was so heavy it would slide on the slick concrete, but every time at the very end of its slide, it would turn sluggishly over to make every point it was not supposed to make. They got some four-eleven tops, and missed out every time. They borrowed a five-dice combination with a five-deuce buster, and Wrinklehead made so many fours and tens with the buster down that Jimmy thought he was going blind. The luck was all against them, and as Blocker said, "They ain't no cheat in the world that'll beat it down, kid, until it changes."

At first, he and Blocker divided sacks of Bull Durham and penny boxes of matches. The matches they split into four parts each to make them last longer. When they ran out of cigaret papers they used their toilet tissue. When they ran out of Bull Durham, they toasted their twists on the cell lights and crumbled them into flakes. When they ran out of matches, they used an iron wheel, a string, a piece of flint, and a can of half burnt cotton taken from their mattresses for lights. When they ran out of twists they grated their sweet plugs and dried them out. When they ran out of toilet tissue, Jimmy tore the thin, yellow leaves from his mother's priceless Bible. He never knew how many times they smoked the name of God.

All day long he sat in his chair with his feet propped up on the bars and looked from underneath the pulled-down visor of his cap at the grayish-white cell house wall. Every time a spider built a new web, he knew it at a glance. All day long he heard the Negro convict up above singing a monotonous ballad: "*Ah'm blue, but Ah wont be blue always, 'cause de sun gwine shine in mah backdo' some day. Ah feels lak layin' mah head on some railroad line, and let de midnight special pacify mah mind . . .*" His nerves ran out through his skin like crawling worms; he dug his nails into his palms, drawing blood, trying to get a handful of them to mash.

Now and then when they could borrow some old greasy deck, he played head and head cards with Cook. At other times he argued with Gay about the Bible; one of those perpetual, stupid, pointless arguments which never ceased and in which neither of them were ever convinced by the other's logic, which flared and waned and dragged and picked up again and changed characters and shifted Books, always and forever and eternally on the Bible, which Gay had read and had never understood and never would, Jimmy felt, and which he, himself, had never read, and never would, he thought. But, queerly, they did not once become angered, thereby earning the other's respect. Years afterward, Jimmy was to learn that Gay grew to think of him as his best friend during that time.

After Boyer, they did not seem to keep any cell mate long in the fourth bunk. The first to come was Harrison, a slow-drawling, cantankerous, evil-eyed, lanky Arkansan, who had the strength of four men in his rawboned frame, and who was wanted in Little Rock to finish a life sentence which he had left AWOL. He stayed for a time, lying fully dressed on his bunk all day, stinking as if he never washed, answering in his laconic "Yassuh's" and "Nossah's", until one Sunday morning he awakened and said, "Gawdamighty spit on a razor-back hawg, Ah'm evil this mawnin' as an ovah-worked mule."

When the guard knocked for breakfast, he said, "Tell ole Button Ah ain' goin'."

And he did not go until a couple of lieutenants and four more guards came after him. He was transferred into 1-D, the heart-trouble company, where he was given special diet and range privileges, and there he remained until the day he got to thinking about the long life down in Little Rock and set his bunk on fire with himself in it. They got him out before he burnt to death, and when he had recovered, sent him to the asylum, from which he escaped.

The inventor came next. Casserton by name, he had invented an automobile to be operated by hot air. He had fashioned a tiny model from tobacco cans and strips of aluminum; and nights, he talked to them hours on end of how it would revolutionize the automobile industry.

"Simple, isn't it?" he would ask, looking about, and Jimmy would say, sotto voce, "Not so much as you."

After a week or two he was transferred. Jimmy never learned what became of his invention, although a couple of years later he heard that Casserton was over in the L block, passing the time of day fishing in his commode.

There were others who came and went, whom afterwards he did not recall. Finally Cook was transferred, and he and Gay were left to argue about the Bible. And all the time, thoughts of Lively, whom he had grown to think of as a martyr, ran through his mind like tiny streamers of flame, consuming it. He wrote long, impassioned letters, trying to cheer him. Oddly, his interest changed character, and pity took the place of the sex attraction. More than anything else, he wanted to do something noble for him.

Many times, in the long rambling letters, he quoted inspiring verses. "*Friend,*" he once quoted, "*there must be happiness ahead. I'm sure we'll spend a day of cheer for every little tear we've shed;*

why don't we make light of our sorrows and smile 'til they are done. We've got so many tomorrows to find our place in the sun."

Along about the last of January he received a check from the Industrial Commission for five hundred and fifteen dollars, the accumulation of back compensation, and was awarded thirteen dollars and sixty-nine cents weekly for the duration of a year, and strangely, or perhaps only naturally, his first thoughts were not of Lively, but of freedom. In fact, he did not think of Lively at all until the thoughts of freedom had worn themselves completely out.

It was so unlike the first freedom of those first scared months which had haunted him, and of which he had tried so hard not to think, the completely lost, completely remote, completely unseen, merciless, indifferent, impossible freedom at the end of twenty years, always at the end of twenty years, which left him feeling that he walked upon a treadmill, trudging doggedly, persistently, continuously, deliberately onward, but never coming closer. It was a bright, tantalizing, luring freedom, so close and so beautiful and so possible, it seemed, lifting him up into heights of hope of which he had never dreamed, throwing off the years as the casting aside of a cloak. Other convicts had bought their freedom for less, and he had five hundred dollars to spend.

He secured the addresses of several attorneys whom had been recommended to him by other convicts in the past, and early in February wrote to them. They did not get him out, perhaps he was in too great a hurry, but from them he learned that second to money, an attorney seems almost always to want time. His five hundred dollars would not wait for them. His was the most impatient five hundred dollars in all the world.

After a couple of weeks had passed, he wrote to the warden, who convicts claimed could get him pardoned overnight, and offered him the five hundred dollars for his release. Sealing the letter in an envelope, he dropped it into one of the mail boxes marked *Private-warden*. If the warden received the letter, he gave no sign of it; although Jimmy was fortunate he was not put in the hole.

Next, he tried the parole and record clerk, a Mr. Bronsen, whom the convicts said could put him on the bricks in a breeze. He received no reply from Mr. Bronsen, either. He tried old Pete Becker, the tin shop guard, who informed him, "Now, son, there are strings and there are strings. It's just like a lot of strings which look just alike are hanging from a ceiling. If you pull the right one the gates open, but if you don't know the one, you can stand there pulling for twenty years."

"But how do I know the right one?" Jimmy asked.

"Son, you don't, but I do," captain Becker informed him.

But in the end, he had to give up captain Becker, too. He tried the inspector, the cashier, the governor's secretary, and every attorney out in the city who had any sort of reputation whatsoever. They all told him practically the same thing: He was not ripe, yet; he had not served enough time on a twenty year sentence; after two or three more years—

But he could not think ahead for two or three years. If he could not have his freedom then, to hell with it. For a time he devoted his efforts in an attempt to get transferred to the prison farm, which was the road to freedom. It was the same, however; he had not served enough time.

Failing in this, his thoughts turned back to Lively. But they were different, now, although he did not know it. There was a slight bitterness in them, a slight chagrin, something of the emotion of one who returns a failure.

IN THE SEMI-GLOOM of early morning, a sand-fine drizzle laid a wet, gray blanket over the prison yard, and the lights in white-enameled reflectors, hanging from the above darkness, cast a million, elongated, crazy-angled shadows. The eternally lighted cell houses, seen from without, were huge stone mausoleums containing a thousand yellow eyes crisscrossed by bars, casting long yellow shafts over the wet sidewalks. It was like a dead city in a strange dead world, outlined in the pale, continuous, eternal yellow light; it was old and weird and sinister.

They marched close together, with bowed heads and turned up collars, with something of abjectness in the droop of their shoulders. It was when they shuffled up the worn, wooden stairs, into the brilliantly lighted chapel, that it touched him. Just inside the doorway, as he reached toward the basin of Holy Water to form the sign of the cross, it touched him, filling him with a clear awe.

Above, streamers of colored tissue swung from chandeliers, striping the sky-blue ceiling with a suggestion of rainbows; while below, gray clad convicts, some bent forward on their arms on the backs of the benches ahead, others kneeling, filled the brown-painted pews like muted stripes of undertone.

Great corsages of freshly cut flowers and potted evergreens made a flower garden about the altar railing; beyond, the altar stood, white, and chaste, and untouchable. Yellow candle flame, eternally burning, reached pale fingers toward a crucifix of beaten bronze, and the plaster Saints looked down with their benign countenances.

There was a Rosary of tiny lighted bulbs to one side; to the other, a miniature replica of ". . . the sepulchre at the rising of the sun . . ." The windows were covered with stained paper, cutting out the sight of prison. There was a cathedral air about the scene which went down into Jimmy. Coming from the sinister semi-gloom of the prison yard, he felt lifted into heaven.

And then, looking toward the altar again, he saw chubby, pink-faced Mike, one of the acolytes, as rotten a girl-boy as was in prison, and it came back to him, like a smut on clean white linen, that beneath that white, chaste, untouchable altar, he had seen convicts in lewd embrace following the fire the year before, and everything was gone—the touch of God, the pure, clear awe, the sight of heaven. It left him feeling as sloppy as a jag on beer. And then he turned into the pew and squeezed in beside Lively.

"Why the hell don't you sit somewhere else, fellow," Lively

rasped in a high, tight voice, turning red. "You see this seat is filled."

"So that's the way you're going to act after I go to all the trouble to come up here to see you?" Jimmy whispered tensely, keeping his lips stiff so the lieutenant, who was directing the seating, couldn't tell that he was talking.

"Don't speak to me!" Lively yelled.

Hearing him, the lieutenant came down the aisle.

"Don't talk so loud," Jimmy cautioned. "Joe Ayret's coming down this way."

"I hope he comes in here and throws you out," Lively said, still talking loudly. "You're not a Catholic anyway."

The lieutenant stopped in the aisle and looked at him.

"Go on and rat, that's what you want to do," Jimmy whispered.

"The next time there's any talking in here, I'm going to clear out the whole bunch of youse guys," the lieutenant said, staring at Lively for a moment before moving down the aisle.

As the priest, followed by his convict acolytes, entered from the alcove and approached the altar, everyone became quiet. "*I will go in unto the Altar of God,*" he said, forming the sign of the cross.

"*Unto God, who giveth joy to my youth,*" the congregation responded.

"What's the matter with you?" Jimmy asked Lively. "What the hell you so shirty about?"

Lively didn't reply. From the back of the chapel, the soft strains of an organ floated gently over the congregation, spreading a flow of motion as the convicts formed the sign of the cross.

"What have I done now?" Jimmy wanted to know. "Every time I want to talk to you, you freeze up and get shirty, but Kippy Mike and Matt Brock can—"

"You're the lousiest convict I know," Lively grated.

"So that's the way I get treated when I come up here with all good intentions of doing something for you?"

"I don't need you to do anything for me."

"Well, if that's the way you feel—"

"That's the way I feel!"

Jimmy looked toward the altar where the two acolytes were moving about, assisting the priest in the service of the mass.

"*Send forth Thy light and Thy truth,*" the priest chanted in his flexible voice.

"I know I haven't been acting so hot since I got my money," Jimmy began defensively.

"Money! Money! *Money!*" Lively grated. "That's all you think of. I don't see how I could have ever thought you a friend."

"I like you a hell of a lot, kid, no matter what you think," Jimmy declared.

"You have a lousy way of showing it," Lively snarled, but Jimmy could see that he was weakening, so he said quickly.

"That's what I want to talk to you about. I saw some shoes advertised in Thursday's *Dispatch;* I want to get you a pair. I didn't know your size so I—"

"I don't need any shoes," Lively interrupted. "I don't want you to get me anything."

After that, they were silent for a time, listening to the service of the mass.

Then Lively said, "You think you can buy me with your money. Well, you can't! I'll stay up there and smoke twists until I rot before I take anything of yours."

"That's what you've always said, but you're wrong," Jimmy contended. "I don't want to make you, kid, I just like you, that's all. The only reason I want to buy you things and share my money with you is because I'm your friend, that's all."

"I wish I could believe that, Jimmy," Lively said, his voice softening. He looked at Jimmy through the corners of his eyes, looked away.

"I mean it, kid," Jimmy said, looking at him. "Look at me, don't you think I mean it?"

Lively glanced at him, and suddenly blushed, his eyes becoming bashful and smoky gray. All of the hard-edged antagonism went out of him, leaving him soft and pliable. "You look funny," he drawled in his high, choir-boy voice, and began laughing, low and muffled.

Hearing that laugh again, Jimmy filled with a maudlin affection. Realization of how much he had missed it surged through him, and he said, "Listen, kid, I'm the best friend you ever had—don't ever forget that."

After a moment, Lively asked, "Why didn't you answer my notes?"

Jimmy started to lie and say that he had, then thought better of it. "I would have but I hadn't made up my mind," he said. "I didn't want you to be expecting something when I wouldn't be able to do it."

"What were you trying to do?"

"I've been trying to get you out of that company. I tried Brownie first—"

"That rat!"

"How did I know he was a rat?" Jimmy flared defensively. "He's been all right with me all along. You think everybody's a rat."

"That's the trouble with you; you don't know who is a rat?"

"Hell, he's been taking my notes to you all along—"

"I was gonna tell you to stop sending them by him. He takes them all to the deputy to read first."

"Does he?" Jimmy's stomach went hollow. "I won't after this," he declared.

After a moment, he said, "I tried Dean and Schooley, and then I tried Fats over in Stout's office. I even offered Fats a hundred dollars if he could get you out of there."

"You're a fool, Jimmy," Lively said angrily. "Now you've gone and queered me sure enough. It'll be just the same after this as if they'd caught me dead to rights."

"I'm sorry," Jimmy mumbled, slightly piqued. "But how in the hell was I to know they'd take it like that?"

"Shhhh, here comes Joe Ayret," Lively cautioned.

Stopping at the end of the pew, the lieutenant said, "Come out of there!"

They looked at him, but neither replied.

"You! I'm talking to you," the lieutenant said, pointing to a convict on the bench ahead. "Come on out of there!"

They breathed again. After a moment the convict arose and reluctantly squeezed out into the aisle. The lieutenant took him by the arm and started to the hole.

"I thought he had us," Jimmy said.

Lively nudged him.

After waiting a time, Jimmy said, "What I was thinking about doing was trying to get over in the company with you."

"Don't do that, Jimmy, it's tough over there."

"It can't be any tougher than where I am."

"Oh, yes it is. Those guys up there will drive you nuts. All they talk about all day long is men." He blushed.

"You make it all right," Jimmy pointed out.

"Not because I want to."

"What I was thinking about doing is making a list of the things you need and buy them for you."

Before Lively could reply, the priest began communion, and they gave him their attention. Convicts who had attended confession the day before had been given pink passes which permitted them to receive communion.

Standing before the altar, offering the chalice in outstretched hands, the priest chanted, "*We offer unto Thee, O Lord, the chalice of salvation, beseeching Thy clemency that, in the sight of Thy Divine Majesty, it may ascend with the odor of sweetness, for our salvation, and for that of the whole world . . .*"

After a moment the convicts went forward and knelt at the altar railing. One of the acolytes passed and collected the pink passes; the priest followed, reciting the Latin ritual, and pressing a Holy Wafer into each open mouth. The second acolyte came behind and held the empty chalice to their lips.

Again and again, the altar railing cleared of kneeling convicts and others took their places. Lively went forward in the third group. Watching, Jimmy wondered detachedly what he got out of it; if he got anything which he could take back to the cell up on 5-D.

When Lively returned, he said, "I'm going to get you some socks and underwear and smoking. And the next candy day, I'll get you a box of candy. Sometime next week I'll turn ten dollars over to your credit so you can order for yourself. I'll tell the deputy I owe you ten dollars for, er—I'll tell him I borrowed it from you and am just now paying it back."

Waiting until the wafer had dissolved on his tongue, Lively replied, "You don't need to get the rest if you just get me some candy and smoking."

"Oh, I'll get the shoes, too," Jimmy said.

"You're all right, Jimmy," Lively acknowledged, smiling. "You mean well, but you're awfully crude."

Jimmy laughed. "Get any mail recently? How's your mother and sisters?"

"I got a letter from my mother last week. She's been sick."

"I'm sorry; I hope she get's better."

"How's your mother and brother?"

"Oh, they're fine. The old man's okay, too."

After leading a congregational prayer for the convicts who had died in the fire a year ago, the priest pronounced benediction, closing the service. The convicts stood up and filed out.

"See you next Sunday," Jimmy said. "I'll bring the shoes out then."

"So long, Jimmy."

They parted at the bottom of the stairs. As always, Lively had done Jimmy all the favors.

ON THE WAY BACK to his cell, Jimmy asked the guard, captain Rizor, a fat, red-faced man, for permission to stop at Blocker's cell and get a newspaper.

"Well, make it snappy," Rizor consented grudgingly.

Breakfast was over, but the convicts had not been called out to the Protestant service, and only the cells in which Catholics bunked were unlocked.

Stopping at Blocker's cell, Jimmy said, "Lemme have last Thursday's *Dispatch*. I want to get an ad out of it."

Blocker got up and began leafing through a stack of old newspapers on the shelf. "How's the kid making out up there in the gal-boy company?" he grinned.

Jimmy laughed. "It's bearing down on him, but it hasn't started mashing him yet."

"Hurry up, hurry up there, Monroe!" Rizor called.

Jimmy didn't reply.

"I had that paper right here in this stack," Blocker said, then turning to one of his cell mates, he asked, "You see that Thursday's paper that was here?"

"Get on down to your cell!" Rizor called. "You've had time enough."

"Aw, go to hell!" Jimmy said under his breath.

Rizor jumped up and started down the range. "Now by God, you get on down to your cell or I'll kick your ass!"

Jimmy shot him a glance and saw that he was red and puffing, so he turned away and started slowly down the range. But Rizor kept after him. As his footsteps grew closer, Jimmy became tighter and tighter until all of his senses pulled bloodless taut, and when Rizor ran up behind him and tried to kick him, a great white flame enveloped him, blasting out all reason and thought and mental perceptions and he wheeled savagely and gripped Rizor and slammed him against the bars and shook him like a rat. And then, with his fist cocked shoulder high as he was about to hit Rizor, his reason and sanity flooded back, dispelling his fury and draining his strength, leaving him weak and limp. And that was the cruelest trick his reason ever played on him; for he didn't hit Rizor. And forever afterwards he regreted it; regretted not beating him unmercifully right then, beating his porcine face into a bloody, unrecognizable mask, while his body was possessed with the strength of fury and insanity.

214

Sensing his return to reason, Rizor ceased to look alarmed, and became infuriated himself in turn. He struck at Jimmy with his stick, but Jimmy caught the stick, and holding it, backed down the range.

Locked in their cells and unable to be of any help, the convicts began to yell and scream, "Don't hit that boy! . . . Don't hit that boy, you dirty rat! . . . Let go of that boy, you bastard!"

Suddenly realizing that should the guards, assembled down in the well to take the companies to chapel, hear them and come up on the range and find him scuffling with Rizor, they would beat him without mercy. Rizor became the hottest piece of flesh he had ever held.

"I'm not trying to hurt you, captain," he began, holding to the stick and backing away. "I'm not trying to hurt you, captain. I'm not trying to hurt you, captain."

In an effort to wrench the stick from his grasp, Rizor lost his grip on it, and Jimmy found himself with a stick and no desire to use it. Rizor reached toward his hip pocket, and thinking he was reaching for a gun, Jimmy went paralyzed with fear. He knew that if Rizor did have a gun, he would shoot him in the belly at point blank range with no hesitation. He stood there, unable to move, and watched Rizor draw the object from his pocket.

When he saw that it was only a blackjack, he threw back his head and sucked in air; and then laughed, abruptly, loudly. Rizor swung with the blackjack. Jimmy ducked and caught his wrist. And then again began, "I'm not trying to hurt you, captain . . . I'm not trying to hurt you, captain . . . I'm not trying to hurt you, captain . . ."

Finally, Rizor pulled away. "Get on down to your cell," he grated. "I ought to report you. Get on down to your cell. Don't you never disobey me again. Get on down to your cell."

Again laughter bubbled inside of Jimmy, but he was wary. He stepped cautiously past Rizor, turned and backed away from him, watching him. Down the range, he stooped and picked up his cap where he had dropped it in the scuffle, never taking his eyes of Rizor. When he came to his cell, he backed inside, pulled the door behind him, then straddled a chair facing the front.

"Whew!" he exclaimed, mopping the sweat from his face, and still feeling that queer, inner desire to laugh.

"You better watch out, Monroe," Gay warned. "Captain Rizor's a mighty treacherous man. He'll slip up behind you and hit you in the head."

"Aw, he's cooled off now," Jimmy said.

A moment later Rizor and two other guards appeared before his cell. Rizor opened the door and started inside, but when Jimmy jumped up and gripped the chair, he backed out again.

"Come on out, I'm going to take you to the hole, you smart bastard," he said.

Jimmy had but one short minute to decide whether to remain in his cell and try to fight it out, or go along with the guards and take a chance on them not hitting him.

Rizor stood to the left of the door, gripping his stick; captain Davis, a big, head-whipping, convict-hating guard, stood to the right. Only the presence of the hall guard, a slim, gray-haired man by the name of Gabardine, who by reputation was a square-shooter, never allowing another guard to hit a convict in his presence, gave Jimmy the courage to obey.

Assuming a posed bravado, he stepped from the cell jauntily, his eyes on Davis, placing a confidence in Gabardine to protect him from behind. As he turned, a sheet of living, burning flame, studded with a million bright yellow and reddish and orange stars, exploded just behind his eyes, as if the nerve which led from his eyeballs to his brain had been dynamited, while his eyes still contained the picture of the range jerking suddenly to within a foot of his face. He reeled twenty feet down the range before he realized that he had been hit, then he began running, slowly and sluggishly and slanting precariously forward. He had to keep running faster and faster to keep from falling on his face, he felt so top-heavy and utterly unreal.

At the end of the range he passed another guard, and another one on the steps going down to the well, but neither of them tried to stop him. He ran out of the cell house, down the stone steps, down the walk in front of the Catholic chapel, and turned into the deputy's office. Blood, spurting from a wound in his scalp, poured down the back of his neck and caught in the collar of his shirt, flowing around to the front, so that it appeared to the clerk in the deputy's office as if his throat had been cut. He gave Jimmy a look and his eyes stretched into huge, white buttons.

"The deputy in?" Jimmy gasped.

"No, but—"

Without waiting for him to finish, Jimmy wheeled and ran outside, turned down the sidewalk toward the hospital. Lieutenant Joe Ware, coming from around the corner of the building, stopped him, holding to his arm.

"Hey, wait a minute there, boy, what's the matter? Where you going? What you been doing? Who cut you?"

"Captain Rizor hit me over the head," Jimmy gasped.

"Well, come on back and talk to the deputy," Ware said, turning him about.

They met the deputy's clerk at the door, and Ware asked, "The deputy in?"

"No sir, he hasn't come in yet."

"Did you see this boy when he came in?"

"Yes sir, I was standing here."

"Was he fighting any of the guards?"

"No sir, he came in by himself."

"What was the trouble, boy?" Ware asked Jimmy.

"Captain Rizor told me to step out of my cell—he and captain Gabardine and captain Davis were standing out on the range—and when I stepped out and turned my back, he hit me on the head." He could still feel the blood running down his scalp and the back of his neck, saturating his shirt and underwear down to his waist where its flow was stopped by his belt.

"Come on, I'll take you to the hospital," Ware said, leading him outside again.

At the hospital, they shaved the hair from about the wound and closed it with three metal clamps, then applied a dressing. The doctor gave him three pills to take then, and a bottle of medicine to be taken every hour with water. They found the deputy in on their return to his office, and he sent Jimmy back into the hole without questioning him.

The convict attendant was absent and the lieutenant could not find Jimmy a change of clothing, so he locked him in the cell as he was clothed. All that night he stayed in the hole with the blood drying to his skin, and his head aching with a living pain. The next morning, the deputy sent him back to his company.

For a time he was filled with being mean and looking tough and carrying a chip on his shoulder. He bought a knife and slung it down his sleeve and hoped another guard would try to hit him. Every time he stepped out on the yard, death perched on his shoulder.

But after a week he threw away the knife. And later, after he had bought the things for Lively, he sent his mother a check for one hundred dollars. Her reply, stating that the receipt of his check was one of the most wonderful things which had ever happened to her, as the servants in the home where she worked as a companion treated her like a dog, thinking that she had no friends or relations and no place to go, set him up as nothing Lively had ever done. Reading, "I carried that check around for a week and waved it under their noses," gave him a feeling of importance which lasted for a time, compensating in part for all the humiliation he had suffered. Only, whenever he saw Rizor, he remembered that he had run.

JIMMY HAD SENT HIM fifteen dollars for railroad fare, and he came down to the prison one Thursday afternoon, looking so thin and haggard and gray that Jimmy was frightened. He was wearing

Jimmy's shoes and hat and gloves and overcoat and suit, which he had left at home. Shorter than Jimmy, he had had the suit cut down.

All during the visit he cried, sobbing again and again, "Oh, if I just had my life to live over," until Jimmy felt like saying, "It's all right, but please don't cry. After all, you can at least leave in a few minutes."

It was as if he had robbed the people and had been sentenced to twenty years in the penitentiary instead of Jimmy; and it was Jimmy who tried to comfort him, "It's all right, dad. Don't cry, dad. You did the best you could, dad," until his voice clogged in his throat.

He told Jimmy that he could go into a business and make some money and establish another home for them in the place of the one which they had lost when he and Jimmy's mother had become divorced. He could make a home for Jimmy to come to upon his release—if he only had some money to start him off. All of his thoughts centered on establishing a home for them, he said.

"It's all my fault," he sobbed. "I tried to do the best I could for you children, but when your mother and I were divorced—"

"I know, I know, dad," Jimmy tried to comfort him. "You did the best you could. It's all right, dad. It's all right. I'm going to give you four hundred dollars to get started in business—that's all I've got."

"If I just had my life to live over," his father cried.

Jimmy called the guard and filled out a money order for four hundred dollars, which he gave to his father, and which his father accepted, crying, and left. For a time, he sent his father forty dollars a month.

His father never visited him again.

8

THE LAST WEEK in June, 1932, Jimmy was moved into cell #9 with Chump Charlie, Big Brown, and a tall, dried-up Mississippian called Pappy Calhoun, so that colored convicts could be put in #12.

Chump had a deck of cards and at night they played seven-up. It was extremely hot that June, and each evening, after supper, Dean brought Chump a bucket of warm water in which to take a bath. Chump had a safety razor and all kinds of lotions and powders and perfumes, and after bathing he shaved, twice each week shaving the hairs from his chest and legs and underneath his arms, after which he massaged himself with lotions and perfumes and dusted himself with powder until the cell smelled like a whore's boudoir. Convicts in the cells on each side and above and below and some-times in cells farther removed would yell at him, "I hear you, Chump."

"Do you hear me?"

"We hear you over this way, too, kid."

"How do I sound?" he would ask, winking at Jimmy and looking pleased with himself.

"Like a mel-o-dee . . . Sweet-lee and loving-lee . . . Like ready for—"

Chump got a kick out of it. Later in the evening while they played cards, he wore silk shirt uppers and silk pyjama trousers with his smooth, powdered and lotioned arms showing, and his face powdered and shaved, and his hair parted in the middle and falling down on each side like a careless bob, smelling as bitchy as a wench on the make, which is what he was because he had his mind set on Jimmy.

The third night, as he lay on his upper bunk across the cell, in his silk, tight-clinging underwear, with his perfumed scent and his white, shaved, lotioned limbs slightly dusted with dark ancestry,

220

his hair down in his eyes, he winked at Jimmy, forming words with the mold of his lips, "Come over when they go to sleep, I'll be nice to you," begging with his eyes.

Choking on the perfume, looking into Chump's begging eyes, Jimmy thought of all the whores he should have had to carry him womanless through those endless years; thought: What the hell, it's night now and when Big Brown and Pappy go to sleep nobody will ever know; thought: What the hell, all these sons of bitches in here do it and if you don't think about it afterwards how can it hurt you, anyway, because nothing can hurt you that you don't think about; thought: I'm a convict now, a goddamned convict doing time. What have I got to lose? thought: I could this time because I don't see how I'm going to be able not to if he keeps looking like that and I keep feeling like this; thought, finally: Oh well, I've done a whole lot of things probably a hell of a lot worse.

And then, at the last moment, reneged, lost all desire and wanted to hit Chump in the mouth for making him think of it at all. Afterwards, he cursed Chump, called him everything he could think of because he had come so near.

But the next morning Chump said, "Hello, Jimmy," in a tenor lilt and winked as if they had a secret.

Jimmy said, "Good morning, Brown. What do you say this fine morning, Pappy." And finally, " 'Lo," to Chump.

He felt a deep chagrin. Last night is gone and past and lost and as dead as if it had never been, he told himself because he needed to know it, and then to Chump he said, but not aloud: And to take some of the smug complacency out of you, bitch, I ought to let you know that the actual peak could never have come from you even if I had gone through with it, but was only within me when my desire was at its highest, like the peak which comes when the woman you've wanted for so long at last undresses before you, taller than you'll ever get again no matter what she does; and after that, even if I had taken you, which God forbid, you would have only been anticlimax. And anyway, it'll never come that close again because it wouldn't be nearly so tall as it was then, because it never is.

But Chump kept after him, getting something it seemed from

his abuse, until Jimmy hated the sight of him. In the light of the day and the darkness of the night, he hated him. With the sight of his begging, sickening eyes, and the scent of his rank, sweet, clogging perfume, he hated him, utterly contemptuous of him.

It was not what Chump was that made Jimmy hate him so, but what he thought he was, so very clever and smart and wise, sitting there day after day talking about the other fags in prison, so condescendingly. "The dumb, simple bitches," he'd say. "Out there on that stem for a sack of smoking. And they call themselves smart."

Looking at him, Jimmy thought: Why, you half-witted slut, you've given your soul to me and thrown everything you ever had at me, and you're not even going to get a sack of smoking for it. You're not going to get anything. And just to prove how dumb you are, who think you're so smart, I'm going to make you so low that you can walk on stilts underneath a snake's belly. I'm going to make you so sick of yourself that you're going to throw away your silk lingerie and let the hairs grow back on your body and start wearing the long gray cotton drawers that scum convicts, like what you are, and don't know it yet, wear. And you never will get anything for it but plenty of abuse.

And yet he could see no reason why he should think like that.

Each candy ordering day he bought two boxes of candy and sent one to Lively and the other to Blocker, and then ate from Chump's boxes, the one Chump ordered for himself and the extra one Dean brought him. Three or four times a week Dean sent Chump hot sandwiches from the kitchen. Jimmy ate the best of them and gave Chump what was left. On top of which he bought Lively underwear and handkerchiefs and sox and then wore Chump's pyjamas. When his clothes became soiled he had Chump wash them, although Chump sent his own out by Dean to have them laundered. He wrote long, mushily passionate love letters to Lively, none of which he ever sent, and let Chump read them, acting all the while as if he did not want him to. When they went out on the yard, he avoided Chump, and on occasions barely replied when Chump addressed him directly, and then in the most brusk manner.

Once when Chump said, "God, Jimmy, you treat me so rough

when I love you so much. You're asking me to take a hell of a lot, Jimmy, a hell of a lot." He replied, "You know what you can do when you get tired."

And when suddenly Chump began to cry, he said, "I can stand much of what you say, but you're just contemptible when you try to impose your tears on me because I'll never feel sorry for you."

"What do you want with me, anyway, Jimmy?" Chump asked.

"I've never thought about it," Jimmy said.

"I'd kill you for that if I didn't love you so much," Chump told him.

"You've had a hell of a lot better reasons than that if you had wanted to," Jimmy thought, but didn't say it.

It was sometime during then that Lively started another campaign to get pardoned, and Jimmy had him send to Akron for the judge, John Stephens, who had sentenced him. Stephens was off the bench and was practicing law. When he came down, Jimmy went out with Lively to see him, and paid his fee of twenty-five dollars and his fare.

That night Dean stopped by the cell and gave Chump a five dollar bill, and after he had gone, Jimmy said, "Let me have that five, will you, Chump. I'm a little short right through here. I paid out all I had to have Lively's judge come down and see him. That's where I was when they called me out this afternoon."

"You certainly ask me to take a lot," Chump said, his eyes hot and feverish.

"So it's like that now, is it?" Jimmy said, feeling all the contempt for Chump that it was necessary for him to feel in order to keep from utterly despising himself, which he did anyway, which he could not help.

He was getting tired of prison and disgusted with himself. Tired and disgusted! Everything was stale flat beer sitting warm and pallid in the sun; or rather like a bloated corpse just before it begins to rot and stink. Tired and disgusted! Tired of the prison and disgusted with himself.

But the prison was indifferent. The days did not give a damn and the nights were no less long. Sunsets came and sunsets went and the walls were rooted just as deeply into the everlasting earth. Stone and steel and time coming and going but never staying and ever the eternal same. And he was getting tired of it. Tired of hearing and seeing and feeling and learning of the perfidy and degradation of convicts. Tired of murder and rape and jobs and hacks and sexual monstrosities.

Lively chose that time to accuse him, in a fit of pique, of trying to buy his friendship. They were up in the Catholic chapel one Sunday.

Stunned, Jimmy turned toward him, his mouth half open and his eyes out of focus. "What did you say?"

"You heard me! I said you are just trying to buy my friendship. That's what I said, and you know it's the truth."

He had said the same thing before, but this time it took hold. Jimmy started to hit him, but thought better of it. He simply got up and walked out of the chapel, and never went back.

It was gone and dead, everything that had ever been between them. And in going it left nothing, nor did anything come to take its place, no regret, no remorse, no loneliness. Loneliness would not have come, anyway, because Lively had never done anything to help the loneliness. It had been with Jimmy before he had ever seen Lively, and all the while he had known him, and would still be with him.

That was Lively. He was gone and that was that.

And then one night Chump said, "Kiss me, please, Jimmy."

"I wouldn't stoop so low as to kiss you under any circumstances," Jimmy replied.

Chump went for his knife, and for a moment Jimmy was frightened; but Chump didn't try to use it. Instead he said, "I'm through, Jimmy. I still love you but you ask me to take too goddamn much."

After that Chump let his beard grow long and gave away his silk underwear and pyjamas, and began wearing the state issue underwear again and sleeping in them. But in the end, when Jimmy had put him as low as he had to put him in order to feel that there was at least some one lower than himself, he still didn't get anything out of it.

That was Lively and Chump and 1932. Another year. That was the way the years went by. The things they brought, they took away. And the things they left, he didn't want, such as the shame and the self contempt and the feeling of being a convict. The weariness and disinterest. Those years! Those years! Another gone! And he was getting tired of it. Tired and disgusted!

THOSE WERE THE DAYS; the moving, living, endless days with legs that dragged but yet kept marching through the stone and steel and five-foot thicknesses of concrete walls. The days with bloody guts filled with the gory slime of degeneracy, enclosed with the gray stone blankness of walls, lashed with bars falling in steady monotonous blows—the bleeding, living, peopled days of convicts doing time.

Those were the indifferent, impersonal, unsympathetic, pitiless, merciless days that did not give a damn if a convict lived or died. Days that moved on and never returned, taking with them his shame, his prayers, his hopes, his disappointments and humiliations and sorrows and virtues and vices, indifferently, mockingly, deliberately, in which he either swam upon the crest or sunk below—either way no one particularly noticed and no one gave a damn.

But there were the nights, which were not nights at all but were the moments alone when he escaped the days. The moments when no one was with him, neither the convicts nor the guards nor the routine nor the discipline nor the rooted, immovable prison.

The nights of loneliness of which no one knew, which had no past, no future, no hope or perspective or foundations in respectability or beliefs or faith or love or hate, but which were only the times immediately present with thoughts which grew out of nothing and conclusions which grew out of them.

Those were the nights which were not nights alone but days and nights with moments when he was alone and were the times for crying and laughing, too, but were his own and were separate from the days which belonged to the slime and dirt and indifference of the peopled prison.

When locked in his cell those nights with nothing more exciting to occupy his mind, he turned to pondering (pondering in the manner in which I employ the term being that pastime devoted to asking yourself unanswerable questions).

To break the monotony of pondering he bought and read such magazines as *Liberty, Colliers, Cosmopolitan, Redbook, the Post,* and others. He became sickeningly romantic.

"Living up and down to a choice made because a bar of music struck obliquely across his heart and a hint of gentle spring was in the air . . ." He read that line and it made him cry—those deep, unshed tears that cry inside of you, which you feel trickling from your heart down into your hollow stomach.

How beautiful and desirable he found life in those wonderful love stories. Beautiful without comparison to past or future thoughts, beautiful for the picture they created out of the words, the night, the aloneness with his thoughts. They never brought regret or remorse or tried to pierce the gray veil of the unseen future, but only a poignant stab of yearning to be like that himself, then, at that immediate moment.

He read of those story-book characters' dilemmas and loves and hates and misfortunes and projected himself into their story-book lives and suffered with them, loved with them, sympathized with them, pitied and fought and prayed alongside of them, and experienced all the soft, mushy emotions which he could not experience in the brutal, rotten, fighting days. He made lonely crusades into fantastic dreamlands that grew out of the printed pages like skyrockets into the nights, and broke his heart a hundred thousand times.

And afterwards, after the nights had gone and the days had come he felt ashamed for those sentimentalities and was invariably more vulgar, obscene, callous. It was all very queer how the two parts of him were so ashamed of each other, the day of him and the night of him. It was also very queer how unrelated those thoughts were to the past, as if they had grown anew within him from nothing that had ever happened.

They slipped up on him and surprised him and oftimes confused him, for he knew not whence they came, nor in fact just what they were, unless they were in fact some stage of insanity through which he was passing, or which was more to be feared—into which he was entering. There were those two things that he did not want to do, and going crazy was one of them. The other was to die. So many times he did not like his thoughts, for they would woo the one and mock the other. They were too new, too uncontrolled, too grisly, too bloody, too fantastic, too sheerly lovely; they were too extreme to go along with his clogged senses of comprehension. They led him merry chases, and chases which many times were not merry but were in fact gruesome and horrible. They remained with him when the night remained with him and his only escape from them was into the day itself where they could not follow. In the day he was safe from them. But so many times they were pleasant, and being safe from them was not to be desired. And there were so many, many times when they supplied the haven and were not the storm at all.

All those confused and not very clear and not very old and too touching thoughts and emotions which grew out of those nights, out of hackneyed, tear-squeezing stories, out of lying awake when he should have been asleep, or from an old tune in clear notes on some distant convict's mandolin—a sudden lilt of melody across a moment's mood like an eccentric artist's fingers upon the chords of chaotic groping, weaving into romantic confusion or violent rebellion the new and jumbled and not very clear and too touching thoughts and emotions of those nights alone.

Feeling the desolation of night when the sounds were dim and the voices gone and the cells were dark—and hearing a Negro's stirring voice break through the hammered quietness, singing low:

"W'en Ah had moneeeEEE, Ah had fren's fo' miles aroun'; but since Ah done got busted, Ah ain' got a single fren in town . . ."

And those thoughts, like tongueless words, like the sidewalks trying to speak, like the mute prayers of the black scared night, weaving fantastic, unsleeping dreams into patterns of girls who were never born, and muted tones that were never played, and poems that were never written; into tense emotional situations wherein he always acted in a brave and noble manner; into horses breaking the barrier at Saratoga while he leaned against the railing, cigaret curling a nonchalant ribbon of smoke into the blue, sunny sky, with fifty thousand dollars on *Red Rosebud* . . . "They're off! . . . She's trailing at the half . . . She's fifth at the three-quarters . . . She's third at the turn . . . She's second down the stretch . . . Here they come! . . . It's a race! It's a race!" RED ROSEBUD BY A NOSE! Fifty thousand dollars at three to one . . . Grinding the cigaret under heel; strolling over towards the club house . . . "Look, Tony, see if you can string this two hundred grand out on *Blue Moon* in the seventh." Once in a blue moon . . .

Only in his thoughts. The lovely, stimulating, bittersweet sensations—so utterly unreal. Like something from another world.

And the next day, ashamed of them. Ashamed as if they were the clap, or syphilis, or cancer.

I N JANUARY, 1933, 2-B company, along with several convicts from 1-B, and a number of others from the G&H block, were transferred to the 2-E&F dormitory. No reason was given, and no one cared; they all liked the dormitory best, anyway.

It was wonderful in the dormitory this time, the convicts said;

it was marvelous, it was solid rickey. Every one had money; the guards were easy; nothing to do but lie around and spoil. Jimmy and Blocker began their poker game again; it was expected of them.

The United States government had paid off the veterans' bonus, and many had been granted monthly compensation. About one-third of the convicts in the dormitory were veterans; and most drew bonuses in excess of five hundred dollars. At the ratio of five for four, they bought cash money for credit in the front office. Shortly, there were hundreds of dollars in cash within the dormitory.

Frank Steeplecross, the head guard, had once been county sheriff, and had owned the largest house on the highest hill in town, it was said. He had been the most notorious fence in the state, open to any and all kinds of graft; and his income had been tremendous until an investigating committee had caught up with him. Now, fat and sixty, with gray-shot hair and a heart as bad as Jesse James was a man, he was a prison back at one-thirty per month, and only that through the grace of the warden who had known him in better days. Though the world had moved beneath him, and time had taken its toll, he had not changed; he was the same old Frank, open to any and all kinds of graft.

At Christmas the convicts had been given safety razors, but afterwards no blades had been issued. The convicts asked captain Frank to bring them blades. He got the idea. His nephew worked in a drug store downtown. That was all captain Frank needed. His nephew pilfered the goods, and captain Frank smuggled them into the dormitory—safety razors, blades, lotions, creams, shaving creams, toothpaste, soaps, powders, tooth and hair brushes, rouge, mascara, anything which he could sell. He got Big Wicks to handle the stuff for him; shortly Big Wicks had four boxes of toilet articles and was doing a rushing business all over the institution.

With so much cash in circulation, there arose disputes over the gambling games. The competition became so intense that gamekeepers, in order to reserve table space, had to arise before the lights were turned on and spread their blankets. Captain Frank come in one morning and found the tables covered from end to end with blankets.

He sent for Jimmy. "Jim," he said, "these fellows who can't get to run a game keep writing out to the warden and over to the inspector telling about us gambling up here." He laughed deprecatingly, spreading his hands. "You know, I don't want to get transferred to one of those working companies. It'd kill me climbing up and down those stairs with my heart." He had a voice like a ward-heeler's whisper.

"We'll take up a while and stop if you say so," Jimmy suggested.

"No, I don't want to stop them from gambling. You know, that's all the fun they have. I tell you what we'll do; I'll make you my head deputy and put you in charge of the gambling. Now this is the way we'll work it; we'll have four games a day, two for the white, two for the colored. You pick out fellows who got money and give them each a game for one day a week. Rotate 'em, see. The white fellows can have one poker game and one blackjack game; the colored fellows one poker game and one skin game. I don't want no dice. Now you can take the poker game for one day, and Blocker the blackjack game."

"Okay, Frank," Jimmy said. "I'll see what I can do."

"And listen, Jim, tell them that it will cost them a buck a game, and you collect it for me." He winked. "A buck from each game-keeper every day."

"Okay, Frank," Jimmy grinned, and started off.

"And wait a minute, Jim," captain Frank called. "I've been thinking about taking a day for myself. I'll tell you what I'll do; you pick out four good fellows, two white and two colored, and I'll take Wednesday and bank all the games myself and split fifty-fifty. No, I'll tell you, you run the poker game for me, Jim, and get Blocker to run a blackjack game for me. Then you and Blocker take a day for yourself and get you a couple of good colored boys who know how to keep their mouths shut and have them run the colored boys' games, and that'll give you a whole day and me a whole day, and the rest of them can split up what days as are left."

"I'll straighten it out for you, Frank," Jimmy promised.

And that was the way they ran it. Jimmy and Blocker took Sunday, which was the best day, and gave the bonus boys Saturday,

Friday, and Thursday, which were the next best respectively. Captain Frank had Wednesday, and all the gamekeepers had to play with him. They gave the rats Monday and Tuesday, on which days every one else played whist. It worked perfectly.

The manner in which the veterans got fleeced out of their money was an education in itself. Wives who had not visited them before, turned up on visiting days with hard luck stories, with sagas of misery, with rouged cheeks and mascaraed eyes and shiny smiles, with hands full of gimme and mouths full of much oblige. And those who did not have wives were tricked into affairs with other convicts' sisters or mothers or aunts or cousins or sweethearts and even in some cases with other convicts' wives. There was no risk. They told the bonus boys about these women, and had them write. The letters were smuggled back and forth by captain Frank. Almost immediately the women fell in love; but somehow, they all needed something, mostly money, the amount depending upon the size of the convict's bonus. And though the officials tried to restrain them, the convicts sent to their newly-discovered loves and prodigal wives all the money for which they asked.

No one could really blame them. For years they had gone along woman-starved and friendless, and suddenly they had five hundred, seven hundred, a thousand dollars. They were ripe for plucking by the first woman who said, "I love you," or by anyone, man, woman, or child, who wrote in from the outside on some lavender-colored stationery scented with narcissus perfume with an enclosed snapshot of a pretty girl.

Captain Frank got his, however, and Jimmy and Blocker got theirs. And when the officials saw how the wind was blowing, they got theirs.

In February the laws were changed, and Jimmy became eligible for a hearing by the parole board at the end of six years and five months, which threw him up in May, 1935. It had grown out of the prison fire. There had been a great deal of subsequent agitation about the congested condition of the prison, and public sentiment had turned against the severe, harsh laws. As a result, three laws had been passed: The first, which was retroactive, established statutory minimums and maximums for all offenses, thereby reducing Jimmy's minimum from twenty to ten years: The second provided for a graduated scale of time off for good behavior, which cut another three years and seven months from Jimmy's sentence: The third created a new parole board of four members.

Jimmy, along with the others, was greatly excited. He could see it now; he could see the end. Those two and a half years seemed so short. He could do them on his head, he told Blocker; he could do them standing on one leg. Although passage of the laws had been almost a certainty since the summer before, when word came in about ten o'clock that night that the first had been passed, the shouting of the convicts could be heard downtown.

Softball games were initiated that spring. It was the reaction. "Rehabilitate the convicts," the press cried. So the prison went "easy" again. By then both the I&K cell block and the new industrial building had been completed, and the ball diamond had been cleared of scrap and laid out into two softball diamonds. Three leagues were drawn up: a school league, a working league, and an idle league. The companies within the leagues organized their own teams; and schedules were worked out by the convicts in the print shop.

Two students of physical education from the university took charge of the program. Twice each week, directly after dinner, the companies in each league were marched down to the diamond, where first, for fifteen minutes, they were put through a series of calisthenics. Then four teams took the fields while the others retired to the grandstand, and two games were played.

Softball took hold of the convicts as nothing else ever had, and rivalry between the teams grew tall as trees. It was all softball that summer, the beginning and the end, just softball. They talked it, slept it, walked it, played it, fought it. They dreamed it, loved it, ate it, argued it. It was in their blood like the red corpuscles. And though the convicts in 2-E&F were supposed to be cripple in some manner or other, they were in the thick of it from the first.

Early in March, when it was first rumored they would have softball, captain Frank brought in a half dozen balls and took them back of the old wooden dormitory, down by the death house, to practice. They cleared away some of the rocks and made a small diamond.

Jimmy was elected manager of the team, and since they could find no one else to do it, he became their catcher also. Their first baseman, Johnny Brothers, shortstop, Baldy, and left fielder, Snakehips, were colored. Candy was at third, Chink and Jerry infield, and every one had a chance at second because they never found one who could play it. For pitchers they had little cripple Boyer, who was very wild, and a big, black fellow called Mose who could really throw them in—he could pitch so fast that every team they played would have the umpire go out and watch his delivery to see if it was legitimate—but he was so "evil" no one could tell what he would do next. Jimmy was the only one who could handle him at all, and even he had to beg him, and plead with him, and pay him to pitch.

But he and captain Frank had their chips down; they were playing for blood. And they had to keep Mose pitching in order to win. But it was a job. Captain Frank would say, "Whew," wiping the sweat out of his eyes, "these fellows have the goddamnest dispositions of any people I ever saw."

And Jimmy would reply, "You don't know the half of it."

However, captain Frank stuck with them right through the season. He went softball crazy. Sometimes he'd get so angry he would put his players in the hole for making an error. All one morning before an important game he had Mose out back of the death house warming up, and that afternoon his arm was so tired he couldn't get the ball up to the plate. Captain Frank swore that he had sold out to the other team and would have had him transferred had it not been for Jimmy and Johnny Brothers. He would try to bribe players on the other teams, but don't let one of his own players drop a ball or strike out with men on base. He'd swear the other guards were bribing his players.

Jimmy would watch him walking up and down the first base line with his big belly sweating in the sun, his white shirt sticking to his body, face red as paint, hat cocked on the back of his head, a lock of hair down in his eyes, talking a mile a minute in a disjointed babble of sighs and prayers and curses and cheers, and say to himself, "Jesus, don't let us lose this one."

At the end of the game captain Frank would be utterly exhausted, his shoulders sagging and his eyes registering the beginning of a heart attack. His unlighted cigar which he had lighted a hundred times would still be unsmoked but now chewed to a frazzle with slimy strings of tobacco hanging from his slack mouth.

The first thing after supper, even before the ball players got their rub-downs, some one would have to get a bucket of warm water for him to soak his feet and some one else would have to apply hot towels to his arms and cold towels to his head and work on him until his quitting time so he could get away under his own power.

That was captain Frank; he played each game harder than all the twenty players combined.

And then the very first thing the next day, as if he had lain awake all night thinking only of his team, he would be out scouting some new convict who had just entered the institution, trying to find out if he could play softball. He would go over to the cell block and slip up on 5-K and interview every new-comer he saw, and if he found one who said he could play he would start right off getting him groomed for the cripple company.

"You act cripple now, and I'll get you over in the cripple company," he'd say, talking through the corner of his mouth in that ward-heeler's whisper and acting as confidential as a tout on Derby Day. "Listen, I'll get you over there before they have a chance to ship you down into the mills." Just by implication he could make the cripple company sound better than freedom itself.

"Hey," he'd say, his face against the bars. "Pst, come closer. Got any smoking?"

"Why, er, no sir—"

"Take this and buy some," he'd say, giving the convict a dime. "And don't forget, there's plenty more where that came from. We have everything over in the cripple company. Best company in the joint. Nobody's cripple. All stiffing." And then he'd look up and down the range, knowing full well that there wasn't another guard in sight. "Now don't forget, just act cripple. Fall back in line. Act like you can't keep up. Let the line get away ahead and just keep on hobbling across the yard. Don't let any of those lieutenants bluff you. Just tell them you can't keep up. I'll get you."

"Yes sir."

"Get it?" he would ask, stretching his eyes interrogatingly.

"Yes sir, fall back, act like I can't keep up, don't let the lieutenants bluff you, just tell them you're cripple and I'll let the line get away ahead and then I'll get you, er-rer, I mean you'll get him, er-rer—"

"That's right, just—er, wait a minute, what did you say?" captain Frank would ask, his eyes stretching in earnest this time. "Say that again," he'd bark, not so certain that the convict had sense enough to act cripple, much less to play softball, and getting a vague idea that he had lost another dime.

Returning to the dormitory he'd send for Jimmy. "Hey, Jim, call Johnny Brothers. Tell him to come down here a minute. Tell him I got a kid coming in soon that can really play that second base . . ."

It was a good thing they won most of their games because captain Frank could not stand to lose. He almost died the time they lost to 3-D, which was supposed to be a breather. They were leading by a score of one to nothing going into the last half of the last inning when Mose blew up and walked the first two hitters. Captain Frank walked out on the diamond and talked to him and he steadied down after that and struck out the next two. Frank got his breath back. But Baldy fumbled a grounder to fill the bases. And the next hitter swung blind and hit one on the eye, sending it high and far into deep left-center field.

Snakehips and a new fielder they had, called Cat, started for it at the same time. When it became apparent that they were going to collide, captain Frank could be heard for a mile, yelling, "Let it alone, you black son of a bitch! Keep away from it! Oh, you dumb bastard!"

When they bumped and dropped the ball, captain Frank had a

235

heart attack and fell flat on his face. He had to be carried to the hospital on stretchers.

Snakehips was salty for days afterwards, and though Jimmy tried to placate him, in the end captain Frank had to apologize before he would play again.

"Aw, Snakehips, old boy, you know how a man says things when he gets excited," captain Frank said. "Don't take it so to heart. Here, take this dice and go down and win yourself something."

After Snakehips had left, he turned to Jimmy and said, "It's a hell of a racket, ain't it, Jim?"

The softball team ran that dormitory that summer. All they had to do was win games for captain Frank. After they had knocked over the colored convicts in the coal company who were supposed to be so good, they could name it and he would pay it. On rainy days they'd move the bunks and tables and practice in the dormitory.

It got to the place that all the officials would run when they saw captain Frank coming. He'd either want to get some player transferred into the cripple company or else he'd want them to arrange a game for his team on Sunday afternoon. He'd want something for his team.

It was fun while it lasted. It kept Jimmy from thinking about himself. It made those two and a half years seem so short. But the 10th of August it was stopped. No reason was given. And Jimmy was right back where he started. Right back with the degenerates and the stir bugs and the poker games and the rats and the envy and the stone and steel and bars. Monotony beat down the excitement of his shortened sentence and the years looked long again. Right back at the same old thing, doing time. Doing two and a half more years. That was plenty time.

And he was getting tired of it. Tired and disgusted.

11

BLOCKER WENT OUT on the 26th of August. Jimmy certainly hated to see him go. All down the line Blocker had been solid with him, on the high spots and on the low, in trouble and smooth sailing. They had been flush together, broke together; what had been one's had been the other's. Blocker had always been on his side, right or wrong; and not once since they had met in September of 1929 had one spoken a harsh word to the other.

Between them, they had about twenty-five dollars in cash at the time. Blocker kept twenty dollars of that, and Jimmy turned over thirty-five dollars to his credit and bought him a pair of shoes. He was given sixteen dollars and thirty cents by the state, so in all he had about seventy-one dollars to take out with him.

"Well, kid, I certainly wish you were going with me," he said when they called him.

"I wish so, myself," Jimmy replied.

"Is there anything you want me to do for you, kid?"

"Nope. I'm okay; just stay out of trouble yourself."

"I'll write to you," he said, "and if I don't it won't be because I ain't thinking about you. And if I get lucky I'll send you some dough."

"You needn't bother," Jimmy said.

"I'll try to write, anyway, kid."

"I won't look for it," Jimmy told him, "so if you don't, I won't be disappointed."

"Come on, Blocker, they're waiting for you," the runner called.

"Well, don't shoot no blanks, kid," he said to Jimmy.

They shook hands.

"When you get out, look me up around Akron or Detroit."

"I will," Jimmy said. "I hope you're in the money."

"Never give a sucker a break, kid," Blocker said, grinning

wolfishly. "Never give a sucker a break." He turned and went down front.

Jimmy threw up his hand and called, "See you." Blocker turned and went out. He never wrote. Jimmy never heard of him again. He certainly missed Blocker. It wasn't the same as he had missed Walter back in 1929. He missed Blocker as he would have missed an arm.

After that their game went to seed. He began losing while dealing. That had never happened to him before. He and Candy began doubling. But Candy could not win, either.

The convicts had said that he could not win without Blocker, that all along Blocker had been holding him up. They had prophesied that he would blow like a balloon bursting if ever Blocker left him; and they had prophesied correctly.

Jimmy lost steadily from the day Blocker left. Maybe he was trying too hard. He sat in those games and tried to play dead cinch, and chewed up cigaret holders as if they were match stems. He chewed a twelve-inch cigaret holder down to a stub within a week. He wanted to win so badly it became an obsession. But he couldn't get the hands, he told himself. That was all, he just couldn't get the hands.

But soon afterwards he sent his mother to come and establish residence in the city where the prison was located, and began sending her the forty dollars each month which he had previously sent to his father. He did not know what he had expected to get out of it, the feeling that he was not alone or the feeling that he was helping some one whom he loved. Whatever it was, he did not get it.

Only the days, the days, the goddamned days.

12

WHEN THE TALKIES CAME on Saturday afternoons, they helped. According to the statement which the warden made to the press, the six thousand and seven hundred dollars paid for the machine and screen had been taken from the convicts' amusement fund, a fund which the convicts had never heard of before. The way they figured it was that the warden had some money on hand which he could not explain. He was being investigated again.

In the Protestant chapel, where the pictures were shown, the seats were graduated like those in an arena, providing good visibility, although they were so congested there was not sufficient knee space. But the convicts put up with that; they did not even kick about it much. If they had not kicked about some feature, it would have been unnatural. And they liked the pictures too well to kick about them. They really went for the pictures, all of which were very, very good. No "bad" pictures were ever shown in that prison until the novelty of seeing them had worn off. Jimmy, along with most of the others, had never seen a talkie before, and he was amazed; they were all amazed. If they had been the movie-going public that year, every picture that Hollywood turned out would have been a box-office hit.

They saw Nancy Carrol in several of the early pictures. She played opposite Buddy Rogers in *Follow Through,* the second one they saw. They saw Clara Bow and Helen Kane in several of the early pictures, also. They went for all the women in an extravagant way, but Helen Kane, with her "boop-boop-bi-doop" and her rolling eyes and shaking hips, was their favorite . . . "Man, I'd do an extra life for some of that," they said . . . "Just take me out and hang me."

They liked everything about all of the pictures, the situations, the scenery, the stories, the action, the dialogue—everything! But those women's voices got the closest to them. Those and the songs. They were a little song-starved then, not having had radios since the fire, and always woman-hungry. When an actress began to speak, they leaned forward in a solid wave.

Out of all the really first-rate pictures which he saw, *Cimarron* and *Calvacade* and *Ben Hur,* and the musicals such as *Gold Diggers of 1933,* the picture called *Laughter,* starring Nancy Carrol and Fredric March, touched Jimmy more than any other.

When he said to her, "You're dying for want of laughter," Jimmy sailed like a kite, he caught a tear jag wet as the Pacific Ocean. *Dying for want of laughter!* Maybe you have to serve four years and get tired of it in order to understand. But out of all the ways which he could think of to die—jumping off a bridge, walking into the belch of a tommy gun, being electrocuted for first-degree murder, bumping off in bed with double pneumonia—dying for want of laughter was a hell of a thing to contemplate. There was a joker in it. Being in prison and hearing it said, and thinking, "So am I who came through the prison fire alive, dying in the end with only two and a half years to go simply because nothing is funny anymore."

He cried when he saw *Skippy.* Every tough, lousy, low convict in the audience cried when they saw *Skippy.* They sat up there and tears streamed down their faces. But it was good for him; it gave him a chance to cry out some of those tears he had been saving up so long. It was good to see *Skippy* and get a chance to cry.

They saw a young actor named Richard Arlen in *The Virginian.* Gary Cooper was the star of that picture, but Dick Arlen, playing the part of the no-account Steve who was hanged for horse stealing was the one whom the convicts liked. They sure did hate to see him hanged. Old Steve!

"He took it like a man, didn't he, jazz?"

"Like a thoroughbred; not a whimper."

They saw *The Big Broadcast* and heard Bing Crosby sing their never-forgotten *Please lend your little ear to my plea.* That one sent them; it wound them up and let them go. For weeks following, all day long, all over the prison, in the dormitories, on the yard, in the cells, all that could be heard was, *Your eyes reveal that you have the soul of an angel, white as snow* . . . And late at night, in the silence, a defiant guitar spelling out the word in plaintive notes: *P-L-E-A-S-E.* A sender! A solid sender!

They went for Bing. They loved him like a mother. They saw him in several other pictures, the titles of which they soon forgot, because Bing's songs were everything for them . . . *I Surrender Dear* . . . *Learn to Croon* . . . They tried hard enough even though they never did. They were not killed for trying . . . *If you want to win your heart's desire, learn to croon* . . . Aw, lay it, Mister Johnson . . . I'm laying it, ain't I? . . . Turn it over and lay it on the other side . . . *If you want to win*— Just one side. Bing's songs. Over and over again until that prison became a music school.

They saw Joan Crawford and Franchot Tone . . . "Man, look at that sucker kiss that gal . . ." And Maurice Chevalier in *The Smiling Lieutenant.* And Ernest Torrence and Will Rogers. They liked old Will, too.

But that Louis Wolheim in that railroad picture, the title of which Jimmy could never recall. It should have been *Lookout There, Here I Go!* because that was the way that train went through that prison with all those convicts aboard. Riding that train right on down those tracks, if they never rode another one.

They worshipped old Louis Wolheim who was riding it with them; they worshipped him for his toughness, and that kid, Dick Arlen, at the throttle for his gameness. Odd how they admired those actors for portraying the very qualities the lack of which made them what they were. They loved the women, they wanted to go to bed with them; but they worshipped those tough guys, those game guys, those guys who had the guts to fight it out and win. There never was an audience that pulled harder for the game kid to win out in the end. They got excited about it.

"The dirty rat! Get 'im, kid, get that dirty rat!" Jumping up and down in their seats. "Get that dirty fink!"

But let the police keep out of it; they and the kid would do it, they didn't need any police. They even booed the picture cops, while at the same time they pulled for the old gray-haired widow whom the police were trying to help.

They saw Clive Brook in *The Night of June 13th,* and called him slick. They saw Laurel and Hardy in a number of pictures. And Cab Calloway going to town in *Minnie The Moocher.* All that Jimmy could hear the following week was those colored convicts chanting, *She was a red hot hoocher choocher, she was the roughest, toughest frail, but Minnie had a heart as big as a whaaaaaAAAAAALLLLLEEEEE . . .*

They saw many pictures, all of which impressed Jimmy for a day. And out of them, like clear-cut emeralds on white satin, stood the unforgettable scene, the shocking shot, as when the lovers turned away from the life preserver in *Calvacade* and he saw the name *Titanic,* that lasted forever. And the girl going crazy with jealousy, before she killed herself, in *The Night of June 13th.* George Raft fingering his tight-tied tie in *Taxi Dancer.* And a girl in a picture, the names of both he could not for the life of him recall, saying, "Because I love you, that's why," which he never forgot.

The talkies helped that fall. They made him softer, more human. They helped him regain a semblance of his perspective which he had lost in the prison fire. They did a great deal for him, morally, spiritually, emotionally. But they hurt him, too. He had to go back to the dormitory, back to the goddamned, rooted, immovable, eternal, everlasting prison of stone and steel, back to the goddamned, gutless, degenerate, callous convicts. And it solid hurt, too.

13

THE DAY GOT OFF to a lousy start in the first place. It was a gray October day with a cold, fine drizzle. They were clad in their coats and vests with their caps pulled down over their eyes. The grass was gone and the walks were wet. It was the end of fall and winter was in view with all its barren bleakness.

Oatmeal and chalk for breakfast. They hadn't had that for some time. Jimmy had been expecting doughnuts and ham-gravy. He was disappointed. It was a little thing, but afterwards, in the stuffy, stinking dormitory, with the wet, gray drizzle looking in from the outside, it grew.

Standing by his bunk after breakfast, idly puffing on a cigaret, he felt traces of an irritation. His dreams the night before had been rather putrid, and his thoughts before he had gone to sleep had been rotten, too.

He watched the convicts preparing for their morning session of gambling, detached, remote, apart. It was as if he awaited something, but could not think of what. Captain Frank took off his overcoat and slouched down in his padded chair, opening a *Detective Story Magazine*. To Jimmy, he looked repugnant, like a fat red toad.

Candy stopped by and asked Jimmy if he was going to play, and he said no, and then Signifier came over and said, "Let me have a buck, Jimmy."

"I only got a half besides a fin," he replied. "You can have that." His voice sounded flat and his lips felt dry.

"Let me have the fin, then," Signifier said. "It ain't nothing but money."

"Do you want this half?"

Signifier took it and said, "Didn't you know this morning was coming?" in that baiting voice of his.

Getting annoyed, Jimmy snarled, "Get up, Johnson!"

But Signifier kept on. "Monday morning always comes; it came last Monday and—"

Jimmy wheeled away, swung up on his bunk, stretched out. Suddenly, he filled with a violent distaste for everything. For Signifier and Candy and captain Frank and the convicts and the guards and the prison. Then he remembered that his mother was going to visit him that afternoon, and he thought, Maybe I'll be all right after she comes.

Pulling the morning paper from beneath his pillow where the paper boy had stuck it while they were at breakfast, he scanned the headlines. Three gunmen had killed a sheriff by the name of Jess Sarber, and had released an ex-con by the name of Dillinger, who was being held on a bank robbery rap. He read a few lines of it. One of the trio had asked to see Dillinger, stating, "We're officers from Michigan City . . ."

He balled up the paper and threw it into the aisle. Treadwell got up from the table and picked it up. "Let me look at your paper, Monroe?"

Jimmy nodded. Treadwell straightened it out and read the headlines. "Killed a sheriff," he announced. "I bet that son of a bitch needed killing."

Jimmy jumped down from his bunk and walked away without replying. Johnny Brothers, Black Boy, and another Negro convict were trying to get a fourth player for a game of whist.

"Sit down and pick 'em up, Jimmy," Brothers said, dipping his head and grinning as was his habit.

"What are you playing?" Jimmy asked, sitting down.

"Whist," Black Boy replied.

"Okay, Black Boy, you and I got 'em," Jimmy said.

They played until dinner, which also turned out to be another blank. Spaghetti and tomato sauce. Like dead white worms in clotted blood. He gagged.

After dinner he sat around and looked out the dingy window at the gray day and waited for his mother. But she didn't come that day. He felt a sense of letdown. Then slowly, he filled with a dull brooding, a general hatred for everything and everyone. He forced down some supper because he knew that he should eat something, but it tasted like dishwater. On the way back from the dining room, the day seemed colder, the rain wetter. The prison seemed bleaker and uglier. Freedom had never seemed so far away.

When mail was called, he received a letter from his mother.

"Dear Son," he read, "Your letter came Wednesday. I had written to you before receiving it but if I had known that you were going to write I would have waited to write to you, but I thought perhaps you were going to write to your father."

"Damon and I planned coming over there today, as I told you, but it was raining this morning and I didn't want to risk it."

He looked at the postmark and saw that it was postmarked that morning.

"I think I told you that I am not very steady on my feet anymore and can't get around so well. My arthritis troubles me when I go out in wet weather and I try to avoid it as much as possible. Your mother is getting to be an old woman. I will be sixty-one years old next month."

He could feel the muscles knotting and pulling down his face.

"Damon says he is muddling along with his work. He certainly has plenty. He is going to apply for his doctor's degree this fall. I certainly am sorry you are not out here to help with him. We need you so very badly. My arms get so weak at times I can't raise them. I had to go to a specialist. He told me that I am overworking myself and that I just need a rest.

"Now, James, I know that prison must be a very trying place and that you are getting tired of being there, but you must remember that you brought it all on yourself. I am doing all I can to get you out, but there are some things that you must do for yourself. You have not been a very good boy and the warden told me that you have given the officials considerable trouble since you have been there.

"Your father might be able to help you get out of there. But the thing for you to understand is that he *hasn't,* and neither have any of all those people with whom you associated and on whom you spent your time and money when you were free. You cannot control the rest of the world, but you *can* and *must* control yourself. Remember that. And if you are a good boy you will come up for parole in two more years. All you need to do is to behave yourself. And you will not need to ask the help of anyone. It is all left with you."

He was struck with the impulse to ball up the letter and throw it away. But he read on from a sense of duty.

"I want you to understand, James, that I *am* trying to help you. Damon is howling, too, because he hasn't been able to have all the things he wants this year. I give up. I am only one person. I give you and Damon all my time and thought. But neither of you is ever satisfied. You make things hard for yourselves. You are both so hardheaded that you will never listen to me, you think I don't know anything.

"I am almost down and out. Some days I can make it and some days I can't. Some days my legs will not carry me to the store. Pretty soon, I hope, it will all be over and I can rest . . ."

Without reading to the end, Jimmy folded the letter across and tore it into very small pieces, then took the pieces out into the aisle and carefully dropped them into a cuspidor . . . Now I wonder what I said to start all this, he thought.

And then suddenly and very queerly he wanted to do something for his mother to make her happy. Right then he would have died for her, lied, killed, stolen—anything for her. He stood there, wanting to make the greatest sacrifice that anyone has ever made for the love they hold their mother, wanting to die a thousand tortured deaths for her in his ardor of self-immolation.

Instead, he went down to the poker game and took out a dollar's worth of chips. In an hour they had him. He was hot and sweating and broke. He had lost the whole five dollars. He looked at the table, looked at Candy. But Candy had been losing, too, and only had a few chips left himself. He split what he had, however, and shoved half, Jimmy's way. But Jimmy shook his head. It wasn't the money. It was the losing. Losing all the time. "I must not be living right," he thought sourly.

Signifier had three penny chips left out of the half he had started with that morning. "You can have half of these if the dealer will lend me his knife," he said, signifying. Jimmy didn't look at him. His eyes slid across the table . . . All that stuff about begging her for help. When did he ever beg her for help? He just said he was tired. Well, he was tired. Tired! TIRED!!!! . . .

He let the smoke dribble from his mouth and nostrils, trying to control himself; watched it eddy upward toward the cardboard sign that hung from the light by a string—SPITTING ON THE FLOOR AND WALL FORBIDDEN . . . He didn't see but one word, FORBIDDEN, and his gaze bruised against it.

The deal began, stopped at him tentatively. Starrett said, "Going or gonna get left?"

He picked up the card, sailed it down the aisle. There was no anger in him, no thought behind the action. Just an answer.

And then, suddenly, it all boiled up in him, the accumulations of all his feelings and sensations and emotions and thoughts; all his hates and fears and humiliations and irritations and stagnations; all the putrid, rotten filth of all those years. It spewed up in his mind like the gaseous belch of rotting slop and gagged him.

All the rotting bog of repressions and inhibitions and shames and scares and those dark and secret impulses and passions and loves and hates and degeneracies and loathings; and those stale flat tears that had soured and spoiled inside of him; and all those dreams and ambitions and desires and aims that had rotted into wormy crusted filth were belching out. Those secret, hidden things inside him were breaking through. He could not hold them inside of himself any longer; he was beginning to flare, to blow; he was like a burning fuze on a dynamite cap.

It was spewing up in thick green slime from those years of being half-afraid of everything and trying not to show it; half-afraid of some one thinking he was a girl-boy and running over him and taking advantage of him; half-afraid that he might be sorry for his crime, or for his mother, or for himself, so that in the end he had wasted all of his sorrow on those indifferent convicts. And those years of being so terribly afraid to think about the past or the future; and all the while being touched by the actual brutalities and cruelties and bitchery and abomination and sodomy of the living, rotten, everlasting prison; and never letting on that he had, or that anything had ever touched him, or could touch him. All those years of trying to convince himself that he had not come there a nineteen-year-old punk and scared.

But it was breaking through.

It was vomiting from those years of trying to be touched and trying to be smart and trying to prove he was not weak, as if there was a penalty on tears; and trying to know so very much more than a nineteen-year-old boy has any business knowing. Those years of trying so awful hard to make them recognize him as a convict, as if it was a special distinction, such as receiving a degree of Doctor of Philosophy; when all the while he was afraid to admit even to himself how afraid and repulsed he had been, and how utterly different everything inside of him still was when he let it be; trying all the while to push it down and throw filth on top of it and bury it and forget it and become some one else whom he never really was and would never be.

And all those convicts on whom he had leaned so heavily in his need for companionship, a need which he would not admit, having convinced himself all along that they leaned on him, Walter and Chump and Lively and Blocker, rose from the gooey bog like a row of slimy specters and leered at him, whispering in their soundless voices that he had never been anything by himself, that he had always needed the feeling of not being alone in that prison.

And now it was oozing out of him, through his mouth and eyes and ears and nostrils, coming out of the days filled with dullness and sameness and death and violence and absoluteness; the brooding days with the slow change of shadows, but the everlasting scene, eternal and the same; the mocking days and the indifferent days and the deliberate days with their pieces of sunset wedged in between two buildings, with their distances horizoned by a wall, with their bar-checked squares of stars and their three-foot parades of moons from window casement to window casement.

The past and the future were meeting, the one had stopped and the other had caught up—fusing together into red hot chaos like a furnace in his brain. His mind rippled and bucked and shot off bright, spurting fuses. He fought for control. He gritted his teeth, tensed his muscles, fighting. He put his hands palms downward on the gray blanket stretched over the table and stood up, straddling the bench. He spit the cigaret butt from his lips. It broke up, scattered tobacco shreds over the shiny cards.

Candy, Johnson, Starrett, Wicks, Joe, Tony, Dutch, looked up at him, looked away. He swung out from the bench, moved down the aisle. He could feel the sticky heat in his eyes, blood in his face. His lips felt thin and stiff as paper, his muscles jerked. Convicts walking up and down the aisle for exercise got out of his way.

At the front, the night guard, captain Charlie, threw up his hand, " 'Lo, Monroe."

Jimmy wheeled, strode back down the aisle without replying. His shirt felt cold moldy on top of the sweat; his trousers chafed him. His shoes felt slimy. And then the dormitory began seeping into his consciousness. A steady hum of noise swirled about his ears. Air, thick with the odor of tobacco fumes and unwashed bodies, clogged in his nostrils. Faces drifted in front of his gaze; faces stamped with that queer docility common to prisoners. Rows of bunks were ugly in his mind. Steel bars formed a grilled background for his thoughts.

Four years of it! Jesus Christ, he was tired . . . *tired!* The unvarying monotony: Up at six; breakfast at seven; dinner at eleven; back in the dormitory; lights out at nine; then the gnawing silence until six; the same thing over the next day. Gray uniforms! Gray weather! Gray faces! Angles, stone, brick, bars! Convicts—all alike! You knew what a guy was going to say before he said it. An endless cycle, as unvarying as eternity. And endless chain of days, gray days, beginning at six, ending at nine, never changing. All alike! Dead days!

God Amighty Knows stopped him. "Wanna buy some cracklin's, Jimmy? Gred big brown 'uns ri' frum de frigid zone!"

Jimmy looked at him. "Huh?"

"Wanna buy some brown 'uns ri' hot outen de oven?"

Jimmy did not want them but he asked mechanically, "Where are they?"

"Ah'll get 'em tomorrow. Uh boy ovah to—" he broke off, looking at Jimmy.

Jimmy bit his lips. He wasn't angry. But he wanted to hit God Amighty Knows in the mouth. No, on the neck just below the ear. A swift chop to the jaw with his left, cross a right to his neck, watch his eyes pop out in his face. God, he wanted to hit him; he wanted so badly to hit him it came all up in his eyes.

He leaned forward on the balls of his feet, tensed his body. God Amighty Knows backed away from him. He walked on; after a couple of steps he turned, caught God Amighty Knows staring at him. His eyes burnt red. Insensate fury shocked him like a current. God, he wanted to hit him! But he didn't. He shook himself like a dog coming out of a pond, walked on, lips stretched in a turned-in smile. He should have hit him, he was thinking. Should have hit him once, anyway. Four years before, when he had first entered, he would have popped him if he had felt this way. Even three years ago, perhaps. But now? Not now! Too much discipline for too long, he thought. His laugh was ragged.

Looking up the aisle, he saw captain Charlie. Captain Charlie was his friend, used to give him candy. He ought to go up and bust him one, he thought. His old gray-headed friend, captain Charlie. Ought to hit him one for luck. Like captain Rizor hit him; captain Rizor hit him for luck that day, split his skull, he bled like a hog . . . Got to kill captain Rizor for that some day, he thought . . . Ought to hit him to make him know he's guarding convicts, he thought, going back to captain Charlie—convicts like me! Me! Yes, me, *ME!*

His feet carried him in captain Charlie's direction. He didn't see anyone but captain Charlie. Wonder what he'd say if a convict hit him in the mouth—his old pal, a guard, a lousy hack, wasn't no pal of his, he was a convict. Wonder what they'd do to him. Put him in the hole for thirty days, maybe. Damn the hole! Damn him!

He walked faster. Wondered if he had the nerve. He stopped in front of captain Charlie's table.

Captain Charlie looked up from the paper. "How're you getting along, Jim?"

Jimmy's lips cracked into a smile. He licked them. "Fine cap, how're you getting along?"

"Oh. I'm doing pretty good for an old man. My wife was asking about you."

Jimmy licked his lips again. "Tell her I'm doing fine. I hope she's doing fine, too."

"She's getting along nicely, thank you."

Jimmy turned away.

"Well, stay out of trouble, Jim," captain Charlie called.

Jimmy rocked down the aisle. That was it, he thought. You're a convict and you can't hit a guard. A guard hit you once but you can't hit a guard. You're scared to hit a guard, that's it. And then you get up enough nerve to hit a guard. But the only guard you can find is old and gray-haired and a friend of yours and his wife asks how you're getting along.

He walked back down the aisle, feeling the muscles jerking in his face. He wanted to scream. He couldn't see. He was going nuts. Heat rolled up from the base of his brain. He wanted to lose his reason, his balance, his perspective, his sight and all of his senses; he wanted to lose everything that held him to the semblance of a human being—a convict. He wanted to become a blankness, unrestrained, unemotional, so he could do a blindly dangerous act. He wanted to kill some one. He wanted to shoot some one in the guts, watch them bend over and take their guts in their hands, watch them topple over and die.

Nuts! He was going nuts!

Sweat trickled into his eyes, stinging them. The warm salt taste of blood came up in his mouth where unknowingly he had bitten his tongue. He moved down toward the latrine, on the other side where the Negros bunked.

A group of black faces ringed in the table, cards spun with a blur of white from the skin box, soft intense curses rose like smoke. Black Boy was dealing.

"Wanna pike, Jimmy?" some one asked.

He shook his head. Black Boy looked up, looked down, wearing his perpetual grin. "How ya be, Jimmy?"

A card fell. A tall light complexioned Negro convict with a pressed shirt, and shiny tan shoes, turned over the card he was playing. Hands reached for the stacks of chips beside him. He picked up the trey of spades from the dead, said, "Throw back, all you niggahs who caught me."

Black Boy carried him a tall stack of chips. Others carried their bets to him. He paid the bets. Black Boy spun the cards. The eight spot fell . . . "Mah hatred," some one said . . . The tall mulatto, called Cincinnati Slick, picked up a stack of chips.

Black Boy said, "Ah ain' got no hatred. Wanna bet some mo', Slick?"

"Throw down."

They pressed their bet. Black Boy turned a card. "Some mo'?" . . . "Throw down." . . . Turned another card. "Some mo'." . . . "Throw down." . . . Chips were stacked high. Black Boy drew a card half out of the box, knocked it back. "Hotdammit, betcha some mo'!" . . . "Throw down." . . .

Johnny Brothers stood up and called over his shoulder. "Hey, Cue Ball Red, come look at this one. Chips stacked knee deep."

Black Boy spun the card. The trey of clubs flashed in the spill of light, fell on its face.

"Dead men fall on their face," some one said.

Black Boy raked in the stack of chips. Slick turned ashy. "You shot me, din yer!" he stated in a flat, accusing voice. "Shot me!"

"Who, me-e-ee? Me shot yer? Whataya mean, Slick." Black Boy was all innocence; his grin stayed white.

Slick snatched up the card box, flung cards through the air. "Now ast me tuh pay for 'em."

Black Boy said, "Sho, Slick, pay for 'em!" His voice was broader, deeper, but untroubled.

Jimmy turned away.

Off to one side, a black boy strummed a uke. Feet patted time. A slurred baritone recited: "Dat's whut Harlem means to me . . ." Another convict cut a step, shoulders swaggering. Hands clapped in rhythmic beat. The days passed and they didn't know it, Jimmy thought.

He took a few steps, was stopped by a voice:

"He had hipped de jedge, yer know, so w'en dey hails 'im in co't dat Sat'dy night for raisin' a rumpus down de street, de jedge says, well, cool dinge, Ah heahs yo is been nabbed by de object John for pitchin' a boogy-woogy dis pas' darkness on de Broadway. W'ut is yo' buzz, cool dinge? And ol' Scagmore, yer no' he done hipped de jedge how to spiel de jive hisself, but de jedge is outspieling him, an' he says, spiel again, yo' cool, kind honor, Ah din quite git yer. And de jedge says, cool dinge, Ah heahby sentences yo' to thirty brightnesses in de wearyhopper and orders de object Jeff to heahby peel yo from dis prominence. You cops dat, doancha, cool dinge? An' . . ."

The days passed.

His feet felt weighted, his mouth sour. He wanted to break something in his hands. Anything to get away from the prison scene. He bit his lip, wet it with his tongue, took a squashed cigaret from his side pants pocket and lit it. His hands had to do something. They trembled. The cigaret tasted like straw.

Then the dormitory got into his eyes again. He closed them tight, stopped stock still, but he could still see it through his closed eyelids; he could see all those rotten years strung out, like putrid stinking corpses that refused to be buried. He couldn't stand it. He wheeled away, toward a window, looked out into the night. Search lights illuminated the yard in sketchy brilliance. Buildings loomed dark and ghostly. A prison guard turned the corner of the chapel building, trudging his weary rounds, coat collar turned up, cap visor pulled down. It was raining.

And then a queer, rushing kaleidoscope of faces and places and things came to him out of the past as if he was drowning . . . He and the girl were sitting on the stairs of the darkened apartment, making love. He was kissing her, wondering why she wouldn't when he knew she wanted to so badly. A dim light on the landing above made her face a white blur beneath the black hair . . . He was saying, "Stick 'em up!" and the man's face was turning suddenly, desperately white . . . He caught the high, skyey punt running back, turned in a wide sweep, whirled away from the first tackler, stiff-armed the second; the stands were yelling frenziedly for a touch-down, the din was a tangible quality about him, inspiring him with a wild desire to push on . . . The girl across the bed from him hesitated before stripping off her underclothes and slowly he turned his gaze from her . . .

He came out of it feeling stifled. A wet towel steamed on the table beside him. The vapor caught in his nostrils. He couldn't breathe. He opened the window. The cold wet air blew against the hot haze of his mind. He took a deep breath and the air was raw in his lungs.

Standing there, rigid and unseeing, he stared into the night. His mind sped up as if a foot had been jammed down on the accelerator of his thought impulses, began whirling like the flywheel of a racer coming down the stretch. His thoughts ran together like white hot melting glass. He wanted to scream out to all eternity.

Some one on a nearby bunk, talking to some one else, said, "Aw, go to hell, you convict bastard!"

He caught a crystal clear view of himself in his proper perspective—*a convict bastard.*

He went down to the latrine and leaned against the wash-trough, took out his last squashed cigaret, and tossed away the package.

It was comparatively quiet down there. The cigaret tasted better. He tried to relax. And then sound creeped into his mind. A broken commode leaked with a monotonous gurgle. The skin on his face crawled like the skin of a snake's belly. He started on the move again, stopped. A wail arose, poignant, stirring—"*All-ll night lo-o-ooo-OOONG Ah set 'n mah cell an' mo—o-o-aaaOAAAAAAAAANNnnn!*"

The muscles tightened all over his body. Heat burned white hot through him. He could feel his right eye jumping in his head, feel his lips twist.

Crazy! He was going crazy! He couldn't stand it anymore! God! God in heaven, he couldn't stand it!

Visions lost all sense of perspective. Steel bars closed in upon him from all ungodly angles. He groped forward, feeling his way through a sense of motion stopped. Life couldn't be going on now, he thought. He was standing still through the relentless march of all eternity. He was being left behind, forever and ever more. His thoughts rose to a scream. He felt an uncontrollable desire to run, to catch up with the march of eternity. His thoughts were breaking up into bits. He bent forward, tensed himself for a running start . . .

The lights flashed . . . And flashed again . . . It was bedtime. That's it, he thought, with a twisted, bitter smile—he couldn't go crazy because he had to go to bed . . .

But after that the feeling of insanity remained with him. The outside world began to leak into his consciousness; the past and present and future, all, became muddled in his mind. He lay awake nights and thought of all those years of youth and vitality which were lost to him. He had never been a full-grown man anywhere but in prison; he had never voted. He thought of all the chances he had thrown away and of all the people he had hurt and disappointed. He thought of the outside, and he thought of it alone, unsleeping in the night. He knew as surely as he lay there that it would kill him if he kept it up. It frightened him.

He became frantic in his desire for freedom. He wrote to his mother and asked her to see the governor and plead for his release. "Tell him how badly you and Damon need me," he wrote. "Tell him you are old and can no longer support yourself and tell him about Damon being blind and trying to get an education and all. Play on his sympathy. And have attorney Bossman and Reverend Hill and all the influential people you know write to him in my behalf." And then he sat down and wrote the governor himself.

It was as it had been that October in 1928. He came to feel, as he had felt then, like a powder keg on fire. It was the bitter thought of winter coming on; he could not stand it, he never could stand it. In November in 1928, he had gone out and robbed a man and his wife in their home. And now that same sick tightness was inside of him. He kept to his bunk, sullen and uncommunicative and tense. He tried reading, but that only brought his emotions to the surface so that everything made an impression on them. He read of love and life and of people achieving things and finding happiness; and could not take it. He tried writing. He bought a typewriter and began to learn typing. He wrote hysterical short stories, pouring out torrents of illiterate protests. Protests against what? He didn't know. And all the while, the rooted, immovable, solid prison was getting next to him.

It was then that he met Rico.

Book IV

What Is the Real and What Is the Unreal

JIMMY HAD GOTTEN as far as the title, A CONVICT IS HUMAN, TOO, but the words would not come. Sitting there, hunched over his typewriter, glumly glaring at the capitalized letters which by now did not make any sense at all, he suddenly became aware of the silence which had descended over the dormitory. Glancing about, he noticed that Wrinklehead, Dutch, Signifier, and Jew Baby, who had been enjoying a hilarious whist game down the table, had stopped to stare at some one. He turned just as Brownie, the deputy's runner, and the newcomer passed behind him. His gaze followed them down the aisle to an upper bunk where the newcomer hung his label.

There was a picturesqueness about the youth which immediately set him apart from other convicts; even his infirmity was original. Wearing a banjo ukelele strung from his neck by a woven chain of shoe strings, he carried his other belongings in a small, grimy sack which he tossed carelessly atop his bunk. His shoulders were rather wide, and standing straight, he was perhaps an inch taller than Jimmy, but when he walked, his shoulders stooped and his body slouched, and every third or fourth step his knees would suddenly knock together as if all the strength had drained from them, and his feet would fly out at grotesque angles, reminiscent of the first wobbly motions of a colt. This gave a precariousness to all of his movements, so that his every step seemed to border on actual disaster.

"Who's the kid?" Jimmy heard Signifier ask when Brownie had returned.

"Prince Rico," Brownie replied.

"You don't mean the Prince of Wales?" Signifier cracked.

"What's the matter with him?" Dutch asked. "Is he stiffing?"

Brownie grinned. "He's got it bad, ain't he?"

"He's about to fall out with it," Signifier said. Then standing, he smirked, "I better go down and help him make his bed. Never let it be said that Signifier didn't help a new kid get straightened out."

"What you gonna do, you gonna sound him out?" Jew Baby asked, getting excited.

"Naw, I was just kidding. I'm gonna get a drink of water."

"I'm coming with you," Jew Baby announced, talking hold of his arm.

Signifier shook him off. "Naw, he'll think we're ganging up on him if you go down there blinking your eyes. He'll think you're Pretty Boy Floyd and get scared."

"Aw, Signore," Jew Baby protested, falling all over Signifier. "Aw, Siggy."

"You fellows rush a kid too fast," Dutch said. "You don't do nothing but queer everything. You make a kid freeze up." He was serious.

Signifier started away. "You can have him when I get through," he called back.

Jimmy watched him saunter down the aisle, saw him stop at Rico's bunk, saw the ensuing pantomime. Then abruptly he quit watching, banged his typewriter closed and stalked over to his bunk, an upper on the center aisle, feeling a wave of aversion. Once he would have been up with a play such as that, he reflected. Now it disgusted him. God, he was tired of it.

He climbed onto his bunk, stretched out, opened a magazine. Hearing Jew Baby ask, "Did you sound him out, Siggy? What do you think about him, Siggy?" he glanced up and saw Signifier coming down the aisle, red-faced and chagrined. He laughed out loud.

Rico had followed Signifier unobserved, and hearing Jimmy laugh, evidently thought it was directed at him. He jerked a glance in Jimmy's direction and the strike of his eyes was like a slap. Still wearing the banjo-ukelele swung from his neck, he raked a slashing discord on it, cutting off the laugh as with an axe. His chin lifted, tilting his head to one side, and a contemptuous sneer grew wide across his mouth. Riveting his eyes straight ahead, he wobbled on, chin high, head tilted, lips sneering.

There was little to be achieved in a walk which, at each step, seemed on the verge of collapse. But his sneer was almighty. It was the sneer of an Omnipotence who would have turned the convicts of that dormitory into swine, and then have concreted the face of the earth.

Jew Baby, Dutch, Signifier, and Wrinklehead stood and watched him pass without a word, all the fun taken out of the incident. But oddly, Jimmy experienced an almost overwhelming admiration for Rico, knowing that it took plenty of courage, or a genuine indifference, for a new convict in a dormitory, especially a kid who looked both weak and broke, to make enemies as recklessly as that.

He followed Rico with his gaze, touched with the desire to know him. Long, black hair was a tangled mass above his head, growing long and thick down the back of his neck and over his ears as if it had neither been combed nor cut in months, and his clothes, all of which were state-issue, were in a state of rags. His brogues were battered and run over and half laced, and his trousers were bagged to a resemblance of chimney elbows. Every now and then he raised his arms and struck a careless note on the uke, his elbows coming through holes in his shirt and coat. Halfway down the aisle he stopped to watch the poker game.

"What did he say to you, Johnson?" Jimmy asked curiously.

Signifier came over to the bunk, grinning sheepishly. "He didn't say anything, he just said he didn't need no help."

Jimmy grinned. "I wonder if he gambles," he mused, his thoughts going back into the prison groove.

"Sure, that punk gambles."

"Why don't you try him out, Jimmy?" Jew Baby leered, coming up. "Give him half a buck and put him on the track. All the kids fall for that."

"I don't know anything about him, though," Jimmy pointed out. "He might be straight for all I know."

"Aw, he's a fag if ever I saw one," Signifier argued. "I can look at 'em and tell. He'll go. If somebody don't turn him out before this week is over I'll walk up and pop old Frank Steeplecross in the mouth."

Wrinklehead joined them to say importantly in his tongue-tied voice, his eyelids fluttering and the whites of his eyes showing, "What you muggs talking about? You talking about that fag?"

"How do you fellows get so sure about the man?" Jimmy wanted to know.

"You can't fool me," Wrinklehead said.

"That's what Johnson's Belle used to say about you," Jimmy informed him. "He said the way he knew it was because he was one himself."

"Aw, that—" Wrinklehead couldn't get the words together.

"Go on and sound him out, Jimmy," Jew Baby persisted.

"Not me," Jimmy declined. "I'm trying to get out of this joint. I don't want to get into any jam now."

"Trying to get a pardon?" Jew Baby was suddenly envious.

Jimmy nodded. They lost interest after that and drifted away, Jew Baby falling all over Signifier and Wrinklehead still trying to get out what he wanted to say about Johnson's Belle.

When Jimmy looked up again, he noticed that Rico had taken a seat in the poker game. After supper, he stood around the game to see how Rico played, but Rico did not play anymore although he passed a couple of times and once stopped to watch. Later, after returning to his bunk, Jimmy heard him beating out a tune down in Black Bottom for a breakdown.

The next day was Sunday, Jimmy's day, and if Rico played at all he'd have to play in one of his games. So when they opened after dinner, he took over the poker game. But Rico did not show up.

After the coffee had been brought around, Jimmy turned the deal over to Candy, directing, "If Rico starts to play send for me. I want to look him over and see what he knows."

"Who's Rico?" Candy asked.

"He's the kid who moved in yesterday."

"Oh!" Candy looked at him.

"That slouchy bitch was playing yesterday afternoon," Starrett broke in. He had been standing behind Jimmy.

"You've got a nasty mouth," Jimmy said.

Then they both looked at him.

"Can he play?" Candy asked Starrett.

"Naw, that bitch can't play," Starrett replied, emphasizing the word *bitch*.

Rico walked past and looked at him curiously as he might have looked at a strange worm.

"Give me some chips here, boy, let's get to gambling!" Starrett shouted to hide his confusion.

Returning from the head of the aisle, Rico stopped to watch the game. Hoping he would sit in, Jimmy took the deal again. For a time Rico stood there, watching them play. Once he glanced up and caught Jimmy's gaze on him. Jimmy nodded. Rico's expression did not change. He stared at Jimmy for a moment, then dropped his gaze to the table, and after a while wobbled off, strumming a slow melody. It was late that evening before he returned and took out a dime's worth of chips.

Jimmy shot him some aces and kings for hole cards which he was lucky enough to hit. But it was obvious from the first that he was an absolute chump in a poker game. He tried to play every hand, and he had no judgement whatsoever. When some one raised a bet that he had called, he took it as a personal challenge and called the raise no matter what he had. His playing was all emotion.

However, he began winning. The others "horsed" at him on the sly, but he continued to hit the aces and kings which Jimmy shot him. Pretty soon he discovered that Starrett was betting pointedly at him, and he made a duel of it. To keep Starrett from beating him, Jimmy began topping the deck and flipping bottoms to hit him out. But winning went to Rico's head. His plunging became more and more reckless, as if something had caught afire within him. His hands trembled and his face became flushed.

He's got it bad, Jimmy observed. He thinks he can gamble and he can't, but he'd lose his soul trying.

After a time Wicks caught on to the cheat and barred a deal. Jimmy had to pay off sixty-five cents. Then the others became suspicious although they did not know why he had paid Wicks off. On the next deal Starrett was backed up with kings. Jimmy hit aces out of sight on the third card. Rico stayed with a trey, six, and ten up, and Jimmy figured him to have six'es.

Wanting so badly to get Rico broke, Starrett kept raising him into Jimmy, knowing that Jimmy had aces, but willing to go broke himself. Jimmy tried to hip Rico to the play; he kept saying he had aces and winking and flipping his hole card, doing everything he could to make Rico turn down. But it was Starrett who turned down.

With only the two of them seeing the last card, Jimmy bet a nickel and said, "Well, I guess these two big red aces take it, eh, kid?"

Rico looked up at him and set in his stack. "That's what they got to do," he said slowly, his voice low and husky.

Starrett burst out laughing. Jimmy turned red. "Take out your chips, kid, I've got you beat," he said.

Rico's chin came up and his head tilted. His eyes became wild and feverish, his face became flushed, and his whole mouth twisted into a sneer. "Where I come from, when you win, you put your money in, turn your hand over, and take the pot," he said, his head bobbing up and down, the sneer also in his voice.

Jimmy looked at him solidly for a moment. He had a longish, reckless face with high cheekbones and too much thinness down the cheeks, and a high, smooth forehead topped by that mat of blue-black hair. His face was sweaty and greasy and his sloe eyes, slanting upward at the edges, gave a slight Mongolian cast to his features. Now his eyes glittered, like those of a cornered animal's.

Jimmy turned his ace out of the hole. "See, I wasn't joking, I've got aces. Take out your money, I'm not trying to beat *you*."

Rico turned sheet white. Emotions dropped across his mobile features like quickly changing scenes. "Call it and win," he grated hoarsely, licking his lips and lifting his chin higher still. "That's what you've been sitting there on that hard seat for all day, isn't it?" His mouth was ugly with the sneer.

Jimmy burnt up. "Call it," he said, tossing in a chip.

"Pay it off," Rico demanded. "Put in the rest of the chips."

"I'm the dealer," Jimmy snarled. "I'm forced to pay if I lose."

"Aw, come on and take the pot and let's get to gambling," Starrett growled, counting his chips. "I'm four bucks loser."

Rico turned and looked down his nose at him; but before he could speak, Jimmy wheeled on Starrett and shouted, "Damn you, I'm running this game!" Then he paid off the pot, counting out the chips one by one.

Watching Starrett fume as he did so, Jimmy hoped he would start something so he could knock out his teeth. But by then Rico had regained his indifference. Waiting until Jimmy had finished, he turned down his cards, said, "You win," and stood up, utterly disdainful of every one.

For several minutes he stood there with his foot on the bench, aloof and contemptuous, strumming an aimless chord on his uke every now and then. Starrett glared at him and Jimmy eyed him furtively. Then Dutch came up and asked loud enough for all to hear, "Want to play some more, Gypsy Kid?"

Jimmy frowned with a quick, involuntary jealousy, wondering if Dutch had staked him.

Rico turned and looked down his nose at Dutch. "I see I made a mistake," he observed, and turned his back.

Jimmy gave a sharp snort of laughter and Dutch turned a dirty red. "You can take it over, Candy," Jimmy said, getting up.

He went over and put on his flannel pyjamas and climbed onto his bunk. There was a novelette in *Cosmopolitan* that he wanted to finish, but he could not keep his mind on it. He was still reading the same paragraph when Signifier and Rico turned in from the aisle. He looked up, surprised.

"Prince said he wanted to meet you," Signifier winked.

"You're the Jimmy Monroe who writes," Rico greeted smiling. "I've read a lot of your stories."

"Really?" Jimmy laughed. "I haven't had any published."

Rico blushed. "I was only trying," he said in a tiny voice. "Tell me I'm not ridiculous for trying." His manner was shy.

Both Jimmy and Signifier were looking at him queerly. Finally Jimmy said, feeling the beginning of a laugh, "You're not ridiculous; you, well, you were just trying."

This was too polite for Signifier. Turning away, he said, "You owe me a buck, Jimmy."

"What do you owe him a buck for?" Rico asked, making conversation.

Alone with him, it was Jimmy's turn to become shy. "Well, er, I was trying, too," he confessed.

They looked sharply at each other, and a small thin smile, like a thread, grew into Rico's lips. Then suddenly, without preamble, he said, "Signifier didn't tell you my name. It's Prince Rico, silly isn't it; they call me Gypsy Kid sometimes, but I don't like it." And in the same breath he continued, "And I'm sorry I put you in the middle out there in the game, I was so excited that I didn't realize until afterwards that you were trying to help me." The words bubbled out in a quick, live rush, drawing Jimmy's stare to his mouth. He had full, deep-red lips, and his skin was smooth and slightly olive-tinged. When talking, his red lips were a smear of mobile motion across his face, shadowed by a line of fuzzy down on his upper lip. "You'll forgive me, won't you?" His eyes were serious and intent, like those of a child's, and he looked very young, perhaps nineteen, and utterly naive.

"Oh hell, that was all right," Jimmy said grandiloquently. "I-I figured you were a little out of practice."

Rico became suddenly rueful. The abrupt change was startling. "You mean you saw I couldn't gamble and took pity on me," he said, the life gone out of his voice. "I know I can't gamble but I don't like to be shown up." It was serious with him.

"I wasn't trying to show you up," Jimmy defended. "I wanted you to win."

"Did you?" Rico's eyes lit. "Why?"

Jimmy became flustered. "Oh, I don't know. I guess it's because I admire you in a way."

Rico was thoughtful for a moment. "I wonder why," he said finally. "I don't always admire myself."

"But you do sometimes?" Jimmy grinned.

"Oh yes, lots, but why would you?"

"Oh, the way you treated Signifier and all of us yesterday. It's so much easier to compromise."

"You don't like a person who compromises?"

"*Like* isn't the right word. I might *like* them, but I won't *admire* them."

Completely and abruptly Rico went through another change of expression, and laughter bubbled from his lips, giving a disturbing girlishness to his face. "In other words," he slurred in a laughter-filled voice, "You admire me but you don't like me."

Jimmy had never seen anyone with such mobile features. They seemed to ripple with a thousand continuously changing expressions as the play of lights and shadows in a movie musical. He was thoroughly entranced. "I admire you," he grinned, "but I don't know as yet whether I like you or not. Is it important?"

"Which way, whether you do or you don't?" He came very close to Jimmy without moving.

"Either way."

He sighed, going away again. "The question is unfair." And then he was completely gone. "When you know me better—" he paused, then amended, "if you ever do, you might not even admire me." He looked away, adding cynically and a little bitterly, "I'm the old original compromiser. Do you know where I got that dime today?"

Jimmy nodded.

"You heard him then?" Rico asked, remote and brooding. "You know why he let me have it, too, don't you?"

Again Jimmy nodded.

"Say it," Rico commanded. "Tell me why I took it?"

Their eyes looked. Everything hung on the answer.

"Like anybody else," Jimmy replied, very matter of factly. "Like me. Because you're going to pay him back." And then he grinned. "Or else because you're not."

At first Rico looked startled. Then he blossomed like a morning glory, and smiled, showing large, white, even teeth. At that moment, Jimmy thought that he was beautiful. It was as if his face had a distinct and separate life which changed his whole appearance with each passing emotion. It was so delicately alive Jimmy felt a strong impulse to touch it with his finger tips. His eyes would grow bright, dim, serious, earnest, mischievous, bitter, cold, and then suddenly sparkling, so that one knew instantly, as if touching piano keys, which note had been sounded. Jimmy had never seen anyone so demonstrative of moods.

"You're rather swell, Jimmy," Rico murmured, and turned away.

Jimmy did not get a chance to talk to him again until the next night. Once during the morning, he saw him down in Black Bottom, flanked by two colored convicts, one with a banjo and the other with a guitar, beating out a swing tune. Rico caught his eye and waved for him to come down, but he shook his head. Another time he saw him playing cards with Signifier.

Monday was slow, and Jimmy spent most of the day working on his story, A CONVICT IS HUMAN, TOO. That evening after supper, he received a letter from the governor's secretary in reply to his recent letter to the governor.

November 24, 1933

Mr. James Buchanan Monroe,
Serial no. 57232

Dear Sir:

Governor Blackwell directs me to acknowledge receipt of your letter of recent date giving additional information on your case.

We are glad to get this comment.

Yours very truly
S.P. Dinkle,
Executive Secretary to the Governor.

Reading it, all of his desire for freedom surged back. Convicts became detestable again, and Rico became just another convict. He resolved to quit thinking of him, to nix him out. This is my chance, he told himself. If I don't get out now I might never get out. He didn't want to get involved in another sordid prison "friendship"; he had been through it with Lively, and he knew how easy it would be to lose his reason, his sense of balance. *Never Again,* he had said, and he meant it.

Rico chose that moment to approach him and say, smiling, "Hello, Jimmy, good news?"

Jimmy got up and walked down to Candy's bunk without replying. "How did we do yesterday?" he asked.

"We made nine-forty altogether," Candy replied. "Johnny Brothers and Black Boy are swinging out with their cuts from the skin game. They claim they didn't make but one-fifty."

Rico passed them, returning to his bunk, head high, mouth sneering, looking straight ahead. Jimmy winced. "Oh hell, let them keep the whole damn take if they want to," he said. "Who am I to have a gambling syndicate?" He wanted to say, but not to Candy, "Who am I to pass judgements?" But he didn't.

Candy looked at him peculiarly. "Better lighten up on that story-writing," he advised. "You'll blow your top."

"Oh, I'm all right," Jimmy said. "How much of the take was in cash?"

"Four-eighty. You want it?"

"Give me two and some weed. Got any cigarets?"

"A couple of packs."

"Give me those and some soap and a few bags of weed and some tooth paste if you got any."

"Got some *Ipana.*"

"That's fine. I'll pick it up after a while."

Returning to the table where he had left his typewriter, he tried to work on his story, but he could not get his thoughts together. His mind kept going back to Rico, and he felt ashamed of the way he had acted. He wanted to go down and apologize, but he could not bring himself to do it.

For a time he banged savagely on the keys, writing over and over, *The quick sly fox jumped over the lazy brown dog.* Every now and then some convict would stop to watch him as if the miracle of touch typing never ceased to amaze.

When the guard shift changed, captain Frank threw up his hand. "G'night, Jim." Jimmy waved. Captain Charlie stopped for a moment to ask how he was making out with the governor.

"I got a letter from Dinkle, but it was just a form letter," Jimmy told him. "Anyway, they're keeping me in mind."

"Well, if there is anything I can do for you, let me know," captain Charlie offered. "You're one boy who deserves to be out. I don't believe you'd ever get into any more trouble."

"I'll get you to write me a letter of recommendation later on," Jimmy said.

"Any time you say, Jim."

When he had gone, Jimmy balled up the pages he had written and stuffed them into the waste paper container. Then he locked his typewriter, went down and climbed onto his bunk.

About a half hour before bedtime Rico stopped by. He was tremulous, undecided. His face was loose and quivering and his lower lip trembled. "Howdy," he greeted tentatively.

"You caught me again," Jimmy grinned a welcome, holding up the magazine.

"Same story?"

"Same paragraph," he admitted, rolling over on his side.

Rico came closer without moving. "You must be in love."

"I'm not sure yet."

"Is she beautiful?"

Jimmy lowered his lids, let his gaze play over Rico's face. "*Beauty* is a term of relative meaning," he replied. "It depends entirely on the viewpoint."

"What is your viewpoint?"

"I'm not sure yet."

Rico laughed low and silently. It reminded Jimmy of the wind in the trees. "It's getting too deep for me," he murmured.

"It's too deep for me, too," Jimmy confessed. "That's why I'm not sure yet."

Rico came closer still. "Was it I again this afternoon?" he asked.

"No, it was I this time."

"Why?" he asked, trying to read Jimmy's eyes.

"Oh, I don't know, I'm trying to get a pardon and I want to stay clear."

For a moment Rico was blank. And then he was instantly, utterly angry. "You're taking a lot for granted, aren't you?" he choked. Anger rode him with spurs, raking him. It showed tightly in his face, thinned his lips, dulled his eyes. "You couldn't be wrong, could you? Just this once?" The sneer was back in his voice.

"I'm humbled," Jimmy said. "I apologize sincerely."

Rico thawed very slowly, as if half afraid he was wrong in doing so. "I accept the apology in the spirit in which it was given. Now what kind of a spirit was that?"

They looked at each other and began to grin.

"Was I?" Jimmy persisted.

"Was you?" Rico echoed.

"I don't know, I'm asking you. Was I wrong?"

"I stand upon my constitutional rights and refuse to answer, suh, on the grounds that the question is incriminating."

They laughed. "That isn't the way it goes," Jimmy said, "but I gather the general meaning."

"Why didn't you come down and listen to us play when I called you today?"

"Oh, I don't know, there were too many colored guys about."

"Why, what's wrong with them? They're like little children, they have a song in their hearts."

"They need a bath, too."

"We all need a bath," Rico pointed out, then added impishly, "That is, all of us except you. You look as if you don't ever need a bath."

Jimmy blushed. "That's an ambiguous remark, suh," he accused, imitating Rico's voice.

"I mean only the best interpretation," Rico smiled. "You look so cosy under your linoleum-checked blanket and two feather pillows— They are feather pillows, aren't they?" It was the week of Thanksgiving and Jimmy had gotten out his winter bedding. "May I feel them?" Rico asked.

Jimmy began to suspect that he was being ridiculed.

Rico felt them. "Oh, grand!" he exclaimed delightedly. He was laughing all inside and his eyes sparkled. "I knew they would be. I just love to feel feather pillows. May I come down and feel them sometimes?"

Now Jimmy was certain that he was being ridiculed. He became angry.

"How does it feel to be a big shot and have every one running after you?" Rico teased.

"I don't know," Jimmy snarled. "When I get to be one I'll tell you."

"I'm not making you angry, am I?"

"No, but don't particularly like it."

"Oh, I'm so sorry. I just want to ask you one more itsy bitsy question." His eyes were wide and bright with mischief; he was enjoying it.

"Now you're simpering," Jimmy grated.

Rico drew away slightly without moving. "But I was just playing," he protested. "Now you've gone and spoiled it." He sounded disappointed.

"I was the dupe," Jimmy said. "I always spoil that."

"But I was just playing," Rico said again in a small, hurt voice. "You weren't a dupe, honestly. I—" Then, abruptly, he went a long way off. "That's what's the matter, isn't it?" He had gone remote and brooding. "The play is so cheap, but the stakes are so high. Don't ever be human in prison. That's the first rule, isn't it? Don't be natural! Don't laugh! Don't play! And most of all don't like anyone. Just use them. That's it, isn't it? Always be tough, slick, smart, a wolf. That's the way it's played, isn't it?" Then suddenly, he changed. "Do you think I'm crazy?" he asked.

It was a long time before Jimmy replied, then his tone was solemn. "No, I've had it, too. It's a little game you play with yourself when you get fed up with playing their game. You make as if you're protesting against it, but you're not, not really, not if you want to make it and get out."

"You do understand, don't you?"

"I understand everything," Jimmy replied. Then he looked at Rico and felt a wave of pity. "I'm terribly sorry for you, though."

"Why?"

"Because you're going to hurt yourself."

"How?"

"Well, some one is bound to get too close to you. You're too vitally alive to keep it all to yourself. You're too emotional and-and—"

"Unstable," Rico supplied.

"Well, yes. And you like to gamble. That's a pity—because you can't. And you're too young. And you haven't got the right sort of armor. You haven't got a chance."

"What is my armor that you speak of, grandpa Monroe?" Rico asked facetiously.

"Your sneer. Looking down your nose like every one is dirt and trying to feel so awful contemptuous. It's not real. Can't anyone feel that much contempt. It's more of a defense mechanism. Isn't it?"

"The trouble with you, Jimmy, is that you understand too much," Rico told him. "Well, get this, I might be gotten next to, as you put it, but none of these lousy convicts in here will ever do it. The prison might—it's inexorable, like death and judgment, but—"

"*Lousy convicts*— that includes me," Jimmy said.

Rico's eyes dropped. "That's not fair and you're not lousy," he said. "Not all the time, anyway." And then, with one of his abrupt changes, he was grinning. "And you're not really a convict," he added, giving Jimmy an up from under look. "You're Mister Monroe."

"Are you Spanish?" Jimmy asked suddenly.

"No, why?"

"Oh, I don't know, you look it."

"No, I'm from a big country that grows big people. We're so big out there that small things are of no interest to us. That's what most people can never understand. I'm from California."

"Are you big?" Jimmy asked with broad amusement.

"Yes." Rico was earnest.

"That's a good thing to know about yourself," Jimmy observed.

"Of course, it's like religion."

"You don't care how you look either, do you?" Jimmy asked, tying the two together.

But Rico didn't get it.

"Clothes, shoes, hair," Jimmy pointed out.

"Oh!" Rico laughed. "Why should I? I don't get any visitors; I just haven't any one to dress for." His eyes fell again.

Jimmy lit a cigaret. "Smoke?" He held out the pack.

Rico took one, lit it, held it in the corner of his mouth. "Are you disappointed in me?" he asked, head tilted, talking around the cigaret and squinting one eye against the smoke.

"I'm not decided," Jimmy replied.

Their eyes met and they got charged from each other, full and violently. Their faces were less than a foot apart before Rico broke his gaze away. "Remember the pardon," he said, sounding gaspy.

Jimmy felt choked himself. "Damn the pardon!"

"You wouldn't mean that—say next week."

"I know I wouldn't."

"Don't ever do anything you wouldn't mean next week," Rico said in a distant, older voice. "It's never worth it."

"I don't know, it depends—"

"Anyway," Rico cut him off. "I don't go up until five and a half years, and then I might not make it. So it would be better if it never came to that. I'd be here so long after you left."

"Maybe I'd make it worth it," Jimmy argued.

Rico's eyes struck up. "That's a hell of a lot of loneliness. Is anything worth it?"

Jimmy asked, "Want a couple of bucks."

Everything went. "Now you've gone and done it again," Rico

accused, going dopey-faced. "You just can't help it, can you. And I had so hoped you wouldn't."

Jimmy took a deep breath. "I'm a gambler," he said.

"Just to think," Rico reflected in a low voice. "A moment ago you were rather grand. It would be better if I hated you from the go; better for both of us."

Jimmy went smart. "That's better than your being indifferent, anyway. My old grandpa used to say, grandson, if you can't make 'em love you—"

"I could hate you very easily," Rico said, turning away.

That was Monday.

TUESDAY WAS BATH DAY. The first section, to which Jimmy belonged, was called right after breakfast. When they came out, the second section was waiting. He located Rico and called, "Catch," tossing him a bar of *Lux*. Rico smiled delightedly.

When they had returned to the dormitory, the convicts teased Jimmy, but he denied everything. "You got me wrong this time. I'm not making any play, I just like the kid. The field's wide open for any of you Casanovas with leanings."

"That's what you said about Lively," an old timer reminded him.

"And there was 'cousin' Walter. The straight of that never did come out."

"This is another cousin you stumbled up on, ain't it?" Signifier jibed. "You're finding all your cousins, ain't you?"

"I'm going to get a pardon and I'd be a fool to get involved in something like that," Jimmy pointed out.

"That ain't nothing," Signifier said. "That ain't no more than you've always been."

"All right, you got it," Jimmy growled, annoyed. "Take it and go." Turning away, he went over to his bunk and oiled and massaged his scalp, a ritual he always performed after his weekly bath. No sooner than he had finished, Rico stopped by.

At sight of him, Jimmy whistled. "Why, you look nice and shiny, like something new."

Rico's hair had been meticulously combed and brushed and his skin looked scrubbed. For once he did not have the ukelele strung about his neck. "I washed behind the ears and when we go to the barber shop I'm going to get a hair cut," he said. "And guess why?" His eyes were radiant.

"I give up—why?"

"So I can look pretty for you. Aren't I brazen?"

"I should say so," Jimmy grinned.

Returning the soap, Rico thanked him. "You're thoughtful. I can't repay you until the first of next month; my mother only sends me two dollars a month and I've spent this month's already."

"Smoke?" Jimmy offered him the pack. He took one. "Where is your mother, in California?"

"Yes, Los Angeles." His voice was different when he talked of her, tender and containing a note of reverence.

Jimmy pulled down his typewriter and gathered together his paper.

"Did you learn to type in here?" Rico asked.

Jimmy nodded. "Can you?"

"A little, but not so well as you."

"You can practice on this sometimes when I'm not using it."

"Oh, can I? Thanks, darling." Enthusiasm raced through him.

Jimmy's head jerked up. "*Darling?*"

Rico was suddenly blushing. "That slipped out. It's a habit I took from my mother."

276

"Listen," Jimmy said, going fatherly. "You haven't been in here long, have you?" He put the typewriter back on the bunk.

"About a year. Are you going to lecture?"

"Yes."

"Must I listen?"

"That's up to you."

"I'll listen. Who's the first heel you're going to tell me about?"

"Me. I'm heel number one. I've been here for almost five years and I'm rather lousy. It won't do you any good to be seen with me; everybody will think the worst of you and give you a tough way to go. They'll swear you're—well, a girl-boy, because I've got the reputation of going for that sort of stuff. It's a bum rap, though, I was strictly a chump—but, well, you've been here long enough to know how it is. You'll have the name without the game." He paused.

"Is that all?" Rico asked. Jimmy could not tell how he was taking it.

"That isn't all I'd like to say, but that's all I'm going to say."

"Aren't you going to say anything about Dutch Henry?" Rico asked, feigning surprise. "Dutch told me never to smoke behind you. He said you had the syphilis. He said you caught it from wetting pencil points when you were writing. He said all writers have the syphilis."

They both began laughing at the same time.

"Dutch is all right," Jimmy grinned. "He's boosting me. In the first place, I'm highly flattered to be classified as a writer, and in the second place, he's probably the one who has the syphilis." Then he became serious. "But I mean what I said."

"It's a new approach to me," Rico observed.

"So you know all the *old* approaches?"

Looking suddenly trapped, Rico denied quickly, "I don't know any." Then laughter came into his voice. "But it must be a new one or you wouldn't use it. You're not the man to follow in a rut."

"You're clever, too, aren't you," Jimmy said, running his hand into his pocket. Palming a dollar bill, he brought out his hand and said, "We're friendly strangers; let's shake on it."

Rico looked at him for a long moment. His shoulders sagged a little and his smile was forced. "So I'm not being given a say?"

Jimmy reached down and took his hand, placed the bill in it, folded the fingers. "It's only a dollar," he said. "It won't break me. Consider it as a gift from me to myself. I've always wanted to be as big as a dollar bill. Remember we're strangers."

Turning quickly away before Rico could reply, he went up front and planked down his typewriter. Signifier came out and joined him. "How're you and the kid making out?" he asked.

"He won't go," Jimmy said. "He's a straight kid. I'm cutting out."

"I wouldn't argue with you," Signifier smirked.

Dutch and Jew Baby came up and sat across the table from them. "You got the best go, Monroe," Dutch conceded, sounding him.

Jew Baby blinked.

"And you got the wrong fellow," Jimmy replied. Taking a pencil from his shirt pocket, he laid it on the table, and when Dutch wasn't looking, knocked it over into his lap.

When Dutch picked it up and started to return it, Jimmy cried, "Watch out, don't stick that in your mouth! You'll get syphilis."

Dutch gave a start. The others turned and gaped at him.

"That's the way I got the syphilis," Jimmy grinned. "Sticking pencil points in my mouth. All writers get the syphilis that way."

Dutch grew sheepish. "Did he tell you what I said?"

"I don't want none of that," Signifier said. "It's run both of these sonabitches crazy already."

"Dutch told Rico I got the syphilis from wetting pencil points in my mouth," Jimmy explained.

They laughed. Dutch turned red. Signifier said, "All's fair in love and war. And this ain't war. Did you tell him about Dutch's shankers?"

"No, I told him Dutch was an epileptic."

"You didn't tell him that sure enough?" Dutch asked.

"Sure enough," Jimmy lied.

Rico came up and sat down beside him. "It's all right for me to talk to you out here, isn't it?" he asked. There was a slight note of sarcasm in his voice.

"Sure, as long as I'm out here it's all right, *clever*," Jimmy replied, then turning to the others, explained, "I just told Prince it wouldn't be advisable for him to talk too much to me because some one might get the idea that he was my kid."

"Or some one might get the idea that you was his kid," Signifier cracked.

Dutch asked Rico, "What did he tell you about me?"

"He didn't tell me anything about you," Rico replied, lifting his head in the beginning of his sneer. "He didn't consider you that important."

"Now take you for instance, Jew Baby," Jimmy continued. "Both you and Dutch. If you saw Prince hanging around my bunk all the time and talking to me the first thing you'd say was that I'd made him, wouldn't you? Of course you would. But if you never saw him talking to me you couldn't say it, could you?" Neither replied. "Could you?" Jimmy persisted.

"Aw, Jimmy," Jew Baby whined. "Old Jimmy."

Dutch jumped to his feet, red and angry. "You're not so god-damned slick," he gritted.

"Here's the dime I owe you and another for interest," Rico said, tossing twenty cents across the table, lips curled, head tilted. "Thanks."

Dutch picked it up and tossed it back. "Keep it and buy yourself some teddies," he snarled, in an ugly mood.

Rico reddened. Snatching up the coins, he hurled them into Dutch's face. Dutch turned sheet white, began climbing over the table. Rico scrambled to his feet and started in to meet him. Then Signifier jumped up to stop Dutch, and Jimmy grabbed Rico by the arm, pulling him away. But Dutch had drawn a knife, and seeing it, Signifier backed up. Rico wheeled and snatched a wooden label from a bunk frame. Then Jimmy stepped between them, weak from a sickening fear he'd always had of knives, but being impelled by some emotion greater than his fear. Before anyone was hurt, captain Frank rushed up and jerked Dutch away.

"We don't want any fighting in here," he puffed. When he saw the knife his voice grew sharp, "You know better than that, Dutch. Give me that knife." Dutch gave him the knife. "Now cut it out," he grated, then looked at Jimmy.

"Just a mistake, Frank," Jimmy grinned.

Turning away, captain Frank caught sight of Rico, then turned back and looked him over long and carefully. All of them looked at Rico. Standing at the foot of the bunk with his hair disordered and his eyes blazing, he appeared wild and reckless and utterly disdainful, but what impressed Jimmy most was that he did not look in the least afraid.

"We don't want any of that in here," captain Frank warned him, then turned and looked at Jimmy again, questioningly.

"He's a ball player, Frank," Jimmy winked. "Got five more years, too."

Captain Frank appeared suddenly interested, but when Signifier laughed, his interest turned sheepish. He ducked his head and returned to his stand. Rico looked at Jimmy as if he wanted to say something, then without saying it, he turned and pushed his way through the crowd that had collected. A moment later Jimmy saw him sitting on his bunk, strumming his uke; he felt relieved.

"Who got my two dimes?" Signifier blustered.

"Here they are," a convict replied, passing over the coins.

"You chump," Jimmy said. When he had put away his type-writer, he went down to the poker game and stood behind Candy.

"What was the matter with Dutch?" Candy asked.

"Aw, that fellow's crazy," Jimmy said. "He wants to jump on every kid he can't make."

When the company went to the barber shop that afternoon, Jimmy, along with a number of others who shaved themselves, remained in the dormitory. Captain Frank came down to ask about Rico.

"Can that fellow really play ball?" Already he was thinking of next year's team.

"Sure, he's good," Jimmy replied. "He's out of California. You know, every one plays softball out there." He didn't know whether they did or not, but he felt certain that neither did captain Frank.

"What position does he play?"

"Field."

"We need a good fielder," captain Frank said. That's what Jimmy knew. "Can he hit?"

"A slugger," he enthused. "When he smacks a ball it's smacked."

Captain Frank nodded. "Keep him out of trouble, Jim."

When the company returned, Jimmy stopped Rico. "Can you play ba—" He broke off, noticing Rico's hair cut. "Say, how did you ever get in this joint?" he asked, stretching his eyes. "You can't be more than fifteen."

"They took me for my big brother," Rico grinned.

With his hair cut, he had lost something, however, Jimmy reflected, trying to ascertain just what when Rico interrupted his thoughts to ask, "What was it you were going to ask me whether I played?"

"Oh yes, can you play softball?"

"No, but I can dance."

Jimmy pulled his hair in mock exasperation. "Dance! Dance! What the hell do I care. Softball I'm talking about."

Rico smiled. "Maybe a little, but I can't play."

"Well, from now on you can. You're a red hot fielder and you can swat like the Babe himself—in case any one asks you."

"But I can't though."

"Well, I just told Frank that you could, and if you want to stay in this dormitory and get along, you had better say you can, too."

"But they'll find out—"

"They won't find out until next year and by that time it might not make any difference."

"All right, if you say so . . ."

Watching him walk off, Jimmy was repulsed by the grotesqueness of his carriage. He'd look so much better if he carried his shoulders erect, he thought. But the next moment he shrugged it off. It didn't mean anything to him.

Rico went over on a clothes' order and got a complete new

outfit from shoes to cap. After supper he stopped by Jimmy's bunk and said brightly, "Look what just a casual remark by you has done to me."

Jimmy turned a glance of pleased astonishment on him. "Now it's you who must be in love," he ventured.

"I am; I've spent the dollar and I'm all yours, darling," he lilted, his lips slightly parted and wet red and his eyes abnormally bright.

"Did that slip out, too?" Jimmy asked.

"No, I meant it."

Their eyes locked. It was Jimmy who broke his gaze away. "Life is a funny thing," he meditated.

For an instant Rico's eyes dulled, then brightened again, but this time the light was all on the surface. "Do tell, grandpa."

Jimmy looked at him again and noticed a few beads of perspiration on his upper lip. It gave him such a queer sensation he felt shocked all over. Stifling it, he said, "I've given away a lot of dough since I've been in here, but every penny of it had strings, some kind of strings. It either did something for me or I looked for something in return. I got something out of it for myself. And the one time I wanted to give away something so small as a dollar with no strings at all, the strings come back from the dollar."

"Didn't you want anything?" Rico asked, his eyes wide and enquiring.

"No."

"Lovely," he said. "I've got a quarter left. I'm going out and gamble." He went remote and distant and very tall, like the top of a cloud, and if his knees had not buckled he would have swirled away. But as it was the effect became grotesque. Jimmy was again repulsed.

I'm a solid damn fool, he told himself. I want to write a story and I can't, and I'm trying to get out of here and I'm letting it get close to me again. Because he was worried about Rico gambling in his present state of mind. He would become too excited and treat people too badly and sooner or later get into serious trouble. For a moment he stood there, cursing himself. Then he went out to the game and sat down beside Rico.

"Listen," he said. "Did you ever see a little girl trying to get across the street and say all of a sudden, 'Here, little girl, let me help you.'"

"No," Rico replied facetiously, "but I will imagine it."

"Why?" Jimmy asked.

"Why what?"

"Why did you want to help her?"

"Oh, because she was a little girl and might grow up into a beautiful woman. And I might fall in love with her, whereas if I hadn't helped her she might have been run over and—"

Jimmy went blindly angry. "Go to hell!" he snarled.

When he had finished eating the slice of pie which Wicks had smuggled from the dining room in his shirt bosom for him, captain Frank called the mail. Jimmy received letters from both his mother and father, and after reading them got over his irritation. Signifier stopped by his bunk and asked, "You wouldn't fool me, would you?"

"It seems as if I'm only fooling myself," Jimmy confessed, but before he could explain, Rico joined them. "I'm running after you something scandalous, aren't I?" he gushed.

Signifier broke into a broad grin and his ears stuck out, but he did not say anything.

"I just got a letter from my mother," Jimmy told Rico. "She says she talked to Dinkle, the governor's secretary, and that he says the governor is planning to pardon about fifty during the Christmas holidays and that I was in line for consideration. I think I'm going to make it this time. I feel it in my bones."

"That's swell," Rico said. He sounded as if he meant it. "May I read it?"

"Sure." Jimmy passed him the letter.

"She writes a nice letter," he said when he had finished. "I hope you get the pardon. That would mean so much to you." Then in a different tone, he added, "I received a letter from my mother, too. Would you like to read it?"

"Sure we would," Signifier replied, having been left out long enough. "Run and get it."

But Rico kept looking at Jimmy until he nodded, then turned away and went down to his bunk, walking rapidly, his knees buckling grotesquely. Watching him, Jimmy felt that slight aversion for his crippleness again. But he felt something else, something more.

"He seems like a good kid," Signifier remarked. "Full of life."

Jimmy picked up his mirror so he could watch Rico without turning, and said with an odd seriousness, "I think I'm going to fall in love with him. You're right, Johnson, I'm a damn fool."

Rico returned with his face aglow and gave Jimmy the letter.

"Why, she writes a swell letter," Jimmy said when he had finished.

"Why are you surprised?" Rico asked curiously.

"Oh, I, er—" He was embarrassed. "I didn't expect her to be so intelligent." But that only made it worse. He began to blush. "What I mean is, er, I mean I think she is very intelligent and sympathetic and knows just what to write."

Rico laughed indulgently. "I love you when you get confused. You're just twelve years old."

"She must love you a lot," Jimmy mused.

Rico went away from them then, to California. "She does," he said. His voice was reverent. "She was so young when I was born. We grew up like pals, like brother and sister. She was only fifteen when I was born." Jimmy did not reply, and after a moment Rico asked timidly, "Want to see her picture."

"Sure," Signifier replied.

Rico took a snapshot from his pocket. The corners had been clipped, and in ink, written across the back, was *To my darling Son, from mother.* She was clad in trousers and a sweater with her hands in her sweater pockets.

"She's good looking," Signifier complimented. "How old is she?"

"That's personal, you damn fool," Jimmy snapped. Then he turned to Rico and said in a stilted tone of voice, as if trying to rectify Signifier's breach of etiquette, "She's a very fine looking woman."

Rico began laughing. "You sound too cute for words, darling. I wish I had a better picture, she's much better looking than that."

"*Darling?*" Signifier mumbled.

"Yes, that's what I said," Rico admitted. "Would you like for me to call you darling, too?"

"Naw, just call me old Signifier," he replied with his signifying habits. "Say, is she married?"

"You're a rat," Rico laughed.

"Yeah, that's what to call old Siggy. Call him a rat. Save the *darling's* for Jimmy," Signifier said.

"No, you're not a rat, you're a darling."

"What was the matter you got transferred from the cotton mill? Have you got rickets in your legs or you just stiffing?" Signifier wanted to know.

"The knee-caps have been broken and unless I exercise a lot they slip out of place," Rico replied. "But the reason I got transferred was I got into a fight with my cell mate. He claimed to be a prize fighter and kept trying to boss everybody in the cell. I got tired of it."

It was easy enough for Jimmy to imagine the sneering way in which Rico would challenge his prize fighting cell mate, but he could not conceive of him putting up much of a fight. He reminded Jimmy of the type they called "game" in prison with that broad note of sarcasm, the fellows who would keep getting up every time they were knocked down. "He was game, anyway," they would laugh. But he did not like to think of anyone knocking Rico down; it made him slightly sick to think about it. Rico seemed so incapable of defending himself.

"*Rico* is a Spanish name isn't it?" he asked to change the conversation.

"Yes, it means *rich,*" Rico replied.

Signifier began laughing. "Well it's about time he found a rich cousin. The rest of 'em—"

"Nix up, Johnson," Jimmy warned.

But Rico had picked it up. "Oh, is this some of his past? Tell me about it, Signifier. If I'm going to be his kid I ought to know something of his love life. Was he blond?"

"Lively was blond but—"

"Lively? Is that the Lively in the girl-boy—on 5-D?"

"Oh, cut it out!" Jimmy grated.

"You know him then?" Signifier asked, laying a trap.

"I've seen him from a distance. Some one pointed him out to me; they said he had a sugar daddy—"

"That was Jimmy," Signifier cut in.

"That's very discouraging," Rico said. "If he likes blonds—"

"You shouldn't do that," Jimmy interrupted. "Signifier is very gullible, he'll believe all this."

"Sure, I'm a fool," Signifier said with his signifying laugh. "I'll believe anything." Then he turned to Rico. "So you're going to be his kid? Well, well, how's about old Siggy?"

"Tell me the rest," Rico demanded, snapping his fingers.

"Well, Chump is brunette— Say, what about my ends?"

"Oh, goddammit, cut it out!" Jimmy snarled, getting red.

"Not Chump up here?" Rico asked with raised brows.

"Sure, didn't you know."

Jimmy wheeled toward the aisle, but Rico headed him off, hugging him. "Is my little itsy bitsy darling getting angry?"

Signifier broke out laughing.

"You go too damn far," Jimmy told Rico furiously.

"You can't take it, darling."

"Sure, I can take it, but why should I? You don't mean any of it—"

"And I'll believe it and tell every one in the dormitory," Signifier put in.

"You're saying it for a joke, but you will!" Jimmy shouted.

"How do you know I don't mean it?" Rico asked. His face pumped with an inner excitement and a smile curled slightly his wide red lips.

Inexplicably, Jimmy was suddenly repulsed. "If you do, you're a damned fool," he snapped. "I'm getting a pardon and to hell with you."

286

"You're so delightful when you're angry," Rico lilted in a high tenor voice, rocking with low laughter and holding to Jimmy's arms. "Curse me again, darling. I like to see your lips grow tight and your eyes look stern and forbidding, and you frown just like Jove, himself. Oh, you're—"

Jimmy felt a queer impulse to laugh, but he didn't want Rico to know it. "Get the hell out of the way and let me by," he blustered.

Clutching tightly to his arms, Rico went through one of his sudden changes. "I really didn't mean it, darling," he said with a child's earnestness. "Don't go away thinking I mean it." He was quite serious.

"What the hell did you say it for, then?"

"Damn right," Signifier echoed. "Now you got me believing it, too, and I'm all set to tell everybody and here you go and say you don't mean it."

Jimmy had to laugh. But Rico remained very solemn. "I was just joking, Jimmy. Honestly, I just wanted to see how you would take it."

"Your jokes are silly," Jimmy said. "I don't like to be put in the middle all the time."

Watching the sudden hurt come up into Rico's eyes, he turned quickly away, trying vainly to be angry, and Rico drew back and let him pass. He went out to the poker game and took out a dollar's worth of chips. After a minute Rico came out and sat across the table from him; he had a quarter he'd borrowed from Signifier.

"Hello, Jimmy," he gushed as if he had not seen him all day.

Jimmy did not reply; he was wondering where Rico got the money.

"Let's save, Jimmy," Rico suggested. He sounded complacent.

"Oh, all right," Jimmy acceded gruffly.

But afterwards he was sorry that he had. Rico made him extremely nervous; he talked to the others as if they were dirt, sneering and looking contemptuous until any moment Jimmy expected some one to jump up and hit him. It seemed more of a cat fight than a poker game. When Rico finally got broke, he gave a vast sigh of relief.

And then he found himself saying, "You can play some of my chips, Prince," pushing half of his stack across the table.

But by then Rico had lost all sense of reason. "You're already out on the limb for a dollar," he sneered. "You don't want to go any deeper, do you? You're not getting anything, you know."

Drawing back his chips, Jimmy choked, infuriated, "That tells me just what you are."

"Give me a half dollar's worth of chips," Rico demanded of the chip seller.

The chip seller hesitated. "Where's your money?"

Rico jumped to his feet, blotching with dull red. "Do you want me to break up this goddamn game?" he shrilled in a high, cracking voice.

Jimmy went sick inside. It was Dutch's game, and he was dealing. "Ain't anybody going to break up this game," he challenged. "And you, little punk, put up your money when you want chips."

Rico drew back as if he would slap Dutch, and Jimmy said quickly, his voice brittle with fear, "He's got money, Dutch, give him the chips."

Rico wheeled and snatched a handful of chips from the chip seller. Then he turned on Jimmy. "I don't need any of your goddamned recommendations."

"You've got to live in here, boy," Jimmy told him, trying to talk down the tenseness. "You can't run over people that way. The rules of the games are that you pay for your chips when you get them; you can't tell us how to run our games."

Dutch had drawn his knife and sat waiting with the knife in his lap. Rico passed the chips back to the chip seller, then turned to Dutch. "Give me an ante."

Dutch tossed three penny chips on the table.

Suddenly smiling and subdued with all of the fury gone out of him, Rico turned to Jimmy and said, "I'll take those chips you wanted to give me now, darling." His voice was penitent.

Well, that lets me in for it, Jimmy thought. I'll have the name without the game. He said slowly, carefully, "Go to hell, punk!"

Without again looking at Jimmy, Rico lost the three chips on the first hand, then got up and left. After a moment Jimmy heard him strumming his ukelele down at the far end of the dormitory, loud and defiantly. He began losing, and lost five dollars. He was hot and sweaty and disgusted with himself.

When the lights went out for bedtime, he stalked down to Rico's bunk, tight-mouthed and belligerent. "Listen, how'd you like for me to hit you in the mouth?" he challenged.

Lying on his side with his face near the edge of the bunk, looking at Jimmy intently, Rico replied, "I don't know. I won't until you do it. I might like it." In the half-shadow his face was smooth with a dull, even sheen like old ivory. All of his features were a blurred, soft outline, giving him an exotic appearance, and his sloe eyes were wide and deep and filled with little lights.

Jimmy gritted his teeth. "Let me tell you something—" Then he broke off, watching Rico's tongue come out slowly to wet his lips. He looked at Rico's wet lips parted slightly over an even row of teeth. "Your lips look like crushed strawberries," he said.

"You're so divinely masculine, darling," Rico whispered in a low, husky voice. "That's what first attracted me—because you're so beautiful with it."

"I'd like to crush them my goddamned self," Jimmy choked.

"That's a lovely idea," Rico said, and Jimmy leaned forward and kissed him with long and steady pressure. Beneath his, Rico's lips felt smooth and softly resilent, like those of all the girls of whom he'd dreamed and had never seen during the past five years, and he kept kissing him until the breath had gone completely out of both of them. At that moment, he did not give a damn if the warden was standing just behind him.

When he drew away they both had to gasp for breath.

"Your eyes are filled with stardust," he whispered hoarsely.

"That's a lovely compliment, darling," Rico murmured.

"But you're so damned exasperating," Jimmy continued. "You keep me scared for you all the time. Why do you treat people so lousy all the time?"

"I need to, darling," Rico told him seriously. "Maybe now I won't need to anymore."

"You're a sweet little kid when you want to be," Jimmy said.

"I want to be for you," Rico lilted lowly, looking upward from beneath a lacquered fan of lashes.

That was Tuesday night. Wednesday morning Rico asked, "Do you still mean it this morning, darling?"

"Yes," Jimmy said.

"As much as last night?"

"Yes," Jimmy lied.

"I wonder," Rico said.

*S*HADOWS, *THEY ARE ALL about me. In the stench-laden corners of my dungeon, they are black sentinels at the black gates of death, forbidding me sanctuary. On the slime-encrusted floor, they lie motionless, writhing in the eyes of my fear. They hover alive in the space about me, vampires of thought, drinking the life of my soul. Shadows, flung into space by sharp corners, breaking off at unknown angles, falling on concrete floors, climbing black walls. Shadows, receding before light, racing rapidly off to hide behind bars, in corners. Shadows of bars falling on shadows of bars, making blackness. Shadows of bars swinging out into space to fall with soul-bruising heaviness on shadows of men. Shadows of shadows, no longer men, victims of the night eternal, victims of the shadows . . .*

"Did you write this?" Jimmy asked. His voice was husky.

Rico nodded. "Do you like it?"

"Did you feel it?"

"It came to me one night in the cell."

Jimmy had a sudden picture of him lying on his bunk in a

darkened cell, haunted with horrible fears. He was sick with being afraid for him.

"If you will sit here very quietly, I will write a story," he said.

"I'll be very quiet for you, darling," Rico promised.

Reading the piece again was all that Jimmy needed to write his story, A CONVICT IS HUMAN, TOO. All the old protests boiled up in him, and he wrote a story, all emotion, from beginning to end. When he had finished, he felt drained of all sensations; he sat there looking blankly at his typewriter.

"I've been awfully quiet," Rico said in a small, hesitant voice. "Can I say something now?"

Jimmy gave a start. He had forgotten Rico. "Yes, play me a song," he said.

Rico began picking out melodies in individual notes on his ukelele. He was very adept and the melody was exceptionally clear. Jimmy found it soothing and pleasant.

"Did you finish it?" Rico asked, stopping once.

Jimmy nodded.

"Do you like it?"

"Very much," Jimmy admitted. "I'll let you read it later on."

Rico played *Sweet Sue* and *Memories* and another tune that Jimmy liked immediately. "What's that one?" he asked.

"*Stardust,*" Rico told him. "Remember what you said about my eyes?"

"God, it's a beautiful tune," Jimmy mused. "It's like your eyes, too. Do you know the words?"

"Yes."

"Sing them for me."

"I can't now. I will sometimes, though. For you."

After a time they had an audience. The other convicts, hearing Rico, and seeing Jimmy there, gathered about. "Say, I didn't know you could play like that," some one observed. "Can you play *I Surrender Dear?*"

Rico began picking it out, looking at Jimmy, but strangely Jimmy did not feel embarrassed. Noticing it, Rico became expansive. He played all the requests that he knew, *Please, Me and My Shadow,*

When My Sugar Walks Down the Street, When Day Is Done. The two colored convicts with the guitar and the banjo joined them, and they had a musical which broke up the poker games.

At eight o'clock, the music hour was over and they had to stop. When they were alone, Rico said, "It's better now, isn't it?"

Jimmy did not reply at first.

"Don't you think it's better?" Rico persisted.

"Sure."

"You don't sound very spontaneous, darling. You do think it's better, don't you?"

"Of course I think it's better," he admitted.

"You're not ashamed of me?"

"Of course not."

"I was very nice to every one, wasn't I?"

"You were swell."

"I noticed that you did not feel embarrassed," Rico said. "You won't ever feel embarrassed or ashamed of me, will you, darling?"

"No."

"Honestly?"

"Honestly."

"I'm glad. I couldn't bear it."

The next day was Thanksgiving and the convicts were given a picture show. The idle companies went in the morning and Jimmy and Rico sat side by side in the darkness. Rico wanted Jimmy to put his arm about his shoulder, but he refused. In the end, however, he compromised by letting Rico hold his hand, feeling completely ridiculous all the while.

Reading his thoughts, Rico teased, "You were the one who never compromised."

"You misunderstood me," Jimmy replied stiffly, and felt Rico laugh to himself.

But shortly the picture swallowed them; it was intense drama. Afterwards Jimmy could not recall a single incident shown in the film, but he remembered it vividly because they discovered that the same things touched them both.

"You are full of little surprises," Rico observed when they were back in the dormitory. "One wouldn't think you were so romantic."

"*Mushy* is a better word," Jimmy said.

"*Mushy* is a lousy word," Rico objected, "and it doesn't describe what I mean. You are full of softnesses all inside, but they come out in rather unexpected ways."

"How do you know?"

"By the things that touch you. Do you dream?"

"Sure, when my supper doesn't agree with me," Jimmy chuckled.

Rico brushed it aside, frowning. "You know I don't mean like that. I mean awake. Tall, golden dreams swaying in a summer breeze, like tall-stemmed lilies. I borrowed that, but it expresses what I mean."

Jimmy was startled. "Yes," he admitted slowly, after a time.

Rico said, "We're so much alike, I could cry."

That evening, Jimmy showed Rico his story. When he had finished reading it, Rico said quite seriously, "This is genius. Do you know you are a genius, darling?" When Jimmy didn't reply, he said, "Are you as happy and excited as I, darling? I'm so filled up I don't know what to do." It was real; it was in his eyes and Jimmy saw it.

"Play me a song," Jimmy said.

They went down to Rico's bunk and he played *Stardust* for Jimmy and sang it in a husky, emotion-filled voice with his eyes as bright as stars and his wet red lips parted in ecstacy. Jimmy never forgot him singing that song that night, and the way he looked at him. They were drunk with each other.

"You're like Aphrodite," Jimmy said.

"I'm more like Circe, really," Rico mused, then asked quickly, "You don't feel badly about any of it, do you, darling?"

"Why should I?" Jimmy countered.

"I'm good for you, aren't I, darling?" Rico persisted. "Tell me that I'm good for you."

"You're marvelous," Jimmy told him. "You're so beautifully

unpredictable." He had never known before that he could say such words.

They set each other up.

4

At THE TIME JIMMY SENT away his story he told Rico that he did not think it would sell. "It's too good for them," he laughed. And it didn't. But Rico was the one who was the most disappointed. And it was Jimmy who had to cheer him.

"It's still a good story, Prince," he said. "The fact that they didn't buy it doesn't alter the worth of the story. It probably won't sell anywhere; it's very amateurish."

"That's one of the drawbacks of greatness," Rico said.

Jimmy looked at him sharply, suspecting that he was being ribbed. "You're full of little philosophies, aren't you?"

"They're not mine," he disclaimed.

"That's the trouble with writing about underdogs," Jimmy reflected, reverting to the story. "Of course I knew that from the start. People don't want to hear too much about them; they have just so much sympathy to spare, and they can't spare too much of it on convicts. And I can't blame them," he added.

"I can't blame anybody for anything," Rico brooded. "What deacon may have rung a bell with larceny in his heart? What angel may have carried heaven's tidings to hell?"

"That sounds like Omar," Jimmy said. "Where else could you get so much fatalism?"

"Anyway, it's not mine."

"You said that before," Jimmy reminded. "Whose is it?"

"It's life's."

294

"What wonderful, enormous plates you have, grandpa," Jimmy said sarcastically.

But Rico was serious. "I'm twenty-four," he said.

"That's a lot of living," Jimmy jibed. "You had better tie your long white whiskers off the floor."

Suddenly, Rico went remote. "It might not be so much," he said dully, "but it was plenty for me until I met you."

Jimmy jerked about and stared at him. After a long moment of appraisal, he remarked, "That's a funny thing to say."

"Everything needs a purpose," Rico pointed out. "Even a thing so inconsequential as life."

It didn't sound right to Jimmy, but he could see that Rico was in earnest. "You have a mother," he finally pointed out.

"I'm such a disappointment to her," Rico confessed.

"Sure, I'm a disappointment to my mother, too," Jimmy argued. "She had her heart set on me being president or some such rot. But if I needed a feeling to pull me through the twenty years I started with, I could have gotten it from her." It was strange how easy he could say that when he knew it wasn't true.

"But you don't know my story," Rico told him. "I've gotten all of that already. You see, I was in the reformatory and my mother sent me three hundred dollars to come home on."

Jimmy grew suddenly a hundred years old. "And you got broke and got into trouble and came to prison. Okay, I understand that. But mothers are funny people, little boy. They wouldn't sell you out for that, no matter how much of that stuff called mother love you destroy and abuse. They still have just as much left. It's like a spring that never runs dry. Your mother wouldn't fail you, little boy, ever . . ." Saying it, he began to wonder if it was so.

"She wouldn't," Rico said. "I know. It's not her; it's me. I was out twelve days. You were so right when you called me haywire—" He broke off to ask, "Have you ever been scared?"

Jimmy was slow in replying. "Of life? Of what it can do to you? Of the prison? Of the nights? Of being alone? Scared of thoughts and feelings and memories?" He took a deep breath. "Sure, I've been scared." He had never before confessed that to anyone. "I've been scared a lot of times. I'm still scared a lot of times."

"You're so much like me," Rico choked, his voice filled with tears, "and yet so different."

They were silent for a moment. Then Jimmy said, "But I don't think about it, and if you don't think about it, it can't hurt you. I learned that as a defense mechanism when the judge said *twenty years*."

But Rico had not heard him. "That's some of it, but not all," he said slowly. "Have you ever been afraid of people not understanding you, and grow up feeling that? Grow up feeling that no one understood you, not even your own mother. And then, in the end, when you had given every one a chance to understand you and no one ever had, telling yourself that you didn't give a damn if they never did, that you simply did not care. And then being wild and reckless and uncaring and saying, take me or leave me and to hell with everybody, and not really meaning it. All the time so pitifully scared and lonely and away from everybody in a shadowed world of abnormality, wanting so badly for some one to tell you that you are right. Or if not that, for some one just to be on your side." When he stopped he was crying.

More than anything in the world, Jimmy wanted to comfort him, but he did not know how. He felt so utterly tender toward him. Finally he said, "It's not all quite clear. Would you mind saying it over?"

Rico looked at him queerly for a moment. Then suddenly he was laughing. "But of course you don't understand, Jimmy. How could you? You don't have to be afraid of yourself. You don't have to be afraid ever—" and now he was deeply bitter "—of doing something so sickening that you want to hang yourself a moment afterwards—and still not being able to keep yourself from doing it."

"I don't know, I've done a lot of things that I'm not proud of," Jimmy said.

"But they stand telling, anyway," Rico stated.

"Let's don't talk about it," Jimmy snarled, getting fed up all of a sudden. He had gotten a picture that was sickeningly repulsive, and for the instant he hated Rico, hated him for everything he implied.

"You're wrong, Jimmy," Rico denied, reading his thoughts. "It never came to that."

Relief came, clogging him. Then he became philosophical. "The trouble with you is that you have too much imagination," he said. "You have a fatalism, but it isn't a true fatalism. It's only a veneer and you don't actually feel it or else it wouldn't desert you when you need it most."

"Now you're getting fleas in *your* beard," Rico charged.

In the evenings sometimes they'd stand beside Jimmy's bunk with a magazine between them and read to each other. And sometimes they'd stop to watch the sun setting beyond the bath house.

"God, I wonder what's beyond that horizon," Jimmy said once.

And Rico replied, "You can take it from me, baby, it's not what you think."

"I'd be willing to chance it, anyway," Jimmy argued.

"I hope for your sake you will, and I'll pray to God, darling, that you'll never be as disappointed as I was."

"You sound like you've been a lot of places," Jimmy observed enviously.

"I have," Rico sighed. "But that horizon was always there, between me and the other side." After a moment he added: "But since I met you something is happening to me. I don't know myself yet just what it is, only I know that the horizon doesn't matter anymore because it's all inside of me now."

"You don't have to ever worry anymore, little boy," Jimmy told him.

And he gave Jimmy one of his scintillating smiles. "You're so unutterably sweet, darling."

On Fridays and Tuesdays Rico was taken to the hospital for treatments, and Jimmy asked him why.

"I have sinus trouble," he stated.

"You don't show any of the symptoms," Jimmy said.

"But I have it very bad at times," Rico contended. "It's all up here." He tapped his forehead just above the bridge of his nose. "Sometimes it's so bad it almost drives me crazy. My mother has it, too."

"Really? I never thought of sinus as being serious."

"It is, though. It is very serious and I hope you never have it. Ninety percent of all the people who have it seriously go crazy—"

"Then you'd better go over and have something done right away," Jimmy teased. "You're crazy enough as it is."

"I'm much better now, though, aren't I?"

"You're splendid."

But the next time Rico went to the hospital he signed up for an operation. About the middle of December he was hospitalized. That evening after supper, Jimmy fixed a package of toilet articles and got captain Frank to take him over to the hospital so he could leave them there for Rico; and the next day when Rico was operated on, he had captain Frank take him over again, and he was there when they wheeled him out of the operating room. He walked beside the stretcher and touched his hand and told him not to worry. But Rico did not need him then because the anesthetic was still with him. When the anesthetic left him was when he needed Jimmy, but Jimmy wasn't there then.

However, the long daily letters which Jimmy wrote and sent over by the paper boy helped greatly, Rico said in his replies. And the few lines which Rico wrote helped Jimmy a great deal, too, for he found it dreadfully lonely in the dormitory. He had not known it could get so lonely in the dormitory before. He thought he had known, but he hadn't.

Signifier elected himself to cheer him. "You look terrible," he said. "You look heartbroken. You better get ahold of yourself or you'll take down with tb."

Jimmy subscribed to all of the papers for Rico, and instructed the runner to give him all of the magazines he wanted. And he paid the colored porter and head nurse to look after him. It cost two dollars a day. But he did not tell Rico, for fear he would not like it.

Rico was in A ward where he could be seen from the hallway

through the glass partition. Every day on sick call Jimmy went over and waved to him. They had bandaged up his nostrils and once Jimmy wrote, "You certainly don't look very romantic." Rico's reply was all full of laughter.

They let him out the day before Christmas. They wanted to keep him in a week longer, he said, "But I told them I just had to get out for Christmas, that it was a matter of life and death. I wanted to be with you this Christmas, darling. There might never be another one."

His mother had sent him two dollar bills in a letter, which, in the Christmas rush, the censors had overlooked. With them, he bought two bottles of sodium amatol capsules. The tb patients used them as opiates, but taken two or three at the time with coffee, they produced a form of intoxication. Because the capsules were blue, they called them "blue boys", and their jags told them that no one would know what they were talking about.

Both received boxes from their mothers. It seemed like a real Christmas, especially with the blue boys. They were "gaged" Christmas Eve and sang Christmas carols until midnight in loud off-key voices, while Rico played the accompaniment on his ukelele. And Christmas morning they took some more blue boys with their breakfast coffee and were very tall afterwards when they went to the show. Everything was funny and delightful. They laughed all during the film, except once, when it was very quiet, Rico leaned over and whispered to Jimmy, "Listen, I hear a train."

Jimmy frowned and listened. "I hear it, too," he said after a moment.

"Let's get on it and go somewhere," Rico said.

"Let's go to New York," Jimmy said.

"That dump!" Rico snorted.

"Well, Chicago, then."

"I've been there," Rico said. "Let's go to Arabia. Let's smell Paris in the spring and watch the bull fights in Barcelona and lie on the sand at Lido and help Omnipotence quench the sun in the Mediterranean. Let's pick stars out of the desert nights and sell them in Singapore for diamonds."

"I'm with you," Jimmy said.

"Always be with me, Jimmy," Rico begged. For an instant he sounded lost and scared. "Hand in hand forever. I couldn't make it without you, Jimmy. You'll never know."

"Hey, what the hell you monkeys whispering about?" some one behind them said.

They started and were silent for a moment. Then Rico asked, "Was I saying anything bad, Jimmy?"

"I don't think anyone could hear us."

"Suppose some one had heard us," Rico said, his voice filled with beginning laughter.

Thinking about it, they both began laughing again. Afterwards, at dinner, they took some more blue boys and drank some more coffee and that afternoon they played poker and lost and it was all so funny and exciting.

Everything was wonderful. They laughed at the convicts and laughed at losing pots. Once Rico said, "Darling, your letters were adorable; you write adorable letters, darling. Where did you learn to write such adorable letters?"

And Jimmy replied, "Were they? I'm glad you think they were; I wanted them to be."

"Did you write such adorable letters to your other girls?" Rico asked.

"There weren't any others," Jimmy denied.

"You lie so beautifully," Rico smiled.

They had completely forgotten the other convicts in the game until one of them exploded with pent-up laughter. And then every one was laughing. They thought they would die of embarrassment; they jumped up and ran away.

But it was all like that. They didn't know there was anyone else in the dormitory. Christmas seemed to belong only to them; in a dream.

Every one began talking about them, even the guards. But they thought them all very stupid and funny people and made little jokes about them and laughed and laughed and laughed.

Signifier and Candy came down to help them eat their boxes.

Pressing chicken and cake upon them until they were stuffed, Jimmy and Rico thought themselves very witty and magnanimous; they teased them and made little quips about them which, in their state of entrancement, they thought only themselves could understand. Then they gave them some blue boys.

Candy took his the following morning and went down to the colored convicts' skin game and "Bama'd" an eight spot through. One of the players caught him, but not before every one's money was hopelessly ensnarled. Jimmy had to go down and straighten it out because Candy wanted to fight all of the colored convicts in the dormitory.

Captain Frank called them aside that afternoon and told them to get rid of the dope and not to give Candy any more of it. They could hardly wait for him to leave before they were laughing again.

Rico received a typewriter from his mother for a Christmas present. Jimmy had never seen him so happy and excited.

"Oh, isn't she swell," he gushed. "She's so lovely, she's so adorable. Oh, isn't she lovely, Jimmy, isn't she grand?"

Jimmy was happy and excited also. "She's perfect," he said.

"She and you are the swellest people in all the world," Rico said.

"And you," Jimmy added.

"We're all swell people," Rico said.

It was not a very expensive typewriter, but they never let on that it was not the best. That night Rico took it apart, while Jimmy sat by and watched.

"Maybe you ought not to do it," he cautioned. "Maybe she wouldn't like it."

"She'll love it," Rico said. "You'd love her, Jimmy. She was so young when I was born; she wasn't but fifteen, and she didn't know how to raise me. I'm her love child. People used to think she was my older sister." He worked while he talked. "When I was old enough so we could talk to each other she taught me a swell way to live. Whatever we thought was right, honestly and sincerely thought it, *was* right. And all my life I've felt that way." He stopped and looked at Jimmy. "Don't you think that's a swell way to live?" he asked.

"Yes," Jimmy lied.

"It is, Jimmy," he argued earnestly. "Everything would be wrong if you couldn't feel that it was right. In the middle of the night when I'm awake and can't sleep, when I think about it, I have to feel that it's right."

It was a week later that Jimmy asked, "How do you feel about it?"

"I feel exalted," Rico replied.

And then, the second week in January, all of their blue boys were gone. For several days they had headaches and their mouths were nasty. But they didn't have any regrets.

"You don't know how swell it is not to have any regrets," Rico said. "It was like a sweet delirium." After a moment he added, "I could kiss you."

"Not here," Jimmy grinned, breaking away.

Soon afterwards he received a letter from his mother telling him to be brave and cheerful and not to become despondent because he didn't receive a Christmas pardon; that perhaps he would get one by summer.

"Are you sorry?" Rico asked, reading the letter.

"Yes," Jimmy replied. "But I had forgotten it until now."

"Then I'm sorry, too," Rico said. "But I'm not sorry about our Christmas. I couldn't be sorry for that."

"I'm not either," Jimmy said.

When they wrote the following Sunday, Rico said, "I told my mother about you last time, Jimmy. Do you want to say something to her now?"

"Tell her that I think she is very swell people and that I think of her as my very own mother and that I love her very much."

"I'll tell her; she'll like that."

"I'm going to tell my mother about you," Jimmy said.

Rico looked like a startled deer. "I hope she doesn't dislike me."

"Oh, she'll love you," Jimmy said, but he had his doubts.

Rico looked very queer when he said that. But Jimmy did not think about it until a long time afterwards.

"You never speak of your father," he noticed.

"You don't speak of yours, either," Rico countered.

"Mine's in Cleveland."

"Mine's in San Francisco."

They looked at each other.

During the following weeks they became very literary and read O. Henry together. Once Jimmy said, "You're a sweet child, Prince."

Rico's reaction was abrupt; his eyes became smoky and wistful. "Oh, how too lovely," he said. "Call me that always."

And then they ran across the name "Puggy Wuggy" in one of O. Henry's stories, and Rico exclaimed, "What a darling little name and it just fits you, darling!"

"Me? What the hell!"

"Yes it does," he stated. "You're a Puggy Wuggy darling and you've got a nose just like a little bunny rabbit's."

"That's no compliment," Jimmy said, blushing.

"You're a little puggy wuggy rabbit," Rico went on, his husky voice teasing and his eyes full of mischief and all alight, but his mouth was very tender. "And you have a little puggy wuggy nose that quirks just like a little bunny's nose when you're about to laugh and I love it and I'm going to call you Puggy Wuggy—"

"The hell you are!" Jimmy snarled.

"—and you're going to call me Sweet Child," Rico continued. "Won't that be nice?"

"Hell naw!"

So after that Rico called him Puggy Wuggy to his intense embarrassment, and he called Rico Sweet Child when he was in the mood.

They loved O. Henry. "He knew a lot about people, didn't he?" Jimmy said.

"This is his school," Rico replied. "He learned it here."

"He learned it everywhere," Jimmy argued. "He was great."

"You're just as great as he ever was, Puggy Wuggy," Rico argued.

"Only no one knows about it, eh?"

"They will," Rico prophesied. He believed it.

Jimmy began writing again. He wrote several short stories about convicts, none of which was as good as the first. But he had a feeling that he was learning.

His mother visited him that month, and he told her about Rico. "He's the most intelligent convict I've met since I've been in prison," he said. "He writes a little, too. And he's helping me no end with my own writing. I think I'm going to get somewhere now. He's about my age and his mother is in California. He's a swell friend." It was all about Rico.

From the start, his mother did not like Rico, and she never changed. But Rico's mother was entirely sold on Jimmy. Her next letter was addressed to her "two sons", and she said that as soon as she got enough money together she was coming to visit them; she wanted to see them both so very much.

"If you get out this summer I want you to go and live with her," Rico said.

"Is she as nice as you?" Jimmy asked.

"Oh, she's much nicer. I don't hold a candle to her."

"Maybe I'll fall in love with her, too," Jimmy said. "She seems very young and I go for the Rico family."

"You will, Puggy Wuggy," Rico said enthusiastically. "I'll write to her and tell her you're coming. You *will* love her, you'll—" he broke off. His face settled so abruptly it was ugly in the change. "Just what did you mean?" he asked. His voice was flat.

Jimmy went callous, only he thought of it as smart. He couldn't help it; he did not want to, but there was something inside of him, impelling him to say, "What could I mean? I'm a man, biologically speaking, I like women and—" He broke off, watching the whiteness come into Rico's face.

"But Jimmy, you don't understand," Rico said in the same flat voice.

"Don't I?" Jimmy leered.

"But she's not like that, Jimmy," Rico argued desperately, trying to give Jimmy every chance. "She's just as good as your own mother; she's better than anyone's mother. She's deeply religious." He paused with his mouth open, waiting for Jimmy to say that he did not mean it.

And when Jimmy did not reply, he stood up. His eyes were dull, his face dopey, remote; his shoulders sagged and his head drooped forward; his hands hung lifeless at his sides. "There were some swell moments, Jimmy. I'll remember those." There was a grinding nonchalance to his voice that jarred Jimmy. For an instant his lips twitched as if he was trying to smile, and then they stopped as if he had given up, and his eyes overflowed with hurt. He was very ugly. He turned away as the hurt completely overwhelmed him and wobbled down the aisle, his knees buckling, stoop-shouldered and grotesque.

For a moment Jimmy sat there watching him. Well, that's Rico, he thought. And then hurt hit him in a solid wave. His stomach became hollow and sick, and he filled with a cold, empty fear. He was sitting on the bottom bunk and without realizing what he was doing he tried to get up and go after Rico. But the thousand emotions which rushed through him assumed weight and froze into solidness and the weight sat heavily upon his shoulders, anchoring him into immobility . . . If that's the way he feels—but he never finished the thought.

After a time he began trembling violently as if he had the ague and when he went to supper the food nauseated him. Passing each other in the dormitory, Rico looked away and Jimmy winced. Signifier came over after a time and asked Jimmy what it was all about. Jimmy shook his head; he could not talk about it. Then Candy and Jew Baby and Wrinklehead and the whole click came over. They wanted to get together and make it tough for Rico. But Jimmy shook his head again.

That night, in the poker game, Rico got into a fight with Starrett. He hit Starrett, knocking him away from the table, and Starrett got up and ran for his knife. Dutch gave Rico a knife and Rico stood there in the aisle, waiting for Starrett to return. Signifier came over and told Jimmy about it, and suddenly Jimmy was sick enough to vomit.

He pulled himself up and went out to talk to Rico. But it wasn't any use. Rico was wild and feverish. He had the open knife in his hand and when Jimmy saw the naked blade a flat plane of drawing coldness moved through his body, contracting his lungs and heart. Goose flesh rippled down the back of his legs and his mind strained to the breaking point.

"Don't do it, kid," he begged.

Rico stood there, rigid and unbending, face a dead white, lips a bluish bruise, eyes lidded. There was a drugged remoteness in his face. Then he turned and looked at Jimmy. "To hell with you and everybody else," he said.

Bleakly pitying they looked at each other.

"Honestly, I didn't mean it," Jimmy said. His voice pleaded. But it was too late.

A flicker of life brushed across Rico's face. "But *you,* Jimmy, I put *you* in the *stars.*" His voice was accusing.

Jimmy turned away. After a moment he went over to Starrett's bunk. "Listen, if there's a fight here tonight, you're going to die," he said; he meant it. Then he turned quickly away before Starrett could reply and went back to his own bunk.

He could feel his lips trembling, but he could not stop them from trembling. There are some things which I don't understand, he thought. Who would have thought a person like him would take it like that ... When he tried to unbutton his shirt, his fingers seemed numb and dead. Finally, he got undressed and into bed. No one came and spoke to him.

But there was no fight. After a time the argument died down. Jimmy contemplated killing Dutch. Eternities later the lights blinked for bedtime. The sounds of the dormitory trailed off to a low murmur. In the lull Jimmy's mind became suddenly active. A flood of self-pity washed over him. And then the lights went out. The dormitory became quiet. Silence floated about him like waves of vapor. He smelt cigaret smoke as some convict smoked a furtive butt in bed. He heard a voice say something aloud with childish defiance and then a laugh ripple, and later slouchy footsteps moving toward the latrine.

He turned over on his stomach, buried his face in his pillow.

But he could still see Rico's drugged, remote face through the pillow beneath his eyes, through his closed eyelids, through the concrete floor below. He could hear the grinding nonchalance of his voice, "*There were some swell moments . . .*" the hurting accusation, "*I put you in the stars . . .*" through the stiff, hammered silence. A gray stone blankness of prison walls closed in upon him and squeezed his thoughts into unbearable agony, and bars fell across his consciousness with steady, monotonous blows.

God, please let me go to sleep, he prayed brokenly. Please make me go to sleep. I got to go to sleep! I got to!

But he didn't go to sleep.

That was his most hysterical night. He was so terribly afraid. All the next day he was afraid, mostly of what Rico might do to himself. They did not look at each other . . . He never had a friend but me, Jimmy thought. And then I let him down. I did it knowing how afraid he had been of his mental attitude toward me, and mine toward him.

Rico was with Dutch all that day, and was very reckless and sneering and don't-caring, treating the convicts worse than he ever had.

But the day after that he came over and asked, "Could it ever be the same again, Jimmy?"

"It ought to be better," Jimmy said. "I've learned so much."

"You'll probably never learn that all life is give and take," Rico said. "But I can't blame you for that's mostly a tough lesson."

"The trouble with me is that I've been in prison too long," Jimmy said.

Rico was brooding. "I hate myself for doing this; but remember this, Jimmy, please remember this—I don't have a choice."

"Take me out of the stars," Jimmy said. "They're too damned high for a convict like me."

"You'll always be in the stars for me, Jimmy," Rico told him.

"It'll just be another story of lost illusions," Jimmy argued. " 'Of dreams broken and crumbled to dust . . . ' Who said that?"

"All dreams are true, Jimmy," Rico stated. "They're true as long as you dream them. Somebody said that in India they believe that the great God Brahma is dreaming all existence . . ."

"Let's not be so deep, sweet little child," Jimmy said.

And suddenly they were laughing. They both found it very good to laugh again. But now they knew what it would be like when they were separated. They had only felt the breath of the devastating loneliness that lay in wait for them, the scared cold nights and empty days, but they knew what the full solid measure would be like. It stained their relationship with a hopeless, futile desperation, as if it was only borrowed for a space of time and would in the end have to be returned. That dug a sense of protest within them, and for the moment, standing there, they would have liked to stop creation.

Later in the month some more bunks were placed in the dormitory and Rico was shifted around to the outside corner where he could look out through the barred windows into the outside street. He and Jimmy would stand with their feet on the bottom bunk frame and lean across his bunk, side by side, and look out at the gray winter days. Sometimes they would talk.

Rico liked to talk of Los Angeles and the people there. "They're the most natural people in the world," he would say. "They do the things they want to do and live."

"Every one else seems to think they're all rather queer."

"They're not freaks, they're only—"

"I mean sexually," Jimmy stated flatly.

Rico turned and looked at him. "Queerness is a funny term," he said after a moment. "There's nothing really lost when a physical change is made unless you feel that it is wrong. It's the feeling that it's wrong that makes it queer."

"How do you feel?" Jimmy asked.

"How do you think I feel, Puggy Wuggy darling?" Rico said, his voice caressing.

"Do you think you're right?" Jimmy pressed.

"Of course," Rico stated, then turned and looked at Jimmy again. "But it's an odd question for you to ask; you ought to know."

When Jimmy didn't reply, he asked, "Do you, Jimmy? Do you think it's right?"

"Not particularly so," Jimmy replied, "but that doesn't take anything from it."

For a long moment Rico was silent, hurt. Then he said in a low, pathetic voice, "You're rather brutal at times, Jimmy. I wonder why I love you so when you're so brutal."

They talked of feelings and reactions. Rico told Jimmy that he abhorred fat, greasy flesh. It gave Jimmy a horrible picture, making him so blindly furious that it was all he could do to keep from slapping Rico. And Rico told him of how his mother's best friend had wanted him to have her when he was twelve; and how utterly distasteful the idea had been to him. Jimmy asked him about women, and he replied that although he had had many, perhaps more than the normal person, none of them had ever satisfied him, they had always left him with a vague feeling of incompleteness. "It was a physical satisfaction, but my mind was never satisfied," Rico explained. "It needed something more, probably to be debased," he added.

Jimmy was shocked and sickened and repulsed. But above all fascinated. "Why?" he asked, really wanting to know.

"Perhaps because that would be the only way I could find emotional exhaustion," Rico answered. "The only way I could find completeness. Have you ever felt completeness, Jimmy?"

"I reckon not," Jimmy said. "Not if that's what it takes."

"Does it sound depraved?"

"Not particularly so," Jimmy lied. "I just don't see the reason for it."

"You don't have to, Puggy Wuggy; you give me everything just as you are."

"I hate to hear you talk like that," Jimmy told him gruffly.

"You were the first, darling," Rico swore. "And you'll be the last."

They talked of other things, too, and Jimmy told him of his dreams when he was a little boy. "I read a lot," he said, "and I guess I must have built up a dream world about myself. I came to feel that the things I did and the things which happened to me, such as eating and studying and sleeping, were things which didn't really count; the real things were the things I dreamed, the castles and the soldiers and me being a general and a hero and all that sort of stuff. It sounds silly, doesn't it?"

"Tell me more," Rico urged. "It explains so many things."

"Well, you see, I was born in a small town in Mississippi where the schools weren't very good, so my mother taught Damon and I until we were in the eighth grade. She wouldn't let us play with the other kids down there and we were a lot to ourselves. We got all of our games out of books. Then my father moved to Pine Bluff, Arkansas—he was a school teacher—and we entered high school. You won't believe it, but I still believed in Santa Claus. I was twelve years old, too. That was when my brother lost his sight. Listen, that was tough."

Rico was greatly concerned. "How, Jimmy?"

"Oh, we were playing with some explosives in the basement. I figured God had caused it to happen because just a few minutes before my mother had warned me that God was going to punish me for being so ugly that day. God was awful real to me then. But God made a mistake. Listen, can you understand that feeling. A terribly real God making a mistake when you were twelve."

He was silent for a moment and Rico touched his arm. Then Jimmy said, "I don't think I ever quite forgave God for that; you see, it was supposed to be me." He was silent again for a long time, then he said, "They sent Damon away to school after that and I was all alone. That's a hell of a feeling to have when you're young, or old, too, for that matter. A little kid who didn't know how to play with anybody. Listen, I'm not trying to get any blue notes into this yarn. Damon and I were never together again. They thought it might affect him in some kind of way. It was funny." When he turned to look at Rico, he saw that he was crying. "It does sound like a sob story, doesn't it?" he conceded deprecatingly. "But every convict's story is a sob story."

"Oh God, Jimmy, do I give you anything?" Rico asked. "Do I make up for some of it?"

"You give me everything," Jimmy told him.

"I want to," Rico sobbed. "I want to give you everything."

After a time Rico said, "Tell me about it if you want to."

"There isn't much to tell," Jimmy said. "I was different from everybody and didn't know exactly why. I didn't want to be. That was what caused all my trouble; I didn't want to be different. I've never wanted to be different. It was then I began feeling that I had to prove something; I don't know, prove I wasn't different, I guess; prove I wasn't scared; prove I wasn't a sissy. I guess that was it. At first it was like taking castor oil. It was like fighting. I hated to fight; I'm even deathly scared of fighting now, for all the bluffs I run. But when some one hurt you, you fought them. That was the way they had done it in those books I had read. And if you won they stopped. So I fought. I could fight, too. But I did it so goddamned deliberately for a teen-age boy.

"That was the way it was about proving something. I learned to smoke and curse and play hooky from school because I thought that made me like other boys. Only, being a damn fool, I went to extremes. Whatever some other little boy said he had done, I went and actually did it. It was that way all through school. I didn't care so much for athletics at first because all I had been used to doing was romping through the woods—there're some wonderful woods in Mississippi, some old sunken roads; some of those roads are a hundred feet deep. We used to play Robin Hood in them. But I learned to play every game they played in school. I made the football team and the baseball team and the tennis team and won eleven letters."

"Tell me about the girls," Rico demanded.

"There weren't many girls," Jimmy said. "None that counted, anyway."

"Were you ever in love?" Rico asked.

"Once, I guess, although you'd probably call it puppy love. It's inconceivable, though. I was only thirteen and hardly knew her. I met her on the tennis courts one day and that night I took her out on Cherry Street to a carnival. There was a moon and we walked along, holding hands and not seeing much of the carnival. We talked

311

about ourselves mostly. I could talk to her; I didn't feel lonely with her.

"And then the next day my father took me to St. Louis. I cried all the way." He took a deep breath. "At first I remembered her so distinctly it was like seeing her everywhere I went. I remembered her face and her features and her body and the way she stood and the way she walked and laughed and smiled and the color of her eyes and the different tints of her hair and the crinkles in the corner of her mouth. And then after a week I lost her; I couldn't to save my soul tell how she looked at all. A funny thing; but since I've been in prison, in the last past year, her face comes back to me again.

"That was the way it was. I started off not liking St. Louis, and never changed. I hated that goddamned city, and always will. I smoked in the school basement and slipped out of the building against the rules and went to picture shows and was very brilliant; oh, I was terribly brilliant. And then I got expelled. That was about a girl. But I didn't even like her; she was an awful snob. Everybody said that she was so terribly hard to make; and so I made her.

"And then we went to Cleveland and I went to school there and graduated and didn't like that goddamned city, either. After that I got a job and fell and broke my back, they said. I got some money for it; I'm still drawing compensation from the state and I got three thousand dollars from the company. After that I didn't have a chance.

"I went to college and spent the three thousand and all my compensation in seven months. I wound up three hundred dollars in debt. And then I got expelled again. That was about a girl, too. But she was a whore.

"After that I blew my top. I went solid goddamned crazy. There were a lot of girls—if you want to call them girls. All kinds. One I should have loved, maybe—maybe two. One I should have married anyway, I know. Then my mother and father were divorced. I don't know, I think that took something away from me, too. It took away a home, I know that. I began living in the street, gambling and running around. You know the story; for that last year it was just like any other convict's story."

"I like the way you tell it," Rico said.

"How else could I tell it?" he replied, realizing suddenly that it was the first time he had ever tried to tell his story to anyone.

"You know how you could tell it," Rico was saying. "Like all the others do—with that touch of gaudy glamour."

"But not to you," Jimmy said, and then wondered why not. It was something about Rico which drew him out, which inspired his confidence, but what he did not know. Maybe because they really liked each other.

It was a week later, however, before Rico chose to tell about himself, and then he did it hesitantly, as if he was not quite certain that he should at all. He said that his mother had been a nurse for an invalid member of a very wealthy family in Los Angeles, and that he had grown up with the three grandchildren.

"I imagine you were spoiled," Jimmy said.

"There was no way of keeping me from being. It wasn't until I was eight that I learned I wasn't rich like the other children of the family, and that my mother was working instead of living there. It happened one day when they had a party and their mother sent me outside to play. I was so hurt I put my arm against the doorjamb of the garage and slammed the door closed against it. I broke it. And then I ran inside where they were having the party and showed everybody my broken arm. I was the center of attention." Jimmy laughed. "I was very funny, wasn't I?" Rico said.

"I never saw my father until I was fifteen. That was when my mother went to live with him. I ran away and joined a carnival going to Texas. At first I was a roustabout, then I got a job doubling for a guy who was faking as a Hindu Prince. His name was Harry Smith and he got into trouble with Poochy's wife; Poochy was the guy who owned the act. He had to scale and I got the part steady. That's where I—" he broke off, and Jimmy said, "Got the phony name. I knew, of course, it wasn't yours; your mother signs her letters *Helen Steel*. Is Steel your name, too?"

"No, my father was named Ramon Collins; he was part Spanish

and part Irish. My name is Aubert LaCarlton Collins." He pronounced it *Obert*.

Jimmy grinned. "One is as bad as the other."

Rico pouted. "I like Aubert." Then he said, "I got the *Prince Rico* from the act; I was a prince, and a prince of riches at that, although later it tickled me how a Hindu prince could have a Spanish name."

"So you, too, fell in love with Poochy's beautiful blonde wife and had to scale," Jimmy teased, bringing him back to the story.

Rico gave a start. Then he grinned. "It does sound like a serial story in a confession magazine, doesn't it? But she was beautiful, darling. She had long silky golden hair and cuddled like a kitten. You would have liked her, darling," he teased, looking at Jimmy through the corners of his eyes. "You go for blondes."

"I go for you," Jimmy contradicted.

"I haven't forgotten Lively," he reminded.

"I have," Jimmy said.

After a moment Rico said, "She ruined me for other women. She never got enough; she wanted buckets of it. I was just sixteen and she was the first woman I had ever had. She drained me dry.

"We showed in White City that summer and went from there to Elkhart. That was where Poochy caught us and I had to run away in my stage clothes. I wore a purple gown with a golden turban and I had to run away wearing that."

"Where did you go?" Jimmy asked, amused.

"Oh, to Chicago, of course." Then he added, "I think Poochy liked me for himself. He saw me in Chicago once and wanted to take me to a room."

Jimmy hated him when he talked of that. It made him sick to think of what he might have been to some one else.

"After that I hoboed south," Rico went on, unaware of Jimmy's feeling. "I got caught stealing in Florida and did a year on the chain gang. That was one tough year. My mother sent me some money that time to come home on but I went to Philadelphia instead and got a job as an entertainer in a honky tonk. I had plenty of gall in those days.

314

"I tried to sing but everybody booed me. Then I tried dancing. I was pretty terrible to start off with, but I might have learned if I hadn't broken my kneecaps."

"How did that happen?" Jimmy asked.

"Oh, I was riding a freight coming out of Pittsburgh and got to fighting with a guy. We were in a box car and he wanted to make me, so we got to fighting and he knocked me off the train."

The picture came unbidden; against his will it came. He could see Rico riding freights with different fellows, some of whom he must have liked, some of whom he must have kissed, or had allowed to fondle him in the corner of some damp, chilly box car, on some sacks or straw, perhaps. He cursed himself and cursed his thoughts; if he had to think about it, at least he didn't have to go into the goddamn harrowing details. But he could not help it. Hearing Rico talk thus, he filled with a squashy mixture of jealousy and chagrin and a sort of impotent fury. How could he have ever been anything else? he asked himself, looking at his wet red lips and smoky smoldering eyes. How could I have possibly been the first? But he prayed that he was; he fought to make himself believe it in the face of all contradictory evidence. Because he had to know that he was the only one; but he did not even want to admit to himself why.

Glancing up, Rico caught sight of his expression and instantly read his thoughts. "Must I say it again for you, Puggy Wuggy?" he asked.

Jimmy shook his head.

"You ought to know without my saying so," Rico pointed out.

"How?"

"Can't you tell? Aren't I adorably inexperienced?"

Jimmy blushed. "I don't know that much about it," he muttered.

"That makes us both just babes in the woods," Rico said.

To change the trend of the conversation, Jimmy asked, "What did you do after you got hurt?"

"I began impersonating females in cabarets," Rico said, and Jimmy cursed himself for having asked. "There was a big call for that sort of thing right then," Rico went on, "and I did pretty good. I didn't need legs, of course; I wore long dresses mostly. The toughest thing about it was dodging the patrons. It seemed as if every fat bald-headed man in the joint felt called upon to make me as soon as he had had a few.

"I know you will think this is odd," he said, "but I was a little hysterical about girls through then. Not exactly sexually; I told you how I felt toward them sexually. I took what they offered because I had to mostly. But what I wanted was to keep them up, buy them diamonds and furs and things like that. All the trouble I ever got into came from me trying to get something for some woman or other about whom I didn't give a damn."

Jimmy took out his cigarets and they lit up. Rico strung his ukelele about his neck.

"That's about all of it, Puggy Wuggy," he said. "I joined the army after that and went to a camp in Georgia. And then deserted after three months. When I got arrested before, the army came and got me and made me serve six months for desertion. After that the state authorities sent me to the reformatory. I was there two years and now I'm doing ten."

"You must have had it tough in all those joints," Jimmy observed. He did not want to say it, but he could not help himself. "With your sensitive mouth and the way your eyes get sometimes."

"The year in Florida was the toughest," Rico confessed. "Those wolves down there will try to rape you and the guards don't give you much protection if you're from the North. I carried a big shiv with me and they knew I would use it. But in the reformatory it was different. I wanted sex there, but I wanted to be the man. They were all trying to make me, so I just played the field and took everything and never gave anything. That was a fine way to do, wasn't it?"

After that, Jimmy's feelings for Rico were never steady from day to day, never the same. He wanted to erase all of the possibilities of what he might have been before; he did not want to admit his existence before they had met.

Once when Rico was shuffling through some letters he dropped one addressed to him at the state insane asylum. He reached for it, but Jimmy beat him to it. When the full realization came to him, he was thoroughly shocked.

"When were you in the insane asylum?" he asked.

Rico confessed that he had plead insanity when he had been arrested the last time. "My crime had been so hysterical it wasn't hard to do," he said. "They thought for a time that I was actually crazy. They kept me down there for six months—observation, they said; then they sent me here."

"Were you?" Jimmy asked.

"I might have been. I had lost my perspective. They were catching me too fast."

"I know how that is," Jimmy said. "I've lost mine, too."

"If we hadn't made up again I'd be back there now," Rico told him. "Each of those days away from you sent me nearer there."

Jimmy felt so very tender for the Rico whom he knew and was scared for him and wanted to protect him and change him all over from that Rico whom he did not know, the Rico who repulsed him so and whom he found so repellent on occasions. It must have been that on those times he was afraid that Rico would turn back and become the other Rico, and that he, Jimmy, would be again a goddamned, solid fool.

EVERYTHING TOUCHED JIMMY that spring. He was too emotional; he had never been so emotional. Everything was soft inside of him and at the slightest touch he'd bubble over, like foam.

A single note on Rico's ukelele touched him. A bar of melody. Thoughts of his mother. A bird flying in the window and flying out again. That touched him greatly. Clouds in the sky. A convict with a flop. And those golden spring twilights without any shadows, soft and diffused with a golden glow, tinting everything with vividness.

And the time they put Honest To God in the hole. He hadn't done a thing. Rico had bought the toothbrush from a convict called Davis on the third floor. The toothbrush turned out to be stolen. Jimmy took the rap for buying it because he figured they might transfer Rico and he knew they wouldn't transfer him. Honest To God was knocked off just because he sometimes peddled old toothbrush handles.

Davis told the inspector, who was holding court that day, that he had found the toothbrush and had sold it to Jimmy. Jimmy admitted buying it. The inspector said pompously that there had been a lot of stealing going on and it had to stop. So he put Honest To God in the hole. He didn't put Davis in the hole because Davis was one of his rats; and he couldn't put Jimmy in the hole without putting Davis in. Jimmy began to protest but the inspector got up and walked out.

All that afternoon he brooded over it.

"You did all you could, Puggy Wuggy," Rico said.

"What I can't see," he contended, "is why the hell he didn't put Davis in the hole since it was obvious that he stole it. And if not him, me, I bought it. Why put a poor goddamned nigger in the hole just because he is a poor goddamned nigger?"

It didn't make sense to him. He had seen a lot of things happen in prison that hadn't made sense, but they were just beginning to touch him. It was as if he had been in a shell for all those years, or had been petrified or dried up and was just then coming to life.

Death Row was then in the L block, and on the afternoons the condemned men were taken across the yard to the death house, the convicts in the dormitory could stand in their windows and watch them pass. Watching them, Jimmy would always wonder what they were thinking; long into the night he would wonder. What *could* they be thinking? He could not tell from looking at them. Some walked with shoulders back, swaggering, contemptuous, and he'd think of Rico and wonder how he would walk that last bitter half mile, wonder if in the end his sneer and high and mighty contempt for everything and every one would fail him. Others walked erect and soberly, as if they were silently praying; some slouched indifferently with their hands in their pockets. The priest walked with some and they looked repentent; but how could he tell if they felt that way? Most appeared perfectly natural from where he looked down on them. They talked and laughed with the guards much the same as any convict going anywhere. But all the time he wondered what they were thinking.

On Easter Sunday he and Rico went to mass together and watched the candles burning. They saw Lively but it did not make any difference.

"If anything ever makes me religious, it'll be burning candles on an altar," Jimmy said.

"Why?" Rico asked curiously.

"Oh, I don't know, I've never thought about it," Jimmy replied. "I guess because they're so soft and insistent and eternal, like a good woman's love."

A moment later he caught Rico's stare on him.

And then they saw Helen Hayes in a picture called *A Farewell to Arms*. "Oh my God, she is magnificent," Jimmy said. "She is so splendidly young and gallant. It's wonderful to feel that there are such young and gallant people in this grimy world."

"It was perfect," Rico choked, holding to his arm when the end came. "It had to end like that. It was like climbing up a mountain and then you're at the top and that's the end. It was tragedy, but glorious and exalted tragedy—and so is love, all love," he sighed.

Back in the dormitory he said to Jimmy, "Let's have ours that perfect, Puggy Wuggy, and then when it ends there won't be any regrets."

"We will," he said.

"They were very courageous people," Rico went on. "She didn't care what anyone thought, did she?"

Jimmy didn't reply.

"I don't either," Rico said. "I don't care what anybody thinks of me but you. I know that they all know, anyway. But I don't care; I feel exalted. You're my God, Puggy Wuggy, I'd die for you.

I'm going to die anyway when it's over and I don't care what anyone thinks."

They were both very soft.

Sometime during the week following the magazine man brought around a new magazine called *Esquire* and Jimmy bought a copy. They liked it so well that he ordered several of the back issues, in one of which they came across a story called, "All My Love." Afterwards Rico said, his eyes smoky and his face like a liquid glow, "All my love, from me to you, Puggy Wuggy," caressing each syllable. Just three trite words, but they touched Jimmy when Rico said them.

All of the stories in *Esquire* impressed them that spring. They thought it the swellest magazine ever published.

"They're so real," Jimmy said. "Most people seem to think that reality can only be achieved through vulgarity, but honestly, most of it is only very pathetic."

Rico's gaze jerked up. "That's how I know you're a genius," he said.

Along about that time the evening paper began running a series of photographs from Laurence Stalling's *Photographic History of the First World War*. Those pictures touched Jimmy that spring. There was one, a careless scatter of rotting corpses on a patch of utter desolation, captioned "No More Parades." The death touched him, but the desolation touched him more. *No More Parades*. It made him think of the condemned men strolling across the yard at sunset. He never saw any of them make that stroll again without thinking, *no more parades*.

There was another, a twilight scene of death and desolation, captioned ". . . short days ago we lived, felt dawn, saw sunset glow . . ." Beneath that picture, those ten words were a complete story of life and death, or war and heroism, indifference and finality.

"I'd like to know all of that verse," he said.

Rico recited, "*We are the dead; short days ago we lived, felt dawn, saw sunset glow, loved and were loved, and now we lie in Flander's fields.*"

"That's something to think about," Jimmy said, shuddering

320

slightly as if a foot had stepped on his grave. "It makes you feel insecure, as if no tomorrow is promised."

He could see those burnt-up convicts lying on the prison yard and those murderers death-house bound; he could see all those convicts dying and dead. And he could see himself dead and rotting in the oblivion of a grave, never having been anything but a number on a board in a prison, having in the end lived and died for nothing and left nothing and was nothing even in the end but worms in the ground.

For a time the meaning went out of everything and he filled with a raw sense of protest against something, he did not know what. Everything seemed wrong for a time. There was more to any man than just a number on a board, he thought. There was something inside of every man which could not be put on black painted numerals, or on a report card—a record of *right* and *wrong*. He was choked and filled and bitter, just from looking at those pictures. At nights Rico would play *Stardust* and sing it in his husky, emotion-filled voice "... *and now my consolation is in the memory of a song* ..." or words to that effect. It stirred poignant melancholy in the clogged confusion of his thoughts and when the thousand groping feelings, when all the protest and melancholy and mixed emotions got choked up in him, something began to sprout. But it was all feeling. It wouldn't come out. He couldn't find the words for it.

And then, shortly afterwards, he saw another photograph in the paper taken from the *First World War*. There was no death in this picture, no destruction, just a scraggly line of soldiers with rifles shoulder high, standing in a trench in the immense, eternal desolation, waiting for something. There was no other life visible; there was no war; there were no trees; snow was on the ground; and the soldiers with their tiny rifles standing there in the middle of eternity, like microscopic atoms in the universal scene, seemed so insignificant, so shockingly ridiculous. Waiting for the order to go out there and die, waiting for blindness or for a leg to be shot off, for some cold supper, for the war to end; waiting for some bullets which they couldn't see, fired no doubt by an enemy which they didn't hate; waiting for anything, but let it hurry.

Rico was turning the page, but he stopped him. "What's familiar about that picture?" he asked. His voice was choked.

"What, Puggy Wuggy?"

"I don't know," he said hesitantly. And then he cried excitedly, "I know! It's us! It's every goddamned convict. It's the waiting, the waiting! Waiting for what? Beans or freedom? Standing in the sleet waiting for a soup bowl haircut. For an ice cold shower. That's what kills a convict. Waiting ten years for a six months flop. Waiting for the lights to go off at night and for them to come on in the morning. Waiting all morning for the noon day whistles to blow so they'll know it's twelve o'clock. I can understand that feeling."

The picture was captioned "Ennui".

The story was all inside of him. He wrote *Ennui* at the top of the page and looked about the dormitory and began writing without knowing what the next word would be. All of his emotions and feelings and protests which he had suffered for all those years boiled out of him. When he got up from the typewriter he had a story. He knew it was a freak of literature. He knew it was impossible. But he had written it. And he knew that he had a million more inside of him which only needed a spark to set them off. But could he write them?

After that all he needed was for Rico to recite *Short days ago we lived, felt dawn, saw sunset glow, loved and were loved* . . . and he could see himself dead with all those stories inside of him unwritten and feel all rushed and filled. Or have him play *Stardust* in individual notes on his ukelele and sing in his husky, passionate voice . . . *sometimes I wonder while I spend the lonely nights* . . . only in his mind it went . . . *why I spend the lonely nights* . . . and the stories would boil out of him by the hundreds, none of which he ever wrote. At first he was unable to write them because all that blind, intense, not very clear protest which he felt so vividly was too real, and later because it was too futile.

Why that particular song stirred up so many protests within him, he never knew. But it did, and he developed an extreme sense of protest against everything. Against the prison and the officials and the indifference, the brutality and callousness; against the whole system of punishment as he saw it. It seemed so illogical to punish some poor criminal for doing something that civilization taught him how to do so he could have something that civilization taught him how to want. It seemed to him as wrong as if they had hung the gun that shot the man.

But out of all the things that touched him that spring, Rico touched him more than anything. Rico, with his morbid, brilliant, insane, unsteady mind and his frenzied beautiful mouth and kaleidoscopic moods and Mona Lisa smile and eyes of pure stardust. Rico, with his weaknesses and broodings and peaks of gayety, sparkling one moment and surly the next, so close to him he could feel him in his heart, and then so remote he saw him as a stranger. Rico, whose anger inspired him to anguish and whose pitiful bravado reminded him of a scared little boy whistling in the dark, making him want to stand between him and all the world. Poor little kid, he thought, what a terrible mistake he was not a woman.

Ever since Rico had confessed to being in the insane asylum, Jimmy had thought of him as a little crazy; he could not help from thinking it. He realized how unstable Rico was and he felt that almost everything Rico did was posed. But in that place of scarred, distorted souls, of abnormality of both body and mind, he felt that there was something about their relationship which transcended the sordid aspects of homosexuality, and even attained a touch of sacredness. Because whatever else Rico might have felt, Jimmy knew that he always believed that they were right. And if the gods he worshipped were pagan gods, who could tell him better? Jimmy asked himself. No one in there.

But even then, after all those days and those nights, Jimmy realized that he did not know him. He was so unpredictable, unlike any person whom Jimmy had ever known. He would challenge the best poker player in the dormitory to play head and head, or want to fight the biggest, toughest heel. Jimmy thought always that he was a little crazy. Especially when he would go out to the poker game with a bar of soap to lose and quit and come back seventeen dollars in debt, or when he would have a jealous rage over him talking to Candy or Signifier.

And at nights when Rico wanted to talk. He was extremely, abnormally affectionate at such times, but Jimmy never found him monotonous. Every moment with him had something all its own.

The fresh green sprouts of grass touched him, and the buds on the trees. And the robins when they came. The showers, and the rainbows afterwards. And the words which came back to him from somewhere in the past . . . *God made hope to spring eternal from the human heart* . . . There was the newness in the spring which touched him, and the oldness in the prison. There were the walls and the horizon, and in the distance the rooftops of the city, an etched skyscraper and the scattered church spires, which touched him. There were people there beyond the walls in love whom he could not see who touched him. And there were flowers blooming somewhere which he could not smell which touched him. There was laughter he'd never hear which touched him.

But the normal people in the normal world whom he had never seen since manhood, most of all.

THE SOFTBALL FEVER swept the prison again that summer and captain Frank had it worse than before. Each day he took the company out to the small rocky areaway between the wooden dormitory and the death house so that the team could practice. He wanted them to beat all of the companies that year.

The duties of managing the team fell to Jimmy again and he shifted the players about and tried them out for each position. Rico had to be taught everything, how to catch a ball, how to bat. But he learned quickly enough. "I could learn to do anything for you," was the way he explained it.

A new convict in the dormitory took Jimmy's place behind the bat and he went to second base. In the first game they played, he cut across behind the box and grabbed a popper out of the air—it was a rather sensational play—and from deep center field Rico yelled, "Pug-gee Wug-gee!" and ran in and hugged him. He never did live that down.

In playing softball, Rico was no different than in anything else. When Jimmy was there to see him, he was very good. He learned so well that soon the sports experts on the *Prison News* were selecting him as all-star material. Jimmy bought him some elastic knee supporters and at night had the colored convict who massaged the pitchers' arms to massage his knees. With the exercising they grew strong and seldom buckled.

Captain Frank was elated and Rico was in solid. Any convict in that dormitory who could play softball was like Caesar's wife. Jimmy was pleased and proud of him. Realizing this, Rico became very enthusiastic and excelled in his position. During the games he kept up so much noise out in center field that he could be heard all over both diamonds.

"Like it?" Jimmy asked him once.

"I like to do anything you like to do, or even like for me to do, Puggy Wuggy."

It was rather odd how sensitive Jimmy was to Rico's playing. He, himself, could make a dozen errors, and it would not phase him; but if Rico made just one he became sick with dread. As in all other things, Rico kept him continuously apprehensive. Not because he showed any indications of going haywire; but because Jimmy expected him to. He dreaded seeing the pressure get on a game because he felt that Rico could not take it.

And then he broke his arm, and Rico had to play alone. It happened during a practice game out by the death house. Mose was pitching for the rookies so the regulars could get some batting practice, and Johnny Brothers said to Jimmy and Candy, "Let's knock old Mose out the box and make him blow up."

Brothers batted first, and hit one over the death house. Jimmy followed with a sharp liner which Wicks fielded with his mouth. Rounding first, he saw that Wicks had stooped for the ball and when Candy yelled, "Slide!" he hit the dirt. But there wasn't any dirt, it was rock and hard-baked clay; and when his left arm went down on it the bone broke just above the wrist. Scrambling to his feet, he looked down at it and said, "Goddamned son of a bitch," then clutched it with his right hand and started running around the end of the dormitory toward the hospital.

Smokey Joe, who had been catching Mose, ran over and took him by the arm, then Brothers caught up with them and took him by the other arm. With Candy and Signifier and a half dozen others following, and captain Frank bringing up the rear, puffing and beer-bellied, they surged up the stone steps into the hospital, scaring the wits out of the hospital guard.

" 'Mergency!" Brothers yelled. "Make way, 'mergency!"

The guard ran around from his desk and halted them. "What the goddamn hell's the matter?" he shouted.

"I broke my arm," Jimmy said, holding up his dangling hand.

"Hell, sit down over there," the guard directed. "The doctor's eating lunch."

Captain Frank came in then, looking like the beginning of a heart attack, gave one glance at the guard and kept on back after the doctor. "I don't give a damn if he's hosing Cleopatra," he said. Jimmy was one of his star players aside from being the manager of his softball team.

Dr. Rist, the visiting surgeon who was then head of the medical college at the state university, happened along with a couple of interns.

"What goes on here?" he asked, and captain Frank, stopping, said, "This man's got a broken arm."

"Let's see, boy," the doctor said.

One of the nurses who had gathered about cut off his shirt, and the doctor took hold of his forearm and his hand and pulled, then eased the bone back into place. "Wrap it up," he said.

Joe O'Neil and the convict doctor took Jimmy back to the Xray room and put his arm in a cast, after which he was hospitalized in C-ward. Seeing that all had been done for him that was possible, captain Frank and the convicts dribbled out. Candy said he would send over whatever he needed. Then he thought of Rico; he had not seen him.

But that night when the runner brought over his pyjamas and toilet articles, he also brought a six-page letter from him.

"Dear Puggy Wuggy," it began. "I wish it had been my arm instead of yours. I would break both of my arms for you. Love you so. Wonder why somebody wont let me break my arm for you. Want to so badly. Want to do everything for you. Just got to stand and see you hurt. I could hurt somebody for that. I could hurt *everybody* for that. I could hurt—oh God. It's so hard to say everything that I mean when you mean so much more to me than I'll ever be able to say—any kind of way . . ."

It was a wonderfully passionate and crazy letter and it cheered Jimmy immensely. It was odd how unimportant a broken arm could get in view of all that worship.

Rico came over on sick call and stood outside and waved and once he walked into the ward regardless of the rules, and said, all smiles, "Wouldja, wouldja?"

"Anne Howe," Jimmy grinned.

"That's the girl in the funnies," Rico said. "Little funny Puggy Wuggy with a nose like a bunny rabbit's."

It was all very mushy and amusing and when he left Jimmy was tickled and happy and excited. The next day, his story, ENNUI, was returned from the national magazine to which he had submitted it, but the rejection slip was so encouraging that he became as excited as if he had sold it. Reading it over the second time—"Excellent prison atmosphere—has no plot but does not need any; on the whole, however, too hysterical for publication"—he thought, I'm going on, goddamned prison had me down, but now I'm going on.

He had the paper boy to take the note over and show it to Rico, and in half an hour's time received his reply, "Congratulations,

Puggy Wuggy, aces to you and all of them and I'm so doggoned proud. Sweet Child."

At the end of two weeks he was discharged. He found Rico at the far end of the dormitory, waiting. "Puggy Wuggy, you're going to be great some day," he greeted. "I've known it for some time now."

The unquestioning faith in his voice embarrassed Jimmy; it put a sense of responsibility in him from which his mind rebelled. "If I am," he replied slowly, groping for the right words, "it's because you are making me so."

"I'm flattered and glad so very much you think I am giving you something, honestly," Rico said, and Jimmy looked sharply at him.

"You give me everything, kid," he said. He had said the same thing once long before, but he had forgotten it.

"Hand in hand," Rico said.

"Hand in hand," Jimmy repeated after him solemnly.

"And to the top."

"And to the top."

It was a vow. And then they were laughing embarrassedly at themselves.

"The nights were longest," Rico told him.

They were very close.

Later that night Signifier told Jimmy how Rico had acted the day he broke his arm. "Man, he tried to kill himself. Every time he'd hit a ball he'd slide halfway to first through all those rocks. He ran into the wall once like he didn't see it. And then he stumbled over those rocks out there in center field and fell flat on his face two or three times without even trying to catch himself. Frank had to stop him from playing. He was like a man trying to commit suicide."

Jimmy didn't know what to say; he felt embarrassed.

"It wouldn't have done for you to have broken your neck," Signifier said.

Jimmy had to laugh.

But after that he wanted to be near Rico all the time. So he propositioned the convict who slept on the bunk beneath Rico to swap bunks with him. Securing his consent for a consideration of two bucks, he put it up to captain Frank to get him transferred.

"I'll have to get somebody to help me dress as long as I have my arm in a cast," he explained. "Rico said he would help me. The guy who sleeps underneath him said he'd swap bunks. I want you to make it official."

"Now, look, Jim, take it easy," captain Frank warned.

"You want me to get well, don't you?" Jimmy snapped.

"All right, I'll get you transferred; but take it easy, Jim. This ain't the Gilsy hotel and you ain't no fool."

But Jimmy did not hear the last of it; he had already gone to tell Rico. They were so excited at being so close to each other that for the first night they could not sleep. Rico leaned over the edge of his upper bunk and looked down at Jimmy wistfully. They talked and giggled like two children. Later, when the sharp edge had worn down, they just watched the huge new moon and played it was a magic carpet carrying them all over the world. It was very thrilling, but the next day they were so sleepy every one wondered why—at least they said they wondered.

The next morning, Rico helped him dress, bossing him around. He put on his shoes and laced them; he seemed very pleased with himself.

"I adore waiting on you," he confessed.

"I adore having you," Jimmy replied.

That evening Rico began writing a song. Several days later, he sent it over to the band to have it orchestrated. But he did not like it and tore it up. After that, for hours on end, he would plunk out notes, like the one-finger plunking on piano keys. It was a monotonous dirge, and after a day or two it got on Jimmy's nerves.

"What the hell is it, anyway?" he asked. "It sounds like the *Song of the Volga Boatman*."

"Did you ever hear the woolen mill in operation?" Rico asked.

"Damn right!" Jimmy exclaimed. "That's what it is."

He could hear again the slow clanking melody of the mills in the deathly silence that day, long before, when up in the idle house sergeant Cody had just shot a convict to death, and recall again how it had sounded to him—so eternal, deliberate, mocking. And he could imagine those convicts as he had imagined them then, working at the looms, feeding the stinking, dusty wool, stopping neither for the years nor for the gunshots nor for the death, and he said,

"If you get all that in your song, you've really got something."

"It's going to be a love song," Rico said.

He was sickeningly disappointed. It left him feeling betrayed, for it was the first time Rico had ever disappointed him. "I don't know, I guess there're a whole lot of people in this world who've been disappointed," he said aloud.

Rico was suddenly upset for it was the first time Jimmy had ever said anything he did not understand. "What, Puggy Wuggy?" he asked anxiously.

"It's a story," Jimmy said. There was a bitter note in his voice, a feeling in his mind of something lost. "Everything's a story. Would you mind typing it for me, I'll dictate it slowly."

Rico took down the typewriter, still very perplexed, and Jimmy began, " *'Blessed are they that mourn, for they shall be comforted . . .'* " He stopped. "I don't know why that should keep coming back, that's perhaps the greatest disappointment of all the other disappointments—no, don't type that!" He stopped again. "Listen, up in the Catholic chapel they recite, '*I believe in The Father Almighty, Maker of Heaven and Earth, in Jesus Christ, His Only Son . . .*' They believe in *The Holy Ghost,* too, and in *The Communion of Saints.* I wonder what they believe in, sure enough. All I believe is that I'm going to die, and anything else—" When Rico began to protest, he cut him off, "Listen, don't get excited. I don't want to argue, I want to tell a story. I don't know what this story is all about yet but it has something to do with the prison fire because that's been inside of me so long I'll never be right again until I get it out—I saw so many people die. But did they die? Do people ever die? The Christians say they don't, the Catholics, rather. Maybe they didn't die, maybe they're sitting here to help me write this story."

He was silent for a time. Rico sat over the typewriter, poised and waiting. After a moment he began again, "I've written a lot of things out of me since I've known you. Maybe I'll do it again." But Rico didn't reply. After a moment he said, "Take this—" And it was the story.

He kept it up all that day, dictating a disjointed account of the prison fire as it had impressed him. When night came he was exhausted and bone dry. Something kept telling him that it was impossible; that he couldn't write a story like that; that he was riding for a fall. But he was too tired to think about it. They both went to sleep immediately. The next day was spent in arranging the continuity of the disjointed paragraphs. Finally Jimmy said, "That's as good as I can get it; but I have an idea that I'm a freak, not a writer."

Rico looked at him for a long moment. "You don't know," he said soberly. "You went away up there, Puggy Wuggy, with the immortals. I don't suppose anyone knows. But you'll never be as great again as you were these past two days."

"I think the other one was better," Jimmy said.

"You'll feel differently about this one later," Rico prophesied.

"Maybe," Jimmy admitted, then added, "I don't know what to call it; I've got a story without a title."

"Call it *Death Is a Final Release*," Rico suggested.

Jimmy turned and looked at him. "You sound despondent. Why?"

"I'm scared," Rico confessed.

Jimmy laughed. "What the hell of?"

"Oh, it's just a silly thought, and I'm not very gallant for thinking it."

"What?"

"Oh, just thinking. When I first met you I thought you were just another convict writer, you know, just writing to pass away the time. I could feel all right with you because secretly I always felt that I was smarter than you. I didn't have any reason to be scared. But now I know you're going away up there—and I can't follow." His voice was choked.

"We'll always be pals," Jimmy said, rather lamely. "You'll always be in everything good I do."

"I thought that when you wrote the first piece," Rico said, "but I can't even kid myself into feeling I have a part in this. I didn't even know what it was all about; and then I listened to it come out of your mind. Let's don't talk about it, Puggy Wuggy."

"You've got your music," Jimmy persisted. "You're certain to be a great composer some day."

"Sure," Rico said, brightening. "I love music, and I'll be a great composer so I can still be your friend. And we'll always be friends, won't we, Puggy Wuggy. Mr. Monroe, the great novelist, and Mr. Rico, the great composer."

"Sure," Jimmy said.

After that Rico began working furiously on his song, writing down the individual notes to the melody as he composed it. When he had finished with the melody he began on the lyrics.

"What rhymes with *gloaming?*" he asked once.

Jimmy could think of nothing except *moaning.* That was funny, because this was going to be a love song.

"Maybe if I knew what *gloaming* meant I could help you a little," he said.

"It means the twilight or dusk."

"Oh."

Finally, Rico wrote the lyrics without his help.

"What are you going to call it?" Jimmy asked.

"*Love's Highway,*" Rico replied. And then he sang it for Jimmy:

"*On into the gloaming I'm forever roaming through the dusk and darkness, too. And though twilight shadows cover hills and meadows, still I'm on my way to you. As my way I'm wending to the happy ending with a cottage made for two. There can be no by-way for I know love's highway is the only road to you . . .*"

Then the chorus: "*Tho the way is dark as night, love will ever be my guiding light, leading, dearest, to where you are. First I'll hold you near my heart, then you'll promise that we'll never part, that you'll never ever leave me, dear, never ever go away . . .*"

The way he sang it, it was a prayer.

At the top of the first page he wrote, "Dedicated to Jimmy B. Monroe, my buddy," and then scribbled across the bottom of the last page where the music ended, "To J.B.M. the easiest of the Aces and the Salt of the Earth, from Aubert LaCarleton Collins—Good Morning Glory."

"That's swell," Jimmy said.

"I'm going to send it over tomorrow and have Crip write me another arrangement."

But somehow the enthusiasm had gone out of it all. For a long moment both of them had a funny feeling and could not find any words for each other. Then Rico said recklessly, "Let's get some blue boys and get high."

"Okay," Jimmy said.

But late that night, when the peak flattened out, Rico begged desperately, "Tell me we didn't need them, Puggy Wuggy."

"We didn't need them," Jimmy said.

*A*FTER THAT NOTHING in all the world was real. It was fantasy and frenzy and delirium. It was dread and apprehension; new and weird and shameful, with its peak in the stars and its depths in slop, but above all indescribably fascinating. Jimmy had never known anyone like Rico, and knowing him was unreality in itself.

The days passed through this grotesque unreality, wired together and meteoric, like a comet in the night. At first it was January, now it was July. But each day was filled to overflowing and could not hold it all, and always there was some left over which spilled into the day following. There was not enough time to hold it all; there never had been.

There was no time to think; everything was feelings and actions and emotions, mostly emotions. It was like a fantastic dream; but even in the dream there was the tiny insistent warning of awakening. It was inevitable; they would awaken and the dream would be gone. They both knew that separation was inexorable, like release. Every one left, a lot dead.

They planned against it, thought against it. They talked of how they were always going to be together, like two children planning the grownup future.

"First, I'm going to write a bunch of stories and sell them and then I'm going to take the money and get you a pardon," Jimmy would say.

And Rico would say, "You don't have to, Puggy Wuggy, if you'll just go and see my mother and write to me sometimes and always remember me; I'll get out, it won't be so long, I'll be a model convict and they'll give me a parole the first time I go up."

"But I mean it," Jimmy would argue, "I'll get a recommendation from your sentencing judge and prosecutor and then I'll square the prosecuting witness so he won't protest. How much did you take, anyway?"

"It wasn't but twelve dollars, but—"

"Hell, a hundred will square him easily. After that it'll be a cinch. If you just keep your head and don't go haywire and get into trouble . . ."

And Rico's face would light up like a Christmas tree and he'd say, "And then we'll be together again and nothing will ever be able to separate us and we'll write an opera—*Bars and Stripes Forever.*"

For the moment enthusiasm would race through both of them and they would feel as if they had beat it at last.

"You keep on writing your songs," Jimmy would say, "and I'll go out to California and see your mother and show you how to turn out some real work and then in about six months I'll come back and get you out. It'll take a little time, though. But you keep working—"

"And you'll write every day," Rico would break in, "Or at least once a week."

"Of course I will."

"You won't forget me?"

"How could I? I'll be thinking of you every moment."

"And I'll be the bestest convict ever was; I won't go haywire and I'll keep my head and I'll read your letters and think of you and you'll be proud of me yet."

And then something would fall on the moment like a heavy weight, and blight the mood. Maybe a Negro voice over in the cell block singing, ". . . *leaves are fallin' and I'm recallin' . . .*"

Solid reality would surge back and overwhelm them. Jimmy would be going out soon; and Rico would be staying. And after that they couldn't pretend anymore.

Jimmy would recall what Rico had said on that first night— "That's a hell of a lot of loneliness. Is anything worth it?" It seemed like a long time ago.

Once Rico jumped up and cried in a ravaged voice, "Oh, god-dammit, it's no use!" Then his voice went dull and lifeless and he said, "I was doing time in a Florida chain gang, and a freight went by. And screamed. And the hack grabbed his rifle and stood up on his horse. I was thinking about my mother out in L.A. And for a moment I was there. And then I came back. And the sun was hotter than the hell I'm going to. And I had chains on my ankles. And I said to myself, If I ever do time again it'll be in death row waiting for the chair. And here I am, doing another stretch in another stir. And I'm saying it all over again. The next time I do time I'll be doing it in death row, waiting for the chair." His face was a dead, dopey white. Then he turned and went out to the poker game and ran twelve dollars into debt; and Jimmy didn't even have the heart to stop him.

Whatever they did, it was always there, hanging over their heads like a Damoclean sword, staining every moment with a blind, futile desperation, a dull, hurting hopelessness, as if each moment was the last. They tried to cram everything into each day.

But the days failed to hold it all; some of it always overflowed into the next. And it was always there, even in the middle of a laugh.

Beneath it everything was magnified into a grotesqueness where each minor incident assumed a significance all out of proportion to its importance, so that they were continuously doing or saying something that hurt the other incomprehensibly, creating a continuous need for explanations and assuagements and avowals of affection.

It was that way when the dormitory softball team played its first game after Jimmy got out of the hospital. Rico had been taking care of him, dressing his arm and rubbing it with cocoa butter since they had taken it out of the cast and substituted splints. Jimmy had found it pleasant to have a broken arm and receive so much attention. But when the game came, Rico did not want to play.

"It's just another silly game without you, Puggy Wuggy," he said.

"Hell, I won't always be there with you," Jimmy said. And seeing the sudden growth of hurt in Rico's eyes; he could have bitten out his tongue.

"I'll play," Rico said dully, "but I won't be any good without you."

And he wasn't. The team lost, and when the pressure got on the game, Rico was horrible to watch. He went to pieces, breaking up into sheer hysteria, right before Jimmy's eyes.

Afterwards Jimmy snarled, unreasonably angry, "It seems as if you'd have enough pride to keep from making a spectacle of yourself like that. It was disgusting. I'd be ashamed to let anyone see me break into pieces like that."

"I haven't got any pride," Rico replied dully, "and you should be the one to know it. If I did—"

He couldn't say it. There weren't anymore words. Just a dull, hurting silence.

All that night Jimmy could hear his low, muffled sobs. He wanted in the worse way to get up and say, "Don't cry, kid, I'm with you. I don't give a damn what you did, how you went to pieces, I'll always be with you." But he couldn't; he just couldn't, that was all.

When early morning came, Rico leaned over the edge of his bunk and said, "I didn't mean what I said, Puggy Wuggy. Next time I'll be very good and you'll be proud of me, honestly."

Jimmy was so relieved he could have cried. But something against his will forced him to say, "It isn't that, that isn't it, it's just that— it's how can I ever feel sure about you when I'm gone when you're going to act like that while I'm still here."

"It'll be different, I swear," Rico said.

The next time the team played, Jimmy didn't go out at all. He stayed in the dormitory. He was too scared. And Rico was right. It was not the same; it was worse. The team lost again but this time all the dormitory inmates were sore about it.

"He was so damned sickening I had to take him out," Candy told Jimmy when they got back.

"Who?" Jimmy asked.

"You know who," Candy said.

Jimmy knew, only he had hoped that he was wrong.

"Boy, he's solid nuts," Signifier elaborated. "He'd fall down every time he'd start for a ball, and once he lost his head and picked up the ball and threw it over the wall. When Frank got after him about it, he said he didn't give a damn and wanted to fight Frank. You know that wasn't right."

"And the bases were loaded," Candy supplemented.

Mose joined them and said, "Dammit, you got tuh do somp'in. Ah ain' gonna pitch no mo' long as that fellow's on the team," with his duck-billed lips stuck out a country mile.

Jimmy had to take it without a word; he did not have one defense he could offer for Rico. Then captain Frank came down the aisle, shaking his head.

"We'll have to get some one else for center field," Jimmy said quickly, before captain Frank could say it. "What about Wiggins?"

"That Rico!" captain Frank exclaimed, shaking his head. "What's the matter with him?"

"He's all right," Jimmy said. "He's a little excitable at times, but he's all right."

Captain Frank continued to shake his head as if he wanted to say more, but Buchanon spoke up, "When are you going to be ready to play again, Jim?"

"I'm going to play the next time the team plays," Jimmy replied.

Captain Frank's eyebrows went up.

"That's next Thursday," Brothers said.

"That's when I'm going to play," Jimmy told them.

It broke up after that.

Rico came in later and sat on the board they'd placed across the bunk frames for a seat. His trousers were torn and both of his knees and his left elbow were freshly bandaged. Jimmy was determined not to argue.

"Skinned yourself up a little, eh?"

He was standing over Rico, leaning with his good arm against the upper bunk frame. Rico looked up at him, his face sweaty and his eyes feverish. "Go ahead and say it and get it over with!" he cried.

Jimmy went abruptly blind. It was not until afterwards that he realized that he had struck Rico in the face. And then he was instantly contrite. "I didn't mean to hit you," he said. "Hit me back. Come on and hit me back."

Rico pulled out his handkerchief and pressed it against his split lips. Above, his eyes were unreadable.

"Why don't you hit me back?" Jimmy cried. "I hit you."

Rico took the handkerchief away and now his lips were slightly smiling. He licked the blood from them and said, "Because I love you, that's why."

Jimmy gave a violent start. Why, he had heard an actress say that in a picture he had seen, and he had never forgotten it.

It was not real. None of it was real. And any moment it might be gone. They tried to put everything into each moment. They were frantic and scared and desperate, and being together was like rain drops on the desert sands.

Once Jimmy said, "I don't think I've been happy for one-half hour at any one time in all my life."

"Don't I give you anything?" Rico asked.

But this time Jimmy began, "It isn't that, that isn't it—and could say no more.

It was desperate and unreal and magnified and intense and grotesque and frantic; and above all it was so futile.

On the twenty-ninth day of July three desperadoes were brought to the prison and the convicts in the dormitory watched their approach through the windows. They were Dillinger gangsters, bound for the electric chair, Pierpont, Clark, and Mokley: Heavily armed special deputies rode in the first car; the second car contained the prisoners. Following were three additional cars of armed deputies, and two army vans of national guardsmen with mounted machine guns.

"Looks like the *Big Parade*," some one remarked.

"It's the last parade, anyway," another cracked.

"That's the way they do it when you're tough," Jimmy said.

For some unaccountable reason, Rico was deeply disturbed. "Tough?" he echoed. His voice was dulled. "They're not tough; they're in the second car."

Time went on with its inexorable chain of events which he and Jimmy watched and discussed. And nothing could make Jimmy so angry as when Rico let some part of it affect him.

"What burns me up with you," he would say, "is that you let some cheap, lousy convict get you mixed up in some cheap lousy situation and you make a damned fool out of yourself, whereas neither the convict nor whatever in the hell you're trying to do has the least importance. You let little insignificant things get you so mixed up that you lose your sense of proportion. I've seen you get so worked up trying to beat Johnny Brothers some coon-can that you didn't give a damn about anything in the world except just to beat him; whereas in the first place coon-can's his game and you will never be able to beat him, and in the second place where you lost fourteen dollars, you couldn't have won but a dime if you had beat him all night, and in the third place it wasn't important and never will be important. I don't mind what you do, but don't let it get important. Don't let it touch you; there's nothing worth touching you."

But in the end it was Jimmy who changed; and Rico who remained the same.

True to his word, when the dormitory team played again, Jimmy took his arm out of the splints, wrapped it securely in adhesive tape, and played shortstop. And Rico went back to center field, and was excellent and scored the winning run.

After that everything was swell again between them. The dormitory was still there, and the bars, and the walls, but they did not notice. They did not notice the other convicts or the guards. On those hot summer days they would lie side by side on Jimmy's bunk and look out the window at the clouds, rolling by in great dirty flocks beneath the sun, and Rico would call them his sheep.

Jimmy had his mother buy a tenor guitar for Rico, and Rico's mother sent Rico some pyjamas and underwear and an expensive scrap book. It made a difference; it put them on a more equal footing. Rico gave Jimmy a pair of the pyjamas and that set them both up.

After that Rico carried himself erect and there was a new confidence in his bearings. He looked different, better. On the fly page of the scrap book he pasted an old picture of Jimmy which his mother had sent to him some time before, and beneath it printed the words, "In memory of God."

"I don't like that," Jimmy protested.

"You are my God, Puggy Wuggy," Rico told him, and then went suddenly soft. "I'm simply crazy about you, Puggy Wuggy. I like everything you do, the way you say 'not particularly so' and 'it isn't that, that isn't it' and the little habit you have of running your fingers through your hair when you're upset."

"And I like the way your eyes light up with excitement when you talk about it," Jimmy teased. "I'll always remember your eyes."

"I'll remember everything about you, Puggy Wuggy."

And then the night Jimmy asked Rico if he could see the face in the moon as they lay watching it walk across their window.

"Who, the man eating green cheese?" Rico wanted to know.

Jimmy said irrelevently, "When the moon shines through your window, think of me, maybe I'll be looking at it, too."

When Rico's voice came it was choked. "Don't say that, please don't say that."

"I didn't mean to hurt you," Jimmy said. "Don't take it like that; we can't do anything about it. It was inevitable from the start."

"I know. I'm sorry." Then, from a long way off, his voice came, low and muffled, "Don't ever lean your whole weight on happiness, Jimmy, you fall too hard when it gives away."

"You have a saying for everything, haven't you?"

"Just the words."

They were silent and thoughtful. Then Jimmy said, "Whenever I see a full moon after this, I'll think of you. And I'll think of this dormitory; and I'll see this goddamned dormitory and I'll see you in it, and I don't want it like that." When Rico didn't reply, he went on, "That isn't it, it isn't that; it's a story—When the moon shines through your window, think of a convict in a prison dormitory, think of me, dear God."

The next day he wrote it, a maze of impressions.

Rico was subdued and quiet after that, and when Jimmy asked him why, he replied, "You don't need me at all, anymore, do you?"

"Even if I didn't, you'd always be my friend, kid," Jimmy told him.

Soon afterwards they read a story in *Esquire* called "Something to Remember You By" which touched both of them. There was a line in it which Jimmy never forgot, and always afterwards, when he tried to do something and failed, he was reminded of it—"*. . . consoled somewhat by the thought you made the lonely crusade for something more.*"

Rico cried over that story, and Jimmy could never understand why; it touched him, too, but not the crying way.

And then there was Warren Williams in a picture called *The Match King*. For weeks afterwards the convicts' catch phrase was, "Don't worry about it until it happens, then I'll take care of it."

The countless times that Jimmy said to Rico, "Don't worry about it until it happens, kid, then I'll take care of it."

About the middle of August, Jimmy was called over to the Classification Bureau for an interview. He was not in line for an interview by them that soon for he was not eligible for a parole hearing until May of the following year, so he asked them why he had been called.

"The order came from the governor's office," the sociologist informed him.

He knew then that he was being examined for a pardon.

At first he was very excited. He wasn't afraid that time, like times before. He felt certain then that he was going to get a pardon; it wasn't like the times when he had been so afraid that it would blow away and vanish. He thought of all the things he would do and of how glad his mother would be. And then he thought of Rico. He'll certainly miss me, he thought. And suddenly he was very scared for Rico.

But Rico appeared extremely happy when Jimmy told him the news. He told Jimmy a thousand things he wanted him to do, as if Jimmy was going home that very moment. Then he said, "Lets get some blue boys and celebrate."

"Fine," Jimmy said.

So they got a jag and went out and played some poker. After a time Rico quit, saying he wanted to lie down for a while. Jimmy was winning so he continued to play. Later, he quit, too, and when he went back to his bunk he found Rico typing. There were a couple of typed sheets on the bunk, and one in the typewriter.

"What are you writing, your life's history?" he teased.

Rico gave a violent start, then wheeled and looked at Jimmy, his face turning crimson.

"What the hell!" Jimmy exclaimed.

Rico snatched the sheet from the typewriter and put it behind him.

"Let me see it," Jimmy demanded.

For a long time Rico just looked at him, his face breaking up into a thousand different expressions, then he said, "Sure, Puggy Wuggy, I'll do anything for you."

Jimmy sat on the edge of the bunk and began reading the typed pages, slightly frowning:

"I'm twenty-four and know life. I wouldn't know life if I wasn't twenty-four, and I wouldn't be twenty-four if I didn't know life. I learned life and life and life until I knew it so well that even when they said, no charge to you, baby, I love it, I didn't feel romantic.

"But love makes a difference. It comes like the Assyrian, gleaming in neither purple nor gold but holding fast and hard to the path until its victim is won.

"Is that the wisdom of twenty-four?

"No, this is it. I love a man. I love him with the violence of Lucrezia Borgia poisoning a baby; the poignance of Al Jolson singing *Mammy* and the tenderness of a mother kissing a baby.

"He loves me also but I am a moron. He made me one but he likes it. He doesn't stay drunk and so when he is sober he looks at me and starts to wondering. Drunk or sober I love him though. What difference does it make? Are we happy? He is my God. I worship at his shrine with the undying fervence of a whirling dervish at some shrine in India. Am I a pushover? He thinks so sometimes but nor for long, and then when he isn't thinking I'm a pushover, he's thinking that I am the last word in passion. What man in that state of mind could totally disapprove of me?

"But passion is not lasting so I have to be smart, too. That is love's labor lost for I am not smart. I am a lover and a dreamer and the world is my playground. He is a worker and a doer, a thinker and the world is his workshop. When he is not thinking that I am a moron and trying to make something different out of me then he thinks that I am great. I am. I am great enough not to work. I am great enough to have something to write about, be able to write and don't merely because I don't care to.

"He's the most beautiful creature that God ever made. But then, to me, he is God. So why not?

"It's funny love, too, because he loves me as much as I do him— but not the same way. Funny thing about this love of ours, it makes

343

me goofy. I keep thinking the queerest thoughts ever. To have him hold me in his arms is ecstacy divine. I am going degenerate now. I'm fighting a singlehanded battle against it. He's the single hand. He doesn't know that I have to have it to live—great quantities of it. He only knows that I am passionate to the extreme.

"He doesn't know. He cold waters passion in himself. But he's wrong and he never will know it. I know. If he did not ever feel the way I did, it wouldn't be our kind of love. His beauty inspires me to rapture. When I see him standing naked I want to rush to him wherever his is and beg for love. When I bathe myself and my hand caresses my body I want to scream for him.

"When I see him talking to other people no matter how they look and what they are I go red-raving mad and want to smash things. But that's because he's the most beautiful creature in the world. I would kill him in a minute. That's because I love him that way. I would kill for him the same way and for the same reason. I can't think of anything in the world that he would ask me that I wouldn't do and all because I love him. I went that way not long after I met him when I first got here for robbery because I wouldn't take advantage of the opportunities I had given me. I killed a guy once about love like ours—shoved him off a speeding train right into a river. Another time I dug a guy's eye out for the same reason and took a beating every day 101 days because I wouldn't tell what the fight was all about.

"I don't know why I'm writing this. Because I'm scared, I guess. Because I know that he will never love me as I do him because I don't gender respect in his mind. And people can't love as I do if they don't respect their lovers.

"I know that he has a moral advantage of position on me and I feel inferior because of it. My own opinions of myself are not so hot in the light of the day.

"But now I no longer care one way or the other. It will soon be over. And that will stop the sun from shining. I never knew, I never knew. I always wanted somebody to tell me that I wasn't wrong. And nobody never has. Maybe it's just an act mostly. He seems to think that way; he seems to think I go into an act every time I open my mouth. Maybe I do. But can't you understand? When it's all over, what am I? I'm just a kid begging life for a break—"

When Jimmy came to the end his eyes kept moving with a jerking motion. He wanted to keep on reading, he didn't want ever to stop, because he knew that when he stopped he would start to think— he would recall the lines "*I killed a guy once about a love like ours . . . Another time . . .*" —and he was terrifyingly afraid of that. He would know, if he stopped to think, that he had been wrong about Rico from the very first, that what he thought they had was just the same as all the rest, all over the slimy prison. And after that, there wouldn't be anything at all in it for him. He looked down at Rico, sitting on the board between the bunks, then looked quickly away. Rico's eyes were like a dog's.

He took a deep breath and said, "So that's the way it is." His voice was not accusing, just tired, defeated, disillusioned.

"How do I know?" Rico said. "I never got something for nothing in all my life. How do I know?"

Everything went then. They were just two convicts who were afraid of each other's thoughts, of each other's power to hurt; afraid of their own thoughts. There was a beaten, unsmiling dullness in their faces, and everything which had been between them, keeping them close, was gone.

"To hell with you!" Jimmy said dully, deliberately. "What have you got to say about that?"

"If that's the way you feel, Jimmy," Rico said, "then I haven't got anything to say."

"That isn't the way I want to feel," Jimmy snarled. "Goddammit, do you think I get some sort of masochistic satisfaction out of getting hurt all the goddamned time? Do you think I want to feel that that's all any of it ever meant to you? If that's all it ever meant then I've wasted a hell of a lot of feelings."

Rico stood up, white-faced and remote, and began a dull bitter plea. "Haven't I tried to be what you wanted me to be, Jimmy? Haven't I gone around here and kissed these bastards' behinds just because you wanted me to get along with them and treat them right when I know they hate my very guts? I've changed everything about myself, Jimmy, and just for you. I never did any of it for myself; I never cared a thing for myself or for anyone except you."

"That isn't it; it isn't that," Jimmy tried to explain it. "The things I wanted you to do, I wanted you to do because you would want to, yourself. Do you understand? I wanted us to be different, to be above all this, to be way up there on top. I wanted us to be the best, and what we had to be something that nobody would believe. But it's all sex with you." His voice was accusing. "And no kind of sex was ever worth the value you put on it, much less your kind."

For a moment Rico appeared as if he would faint, then his eyes became haunted and crazy and his face cracked like a new white drum on a banjo. "You don't think so," he said, pushing the words between clenched teeth and paper-stiff lips. "You don't think its worth that much? I'll show you what it's worth to me." His head went up and his chin lifted and the sneer was on his lips again, was all over his face, in his shoulders, in his hands, making him grotesque and ugly. "I'll show you! I'll kill my Goddamned self!"

Jimmy believed that he would try it and he was suddenly sickeningly afraid. It nauseated him. He had to exert an extreme effort to speak, and when he spoke, he didn't say what he wanted to. "That won't prove anything. Anybody can kill himself. The proof's in living."

"Be seeing you, pal," Rico said, and walked away.

Jimmy felt as if he had kicked a cripple or slugged a blind man.

But just before bedtime Rico came back and said in a hoarse, ragged voice, "I didn't have the nerve. I'd like to do something very low, because I didn't have the nerve." His eyes were bruised and dirty.

"Go to bed and sleep it off, kid," Jimmy said. "You'll feel differently in the morning."

But Rico could not sleep. All that night Jimmy heard his dull, racked sobbing, and he thought, One hell of a celebration.

After that Rico was despondent and desperate, although he tried to be very gay and not show it. But Jimmy could see it underneath.

346

It showed in his eyes, in the way he talked; in the way he wanted to take any sort of "rape-fiend" chance to please Jimmy. And nights he kept Jimmy awake talking as if he was afraid that sleep might rob him of some precious moment.

Nothing was real.

I T WAS LIKE being washed away in a flood. Everything happened at once, surging down on them in great waves, before which they were powerless. Everything was violent and chaotic and haywire, happening suddenly and overwhelmingly, washing onward with a great fury that left in its wake consequences. It was in the consequences which they drowned after fighting through the flood.

After the letter the intimacy which had kept them close was lost in the desperate effort to regain it so that they were never quite in attune with the other's mood or unreservedly sympathetic of the other's emotion. Jimmy felt, against his will, a dull repulsion, an indefinable distaste for Rico's affection, and sensing this, a tight-drawn recklessness came into Rico's actions, a despair which seemed bent on self-destruction, creating of him a person lashing himself into suicide.

The separation was deep and dull and hurting, and all the more irreparable because Rico no longer gave Jimmy anything, but now had become his responsibility.

There was an excitement, but it was different. It was the strained, frantic, panicky excitement of rushing onward to one great, final, everlasting explosion. The last week of August burnt through them like a dynamite fuse, each day burning closer to the explosion that seemed so imminent. The explosion that would finally bring their separation into the open, and shatter it into irrevocability.

But it never came. For the first week in September a situation arose of which both were victims, and against which both rebelled. And they were made to become close again; but in a different way.

Captain Frank called Jimmy down to his desk that day, and said to him, "Listen, Jim, I'm not trying to run your business, but you and Rico have got to watch yourselves."

"Why?" Jimmy asked, getting on his muscle. "Why have we got to watch ourselves?"

"Listen, Jim, there's no need of all of that," captain Frank said, spreading his hands. "Three lieutenants have asked me about you and Rico, and last week the deputy called me into his office and showed me a whole stack of notes which convicts up here in the dormitory had written over there about you and him. They told him you two did whatever you wanted to do up here and that I let you do it."

Jimmy's first reaction was that of shock; and then he felt chagrin. He should have known that the convicts would be ratting on them; but he had never given it a thought. He and Rico had been so wrapped up in themselves that they had forgotten that there were other convicts in the dormitory.

"I told the deputy that it was all a pack of lies," captain Frank went on. "I explained how Rico had helped you a little when your arm was in splints, but that I had asked him to do it. Some one had to help him, they discharged him from the hospital with his arm still in a sling, I said. But you know the deputy, Jim; you can't fool him.

"What have they got against Rico, anyway, Jim?" he asked.

"I don't know, Frank," Jimmy lied. "They just don't like him. He doesn't associate with them and doesn't have to ask them for anything—his mother sends him everything he wants—and they don't like that. The truth is, Frank, we've just been getting along too good for them."

"That's what I told the deputy," Frank said. "You're drawing compensation and he gets what he wants from home. You guys stay to yourself and write stories and that sort of thing and these guys just can't stand it. You're just getting along too good for these rats up here, that's all. But you know the deputy; he just sits there and looks at you with his head bobbing and knows more about it than you do yourself.

"You know, Jim," captain Frank became meditative. "I can't understand what makes people like that. I've seen a lot of people outside like that—envious. They did me the same way when I was sheriff—people I'd been feeding. Kept yapping until they got me out. Son of a bitches whom I had supported for years got up before the investigating committee and testified against me. You'd be surprised if I told you who some of the fellows are who wrote notes about you and Rico—"

"You'd better not tell me, Frank," Jimmy interrupted, sucking air.

"What I wanted to tell you," captain Frank said, "is that Stout sent a transfer up here for Rico this morning . . ." Jimmy went white. "He was going to transfer him into 5-D."

In the sudden cold scare which enveloped him, Jimmy was drained of all strength. His stomach became hollow and his knees knocked together. His mouth came open but he could not find the handle to the words.

"I sent the transfer back and then I went out to see the warden," captain Frank told him, and he was able to breathe again. "I've done the warden a lot of favors in my time and I asked him to do me a favor. I asked him to let you and Rico stay here in the dormitory and that I would be responsible for you both. I promised that no more complaints would reach him. Do you know, he had almost as many notes about you two as the deputy."

"What did he say?" Jimmy asked fearfully.

"He promised to let him stay. But listen, Jim, you'd better cut it out."

Relieved of his fear, Jimmy became indignant, outraged. "There isn't anything to cut out, Frank," he snarled. "We're just good friends."

Captain Frank's eyebrows went up.

"I'm not trying to string you, Frank," Jimmy persisted. "Listen, can't a man have a friend in this joint? Is there any crime in having a friend?"

Captain Frank spread his hands again. "I'm on your side, Jim, I don't need convincing. But I didn't write the rules. You know how it is, you're not a fool."

"What do they want me to do, quit talking to him," Jimmy continued to argue. The thing was riding him now. "I guess they don't even want me to look at him. I guess they want to tell me who I can talk to; I guess that's what they want to do. I guess they want me to do like they want or else they're going to make me, I guess that's it."

"Now, Jim, just take it easy," captain Frank cautioned. "You don't have to stop talking to him, but don't do it at night. And don't hang around your bunks all the time; come out and gamble and mix with the other fellows like you used to do. That will help. And tell Rico to stop playing his uke when the colored convicts are having church on Wednesday nights. They're the ones who have been putting up the biggest squawk. You know the chaplain gave them that privilege and they've been ratting to him ever since Rico has been in the dormitory.

"You come out and mingle with them again, Jim. They all like you but they think you've gone highhat since you've been writing stories. They think you think you're too good to associate with them. You know how to handle them. Do it, Jim. And you and Rico take it easy. The next time I won't be able to do a thing."

For a long moment Jimmy stood there without replying, turning the advice over in his mind. He knew that captain Frank was right, but he hated to give in. It was the old trouble, he hated to admit that other convicts, that all of them combined, could affect his manner of conduct. But in the end he said, "Okay, Frank, I will. And thanks," because now he had Rico to think of.

At first he did not tell Rico, but Rico could not understand why, all of a sudden, he wanted to go out and gamble and talk to the other convicts.

"What's the matter, Puggy Wuggy?" he asked. "Don't you like

to talk to me anymore?" There was a small, pitiful entreaty in his voice.

So Jimmy had to tell him.

He became flamingly furious. "The chicken-livered bastards!" he raved. "I wish I knew just one of them."

"That's why I didn't find out," Jimmy said.

"You needn't worry, Puggy Wuggy," Rico assured him. "I won't do anything to hurt you. But oh, if it wasn't that you were getting a pardon, I'd show them."

Jimmy did not tell him that it was for his, Rico's, sake that he had not found out.

But Rico tried to show them anyway, it seemed. After that he wanted to fight every one. If he noticed a convict looking at him, he'd challenge him to a fight. And he went out of his way to show them how utterly contemptuous of them he was. Jimmy lived in a state of continuous apprehension. But by spending his efforts to keep Rico out of trouble, he also kept himself in line.

However, Rico was transferred down front, next to the guard's stand, after all. From the moment the transfer came, he and Jimmy did not speak with good will to another convict in that dormitory. They walked over those who got in their way, and treated the others as scum. Jimmy quit managing the softball team, and they both quit playing; he gave up his poker games, and, borrowing some of Rico's contempt, laid a naked knife blade on Signifier's throat and made him speak an abject apology for a crack which he had made.

Again and again captain Frank tried to reason with him, he pleaded with him, he reminded him of the pardon he was seeking; but Jimmy would not listen.

It seemed as if every one was watching them, waiting for a chance to ridicule or to laugh. But they did not give them the opportunity. Either Jimmy was down to Rico's bunk, or Rico was up to his. They flaunted their relationship, and dared the convicts to show by word or gesture that they even noticed.

"If it hurts you, kid, don't ever let them see it," Jimmy told Rico once.

So they laughed about it, they laughed at the convicts, and

laughed at the rules. At night, after bedtime, Jimmy would go down and sit on Rico's bunk and talk to him while the dormitory lay awake and watched. And on Wednesday nights, when the colored convicts held prayer meetings, he and Rico sat on the end of the table while Rico loudly played his ukelele.

They sat in a poker game one day and began squeezing the players until the gamekeeper was forced to protest. Jimmy jumped to his feet and snatched the blanket from the table, breaking up the game. Only his sheer, cool audacity kept him from getting killed that time.

The next day captain Frank and captain Charlie got together and stopped the gambling. Following, a tightness grew through the dormitory which you could walk on. And he and Rico walked on it. Their insolence was towering.

Captain Charlie tried to talk to Rico. The next day Rico told Jimmy of it. "Old Charlie's trying to reform me. He thinks I'm too nice to be like I am. He told me that if I'd stop coming down here and give you up altogether that he'd go to the front for me and try to get me an honor job. He's kind of nice, Puggy Wuggy, and he's crazy about you. He thinks you are a genius; but he doesn't think we should be friends. He says we're not good for each other."

Another time Rico said, "Captain Charlie told me that we're making it pretty tough for him. He said I'd have to stop coming down here to your bunk entirely."

"What did you tell him?" Jimmy asked.

"He's such a nice old man and he talked so pitifully I couldn't— I just didn't have the heart to refuse him. After all, he asked me if I wouldn't; he didn't order me to. I hope you're not angry."

"Of course not," Jimmy said. "You did just right. He is a swell old fellow. I'll come down to your bunk after this. No one can say anything about that. It's right under the gun."

But it did not help. The convicts were a solid wall of antagonism about them, and captain Frank informed Jimmy that the notes had grown in both volume and vituperation. "I wish you'd get some goddamned reason, Jim," he said, "because in the long run you're only going to make it hard on yourself. You're fighting a human characteristic which you can't beat, but I can't bring myself to blame you for it. I wish I had done the same thing.

"But you needn't worry, Jim," he added. "You'll be right here in this dormitory—both you and Rico—as long as I've got a friend in the Capitol."

"Thanks, Frank," Jimmy said, tears coming into his eyes.

After that he and Rico quieted down. They began reading to each other again, sitting out at the table down at the end near the guard's stand. Once, reading a story in a pulp paper magazine, they came across the line, ". . . *and there was one who forever remained un-named.*"

"That stirs your imagination, doesn't it?" Jimmy said.

"That might be any convict," Rico pointed out.

"Damned right! He forever remained un-named. That's a story."

And he wrote it: About the convict who got the pardon, the officials said his name was Mack, but the body of the Mack whom the convicts knew, which was slipped out of the prison underneath the canvas of the meat truck with its head beaten to a bloody pulp and the six bullet holes in its belly *Forever Remained Un-named.*

In the evenings he worked on it down at his bunk while Rico kept him company. Seeing them together down there, the convicts approached captain Charlie in a steady stream, demanding that he do something. Some swore that they had seen them openly committing acts of sex perversion; some threatened to draw up a petition to have him discharged if he did not report them. Two runners who worked for the inspector threatened to bring the inspector up there and show him what was going on.

Captain Charlie sent for Jimmy. He looked pitiful. "Jim," he began, "I've known you for a long time now. Remember when you were over in the 5-F dormitory in 1929. You were new then. Remember how we used to talk at night and how my wife used to make candy and send it in to you. Remember the time we caught the other fellows with that April Fool candy with the cotton inside of it."

He touched Jimmy then.

"I've always liked you, Jim," he went on, "and I've always

figured that you liked me, too. I'm going to tell you something that I've never told anyone. Remember back in December of 1930 when you and Lively were such good friends and the time they moved you fellows out of 1-E&F and put some of you in 2- & 3-E&F?"

Jimmy nodded.

"Well, that night they caught you down on 2-E&F talking to Lively, I had to sort of, er, speak up for you—"

"I remember, cap," Jimmy said. "You told a lie for me to get me out of a jam. I've never told you, cap, but I appreciate that."

"Well, captain Jenkins, he was up on your floor, knew that I was lying and reported me to the warden. He had the ear of the warden then, and they transferred me to the walls shortly after that. You didn't know it because you had been transferred into the cells by then, but I stayed on the walls at night for almost a year." His voice thickened a little. "It's lonely on the walls, son. You don't know how lonely it can get up there at night on those walls. There isn't any light and you can't read; you don't have any place to walk but aroud the parapet. You sit there night after night watching the sleeping prison. There were some little gray mice up there. I used to feed them scraps out of my lunch and talk to them for company." He sighed. "They were nice little mice."

He paused and looked up, as if inviting Jimmy to speak. But Jimmy could not speak; he was choked.

After a time he resumed, "I was sixty-six last week. I couldn't do another year on those walls.

"Listen, Jim, I don't want to have to report you and Rico because I like you both. I've never seen you do anything. But don't have him down there at your bunk at night. Do that for me, will you, Jim. If you don't, these convicts are going to put me on the wall again."

Jimmy had never in all his life felt so sorry for anyone. "Cap," he said. "You've got a blackjack there. You take it and get up and beat me across the head. Knock me down and kick me. Then take me to the hole for insubordination. I can beat that. And that will help; that will keep them off of you."

For a long moment they looked into each other's eyes. Captain

Charlie did not reply until he felt that Jimmy was sincere, then he said, "Thanks, Jim, but I couldn't."

Jimmy dropped his gaze. "I wish you could, cap. Just close your eyes and swing, cap." When captain Charlie did not reply, he said, "I'm sorry, cap. I can't do the other. Before I'd let these convicts beat me now, I'd die and go to hell. And if it killed you, cap, I wouldn't be here to know it."

He turned slowly and went back to his bunk. Rico was waiting for him. He told Rico what captain Charlie had said.

"I'd better not come back here anymore," Rico said.

"Sit down just as you've been doing," Jimmy grated. "I'm not taking orders from all the convicts in the world."

"Then maybe I'd better sit up on the top bunk where they can see we're not doing anything," Rico suggested.

"That's a hell of a thing," Jimmy flared. "You got to sit up on an upper bunk at eight-thirty in the evening when all the lights are on and everybody is moving about all over the dormitory so some lousy convict bastard can see that you're not doing anything."

He tried to continue writing, but he was blind. He could not think. He wanted to hurt some one. After a moment he put aside his typewriter and stood up. He wanted to talk, but he was too angry.

About a quarter to nine, captain Charlie came down and asked Rico to step down to his desk. When Rico hesitated, Jimmy said, "Go down and see what he wants."

For a moment afterwards he stood there, wondering how it would all end, then he undressed and put on his pyjamas. But he did not feel like lying down; he was filled with a blind, rock-hard frustration.

Just before the lights winked, Chump Charlie came up to him and said, "You better go down to the desk, Jimmy, cap Charlie is writing up Rico."

Jimmy did not think it was strange that Chump Charlie should be the one in all the dormitory to inform him; he did not think about it at all. He reached underneath his pillow for the knife he had hidden there. He didn't think that he would need it, but he wanted to be prepared. And then he thought about the pardon. I'm getting a pardon, he thought. I'd be a fool. He stood there for a long time, thinking about the pardon; thinking, I've been in prison for five years and nine months, I'd like to be free. Then he recalled the different times when his hopes had been built up in vain. But this time he was really booked to go; he felt it in his bones.

He put the knife away. And then he took a deep breath and walked slowly down the aisle toward the guard's stand. Because he could not help it. Because all along he had known that he would do it. The convicts stopped whatever they were doing to turn and watch him.

When he got to the desk, he asked, "What are you reporting Rico for, cap; he hasn't done anything."

"I've got to," captain Charlie said. "I've got to do something."

"You've got to put a charge on the report card," Jimmy said. "What charge are you going to put on the report card?"

The lights winked at that time. But no one began preparing for bed. They were standing out in the aisles, watching Jimmy and Rico and captain Charlie.

"I've got to charge him with sex perversion," captain Charlie replied.

"It will be a lie," Jimmy said. "Did you ever see us doing anything like that?"

"No," captain Charlie admitted, "but that's what every one says it is."

"You're letting them run your job," Jimmy stated.

"I can't help it, Jim; I couldn't do another year on those walls."

"Okay," Jimmy said. "But if you write him up, write me up; he couldn't do it by himself."

Rico was looking at him queerly, but he didn't speak. Jimmy turned and walked away, thinking, I've always been a fool. *Always!*

He went back and stood by his bunk and lit a cigaret. No one spoke to him. Captain Charlie came around and took count. But he would not look at Jimmy. The lights went out. Slowly, one by one, the convicts began climbing into their bunks, but their necks were still craned to see what would happen. Rico still stood down by the guard's stand. He was dressed. Jimmy stood there, watching. He felt as if he was some one else, standing there.

When captain Charlie had turned in his count, he came up to him and said, "Put on your clothes, Monroe, I've got to take you to the hole."

Jimmy nodded. He put on his new tan shoes and his Sunday trousers. When he had finished, he went down front. Captain Charlie was waiting. Jimmy looked at Rico. Rico slightly smiled. There was a quality of unreality about him as he stood there, slightly smiling. His eyes had a dazed, slightly disbelieving expression in them, similar to that in the eyes of a sleep-walker.

Jimmy tried to smile, too. "Don't worry about it until it happens," he said. "Then I'll take care of it." But he could not get it to go off right, his smile would not work and his voice cracked.

"Come on," captain Charlie said.

They turned, Jimmy leading the way, Rico following, captain Charlie bringing up the rear, went down the stairs and through the gate into the anteroom of the main entrance where the gate-keeper sat. Captain Charlie placed them in the charge of the gate-keeper to be held for the night deputy.

They sat close together on the window ledge to wait. Jimmy turned and looked through the window at his back. The fountain in the gold fish pool which had replaced the alligator pond caught little slivers of light which made it appear ethereal and ghostly and unreal, intensifying the feeling of unreality which already possessed him.

"It looks queer, doesn't it," he said to Rico. "Like a little lost fountain in some immense tomb."

"Puggy Wuggy," Rico began. His voice sounded choked. Jimmy turned and looked at him. His eyes were pinned on Jimmy in a rapt, awestruck stare. "No one has ever taken up for me like this before," he went on. Even his voice sounded unreal, Jimmy thought. "Why did you do it, Puggy Wuggy?" Rico asked. "I didn't expect you to and I wouldn't have blamed you if you hadn't. You've got so much to lose, while they can't hurt me, not really, not if you keep on loving me."

"I don't know why I did it," Jimmy replied slowly. "Maybe in the end just to prove something; maybe just to prove that I would."

"You don't know what you've done for me," Rico told him in a queer, ghostly voice. "You've done the one thing necessary to make me different. You believe in me, don't you, Jimmy? You believe we're right, don't you?"

"Let's don't get melodramatic," Jimmy said, trying again to smile. "When I get to analyzing it, I'll probably discover that I had a very lousy reason, after all."

"It's like seeing something for the first time," Rico said in that rapt, ghostly voice. "It's like looking through a mirror, Jimmy, like looking into heaven."

The night deputy came then, and put them in the hole. But all that night Rico kept up a disjointed, one-sided conversation in that queer, light voice, trying to tell Jimmy what he had done for him. There were other convicts in the hole, and they yelled for him to shut up and let them sleep; they cursed him and reviled him and called him names; but he did not seem to hear them. He was tying to tell Jimmy something which Jimmy could not wholly understand.

The next morning they were taken out separately for trial. When Jimmy was brought into the courtroom, he asked the deputy what was his charge.

"Sex perversion," the deputy read from the card.

"That's a joke," Jimmy said. "Send for the guard."

"I don't need to send for the guard," the deputy said. "It's on the card and I believe that you are guilty."

Jimmy reddened. "It doesn't make any difference what you believe," he raved. "This is a court and only what is proved is supposed to count. The charge is a lie and anybody who says it's true is a liar. If the convicts who told you all those lies are going to run this goddamned institution, then—"

"Take him back," the deputy instructed the courtroom guard. "Take him back. I believe he's guilty."

The guard grabbed him by the arm and roughly shoved him back into the anteroom which led into the hole. They had already taken Rico back to his cell.

"What did he say your charge was?" Jimmy asked.

Rico hesitated a moment, knowing that every one was listening, then said, "S.P. Do you understand?"

"Some punk," a convict cracked.

"All right, bastard!" Jimmy flared. "I'll get out of here and catch you on the yard and cut your goddamned throat."

"Oh, let him alone," Rico said.

When his rage had passed, Jimmy replied, "That was my charge, too. What did you tell him?"

"I told him if he believed that, I didn't have anything to say." Then after a moment, he asked, "What else could I have said?"

"I blew my top," Jimmy confessed. "I said everybody was a lie." When Rico did not reply, he said angrily, "And I'll be damned if I let them get away with it, either. Even if I am guilty, no guard actually caught me."

"*We* sounds better," Rico interposed. "Do you mind, P.W.?"

Jimmy laughed. "I stand rebuked."

"It wasn't a rebuke—a request."

They were kept in the hole for five days. Rico took it without a whimper. That surprised Jimmy somewhat. But during that time he came to understand more of what Rico had been trying to tell him that first night. Rico was changed. He had gained something deep inside of him. Jimmy had never admired him so much.

On the afternoon of the fifth day they were taken out and transferred into separate single cells on 5-D, the company of degenerates. The following day, Jimmy got a special letter and wrote to his mother, asking her to visit him right away. When she came, a couple of days later, he told her what had happened. He told her that the charge was not true, and asked her to go to the welfare director and have it taken from his record, and if he would not do it, for her to go to the governor.

She cried. "Now you've gone and nullified everything we've done for you," she sobbed.

"Listen, mother, let's don't go into it," Jimmy said. "I could not help it, so let's don't talk about it. You just see the welfare director. I'll get it straightened out."

But he was sick enough to cry himself. One thing it did for him, however, was to give him back reality. He could see his and Rico's relationship in its true perspective for the first time. But even then, he did not have any regrets. Because there had been those moments that were priceless; those moments which had given him everything. He felt grateful to Rico for those moments. But he knew that they were not anymore. That he had had them all.

He knew if there had ever been a pardon in store for him, that it was gone. But he did not put the slightest blame on Rico, even to himself. Because he knew that in the full, final analysis, the thing he had done, he had done it for himself. He had done it because in his warped and unmoral way it made him something; it made him a man. And if he had lost a pardon, he had never had it anyway. He had served plenty of time and he could serve plenty more. But the way he thought of it, he could not have waited until later to have been a man. But it was for himself. Just for himself.

Company 5-D was the worst company in the prison. Up there, the convicts cursed and argued and fought from lights-on until lights-out, and no one took the trouble to restrain them. In the time that Jimmy was up there, he never once heard a sentence completed without its punctuation of vulgarity. They were taken out of their cells exactly three times each day for meals; the remainder of the time they were kept locked in their single cells to think up new and startling expressions of vulgarity to hurl at each other.

And now they had the *name*, Jimmy thought. He was going out, sooner or later; it couldn't be too long, anyway. But Rico had to stay there for years to come. And when they put the name on you, it stuck. You were a "lousy whore" forevermore. No matter how you played it.

But Rico took it with a smile. His chin stayed up. And if it hurt, he never let the convicts see it.

Jimmy got in quite a bit of writing in spite of all the noise. He wrote mostly because he did not want to think, and although the stories which he wrote were much too hysterical to be of any value, they helped greatly as simple measures of relief. And he began to feel that some day he would write stories that would sell.

Each day when they went out for supper, he left his typewriter and all that he had written during the morning in Rico's cell, for him to copy and correct. It gave him something to do. In every way Jimmy could see the difference in him. He had quieted down, and there was a new quality of serenity in his manner—or perhaps it was resignation—Jimmy could not be sure. However, he did not let insignificant matters affect him anymore.

Jimmy hoped he would remain like that. But only for his, Rico's, own sake. For Jimmy did not need him any longer. He had gone on by him. He felt that Rico understood, though, for once when he sent a story down to be typed, he received a note in reply which was something of a promise.

"Jimmy, here it am! Easy aces all the way. Just like a itsy bitsy mousey wowsey down there you are. I love you, sweets. You are swell people. I am very glad to have met you, Mr— what was the name? Are you O.K.? I'm at the peak. Thought I would be tired but I'm not. Hope there aren't many errors— But if there are, I hope I was never one. Irrelevant, aren't I? I tried to make it perfect. Send down all the errors though that you come to. I will do them. I am like that now.

"Seriously, though, Puggy Wuggy, you've given me more than you'll ever know. I'm doing quite swell. I mean on the inside. And I'll continue to be that way after you're gone. You needn't worry about me, Puggy Wuggy. I'll be swell.

"I understand now what you meant by a lot of things—about putting something into anything you hope to get something out of. Does that sound very confused? And about treating people as people and using good judgement. I've learned that, too.

"And you keep on going up, Puggy Wuggy, and you'll be where you belong—at the top of the heap. I'll be doing swell, though, and you needn't ever worry about me when you get there, Puggy Wuggy.

"What are you doing? Just percolating? Remember when that used to be the word? Let's percolate!

"I may clean up and wash some clothes if I don't feel lazy. Can't know how I feel until I feel myself. I love you again in the same letter. Or is this the first time? Love you—that's the second. Always. Wouldja, wouldja? Remember?"

After that Jimmy felt a great deal better. Maybe Rico knew. Maybe he didn't. But he hoped to God that he did.

Monday of the third week that they were up there, the magazine man told Jimmy that he had seen his name on the list of convicts who were to be transferred to the prison farm. The convict in the next cell heard him and yelled it all over the block.

And that was the way Rico learned. It scared him. The next morning Jimmy could see it in his eyes. But Rico took it with a smile. They had no idea what day he would be called, but they reasoned that it would be soon. That night and all the next day they spent in frantic preparation. Jimmy gave him a number of things which he wanted him to have, things which were associated with some incident, some emotion, some discovery which they had experienced together. And Rico gave him the picture of his mother, and her address, and a copy of his song. Jimmy promised to go out to Los Angeles and see her the very first thing he did when he got out. Then they worked out an elaborate plan whereby they could send letters back and forth to each other with the driver of the milk truck.

But for all their preparedness, when Jimmy was called, they were both shocked into unreality again. On the way out he stopped by Rico's cell to say goodby. Rico was smiling, although his lips were trembling and his eyes appeared as if he had been crying steadily for hours.

"Easy aces, kid," Jimmy said, shaking his hand. He tried to smile, but his lips were too stiff.

"To the stars, Puggy Wuggy," Rico said, gaspingly.

There was no more to say. Jimmy picked up his sacks, looked at Rico again. "Be seeing you, kid." And then he went down the aisle.

"Don't forget to write," Rico called. Jimmy could tell by his voice that he was already crying again; that he was crying and did not care who knew it.

"I won't," he called, looking back. Rico had both arms stuck through the bars and was wildly waving.

When Jimmy went down the stairs he was thinking about Rico. I hope he'll make it, he thought. It'll certainly be tough on him up there . . . And then he thought, he certainly worshipped me. He gave me a lot, too. He gave me everything he had to give. But now I'm going on. I hope I gave him something, too, in passing. I hope he'll understand.

But when he passed through the front gates he began thinking of the farm. It felt strange to be going through the gates again. After a moment a keen excitement filled him . . . I'm going to the farm, he thought. I've got it beat now. Big, ugly prison, but I've got it beat now . . . Because the farm was the way to freedom.